The Laird Of Norlaw

A Scottish Story

by

Mrs. Oliphant

The Laird Of Norlaw
A Scottish Story
by Mrs. Oliphant

ISBN: 978-93-62764-91-1

Published by

DOUBLE 9 BOOKS

2/13-B, Ansari Road
Daryaganj, New Delhi – 110002
info@double9books.com
www.double9books.com
Tel. 011-40042856

ABOUT THE AUTHOR

Margaret Oliphant Wilson Oliphant was a Scottish author and historical writer who usually wrote under the name Mrs. Oliphant. She was born Margaret Oliphant Wilson on April 4, 1828, and died on June 20, 1897. She writes "domestic realism, the historical novel, and tales of the supernatural" as her short stories. Margaret Oliphant was born in Wallyford, near Musselburgh, East Lothian. She was the only daughter and youngest child still living of Margaret Oliphant (c. 1789–17 September 1854) and Francis W. Wilson, a clerk. We lived in Lasswade, Glasgow, and Liverpool when she was a child. In Wallyford, a street called Oliphant Gardens is named after her. As a girl, she was always trying new things with writing. Passages in the Life of Mrs. Margaret Maitland, her first book, came out in 1849. This was about the mostly successful Scottish Free Church movement, which was something her folks agreed with. Next came Caleb Field in 1851, the same year she met publisher William Blackwood in Edinburgh and was asked to write for Blackwood's Magazine. She did so for the rest of her life and wrote over 100 articles, including one that criticized Arthur Dimmesdale in Nathaniel Hawthorne's "The Scarlet Letter."

CONTENTS

CHAPTER I

The house of Norlaw stands upon the slope of a low hill, under shelter of the three mystic Eildons, and not very far from that little ancient town which, in the language of the author of "Waverley," is called Kennaquhair.

A low, peaceable, fertile slope, bearing trees to its top-most height, and corn on its shoulders, with a little river running by its base, which manages, after many circuits, to wind its way into Tweed. The house, which is built low upon the hill, is two stories in front, but, owing to the unequal level, only one behind. The garden is all at the back, where the ground is sheltered, but in front, the green, natural surface of the hill descends softly to the water without any thing to break its verdure. There are clumps of trees on each side, straying as nature planted them, but nothing adorns the sloping lawn, which is not called a lawn, nor used for any purposes of ornament by the household of Norlaw.

Close by, at the right hand of this homely house, stands an extraordinary foil to its serenity and peacefulness. The old castle of Norlaw, gaunt and bare, and windowless, not a towered and battlemented pile, but a straight, square, savage mass of masonry, with windows pierced high up in its walls in even rows, like a prison, and the gray stone-work below, as high under the first range of windows as the roof of the modern house, rising up blank, like a rock, without the slightest break or opening. To see this strange old ruin, in the very heart of the peaceful country, without a feature of nature to correspond with its sullen strength, nor a circumstance to suggest the times and the danger which made that necessary, is the strangest thing in the world; all the more that the ground has no special capacities for defense, and that the castle is not a picturesque baronial accumulation of turrets and battlements, but a big, austere, fortified dwelling-house, which modern engineering could make an end of in half a day.

It showed, however, if it did nothing better, that the Livingstones were knights and gentlemen, in the day when the Border was an unquiet habitation—and for this, if for nothing else, was held in no little honor by the yeoman Livingstone, direct descendant of the Sir Rodericks and Sir Anthonys, who farmed the remains of his paternal property, and dwelt in the modern house of Norlaw.

This house was little more than a farm-house in appearance, and nothing more in reality. The door opened into a square hall, on either side of which was a large room, with three deep-set windows in each; four of these windows looked out upon the lawn and the water, while one broke each corner of the outer wall. On the side nearest the castle, a little behind the front level of the house, was an "outshot," a little wing built to the side, which formed the kitchen, upon the ever-open door of which the corner window of the common family sitting room kept up a vigilant inspection. A plentiful number of bed-chambers up-stairs were reached by a good stair-case, and a gallery which encircled the hall; the architecture was of the most monotonous and simple regularity; so many windows on one side soberly poising so many windows on the other. The stair-case made a rounded projection at the back of the house, which was surmounted by a steep little turret roof, blue-slated, and bearing a tiny vane for its crown, after the fashion of the countryside; and this, which glimmered pleasantly among the garden fruit trees when you looked down from the top of the hill—and the one-storied projection, which was the kitchen, were the only two features which broke the perfect plainness and uniformity of the house.

But though it was July when this history begins, the flush of summer—and though the sunshine was sweet upon the trees and the water, and the bare old walls of the castle, there was little animation in Norlaw. The blinds were drawn up in the east room, the best apartment—though the sun streamed in at the end window, and "the Mistress" was not wont to leave her favorite carpet to the tender mercies of that bright intruder; and the blinds were down in the dining-room, which nobody had entered this morning, and where even the Mistress's chair and little table in the corner window could not keep a vicarious watch upon the kitchen door. It was not needful; the two maids were very quiet, and not disposed to amuse themselves. Marget, the elder one, who was the byrewoman, and had responsibilities, went about the kitchen very solemnly, speaking with a gravity which became the occasion; and Janet, who was the house-servant, and soft-hearted, stood at the table, washing cups and saucers, very slowly, and with the most elaborate care, lest one of them should tingle upon the other, and putting up her apron very often to wipe the tears from her eyes. Outside, on the broad stone before the kitchen door, a little ragged boy sat, crying bitterly—and no one else was to be seen about the house.

"Jenny," said the elder maid, at last, "give that bairn a piece, and send him away. There's enow of us to greet—for what we're a' to do for a puir distressed family, when aince the will o' God's accomplished this day, I canna tell."

"Oh, woman, dinna speak! he'll maybe win through," cried Jenny, with renewed tears.

Marget was calm in her superior knowledge.

"I ken a death-bed from a sick-bed," she said, with solemnity; "I've seen them baith—and weel I kent, a week come the morn, that it was little good looking for the doctor, or wearying aye for his physic time, or thinking the next draught or the next pill would do. Eh sirs! ane canna see when it's ane's ain trouble; if it had been ony ither man, the Mistress would have kent as weel as me."

"It's an awfu' guid judge that's never wrang," said Jenny, with a little impatience. "He's a guid faither, and a guid maister; it's my hope he'll cheat you a' yet, baith the doctor and you."

Marget shook her head, and went solemnly to a great wooden press, which almost filled one side of the kitchen, to get the "piece" which Jenny showed no intention of bestowing upon the child at the door. Pondering for a moment over the basket of oat cakes, Marget changed her mind, and selected a fine, thin, flour one, from a little pile.

"It's next to funeral bread," she said to herself, in vindication of her choice; "Tammie, my man, the maister would be nae better if ye could mak' the water grit with tears—run away hame, like a good bairn; tell your mother neither the Mistress nor me will forget her, and ye can say, I'll let her ken; and there's a piece to help ye hame."

"I dinna want ony pieces—I want to ken if he's better," said the boy; "my mother said I wasna to come back till there was good news."

"Whisht, sirrah, he'll hear you on his death-bed," said Marget, "but it'll no do *you* ony harm, bairn; the Mistress will aye mind your mother; take your piece and run away."

The child's only answer was to bury his face in his hands, and break into a new fit of crying. Marget came in again, discomfited; after a while she took out a little wooden cup of milk to him, and set it down upon the stone without a word. She was not sufficiently hard-hearted to frown upon the child's grief.

"Eh, woman Jenny!" she cried, after an interval, "to think a man could have so little pith, and yet get in like this to folk's hearts!"

"As if ye didna ken the haill tale," cried Jenny, with indignant tears, "how the maister found the wean afield with his broken leg, and carried him hame—and how there's ever been plenty, baith milk and meal, for thae puir orphants, and Tammie's schooling, and aye a kind word to mend a'—and yet, forsooth, the bairn maunna greet when the maister's at his latter end!"

"We'll a' have cause," said Marget, abruptly; "three bonnie lads that might be knights and earls, every one, and no' a thing but debt and dool, nor a trade to set their hand to. Haud yer peace!—do ye think there's no trade but bakers and tailors, and the like o' that? and there's Huntley, and Patie, and Cosmo, my bonnie bairns!—there never was three Livingstones like them, nor three of ony other name as far as Tyne runs—and the very bairn at the door has muckle to look to as they!"

"But it's nae concern o' yours, or o' mine. I'm sure the maister was aye very good to me," said Jenny, retiring into tears, and a *non sequitur*.

"No, that's true—it's nae concern o' yours—*you're* no' an auld servant like me," said her companion, promptly, "but for mysel' I've sung to them a' in their cradles; I would work for them with my hands, and thankful; but I wouldna desire that of them to let the like o' me work, or the Mistress toil, to keep them in idleset. Na, woman—I'm jealous for my bairns—I would break my heart if Huntley was content to be just like his father; if either the Mistress or the lads will listen to me, I'll gie my word to send them a' away."

"Send them away—and their mother in mourning? Oh, my patience! what for?"

"To make their fortune," said Marget, and she hung the great pot on the great iron hook above the fire, with a sort of heroic gesture, which might have been amusing under other circumstances—for Marget believed in making fortunes, and had the impulse of magnificent hope at her heart.

"Eh, woman! you're hard-hearted," said her softer companion, "to blame the Maister at his last, and plan to leave the Mistress her lane in the world! I would make them abide with her to comfort her, if it was me."

Marget made no answer—she had comforted herself with the flush of fancy which pictured these three sons of the house, each completing his triumph—and she was the byrewoman and had to consider the cattle, and cherish as much as remained of pastoral wealth in this impoverished house. She went out with her dark printed gown carefully "kilted" over her red and blue striped petticoat, and a pail in her hand. She was a woman of forty, a farm servant used to out-of-door work and homely ways, and had neither youth nor sentiment to soften her manners or enlarge her mind. Yet her heart smote her when she thought of the father of the house, who lay dying while she made her criticism upon him, true though it was.

"Has he no' been a good master to me? and would I spare tears if they could ease him?" she said to herself, as she rubbed them away from her eyes. "But folk can greet in the dark when there's no work to do," she added, peremptorily, and so went to her dairy and her thoughts. Tender-hearted Jenny cried in the kitchen, doing no good to any one; but up-stairs in the room of death, where the family waited, there were still no tears.

CHAPTER II

Half a mile below Norlaw, "as Tyne runs," stood the village of Kirkbride. Tyne was but one of the many undistinguished Tynes which water the south of Scotland and the north of England, a clear trout stream, rapid and brown, and lively, with linns and pools, and bits of woodland belonging to it, which the biggest brother of its name could not excel; and Kirkbride also was but one of a host of Kirkbrides, which preserved through the country, long after every stone of it had mouldered, the name of some little chapel raised to St. Bridget. This was an irregular hamlet, straggling over two mounds of rising ground, between which Tyne had been pleased to make a way for himself. The morsel of village street was on one bank of the water, a row of irregular houses, in the midst of which flourished two shops; while at the south end, as it was called, a little inn projected across the road, giving, with this corner, and the open space which it sheltered, an air of village coziness to the place which its size scarcely warranted. The other bank of the water was well covered with trees—drooping birches and alders, not too heavy in their foliage to hide the half dozen cottages which stood at different elevations on the ascending road, nor to vail at the summit the great jargonel pear-tree on the gable wall of the manse, which dwelt upon that height, looking down paternally and with authority upon the houses of the village. The church was further back, and partially hidden by trees, which, seeing this edifice was in the prevailing fashion of rural Scottish churches—a square barn with a little steeple stuck upon it—was all the better for the landscape. A spire never comes amiss at a little distance, when Nature has fair play and trees enough—and the hillock, with its foliage and its cottages, its cozy manse and spire among the trees, filled with thoughts of rural felicity the stray anglers who came now and then to fish in Tyne and consume the produce of their labor in the gable parlor of the Norlaw Arms.

The doctor had just passed through the village. On his way he had been assailed by more than one inquiry. The sympathy of the hamlet was strong, and its curiosity neighborly,—and more than one woman retired into her cottage, shaking her head over the news she received.

"Keep us a'! Norlaw! I mind him afore he could either walk or speak— and *then* I was in service, in the auld mistress's time, at Me'mar," said one of the village grandmothers, who stood upon the threshold of a very little house, where the village mangle was in operation. The old woman stood at the door, looking after the doctor, as he trotted off on his stout pony; she was speaking to herself, and not to the little audience behind, upon whom, however, she turned, as the wayfarer disappeared from her eyes, and laying down her bundle on the table, with a sigh, "Eh, Merran Hastie!" she exclaimed, "he's been guid to you."

The person thus addressed needed no further inducement to put her apron to her eyes. The room was very small, half occupied by the mangle, which a strong country girl was turning; and even in this summer day the apartment was not over bright, seeing that the last arrival stood in the doorway, and that the little window was half covered by a curtain of coarse green gauze. Two other village matrons had come with their "claes," to talk over the danger of their neighbor and landlord, and to comfort the poor widow who had found an active benefactor in "Norlaw." She was comforted, grateful and grieved though she was; and the gossips, though they looked grave, entered *con amore* into the subject; what the Mistress was likely to do, and how the family would be "left."

"My man says they'll a' be roupit, baith stock and plenishing," said the mason's wife. "Me'mar himsel' gave our John an insight into how it was. I judge he maun have lent Norlaw siller; for when he saw the dry-stane dike, where his ground marches with Norlaw, he gave ane of his humphs, and says he to John, 'A guid kick would drive it down;' says he, 'it'll last out *his* time, and for my part, I'm no a man for small fields;' so grannie, there's a family less, you may say already, in the country-side."

"I'll tarry till I see it," said the old woman; "the ane of his family that's likest Norlaw, is his youngest son; and if Me'mar himsel', or the evil ane, his marrow, get clean the better of Huntley and Patrick, not to say the Mistress, it'll be a marvel to me."

"Norlaw was aye an unthrift," said Mrs. Mickle, who kept the grocer's shop in Kirkbride; "nobody could tell, when he was a young man, how he got through his siller. It aye burnt his pockets till he got it spent, and ye never could say what it was on."

"Oh, whisht!" exclaimed the widow; "me, and the like of me, can tell well what it was on."

"Haud a' your tongues," said the old woman; "if any body kens about Norlaw, it's me; I was bairn's-maid at Me'mar, in the time of the auld mistress, as a' the town kens, and I'm well acquaint with a' his pedigree, and mind him a' his life, and the truth's just this, whatever any body may say. He didna get his ain fancy when he was a young lad, and he's never been the same man ever sinsyne."

"Eh! was Norlaw crossed in love?" said the girl at the mangle, staying her grinding to listen; "but I'm no sorry for him; a man that wasna content with the Mistress doesna deserve a good wife."

"Ay, lass; you're coming to have your ain thoughts on such like matters, are ye?" said the old woman; "but take you my word, Susie, that a woman may be the fairest and the faithfu'est that ever stood on a hearthstane, but if she's no her man's fancy, she's nae guid there."

"Susie's very right," said the mason's wife; "he wasna blate! for a better wife than the Mistress never put her hand into ony housewifeskep, and it's her that's to be pitied with a man like you; and our John says—"

"I kent about Norlaw before ever you were born, or John either," said the old woman; "and what I say's *fac*, and what you say's fancy. Norlaw had never a thought in his head, from ten to five-and-twenty, but half of it was for auld Me'mar's ae daughter. I'm no saying he's a strong man of his nature, like them that clear their ain road, or make their ain fortune; but he might have held his ain better than he's ever done, if he had been matched to his fancy when he was a young lad, and had a' his life before him; that's just what I've to say."

"Weel, grannie, its awfu' hard," said the mason's wife; "the Mistress was a bonnie woman in her day, and a spirit that would face onything; and to wear out her life for a man that wasna heeding about her, and be left in her prime a dowerless widow!—Ye may say what ye like—but I wouldna thole the like for the best man in the country-side, let alone Norlaw."

"Naebody would, if they kent," said the oracle, "but what's a woman to do, if she's married and bound, and bairns at her foot, before she ever finds out what's been lying a' the time in her man's heart?"

"Then it was just a shame!" cried Susie, at the mangle, with tears in her eyes; "a burning shame! Eh Grannie, to find it out *then*! I would rather dee!"

"Ay, ay," said the old woman, shaking her head; "young folk think so— but that's life."

"I'll never think weel of Norlaw again—I'll never believe a lad mair! they might be thinking ony mischief in their heart," cried Susie, hastily putting up her particular bundle, and dashing a tear off her hot cheek. "They can greet for him that likes; I'll think of naebody but the Mistress—no me!"

Whereupon this keen sympathizer, who had some thoughts of her own on the matter, rushed forth, disturbing the elder group, whose interest was calmer and more speculative.

"Aweel, aweel! we're a' frail and full of shortcomings," said the widow; "but naebody kens how kind Norlaw has been to me. My little Tammie's away somegate about the house now. I thought the bairn's heart would break when he heard the news first. I'm sure there's no one hour, night or day, that he wouldna lay down his life for Norlaw."

"He was aye a kind man and weel likit—most folk are that spend their siller free, and take a' thing easy," said Mrs. Mickle, with a sigh which was partly for that weakness of human nature, and partly for the departing spirit.

Then new customers began to come in, and the group dispersed. By this time it was getting late in the afternoon, and John Mellerstone's wife had to bethink herself of her husband's supper, and Mrs. Mickle of her evening cup of tea. The sun had begun to slant over the face of the brae opposite to them, brightening the drooping bushes with touches of gold, and glowing upon the white gable wall of the manse, obscured with the wealthy branches of its jargonel tree. The minister was making his way thoughtfully up the path, with his hat over his face a little, and his hands under the square skirts of his coat, never pausing to look down, as was his custom when his mind was at ease. He, too, had been at Norlaw, and his thoughts were still there.

CHAPTER III

The sun was shining into the west chamber at Norlaw. It was the room immediately over the dining-room, a large apartment, paneled and painted in a faint green color, with one window to the front and one to the side of the house. The side window looked immediately upon the old castle, and on the heavy masses of blunt-leaved ivy which hung in wild festoons everywhere from this front of the ruin; and the sun shone in gloriously to the sick chamber, with a strange mockery of the weakness and the sorrow there. This bed was what used to be called a "tent-bed," with heavy curtains of dark brown moreen, closely drawn at the foot, but looped up about the pillows. At the side nearest the sunshine, the Mistress, whose place had been there for weeks, stood by the bed measuring out some medicine for the sufferer. A fortnight's almost ceaseless watching had not sufficed to pale the cheek of health, or waste the vigor of this wife, who was so soon to be a widow. Her fresh, middle-aged, matronly bloom, her dress careful and seemly, her anxious and troubled brow, where deep solicitude and hope had scarcely given way to the dread certainty which everybody else acknowledged, made a very strange contrast, indeed, to the wasted, dying, eager face which lay among those pillows, with already that immovable yellow pallor on its features which never passes away; a long, thin hand, wasted to the bone, was on the coverlid, but the sufferer looked up, with his eager, large black eyes toward the medicine glass in his wife's hand with a singular eagerness. He knew, at last, that he was dying, and even in the solemnity of those last moments, this weak, graceful mind, true to the instincts of its nature, thought with desire and anxiety of dying well.

The three sons of the house were in the room watching with their mother. Huntley, who could scarcely keep still, even in the awe of this shadow of death, stood by the front window, often drawing close to the bed, but unable to continue there. The second, who was his mother's son, a healthful, ruddy, practical lad, kept on the opposite side of the bed, ready to help his mother in moving the patient. And at the foot, concealed by the curtains, a delicate boy of fifteen, with his face buried in his hands, sat upon an old square ottoman, observing nothing. This was Cosmo, the youngest and favorite, the only one of his children who really resembled Norlaw.

The caprice of change was strong upon the dying man; he wanted his position altered twenty times in half an hour. He had not any thing much to say, yet he was hard to please for the manner of saying it; and longed, half in a human and tender yearning for remembrance, and half with the weakness of his character, that his children should never forget these last words of his, nor the circumstances of his dying. He was a good man, but he carried the defects of his personality with him to the very door of heaven. When, at last, the pillows were arranged round him, so as to raise him on his bed in the attitude he wished, he called his children, in his trembling voice. Huntley came forward from the window, with a swelling heart, scarcely able to keep down the tears of his first grief. Patrick stood by the bed-side, holding down his head, with a stubborn composure—and Cosmo, stealing forward, threw himself on his knees and hid his sobbing in the coverlid. They were all on one side, and on the other stood the mother, the care on her brow blanching into conviction, and all her tremulous anxiety calmed with a determination not to disturb this last scene. It *was* the last. Hope could not stand before the look of death upon that face.

"My sons," said Norlaw, "I am just dying; but I know where I am in this strait, trusting in my Saviour. You'll remember I said this, when I'm gone."

There was a pause. Cosmo sobbed aloud in the silence, clinging to the coverlid, and Huntley's breast heaved high with a tumultuous motion—but there was not a word said to break the monologue of the father, who was going away.

"And now you'll have no father to guide you further," he continued, with a strange pity for them in his voice. "There's your mother, at my side— as true a wife and as faithful, as ever a man had for a blessing. Boys, I leave your mother, for her jointure, the love you've had for me. Let her have it all—all—make amends to her. Martha, I've not been the man I might have been to you."

These last words were spoken in a tone of sudden compunction, strangely unlike the almost formal dignity of the first part of his address, and he turned his eager, dying eyes to her, with a startled apprehension of this truth, foreign to all his previous thoughts. She could not have spoken, to save his life. She took his hand between hers, with a low groan, and held it, looking at him with a pitiful, appealing face. The self-accusation was like an injury to her, and he was persuaded to feel it so, and to return to the current of his thoughts.

"Let your mother be your counselor; she has ever been mine," he said once more, with his sad, dying dignity. "I say nothing about your plans, because plans are ill adjuncts to a death-bed; but you'll do your best, every one, and keep your name without blemish, and fear God and honor your mother. If I were to speak for a twelvemonth I could not find more to say."

Again a pause; but this time, besides the sobs of Cosmo, Patrick's tears were dropping, like heavy drops of rain, upon the side of the bed, and Huntley crushed the curtain in his hand to support himself, and only staid here quite against his nature by strong compulsion of his will. Whether he deserved it or not, this man's fortune, all his life, had been to be loved.

"This night, Huntley will be Livingstone of Norlaw," continued the father; "but the world is fading out of my sight, boys—only I mind, and you know, that things have gone ill with us for many a year—make just the best that can be made, and never give up this house and the old name of your fathers. Me'mar will try his worst against you; ay, I ought to say more; but I'm wearing faint—I'm not able; you'll have to ask your mother. Martha, give me something to keep me up a moment more."

She did so hurriedly, with a look of pain; but when he had taken a little wine, the sick man's eye wandered.

"I had something more to say," he repeated, faintly; "never mind—your mother will tell you every thing;—serve God, and be good to your mother, and mind that I die in faith. Bairns, when ye come to your latter end, take heed to set your foot fast upon the rock, that I may find you all again."

They thought he had ended now his farewell to them. They laid him down tenderly, and, with awe and hidden tears, watched how the glow of sunset faded and the evening gray stole in over that pallid face which, for the moment, was all the world to their eyes. Sometimes, he said a faint word to his wife, who sat holding his hand. He was conscious, and calm, and departing. His sins had been like a child's sins—capricious, wayward, fanciful transgressions. He had never harmed any one but himself and his own household—remorseful recollections did not trouble him—and, weak as he was, all his life long he had kept tender in his heart a child's faith. He was dying like a Christian, though not even his faith and comfort, nor the great shadow of death which he was meeting, could sublime his last hours out of nature. God does not always make a Christian's death-bed sublime. But he was fast going where there is no longer any weakness, and the calm of the evening rest was on the ending of his life.

Candles had been brought softly into the room; the moon rose, the night wore on, but they still waited. No one could withdraw from that watch, which it is agony to keep, and yet worse agony to be debarred from keeping, and when it was midnight, the pale face began to flush by intervals, and the fainting frame to grow restless and uneasy. Cosmo, poor boy, struck with the change, rose up to look at him, with a wild, sudden hope that he was getting better; but Cosmo shrunk appalled at the sudden cry which burst as strong as if perfect health had uttered it from the heaving, panting heart of his father.

"Huntley, Huntley, Huntley!" cried the dying man, but it was not his son he called. "Do I know her name? She's but Mary of Melmar—evermore Mary to me—and the will is there—in the mid chamber. Aye!—where is she?—your mother will tell you all—it's too late for me."

The last words were irresolute and confused, dropping back into the faint whispers of death. When he began to speak, his wife had risen from her seat by the bed-side—her cheeks flushed, she held his hand tight, and over the face of her tenderness came an indescribable cloud of mortification, of love aggrieved and impatient, which could not be concealed. She did not speak, but stood watching him, holding his hand close in her own, even after he was silent—and not even when the head sank lower down among the pillows, and the eyes grew dim, and the last hour came, did the watcher resume the patient seat which she had kept so long. She stood by him with a mind disquieted, doing every thing that she could do—quick to see, and tender to minister; but the sacramental calm of the vigil was broken—and the widow still stood by the bed when the early summer light came in over her shoulder, to show how, with the night, this life was over, and every thing was changed. Then she fell down by the bed-side, scarcely able to move her strained limbs, and struck to the heart with the chill of her widowhood.

It was all over—all over—and the new day, in a blaze of terrible sunshine, and the new solitude of life, were to begin together. But her sons, as they were forced to withdraw from the room where one was dead, and one lost in the first blind agony of a survivor, did not know what last pang of a long bitterness that was, which struck its final sting, to aggravate all her grievous trouble, into their mother's heart.

CHAPTER IV

Those slow days of household gloom and darkness, when death lies in the house, and every thought and every sound still bears an involuntary reference to the solemn inmate, resting unconscious of them all, went slowly over the roof of Norlaw. Sunday came, doubly mournful; a day in which Scottish decorum demanded that no one should stir abroad, even to church, and which hung indescribably heavy in those curtained rooms, and through the unbroken stillness of its leisure, upon the three youths who had not even their mother's melancholy society to help them through the day. The Mistress was in her own room, closely shut up with her Bible and her sorrow, taking that first Sabbath of her widowhood, a solitary day of privilege and indulgence, for her own grief. Not a sound was audible in the house; Jenny, who could be best spared, and who was somewhat afraid of the solemn quietness of Norlaw, had been sent away early this morning, to spend the Sabbath with her mother, in Kirkbride, and Marget sat alone in the kitchen, with a closed door and partially shuttered window, reading to herself half aloud from the big Bible in her lap. In the perfect stillness it was possible to hear the monotonous hum of her half-whispering voice, and sometimes the dull fall of the ashes on the kitchen hearth, but not a sound besides.

The blinds were all down in the dining-room, and the lower half of the shutters closed. Though the July sun made triumphant daylight even in spite of this, it was such a stifling, closed-in, melancholy light, bright upon the upper walls and the roof, but darkened and close around the lads, that the memory of it never quite passed out of their hearts. This room, too, was paneled and painted of that dull drab color, which middle-class dining-rooms even now delight in; there were no pictures on the walls, for the family of Norlaw were careless of ornaments, like most families of their country and rank. A dull small clock upon the black marble mantel-piece, and a great china jar on the well-polished, old-fashioned sideboard, were the only articles in which any thing beyond use was even aimed at. The chairs were of heavy mahogany and hair-cloth—a portion of the long dining-table, with a large leaf folded down, very near as black as ebony, and polished like a mirror, stood between the front windows—and the two round ends of this same dining-table stood in the centre of the room, large enough for family purposes, and covered with a red and blue table-cover. There was a heavy large chintz easy-chair at the fire-place, and a little table supporting a covered work-basket in the corner window—yet the room had not been used to look a dull room, heavy and dismal though it was to-day.

The youngest boy sat by the table, leaning over a large family Bible, full of quaint old pictures. Cosmo saw the pictures without seeing them—he was leaning both his elbows on the table, supporting his head with a pair of long, fair hands, which his boy's jacket, which he had outgrown, left bare to the wrists. His first agony of grief had fallen into a dull aching; his eyes were observant of the faintest lines of those familiar wood-cuts, yet he could not have told what was the subject of one of them, though he knew them all by heart. He was fair-haired, pale, and delicate, with sensitive features, and dark eyes, like his father's, which had a strange effect in contrast with the extreme lightness of his hair and complexion. He was the tender boy—the mother's child of the household, and it was Cosmo of whom the village gossips spoke, when they took comfort in the thought that only his youngest son was like Norlaw.

Next to Cosmo, sitting idly on a chair, watching how a stream of confined sunshine came in overhead, at the side of the blind, was Huntley, the eldest son. He was very dark, very ruddy, with close curls of black hair, and eyes of happy hazel-brown. Heretofore, Huntley Livingstone's principal characteristic had been a total incapacity to keep still. For many a year Marget had lamented over him, that he would not "behave himself," and even the Mistress had spoken her mind only too often on the same subject. Huntley would not join, with gravity and decorum, even the circle of evening visitors who gathered on unfrequent occasions round the fireside of Norlaw. He had perpetually something on hand to keep him in motion, and if nothing better was to be had, would rummage through lumber-room and family treasury, hunting up dusty old sets of newspapers and magazines, risking the safety of precious old hereditary parchments, finding a hundred forgotten trifles, which he had nothing to do with. So that it was rare, even on winter evenings, to find Huntley at rest in the family circle; it was his wont to appear in it at intervals bringing something with him which had no right to be there—to be ordered off peremptorily by his mother with the intruding article; to be heard, all the evening through, knocking in nails, and putting up shelves for Marget, or making some one of the countless alterations, which had always to be made in his own bed-chamber and private sanctuary; and finally, to reappear for the family worship, during which he kept as still as his nature would permit, and the family supper, at which Huntley's feats, in cutting down great loaves of bread, and demolishing oat-cakes, were a standing joke in the household.

This was the old Huntley, when all was well in Norlaw. Now he sat still, watching that narrow blade of sunshine, burning in compressed and close by the side of the blind; it was like his own nature, in those early days of household grief.

Patrick was a less remarkable boy than either of his brothers; he was most like Huntley, and had the same eyes, and the same crisp, short curls of black hair. But Patrick had a medium in him; he did what was needful, with the quickest practical sense; he was strong in his perception of right and justice; so strong, that the Quixotry of boyish enthusiasm had never moved him; he was not, in short, a describable person; at this present moment, he was steadily occupied with a volume of sermons; they were extremely heavy metal, but Patrick went on with them, holding fast his mind by that anchor of heaviness. It was not that his gravity was remarkable, or his spiritual appreciation great; but something was needful to keep the spirit afloat in that atmosphere of death; the boys had been "too well brought up" to think of profaning the Sabbath with light literature; and amusing themselves while their father lay dead was a sin quite as heinous. So Patrick Livingstone read, with a knitted brow, sermons of the old Johnsonian period, and Cosmo pondered the quaint Bible woodcuts, and Huntley watched the sunshine; and they had not spoken a word to each other for at least an hour.

Huntley was the first to break the silence.

"I wish to-morrow were come and gone," he exclaimed, suddenly, rising up and taking a rapid turn through the room; "a week of this would kill me."

Cosmo looked up, with an almost feminine reproof in his tearful black eyes.

"Well, laddie," said the elder brother; "dinna look at me with these e'en! If it would have lengthened out his days an hour, or saved him a pang, would I have spared years to do it? but what is *he* heeding for all this gloom and silence now?"

"Nothing," said the second brother, "but the neighbors care, and so does my mother; it's nothing, but it's all we can give—and he *would* have heeded and been pleased, had he thought beforehand on what we should be doing now."

It was so true, that Huntley sat down again overpowered. Yes, *he* would have been pleased to think of every particular of the "respect" which belonged to the dead. The closed houses, the darkened rooms, the funeral train; that tender human spirit would have clung to every one of them in his thoughts, keeping the warmth of human sympathy close to him to the latest possibility, little, little though he knew about them now.

"What troubles me is standing still," said Huntley, with a sigh. "I can not tell what's before us; I don't think even my mother knows; I believe it's worse than we can think of; and we've neither friends, nor money, nor influence. Here are we three Livingstones, and I'm not twenty, and we've debts in money to meet, and mortgages on the land, and nothing in the world but our hands and our heads, and what strength and wit God has given us. I'm not grumbling—but to think upon it all, and to think now that—that he's gone, and we're alone and for ourselves—and to sit still neither doing nor planning, it's that that troubles me!"

"Huntley, it's Sabbath day!" said Cosmo.

"Ay, I ken! it's Sabbath and rest, but not to us," cried the young man; "here's me, that should have seen my way—I'm old enough—me that should have known where I was going, and how I was going, and been able to spare a hand for you; and I'm the biggest burden of all; a man without a trade to turn his hand to, a man without knowledge in his head or skill in his fingers—and to sit still and never say a word, and see them creeping down, day by day, and every thing put back as if life could be put back and wait. True, Patie! what would you have me do?"

"Make up your mind, and wait till it's time to tell it," said Patie, without either reproof or sympathy; but Cosmo was more moved—he came to his eldest brother with a soft step.

"Huntley," said Cosmo, in the soft speech of their childhood, "what makes ye speak about a trade, you that are Livingstone of Norlaw? It's for us to gang and seek our fortunes; you're the chief of your name, and the lands are yours—they canna ruin *you*, Huntley. I see the difference mysel', the folks see it in the country-side; and as for Patie and me, we'll seek our fortunes—we're only the youngest sons, it's our inheritance; but Norlaw, and home, and the name, are with you."

This appeal had the strangest effect upon Huntley; it seemed to dissipate in an instant all the impatience and excitement of the youth's grief; he put his arm round Cosmo, with a sudden melting of heart and countenance.

"Do ye hear him, Patie?" cried Huntley, with tears; "he thinks home's home forever, because the race has been here a thousand years; he thinks I'm a prince delivering my kingdom! Cosmo, the land's gone; I know there's not an acre ours after to-morrow. I've found it out, bit by bit, though nobody said a word; but we'll save the house, and the old castle, if we should never have a penny over, for mother and you."

The boy stared aghast into his brother's face. The land! it had been Cosmo's dream by night, and thought by day. The poetic child had made, indeed, a heroic kingdom and inheritance out of that little patrimonial farm. Notwithstanding, he turned to Patie for confirmation, but found no comfort there.

"As you think best, Huntley," said the second son, "but what is a name? My mother will care little for Norlaw when we are gone, and the name of a landed family has kept us poor. *I've* found things out as well as you. I thought it would be best to part with all."

"It was almost his last word," said Huntley, sadly.

"Ay, but he could not tell," said the stout-hearted boy; "he was of another mind from you or me; he did not think that our strength and our lives were for better use than to be wasted on a word. What's Norlaw Castle to us, more than a castle in a book? Ay, Cosmo, it's true. Would you drag a burden of debt at Huntley's feet for the sake of an acre of corn-land, or four old walls? We've been kept down and kept in prison, us and our forbears, because of Norlaw. I say we should go free."

"And I," cried Cosmo, lifting his long, white hand in sudden passion, "I, if Huntley does not care for the name, nor for my father's last wish, nor for the house of our ancestors; I will never rest night nor day, though I break my heart or lose my life, till I redeem Norlaw!"

Huntley, whose arm still rested on the boy's shoulder, drew him closer, with a look which had caught a tender, sympathetic, half-compassionate enthusiasm from his.

"We'll save Norlaw for my father's son," said the elder brother; and, young as Huntley was, he looked with eyes full of love and pity upon this boy, who inherited more from his father than his name. Huntley had been brought up in all the natural love and reverence of a well-ordered family; he knew there was weakness in his father's character, beautiful, lovable, tender weakness, for which, somehow, people only seem to like him better. He had not permitted himself to see yet what harm and selfish unconsciousness of others that graceful temperament had hidden. He looked at Cosmo, thinking as a strong mind thinks of that constitution which is called poetic—of the sensitive nature which would shrink from unkindness, and the tender spirit which could not bear the trials of the world; and the lad's heart expanded over his father's son.

Patie got up from his chair, and went to the little bookcase in the corner to look for another book of sermons. This boy could not blind his eyes, even with family affection. He loved his father, but he knew plainly, and in so many words, that his father had ruined their inheritance. He could not help seeing that this amiable tenderness bore no better fruit than selfishness or cruelty. He thought it would be right and just to all their hopes to part with even the name of Norlaw. But it was not his concern; he was ready to give his opinion at the proper time, but not to stand out unreasonably against the decision of his elder brother; and when he, too, looked at Cosmo, it was with soberer eyes than those of Huntley—not that he cared less for his father's son—but Patrick could not help seeing with those clear eyes of his; and what he feared to see was not the sensitive nature and the tender spirit, but the self-regard which lay beneath.

Which of them was right, or whether either of them were right, this history will best show.

CHAPTER V

Sabbath night; a July night, sweet with summer stars and moonlight, and with no darkness in it: the water running soft with its quietest murmur, the thrush and blackbird beguiled to sing almost as late as the southland nightingale; the scent of the late roses coming round the corner of the house on the faint breeze; the stars clustered in a little crowd over the gaunt castle walls, and in the distance the three weird Eildons, standing out dark against the pale azure blue and flood of moonlight; a Sabbath evening with not a sound in it, save the sweetest sounds of nature, a visible holy blessing of quiet and repose.

But the table was spread in the dining-parlor at Norlaw; there was a basket of oat-cakes and flour "bannocks" upon the table, in a snowy napkin, and butter, and milk, and cheese, all of the freshest and most fragrant, the produce of their own lands. Two candles made a little spot of light upon the white table-cloth, but left all the rest of the room in dreary shadow. To see it was enough to tell that some calamity oppressed the house—and when the widow came in, with her face of exhaustion, and eyes which could weep no more for very weariness, when the boys followed slowly one by one, and Marget coming in with the solemn, noiseless step, so unusual to her, hovered about them with all her portentous gravity, and unwonted attendance, it was not hard to conclude that they ate and drank under the shadow of death. The Mistress had not appeared that day, from the early breakfast until now; it was the only time before or after when she faltered from the ways of common life.

When they had ended the meal, which no one cared to taste, and when the lads began to think with some comfort, in the weariness of their youth, that the day at last was over, Mrs. Livingstone drew her chair away from the table, and looked at them all with the sorrowful tenderness of a mother and a widow. Then, after a long interval, she spoke.

"Bairns!" she said, with a voice which was hoarse with solicitude and weeping, "you're a' thinking what you're to do, and though it's the Sabbath day, I canna blame ye, but me, I'm but a weak woman—I could not say a word to counsel ye, if it was to save the breaking of my heart this day."

"We never looked for it, mother. There's time enough! do you think we would press our plans on you?" cried the eager Huntley, who had been groaning but a few hours ago, at this compulsory delay.

"Na, I could not do it," said the mother, turning her head aside, and drawing the hem of her apron through her fingers, while the tears dropped slowly out of her tired eyes; "this is the last Sabbath day that him and me will be under the same roof. I canna speak to you, bairns; I'm but a weak woman, and I've been his wife this five-and-twenty years."

After a pause, the Mistress dried her eyes, and went on hurriedly:—

"But I ken ye must have your ain thoughts; the like of you canna keep still a long summer day, though it is a Sabbath; and, bairns, I've just this to say to you; ye canna fear mair than we'll have to meet. I'm thankful even that he's gane hame before the storm falls; for you're a' young, and can stand a blast. There's plenty to do, and plenty to bear. I dinna forbid ye thinking, though it's Sabbath night, and death is among us; but oh! laddies, think in a godly manner, and ask a blessing—dinna darken the Sabbath with worldly thoughts, and him lying on his last bed up the stair!"

The boys drew near to her simultaneously, with a common impulse. She heard the rustle and motion of their youthful grief, but she still kept her head aside, and drew tightly through her fingers the hem of her apron.

"The day after the morn," continued the widow, "I'll be ready with all that I ken, and ready to hear whatever you think for yourselves; think discreetly, and I'll no' oppose, and think soberly, without pride, for we're at the foot of the brae. And we've nae friends to advise us, bairns," continued the Mistress, raising her head a little with the very pride which she deprecated; "we've neither kith nor kin to take us by the hand, nor give us counsel. Maybe it's a' the better—for we've only Providence to trust to now, and ourselves."

By this time she had risen up, and taking the candle which Patrick had lighted for her, she stood with the little flat brass sconce in her hand, and the light flickering over her face, still looking down. Yet she lingered, as if she had something more to say. It burst from her lips, at last, suddenly, almost with passion.

"Bairns! take heed, in your very innermost hearts, that ye think no blame!" cried the widow; and when she had said these words, hastened away, as if afraid to follow up or to weaken them by another syllable. When she was gone, the lads stood silently about the table, each of them with an additional ache in his heart. There *was* blame which might be thought, which might be spoken; even she was aware of it, in the jealous regard of her early grief.

"The Mistress has bidden you a' good night," said Marget, entering softly; "ye've taen nae supper, and ye took nae dinner; how are ye to live and work, growing laddies like you, if you gang on at this rate? Ye mean to break my heart amang you. If ye never break bread, Huntley Livingstone, how will you get through the morn?"

"I wish it was over," cried Huntley, once more.

"And so do I. Eh! bairns, when I see those blinds a' drawn down, it makes my heart sick," cried Marget, "and grief itsel's easier to thole when ane has ane's wark in hand. But I didna come to haver nonsense here. I came to bid ye a' gang to your beds, like good laddies. Ye'll a' sleep; that's the good of being young. The Mistress, I daur to say, and even mysel', will not close an eye this night."

"Would my mother let you remain with her, Marget?" said Huntley; "I can't bear to think she's alone in her trouble. Somebody should have come to stay with her; Katie Logan from the manse, perhaps. Why did not some one think of it before?"

"Whisht! and gang to your beds," said Marget; "no fremd person, however kindly, ever wins so far into the Mistress's heart. If she had been blessed with a daughter of her ain, it might have been different. Na, Huntley, your mother wouldna put up with me. She's no ane to have either friend or servant tending on her sorrows. Some women would, but no' the Mistress; and I'm o' the same mind mysel'. Gang to your beds, and get your rest, like good bairns; the morn will be a new day."

"Shut up the house and sleep; that's all we can do," said Cosmo; "but I canna rest—and he'll never be another night in this house. Oh, father, father! I'll keep the watch for your sake!"

"If he's in this house, he's here," said Patrick, suddenly, to the great amazement of his hearers, moved for once into a higher imagination than any of them; "do you hear me Cosmo? if he's out of heaven, he's here; he's no' on yon bed dead. It's no' *him* that's to be carried to Dryburgh. Watching's past and done, unless he watches us; he's either in heaven, or he's here."

"Eh, laddie! God bless you, that's true!" cried Marget, moved into sudden tears. There was not composure enough among them to add another word; they went to their rooms silently, not to disturb their mother's solitude. But Huntley could not rest; he came softly down stairs again, through the darkened house, to find Marget sitting by the fire which she had just "gathered" to last all night, reading her last chapter in the big Bible, and startled her by drawing the bolts softly aside and stepping out into the open air.

"I must breathe," the lad said with a voice full of broken sobs.

The night was like a night of heaven, if such a glory is, where all glories are. The moon was more lavish in her full, mellow splendor, than she had ever been before, to Huntley's eyes; the sky seemed as light as day, almost too luminous to show the stars, which were there shining softly in myriads, though you could scarcely see them; and the water flowed, and the trees rustled, with a perfection of still music, exquisite, and silent, and beyond description, which Nature only knows when she is alone. The youth turned back again with a sob which eased his heart. Out of doors nothing but splendor, glory, a beatitude calm and full as heaven; within, nothing but death and the presence of death, heavy, like a pall, upon the house and all its inmates. He went back to his rest, with the wonder of humanity in his heart; when, God help us, should this terrible difference be over? when should the dutiful creation, expanding thus, while the rebel sleeps, receive once more its fullest note of harmony, its better Eden, the race for whom sin and sorrow has ended for evermore?

CHAPTER VI

The day of the funeral rose with a merciful cloud over its brightness—a sorrowful bustle was in the house of Norlaw; some of the attendants of the burial train were to return to dine, as the custom was, and Marget and Jenny were fully employed in the kitchen, with the assistance of the mother of the latter, who was a widow herself, full of sorrowful experience, and liked, as is not unusual in her class, to assist in the melancholy labors of such an "occasion." The east room was open for the reception of the funeral guests, and on the table were set out decanters of wine, and liberal plates of a delicate cake which used to bear the dismal title of funeral biscuit in Scotland. The widow, who put on for the first time to-day, the dress which henceforward she should wear all her life, kept her own apartment, where the wife of the principal farmer near, and Catharine Logan, the minister's daughter, had joined her; for though she would much rather have been left alone, use and precedent were strong upon the Mistress, and she would not willingly have broken through any of the formal and unalterable customs of the country-side. The guests gathered gradually about the melancholy house; it was to be "a great funeral." As horseman after horseman arrived, the women in the kitchen looked out from the corner of their closed shutters, with mournful pride and satisfaction; every household of any standing in the district came out to show "respect" to Norlaw—and even the widow in her darkened room felt a certain pleasure in the sounds which came softened to her ear, the horses' hoofs, the clash of stirrup and bridle, and the murmur of open-air voices, which even the "occasion" could not subdue beyond a certain measure.

The lads were all assembled in the east room to receive their guests, and with them, the earliest arrival of all, was the minister, lending his kindly support and aid to Huntley, in this earliest and saddest exercise of his new duties as head of the house. One good thing was, that the visitors did not feel themselves called upon to overwhelm the fatherless youth with condolences. A hearty grasp of rough hands; a subdued word of friendship and encouragement, as one by one, or in little clusters, those great rustic figures, all in solemn mourning, collected in the room, were all that "the family" were called upon to undergo.

The hum of conversation which immediately began, subdued in tone and grave in expression, but still conversation such as rural neighbors use, interspersed with inquiries and shakes of the head, as to how this household was "left," was a relief to the immediate mourners, though perhaps it was not much in accordance with the sentiment of the time. It was etiquette that the wine and cake should be served to all present, and when all the guests were assembled, the minister rose, and called them to prayer. They stood in strange groups, those stalwart, ruddy southland men, about the table—one covering his eyes with his hand, one standing erect, with his head bowed, some leaning against the wall, or over the chairs. Perhaps eyes unaccustomed to such a scene might have thought there was little reverence in the fashion of this funeral service; but there was at least perfect silence, through which the grave voice of the minister rose steadily, yet not without a falter of personal emotion. It was not the solemn impersonal words which other churches say over every man whom death makes sacred. It was an individual voice, asking comfort for the living, thanking God for the dead— and when that was done the ceremonial was so far over, and Norlaw had only now to be carried to his grave.

All the preparations were thus far accomplished. The three brothers and Dr. Logan had taken their place in the mourning coach; some distant relatives had taken possession of another; and the bulk of the guests had mounted and were forming into a procession behind. Every thing had progressed thus far, when some sudden obstruction became visible to the horsemen without. The funeral attendants closed round the hearse, the horses were seized by strangers, and their forward motion checked; already the farmers behind, leaping from their horses, crowded on to ascertain the cause of the detention; but the very fact of it was not immediately visible to the youths who were most interested. When the sudden contention of voices startled Huntley, the lad gazed out of the window for a moment in the wild resentment of grief, and then dashing open the door, sprang into the midst of the crowd; a man who was not in mourning, and held a baton in his hand, stood firm and resolute, with his hand upon the door of the hearse; other men conspicuous among the funeral guests, in their every-day dress, kept close by him, supporting their superior. The guides of the funeral equipage were already in high altercation with the intruders, yet, even at their loudest, were visibly afraid of them.

"Take out the horses, Grierson—do your duty!" shouted the leader at the hearse door; "stand back, ye blockheads, in the name of the law! I'm here to do my orders; stand back, or it'll be waur for ye a'—ha! wha's here?"

It was Huntley, whose firm young grasp was on the sturdy shoulder of the speaker.

"Leave the door, or I'll fell you!" cried the lad, in breathless passion, shaking with his clutch of fury the strong thick-set frame which had double his strength; "what do you want here?—how do you dare to stop the funeral? take off your hand off the door, or I'll fell you to the ground!"

"Whisht, lad, whisht—it's a sheriff's officer; speak him canny and he'll hear reason," cried one of the farmers, hastily laying a detaining grasp on Huntley's arm. The intruder stood his ground firmly. He took his hand from the door, not in obedience to the threat, but to the grief which burned in the youth's eyes.

"My lad, it's little pleasure to me," he said, in a voice which was not without respect, "but I must do my duty. Felling me's no' easy, but felling the law is harder still. Make him stand aside, any of you that's his friend, and has sense to ken; there's no mortal good in resisting; this funeral can not gang on this day."

"Let go—stand back; speak to *me*," said Huntley, throwing off the grasp of his friend, and turning to his opponent a face in which bitter shame and distress began to take the place of passion; "stand aside, every man—what right have *you* to stop us burying our dead? I'm his son; come here and tell me."

"I am very sorry for you, my lad, but I can not help it," said the officer; "I'm bound to arrest the body of Patrick Livingstone, of Norlaw. It may be a cruel thing, but I must do my duty. I'm Alexander Elliot, sheriff's officer at Melrose; I want to make no disturbance more than can be helped. Take my advice. Take in the coffin to the house and bid the neighbors back for another day. And, in the meantime, look up your friends and settle your scores with Melmar. It's the best you can do."

"Elliot," said Dr. Logan, over his shoulder, "do you call this law, to arrest the dead? He's far beyond debt and trouble now. For shame!—leave the living to meet their troubles, but let them bury their dead."

"And so I would, minister, if it was me," said Elliot, twirling his baton in his hand, and looking down with momentary shame and confusion; "but I've as little to do with the business as you have," he added, hurriedly. "I give you my advice for the best, but I must do my duty. Grierson, look to thae youngsters—dang them a'—do ye ca' that mair seemly? it's waur than me!"

Cosmo Livingstone, wild with a boy's passion, and stupefied with grief, had sprung up to the driving-seat of the hearse while this discussion proceeded; and lashing the half-loosed horses, had urged them forward with a violent and unseemly speed, which threw down on either side the men who were at their heads, and dispersed the crowd in momentary alarm. The frightened animals dashed forward wildly for a few steps, but speedily brought up in their unaccustomed career by the shouts and pursuit of the attendants, carried the melancholy vehicle down the slope and paused, snorting, at the edge of the stream, through which, the boy, half mad with excitement, would have driven them. Perhaps the wild gallop of the hearse, though only for so short a distance, horrified the bystanders more than the real interruption. One of the funeral guests seized Cosmo in his strong arms, and lifted him down like a child; the others led the panting horses back at the reverential pace which became the solemn burden they were bearing; and after that outbreak of passion, the question was settled without further discussion. Patrick Livingstone, his eyes swollen and heavy with burning tears, which he could not shed, led the way, while the bearers once more carried to his vacant room all that remained of Norlaw.

The mass of the funeral guests paused only long enough to maintain some degree of quietness and decency; they dispersed with natural good feeling, without aggravating the unfortunate family with condolence or observation. Huntley, with the minister and the principal farmer of the district, Mr. Blackadder, of Tyneside, who happened to be also an old and steady friend of their father, stood at a little distance with the officer, investigating the detainer which kept the dead out of his grave; the melancholy empty hearse and dismal coaches crept off slowly along the high road; and Cosmo, trembling in every limb with the violence of his excitement, stood speechless at the door, gazing after them, falling, in the quick revulsion of his temperament, from unnatural passion into utter and prostrate despondency. The poor boy scarcely knew who it was that drew him into the house, and spoke those words of comfort which relieved his overcharged heart by tears. It was pretty Katie Logan, crying herself, and scarcely able to speak, who had been sent down from the widow's room, by Mrs. Blackadder, to find out what the commotion was; and who, struck with horror and amazement, as at a sacrilege, was terrified to go up again, to break the tender, proud heart of Norlaw's mourning wife, with such terrible news.

Presently the mournful little party came in to the east room, which still stood as they had left it, with the funeral bread and wine upon the table. Patrick came to join them immediately, and the two lads bent their heads together over the paper: a thousand pounds, borrowed by a hundred at a time from Mr. Huntley, of Melmar, over and above the mortgages which that gentleman held on the better part of the lands of Norlaw. The boys read it with a passion of indignation and shame in their hearts; their father's affairs, on his funeral day, publicly "exposed" to all the countryside; their private distress and painful prospects, and his unthrift and weakness made the talk of every gossip in the country. Huntley and Patrick drew a hard breath, and clasped each other's hands with the grip of desperation. But Norlaw lay unburied on his death-bed; they could not bury him till this money was paid; it was an appalling sum to people in their class, already deeply impoverished, and in the first tingle of this distressing blow, they saw no light either on one side or the other, and could not tell what to do.

"But I can not understand," said Dr. Logan, who was a man limited and literal, although a most pious minister and the father of his people; "I can not understand how law can sanction what even nature holds up her hand against. The dead—man! how dare ye step in with your worldly arrests and warrants, when the Lord has been before you? how dare ye put your bit baton across the grave, where a righteous man should have been laid this day?"

"I have to do my duty," said the immovable Elliot, "how daur ye, is naething to me. I must do according to my instructions—and ye ken, doctor, it's but a man's body can be apprehended ony time. Neither you nor me can lay grips on his soul."

"Hush, mocker!" cried the distressed clergyman; "but what is to be done? Mr. Blackadder, these bairns can not get this money but with time and toil. If that will do any good, I'll go immediately to Me'mar myself."

"Never," cried Huntley; "never—any thing but that. I'll sell myself for a slave before I'll take a favor from my father's enemy."

"It's in Whitelaw's hands, the writer in Melrose. I'll ride down there and ask about it," said Blackadder; "whisht, Huntley! the minister's presence should learn you better—and every honest man can but pity and scorn ane that makes war with the dead; I'll ride round to Whitelaw. My wife's a sensible woman—she'll break it softly to your mother—and see you do nothing to make it worse. I suppose, Elliot, when I come back I'll find you here."

"Ay, sir, I'm safe enough," said the officer significantly, as "Tyneside" rose to leave the room. Huntley went with him silently to the stable, where his horse stood still saddled.

"I see what's in your eye," said Blackadder, in a whisper; "take heart and do it; trust not a man more than is needful, and dinna be violent. I'll be back before dark, but I may not chance to speak to you again. Do what's in your heart."

Huntley wrung the friendly hand held out to him, and went in without a word. His old restless activity seemed to have returned to him, and there was a kindling fire in his hazel eyes which meant some purpose.

Good Dr. Logan took the lad's hands, and poured comfort and kindness into his ears; but Huntley could scarcely pause to listen. It was not strange — and it seemed almost hard to bid the youth have patience when the vulgar law — stubborn and immovable — the law of money and merchandise, kept joint possession with death of this melancholy house.

CHAPTER VII

Huntley could not see his mother after this outrage became known to her. The widow resented it with all a woman's horror and passion, and with all the shame of a Scottish matron, jealous, above all things, of privacy and "respect." Pretty Katie Logan sat at her feet crying in inarticulate and unreasoning sympathy, which was better for the Mistress than all the wisdom and consolation with which good Mrs. Blackadder endeavored to support her. In the kitchen, Jenny and her mother cried too, the latter telling doleful stories of similar circumstances which she had known; but Marget went about with a burning cheek, watching "the laddies" with a jealous tenderness, which no one but their mother could have surpassed, eager to read their looks and anticipate their meaning. It was a sultry, oppressive day, hot and cloudy, threatening a thunder storm; and it is impossible to describe the still heavier oppression of distress and excitement in this closed-up and gloomy house. When Marget went out to the byre, late in the afternoon, several hours after these occurrences, Huntley came to her secretly by a back way. What he said roused the spirit of a hero in Marget's frame. She put aside her pail on the instant, smoothed down her new black gown over her petticoat, and threw a shawl across her head.

"This moment, laddie—this instant—ye may trust me!" cried Marget, with a sob; and before Huntley, passing round behind the offices, came in sight of the high road, his messenger had already disappeared on the way to Kirkbride.

Then Huntley drew his cap over his eyes, threw round him a gray shepherd's plaid, as a partial disguise, and set out in the opposite direction. Before he reached his journey's end, the sweeping deluge of a thunder storm came down upon those uplands, in white sheets of falling water. The lad did not pause to take shelter, scarcely to take breath, but pushed on till he reached some scattered cottages, where the men were just returning from their day's work. At that time the rain and the western sun, through the thickness of the thunder cloud, made a gorgeous, lurid, unearthly glow, like what it might make through the smoke of a great battle. Huntley called one of the men to him into a little hollow below the hamlet. He was one of the servants of Norlaw, as were most of these cottagers. The young master told his tale with little loss of words, and met with the hearty and ready assent of his horrified listener.

"I'll no' fail ye, Maister Huntley; neither will the Laidlaws. I'll bring them up by the darkening; ye may reckon upon them and me," said the laborer; "and what use burdening yoursel' with mair, unless it were to show respect. There's enow, with ane of you lads to take turns, and us three."

"Not at the darkening—at midnight, Willie; or at earliest at eleven, when it's quite dark," said Huntley.

"At eleven! mid nicht! I'm no heeding; but what will we say to the wives?" said Willie, scratching his head in momentary dismay.

"Say—but not till you leave them—that you're coming to serve Norlaw in extremity," said Huntley; "and to make my brothers and me debtors to your kindness forever."

"Whisht about that," said Willie Noble; "mony a guid turn's come to us out of Norlaw;—and Peggie's nae like the maist of women—she'll hear reason. If we can aince win owre Tweed, we're safe, Maister Huntley; but it's a weary long way to there. What would you say to a guid horse and a light cart? there's few folk about the roads at night."

Huntley shrunk with involuntary horror from the details even of his own arrangement.

"I'll take care for that," he said, hurriedly; "but we could not take a carriage over Tweed, and that is why I ask this help from you."

"And kindly welcome; I wish to heaven it had been a blyther errand for your sake," said the man, heartily; "but we maun take what God sends; and wha's to keep the officer quiet, for that's the chief of the haill plan?"

"I've to think of that yet," said Huntley, turning his face towards home with a heavy sigh.

"I'd bind him neck and heels, and put him in Tyne to cool himsel'!" said Willie, with a fervent effusion of indignation. Huntley only bade him remember the hour, shook his hard hand, and hurried away.

It was a painful, troubled, unhappy evening, full of the excitement of a conspiracy. When Huntley and Patrick communicated with each other it was impossible to say, for they never seemed to meet alone, and Patrick had taken upon himself the hard duty of keeping Elliot company.

The minister and his daughter departed sadly in the twilight, knowing no comfort for the family they left. And Mr. Blackadder returned gloomily from his visit to the attorney, bringing the news that he had no authority to stop proceedings till he consulted with his principal, after which, in good time, and with a look and grasp of Huntley's hand, which were full of meaning, the good farmer, too, took his wife away.

Then came the real struggle. The officer kept his watch in the dining-room, to which he had shifted from some precautionary notion, and sat there in the great chintz easy-chair, which the hearts of the lads burned to see him occupy, perfectly content to talk to Patie, and to consume soberly a very large measure of toddy, the materials for which stood on the table the whole evening. Patie discharged his painful office like a hero. He sat by the other side of the table, listening to the man's stories, refusing to meet Huntley's eye when by chance he entered the room, and taking no note of the reproachful, indignant glances of Cosmo, who still knew nothing of their plans, and could not keep his patience when he saw his brother entertaining this coarse intruder in their sorrowful affairs.

Huntley, meanwhile, moved about stealthily, making all the arrangements. It was a considerable discouragement to find that the officer had made up his mind to spend the night in the dining-room, where Marget, with a swell and excitement in her homely form, which, fortunately, Elliot's eyes were not sufficiently enlightened to see, prepared the hair-cloth sofa for his night's repose. He was sober, in spite of the toddy, but it seemed more than mortal powers could bear, keeping awake.

It was midnight; and Huntley knew by Marget's face that his assistants were in attendance, but still they scarcely ventured to say to each other that every thing was ready for their melancholy office.

Midnight, and the house was still. Yet such a perturbed and miserable stillness, tingling with apprehension and watchfulness! The widow had left her sorrowful retirement up-stairs; she stood outside on the gallery in the darkness, with her hands clasped close together, keeping down all natural pangs in this unnatural hardship. Marget, who was strong and resolute, stood watching breathless at the closed door of the dining-room, with a great plaid in her hands, which nobody understood the occasion for. No one else was to be seen, save a train of four black figures moving noiselessly up the stairs. At every step these midnight emissaries took, Marget held her breath harder, and the Mistress clasped her hand upon her heart with an agonizing idea that its throbs must be heard throughout the house. A single faint ray of light directed their way to the room where the dead lay; all beside was in the deepest darkness of a stormy night—and once more with a merciful noise pattering loud upon the trees without, came down the deluge of the thunder storm.

It was at this moment that Cosmo, sitting in his own room, trying to compose his heart with a chapter in his Bible, saw, for he could not hear, his door open, and Huntley's face, pale with agitation, look in.

"Come!" said the elder brother, who was almost speechless with strong excitement.

"Where?" cried the amazed boy.

Huntley held up his hand to bar speaking.

"To bury my father," he answered, with a voice which, deep in solemn meaning, seemed, somehow, to be without common sound, and rather to convey itself to the mind, than to speak to the ear.

Without a word, Cosmo rose and followed. His brother held him fast upon the dark gallery, in a speechless grip of intense emotion. Cosmo could scarcely restrain the natural cry of terror, the natural sob out of his boy's heart.

It went down solemnly and noiselessly, down the muffled stair, that something, dark and heavy, which the noiseless figures carried. At the foot of the stairs, Patie, his own pale face the only thing there on which the light fell fully, held with a steady, patient determination, and without a tremble, the little rush light, hid in a lantern, which guided their descent, and in the darkness above stood the Mistress, like a figure in a dream, with her hands pressed on her heart.

Then a blast of colder air, a louder sound of the thunder-rain. The two brothers stole down stairs, Huntley still holding fast by Cosmo's arm—and in another moment the whole procession stood safe and free, in the garden, under the blast of big rain and the mighty masses of cloud. So far, all was safe; and thus, under shelter of the midnight, set forth from his sad house, the funeral of Norlaw.

CHAPTER VIII

That night was a night of storms. When the heavy rain ceased, peals of thunder shook the house, and vivid lightning flashed through the darkness. When the funeral procession was safe, Marget fastened her plaid across the door of the dining-room as a precaution, and went up stairs to attend to the Mistress. She found the widow kneeling down, where she had stood, leaning her hands and her face against the railings of the gallery, not fainting, perfectly conscious, yet in a condition in comparison with which a swoon would have been happiness. Her hands clung tight and rigid about the rails. She had sunk upon her knees from pure exhaustion, and kept that position for the same reason. Yet she was terribly conscious of the approach of Marget, afraid of her in the darkness, as if she were an enemy. The faithful servant managed to rouse her after great pains, and at last was able to lead her down stairs, to the gathered fire in the kitchen, where the two sat in the darkness, with one red spark of fire preserving some appearance of life in the apartment, listening to the blast of rain against the window, watching the flashes of wild light which blazed through the three round holes in the kitchen shutter, and the thunder which echoed far among the distant hills. Sitting together without a word, listening with feverish anxiety to every sound, and fearing every moment that the storm must wake their undesired inmate, who could not stir in the dining-room without their hearing. It was thus the solemn night passed, lingering and terrible, over the heads of the women who remained at home.

And through that wild summer midnight—through the heavy roads, where their feet sank at every step, and the fluttering ghostly branches on the hedgerows, which caught the rude pall, a large black shawl, which had been thrown over the coffin—the melancholy clandestine procession made its way. When they had gone about half a mile, they were met by the old post-chaise from the Norlaw Arms, at Kirkbride, which had been waiting there for them. In it, relieving each other, the little party proceeded onward. At length they came to Tweed, to the pebbly beach, where the ferryman's boat lay fastened by its iron ring and hempen cable. But for the fortunate chance of finding it here, Huntley, who was unrivaled in all athletic exercises, had looked for nothing better than swimming across the river, to fetch the boat from the other side. Rapidly, yet reverently, their solemn burden was laid in the boat; two of the men, by this time, had ventured to light torches, which they had brought with them, wrapt in a plaid. The rain had ceased. The broad breast of Tweed "grit" with those floods, and overflowing the pebbles for a few yards before they reached the real margin of the stream, flowed rapidly and strongly, with a dark, swift current, marked with foam, which it required no small effort to strike steadily across. The dark trees, glistening with big drops of rain—the unseen depths on either side, only perceptible to their senses by the cold full breath of wind which blew over them—the sound of water running fierce in an expanded tide; and as they set out upon the river, the surrounding gleam of water shining under their torches, and the strong swell of downward motion, against which they had to struggle, composed altogether a scene which no one there soon forgot. The boat had to return a second time, to convey all its passengers; and then once more, with the solemn tramp of a procession, the little party went on in the darkness to the grave.

And then the night calmed, and a wild, frightened moon looked out of the clouds into solemn Dryburgh, in the midst of her old monkish orchards. Through the great grass-grown roofless nave, the white light fell in a sudden calm, pallid and silent as death itself, yet looking on like an amazed spectator of the scene.

The open grave stood ready as it had been prepared this morning—a dark, yawning breach in the wet grass, its edge all defined and glistening in the moonlight. It was in one of the small side chapels, overgrown with grass and ivy, which are just distinguishable from the main mass of the ruin; here the torches blazed and the dark figures grouped together, and in a solemn and mysterious silence these solitary remains of the old house of God looked on at the funeral. The storm was over; the thunder clouds rolled away to the north; the face of the heavens cleared; the moon grew brighter. High against the sky stood out the Catherine window in its frame of ivy, the solitary shafts and walls from which the trees waved—and in a solemn gloom, broken by flashes of light which magnified the shadow, lay those morsels of the ancient building which still retained a cover. The wind rustled through the trees, shaking down great drops of moisture, which fell with a startling coldness upon the faces of the mourners, some of whom began to feel the thrill of superstitious awe. It was the only sound, save that of the subdued footsteps round the grave, and the last heavy, dreadful bustle of human exertion, letting down the silent inhabitant into his last resting-place, which sounded over the burial of Norlaw.

And now, at last, it was all over; the terrible excitement, the dismal, long, self-restraint, the unnatural force of human resentment and defiance which had mingled with the grief of these three lads. At last he was in his grave, solemnly and safely; at last he was secure where no man could insult what remained of him, or profane his dwelling-place. As the moon shone on the leveled soil, Cosmo cried aloud in a boyish agony of nature, and fell upon the wet grass beside the grave. The cry rang through all the solemn echoes of the place. Some startled birds flew out of the ivied crevices, and made wild, bewildered circles of fright among the walls. A pang of sudden terror fell upon the rustic attendants; the torch bearers let their lights fall, and the chief among them hurriedly entreated Huntley to linger no longer.

"A's done!" said Willie Noble, lifting his bonnet reverently from his head. "Farewell to a good master that I humbly hope's in heaven lang afore now. We can do him nae further good, and the lads are timid of the place. Maister Huntley, may I give them the word to turn hame?"

So they turned home; the three brothers, last and lingering, turned back to life and their troubles—all the weary weight of toil which *he* had left on their shoulders, for whom this solemn midnight expedition was their last personal service. The three came together, hand in hand, saying never a word—their hearts "grit" like Tweed, and flowing full with unspeakable emotions—and passed softly under the old fruit trees, which shed heavy dew upon their heads, and through the wet paths which shone in lines of silver under the moon; Tweed, lying full in a sudden revelation of moonlight, one bank falling off into soft shadows of trees, the other guarding with a ledge of rock some fair boundary of possession, and the bubbles of foam gleaming bright upon the rapid current, was not more unlike the invisible gloomy river over which they passed an hour ago, than was their own coming and going. The strain was out of their young spirits, the fire of excitement had consumed itself, and Norlaw's sons, like lads as they were, were melting, each one silently and secretly, into the mood of tears and loving recollections, the very tenderness of grief.

And when Marget took down the shutter from the window, to see by the early morning light how this night of watching had at last taken the bloom from the Mistress' face, three other faces, white with the wear of extreme emotion, but tender as the morning faces of children, appeared to her coming slowly and calmly, and with weariness, along the green bank before the house. They had not spoken all the way. They were worn out with passion and sorrow, and want of rest—even with want of food—for these days had been terrible days for boys of their age to struggle through. Marget could not restrain a cry of mingled alarm and triumph. That, and the sound of the bolts withdrawn from the door, did what the thunder storm could not do. It broke the slumbers of the sheriff's officer, who had slept till now. He ran to the window hastily, and drew aside the curtain—he saw the face of the widow at the kitchen-door; the lads, travel-soiled and weary, with their wet clothes and exhausted faces, coming up to meet her; and the slumbrous sentinel rushed out of the room to entangle himself in the folds of Marget's plaid, and overwhelm her with angry questions; for she came to his call instantly, with a pretense of care and solicitude exasperating enough under any circumstances.

"Where have the lads been?" cried Elliot, throwing down at her, torn through the middle, the plaid which she had hung across his door.

"They've been at their father's funeral," said Marget, solemnly, "puir bairns!—through the storm and the midnicht, to Dryburgh, to the family grave."

The man turned into the room again in a pretended passion—but, sheriff's officer though he was, perhaps he was not sorry for once in his life to find himself foiled.

CHAPTER IX

"Put on your bonnet, Katie, and come with me—the like of you should be able to be some comfort to that poor widow at Norlaw," said Dr. Logan to his daughter, as they stood together in the manse garden, after their early breakfast.

After the storm, it was a lovely summer morning, tender, dewy, refreshed, full of the songs of birds and odors of flowers.

Katie Logan was only eighteen, but felt herself a great deal older. She was the eldest child of a late marriage, and had been mother and mistress in the manse for four long years. The minister, as is the fate of ministers, had waited long for this modest preferment, and many a heavy thought it gave him to see his children young and motherless, and to remember that he himself was reaching near the limit of human life; but Katie was her father's comfort in this trouble, as in most others; and it seemed so natural to see her in full care and management of her four little brothers and sisters, that the chances of Katie having a life of her own before her, independent of the manse, seldom troubled the thoughts of her father.

Katie did not look a day older than she was; but she had that indescribable elder-sister bearing, that pretty shade of thoughtfulness upon her frank face, which an early responsibility throws into the looks of very children. Even a young wife, in all the importance of independent sway, must have looked but a novice in presence of the minister's daughter, who had to be mistress and mother at fourteen, and had kept the manse cosy and in order, regulated the economies, darned the stockings, and even cut out the little frocks and pinafores from that time until now. Katie knew more about measles and hooping-cough than many a mother, and was skilled how to take a cold "in time," and check an incipient fever. The minister thought no one else, save his dead wife, could have managed the three hundred pounds of the manse income, so as to leave a comfortable sum over every year, to be laid by for "the bairns," and comforted himself with the thought that when he himself was "called away," little Johnnie and Charlie, Colin and Isabel, would still have Katie, the mother-sister, who already had been their guardian so long.

"I'm ready, papa!" said Katie; "but Mrs. Livingstone does not care about a stranger's sympathy. It's no' like one belonging to herself. She may think it very kind and be pleased with it, in a way; but it still feels like an interference at the bottom of her heart."

"She's a peculiar woman," said Dr. Logan, "but you are not to be called a stranger, my dear: and it's no small pleasure to me, Katie, to think that there are few houses in the parish where you are not just as welcome as myself."

Katie made no reply to this. She did not think it would much mend the matter with the Mistress to be reckoned as one of the houses in the parish. So she tied on her bonnet quietly, and took her father's arm, and turned down the brae toward Norlaw; for this little woman had the admirable quality of knowing, not only how to speak with great good sense, but how to refrain.

"I'm truly concerned about this family," said Dr. Logan; "indeed, I may say, I'm very much perplexed in my mind how to do. A state of things like this can not be tolerated in a Christian country, Katie. The dead denied decent burial! It's horrible to think of; so I see no better for it, my dear, than to take a quiet ride to Melmar, without letting on to any body, and seeing for myself what's to be done with *him*."

"I don't like Mr. Huntley, papa," said Katie, decidedly.

"That may be, my dear; but still, I suppose he's just like other folk, looking after his own interest, without meaning any particular harm to any body, unless they come in his way. Oh, human nature!" said the minister; "the most of us are just like that, Katie, though we seldom can see it; but there can be little doubt that Melmar was greatly incensed against poor Norlaw, who was nobody's enemy but his own."

"And his sons!" said Katie, hastily. "Poor boys! I wonder what they'll do?" This was one peculiarity of her elder-sisterly position which Katie had not escaped. She thought it quite natural and proper to speak of Patie and Huntley Livingstone, one of whom was about her own age, and one considerably her senior, as the "boys," and to take a maternal interest in them; even Dr. Logan, excellent man, did not see any thing to smile at in this. He answered with the most perfect seriousness, echoing her words:—

"Poor boys! We're short-sighted mortals, Katie; but there's no telling— it might be all the better for them that they're left to themselves, and are no more subject to poor Norlaw. But about Melmar? I think, my dear, I might as well ride over there to-day."

"Wait till we've seen Mrs. Livingstone, papa," said the prudent Katie. "Do you see that man on the road—who is it? He's in an awful hurry. I think I've seen him before."

"Robert Mushet, from the hill; he's always in a hurry, like most idle people," said the minister.

"No; it's not Robbie, papa; he's as like the officer as he can look," said Katie, straining her eyes over the high bank which lay between his path and the high-road.

"Whisht, my dear—the officer? Do you mean the exciseman, Katie? It might very well be him, without making any difference to us."

"I'm sure it's him—the man that came to Norlaw yesterday!" cried Katie, triumphantly, hastening the good doctor along the by-road at a pace to which he was not accustomed. "Something's happened! Oh papa, be quick and let us on."

"Canny, my dear, canny!" said Dr. Logan. "I fear you must be mistaken, Katie; but if you're right, I'm very glad to think that Melmar must have seen the error of his way."

Katie was very indifferent about Melmar; but she pressed on eagerly, full of interest to know what had happened at Norlaw. When they came in sight of the house, it was evident by its changed aspect that things were altered there. The windows were open, the blinds drawn up, the sunshine once more entering freely as of old. The minister went forward with a mind perturbed; he did not at all comprehend what this could mean.

The door was opened to them by Marget, who took them into the east room with a certain solemn importance, and who wore her new mourning and her afternoon cap with black ribbons, in preparation for visitors.

"I've got them a' persuaded to take a rest—a' but Huntley," said Marget; "for yesterday and last night were enough to kill baith the laddies and their mother—no' a morsel o' meat within their lips, nor a wink of sleep to their e'en."

"You alarm me, Marget; what does all this mean?" cried Dr. Logan, waving his hand towards the open windows.

Katie, more eager and more quick-witted, watched the motion of Marget's lips, yet found out the truth before she spoke.

"The maister's funeral," said Marget, with a solemn triumph, though her voice broke, in spite of herself, in natural sorrow, "took place yestreen, at midnicht, sir, as there was nae other way for it, in the orderings of Providence. Maister Huntley arranged it so."

"Oh, poor boys!" cried Katie Logan, and she threw herself down on a chair, and cried heartily in sympathy, and grief, and joy. Nothing else was possible; the scene, the circumstances, the cause, were not to be spoken of. There was no way but that way, of showing how this young heart at least felt with the strained hearts of the family of Norlaw.

"Ye may say sae, Miss Katie," said Marget, crying too in little outbursts, from which she recovered to wipe her eyes and curtsey apologetically to the minister. "After a' they gaed through yesterday, to start in the storm and the dark, and lay him in his grave by torchlight in the dead of the night—three laddies, that I mind, just like yesterday, bits of bairns about the house—it's enough to break ane's heart!"

"I am very much startled," said Dr. Logan, pacing slowly up and down the room; "it was a very out-of-the-way proceeding. Dear me!—at midnight—by torchlight!—Poor Norlaw! But still I can not say I blame them—I can not but acknowledge I'm very well pleased it's over. Dear me! who could have thought it, without asking my advice or any body's,—these boys! but I suppose, Katie, my dear, if they are all resting, we may as well think of turning back, unless Marget thinks Mrs. Livingstone would like to have you beside her for the rest of the day."

"No, papa; she would like best to be by herself—and so would I, if it was me," said Katie, promptly.

"Eh, Miss Katie! the like of you for understanding—and you so young!" cried Marget, with real admiration; "but the minister canna gang away till he's seen young Norlaw."

"Who?" cried Dr. Logan, in amazement.

"My young master, sir, the present Norlaw," said Marget, with a curtsey which was not without defiance.

The good minister shook his head.

"Poor laddie!" said Doctor Logan, "I wish him many better things than his inheritance; but I would gladly see Huntley. If you are sure he's up and able to see us, tell him I'm here."

"I'll tell him *wha's* here," said Marget, under her breath, as she went softly away; "eh, my puir bairn! I'd gie my little finger cheerful for the twa of them, to see them draw together; and mair unlikely things have come to pass. Guid forgive me for thinking of the like in a house of death!"

Yet, unfortunately, it was hard to avoid thinking of such profane possibilities in the presence of two young people like Huntley and Katie—especially for a woman; not a few people in the parish, of speculative minds, who could see a long way before them, had already lightly linked their names together as country gossips use, and perhaps Huntley half understood what was the meaning of the slight but significant emphasis, with which Marget intimated that "the minister and *Miss Katie*" were waiting to see him.

The youth went with great readiness. They were, at least, of all others, the friends whom Huntley was the least reluctant to confide in, and whose kindness he appreciated best.

And when pretty Katie Logan sprang forward, still half crying, and with bright tears hanging upon her eye-lashes, to take her old playmate's hand, almost tenderly, in her great concern and sympathy for him, the lad's heart warmed, he could scarcely tell how. He felt involuntarily, almost unwillingly, as if this salutation and regard all to himself was a sudden little refuge of brighter life opened for him out of the universal sorrow which was about his own house and way. The tears came to Huntley's eyes—but they were tears of relief, of ease and comfort to his heart. He almost thought he could have liked, if Katie had been alone, to sit down by her side, and tell her all that he had suffered, all that he looked forward to. But the sight of the minister, fortunately, composed Huntley. Dr. Logan, excellent man as he was, did not seem so desirable a confidant.

"I don't mean to blame you, my dear boy," said the minister, earnestly; "it was a shock to my feelings, I allow, but do not think of getting blame from me, Huntley. I was shut up entirely in the matter, myself; I did not see what to do; and I could not venture to say that it was not the wisest thing, and the only plan to clear your way."

There was a little pause, for Huntley either would not, or could not, speak—and then Dr. Logan resumed:

"We came this morning, Katie and me, to see what use we could be; but now the worst's over, Huntley, I'm thinking we'll just go our way back again, and leave you to rest—for Katie thinks your mother will be best pleased to be alone."

"Do you think so?" said Huntley, looking eagerly into Katie's face.

"Yes, unless I could be your real sister for a while, as long as Mrs. Livingstone needed me," said Katie, with a smile, "and I almost wish I could—I am so good at it—to take care of you boys."

"There is no fear of us now," said Huntley. "The worst's over, as the minister says. We've had no time to think what we're to do, Dr. Logan; but I'll come and tell you whenever we can see what's before us."

"I'll be very glad, Huntley; but I'll tell you what's better than telling me," said Dr. Logan. "Katie has a cousin, a very clever writer in Edinburgh—I knew there was something I wanted to tell you, and I had very near forgotten—if you'll take my advice, you'll go in, it's not very far, and get him to manage the whole thing for you. Here's the address that Katie wrote down last night. Tell your mother about it, Huntley, and that it's my advice you should have a sound man in the law to look after your concerns; and come down to the manse as soon as you can, if it were only for a change; and you'll give your mother our regards, and we'll bid you good-day."

"And dinna think more than you should, or grieve more, Huntley—and come and see us," said Katie, offering him her hand again.

Huntley took it, half joyfully, half inclined to burst out into boyish tears once more. He thought it would have been a comfort and refreshment to have had her here, this wearied, melancholy day. But somehow, he did not think with equal satisfaction of Katie's cousin. It seemed to Huntley he would almost rather employ any "writer" than this one, to smooth out the raveled concerns of Norlaw.

CHAPTER X

Common daylight, common life, the dead buried out of their sight, the windows open, the servants coming to ask common questions about the cattle and the land. Nothing changed, except that the father was no longer visible among them—that Huntley sat at the foot of the table, and the Mistress grew familiar with her widow's cap. Oh, cruel life! This was how it swallowed up all the solemnities of their grief.

And now it was the evening, and the eager youths could be restrained no longer. Common custom had aroused even the Mistress out of her inaction, sitting by the corner window, she had once more begun mechanically to notice what went and came at the kitchen door—had been very angry with the packman, who had seduced Jenny to admit him—and with Jenny for so far forgetting the decorum due to "an afflicted house;" had even once noticed, and been partially displeased by the black ribbons in Marget's cap, which it was extravagant to wear in the morning; and with melancholy self-reproof had opened the work basket, which had been left to gather dust for weeks past.

"I needna be idle *now*"—the Mistress said to herself, with a heavy sigh; and Huntley and Patie perceived that it was no longer too early to enter upon their own plans and views.

With this purpose, they came to her about sunset, when she had settled herself after her old fashion to her evening's work. She saw instinctively what was coming, and, with natural feeling, shrunk for the moment. She was a little impatient, too, her grief taking that form.

"Keep a distance, keep a distance, bairns!" cried the Mistress; "let me have room to breathe in! and I'm sure if ye were but lassies, and could have something in your hands to do, it would be a comfort to me. There's Jenny, the light-headed thing, taken her stocking to the door, as if nothing was amiss in the house. Pity me!—but I'll not be fashed with *her* long, that's a comfort to think of. Laddies, laddies, can ye no keep still? What are ye a'wanting with me?"

"Mother, it's time to think what we're to do; neither Patie nor me can keep quiet, when we think of what's before us," said Huntley—"and there's little comfort in settling on any thing till we can speak of it to you."

The Mistress gave way at these words to a sudden little outbreak of tears, which you might almost have supposed were tears of anger, and which she wiped off hurriedly with an agitated hand. Then she proceeded very rapidly with the work she had taken up, which was a dark gray woolen stocking—a familiar work, which she could get on with almost without looking at it. She did look at her knitting, however, intently, bending her head over it, not venturing to look up at her children; and thus it was that they found themselves permitted to proceed.

"Mother," said Huntley, with a deep blush—"I'm a man, but I've learned nothing to make my bread by. Because I'm the eldest, and should be of most use, I'm the greatest burden. I understand about the land and the cattle, and after a while I might manage a farm, but that's slow work and weary—and the first that should be done is to get rid of me."

"Hold your peace!" cried the Mistress, with a break in her voice; "how dare ye say the like of that to your mother? Are you not my eldest son, the stay of the house? Wherefore do ye say this to me?"

"Because it's true, mother," said Huntley, firmly; "and though it's true I'm not discouraged. The worst is, I see nothing I can do near you, as I might have done if I had been younger, and had time to spare to learn a trade. Such as it is, I'm very well content with my trade, too; but what could I do with it here? Get a place as a grieve, maybe, through Tyneside's help, and the minister's, and be able to stock a small farm by the time I was forty years old. But that would please neither you nor me. Mother, you must send me away!"

The Mistress did not look up, did not move—went on steadily with her rapid knitting—but she said:—

"Where?" with a sharp accent, like a cry.

"I've been thinking of that," said Huntley, slowly; "If I went to America, or Canada, or any such place, I would be like to stay. My mind's against staying; I want to come back—to keep home in my eye. So I say Australia, mother."

"America, Canada, Australia!—the laddie's wild!" cried the Mistress. "Do you mean to say ye'll be an emigrant? a bairn of mine?"

Emigration was not then what it is now; it was the last resort—sadly resisted, sadly yielded to—of the "broken man;" and Huntley's mother saw her son, in imagination, in a dreary den of a cabin, in a poor little trading ship, with a bundle on the end of a stick, and despair in his heart, when he spoke of going away.

"There's more kinds of emigrants than one kind, mother," said Patie.

"Ay," said the Mistress, her imagination shifting, in spite of her, to a dismal family scene, in which the poor wife had the baby tied on her back in a shawl, and the children at her feet were crying with cold and hunger, and the husband at her side looking desperate. "I've seen folk on the road to America—ay, laddies, mony a time. I'm older than you are. I ken what like they look; but pity me, did I ever think the like of that would be evened to a bairn of mine!"

"Mother," said Huntley, with a cheerfulness which he did not quite feel, "an emigrant goes away to stay—I should not do that—I am going, if I can, to make a fortune, and come home—and it's not America; there are towns *there* already like our own, and a man, I suppose, has only a greater chance of getting bread enough to eat. I could get bread enough in our own country-side; but I mean to get more if I can—I mean to get a sheep farm and grow rich, as everybody does out there."

"Poor laddie! Do they sell sheep and lands out there to them that have no siller?" said the Mistress. "If you canna stock a farm at hame, where you're kent and your name respected, Huntley Livingstone, how will you do it there?"

"That's just what I have to find out," said Huntley, with spirit; "a man may be clear he's to do a thing, without seeing how at the moment. With your consent, I'm going to Australia, mother; if there's any thing over, when all our affairs are settled, I'll get my share—and as for the sheep and the land, they're in Providence; but I doubt them as little as if they were on the lea before my eyes. I'm no' a man out of a town that knows nothing about it. I'm country bred and have been among beasts all my days. Do you think I'm feared! Though I've little to start with, mother, you'll see me back rich enough to do credit to the name of Norlaw!"

His mother shook her head.

"It's easy to make a fortune on a summer night at hame, before a lad's twenty, or kens the world," she said. "I've seen mony a stronger man than you, Huntley, come hame baith penniless and hopeless—and the like of such grand plans, they're but trouble and sadness to me."

Perhaps Huntley was discouraged by the words; at all events he made no reply—and the mind of his mother gradually expanded. She looked up from her knitting suddenly, with a rapid tender glance.

"Maybe I'm wrong," said the Mistress; "there's some will win and some will fail in spite of the haill world. The Lord take the care of my bairns! Who am I, that I should be able to guide you, three lads, coming to be men?

Huntley, you're the auldest, and you're strong. I canna say stay at hame—I dinna see what to bid you do. You must take your ain will, and I'll no' oppose."

If Huntley thanked his mother at all it was in very few words, for the politenesses were not cultivated among them, the feelings of this Scottish family lying somewhat deep, and expressing themselves otherwise than in common words; but the Mistress brushed her hand over her eyes hurriedly, with something like a restrained sob, intermitting for a single instant, and no longer, the rapid glitter of her "wires"—but you would scarcely have supposed that the heart of the mother was moved thus far, to hear the tone of her next words. She turned to her second son without looking at him.

"And where are *you* for, Patie Livingstone?" said the Mistress, with almost a sarcastic sharpness. "It should be India, or the North Pole to pleasure you."

Patie was not emboldened by this address; it seemed, indeed, rather to discomfit the lad; not as a reproach, but as showing a greater expectation of his purposes than they warranted.

"You know what I aimed at long ago, mother," he said, with hesitation. "It may be that we can ill afford a 'prentice time now—but I'm no' above working while I learn. I can scramble up as well as Huntley. I'll go either to Glasgow or to Liverpool, to one of the founderies there."

"Folk dinna learn to be *civil* engineers in founderies," said the Mistress; "they're nothing better than smiths at the anvil. You wanted to build a light-house, Patie, when ye were a little bairn—but you'll no' learn there."

"I'll maybe learn better. There's to be railroads soon, everywhere," said Patie, with a little glow upon his face. "I'll do what I can—if I'm only to be a smith, I'll be a smith like a man, and learn my business. The light-house was a fancy; but I may learn what's as good, and more profitable. There's some railroads already, mother, and there's more beginning every day."

"My poor bairn!" said the Mistress, for the first time bestowing a glance of pity upon Patie—"if your fortune has to wait for its making till folk gang riding over a' the roads on steam horses, like what's written in the papers, I'll never live to see it. There's that man they ca' Stephenson, he's made something or other that's a great wonder; but, laddie, you dinna think that roads like that can go far? They may have them up about London—and truly you might live to make another, I'll no' say—but I would rather build a tower to keep ships from being wrecked than make a road for folk to break their necks on, if it was me."

"Folk that are born to break their necks will break them on any kind of road," said Patie, with great gravity; "but I've read about it all, and I think a man only needs to know what he has to do, to thrive; and besides, mother, there's more need for engines than upon railroads. It's a business worth a man's while."

"Patie," said the Mistress, solemnly, "I've given my consent to Huntley to gang thousands of miles away over the sea; but if *you* gang among thae engines, that are merciless and senseless, and can tear a living creature like a rag of claith—I've seen them, laddie, with my own e'en, clanging and clinking like the evil place itself—I'll think it's Patie that's in the lion's mouth, and no' my eldest son."

"Well, mother!" said Patie, sturdily—"if I were in the lion's mouth, and yet had room to keep clear, would you be feared for me?"

This appeal took the Mistress entirely without preparation. She brushed her hands hastily over her eyes once more, and went on with her knitting. Then a long, hard-drawn breath, which was not a sigh, came from the mother's breast; in the midst of her objections, her determination not to be satisfied, a certain unaccountable pride in the vigor, and strength, and resolution of her sons rose in the kindred spirit of their mother. She was not "feared"—neither for one nor the other of the bold youths by her side. Her own strong vitality went forth with them, with an indescribable swell of exhilaration—yet she was their mother, and a widow, and it wrung her heart to arrange quietly how they were to leave her and their home.

"And me?" said Cosmo, coming to his mother's side.

He had no determination to announce—he came out of his thoughts, and his musings, and his earnest listening, to lay that white, long hand of his upon his mother's arm. It was the touch which made the full cup run over. The widow leaned her head suddenly upon her boy's shoulder, surprised into an outburst of tears and weakness, unusual and overpowering—and the other lads came close to this group, touched to the heart like their mother. They cried out among their tears that Cosmo must not go away—that he was too young—too tender! What they had not felt for themselves, they felt for him—there seemed something forlorn, pathetic, miserable, in the very thought of this boy going forth to meet the world and its troubles. This boy, the child of the house, the son who was like his father, the tenderest spirit of them all!

Yet Cosmo, who had no plans, and who was only sixteen, was rather indignant at this universal conclusion. He yielded at last, only because the tears were still in his mother's eyes, and because they were all more persistent than he was—and sat down at a little distance, not sullen, but as near so as was possible to him, his cheek glowing with a suspicion that they thought him a child. But soon the conversation passed to other matters, which Cosmo could not resist. They began to speak of Melmar, their unprovoked enemy, and then the three lads looked at each other, taking resolution from that telegraphic conference; and Huntley, with the blood rising in his cheeks, for the first time asked his mother, in the name of them all, for that tale which her husband, on his death-bed, had deputed her to tell them, the story of the will which was in the mid-chamber, and that Mary who was Mary of Melmar evermore in the memory of Norlaw.

At the question the tears dried out of the Mistress's eyes, an impatient color came to her face—and it was so hard to elicit this story from her aggrieved and unsympathetic mind, that it may be better for Mrs. Livingstone, in the estimation of other people, if we tell what she told in other words than hers.

CHAPTER XI

Yet we do not see why we are called upon to defend Mrs. Livingstone, who was very well able, under most circumstances, to take care of herself. She did not by any means receive her sons' inquiries with a good grace. On the contrary, she evaded them hotly, with unmistakable dislike and impatience.

"Mary of Me'mar! what is she to you?" said the Mistress. "Let bygones be bygones, bairns—she's been the fash of my life, one way and another. Hold your peace, Cosmo Livingstone! Do you think I can tell this like a story out of a book. There's plenty gossips in the countryside could tell you the ins and the outs of it better than me—"

"About the mid-chamber and the will, mother?" asked Patrick.

"Weel, maybe, no about that," said the Mistress, slightly mollified; "if that's what ye want. This Mary Huntley, laddies, I ken very little about her. She was away out of these parts before my time. I never doubted she was light-headed, and liked to be admired and petted. She was Me'mar's only bairn; maybe that might be some excuse for her—for he was an auld man and fond. But, kind as he was, she ran away from him to marry some lad that naebody kent—and went off out of the country with her ne'er-do-weel man, and has never been heard tell of from that time to this—that's a' I ken about her."

This was said so peremptorily and conclusively, setting aside at once any further question, that even these lads, who were not particularly skilled in the heart or its emotions, perceived by instinct, that their mother knew a great deal more about her—more than any inducement in the world could persuade her to tell.

"I've heard that Me'mar was hurt to the heart," said the Mistress, "and no much wonder. His bairn that he had thought nothing too good for! and to think of her running off from *him*, a lone auld man, to be married upon a stranger-lad without friends, that naebody kent any good o', and that turned out just as was to be expected. Oh, aye! it does grand to make into a story—and the like of you, you think it all for love, and a warm heart, and a' the rest of it; but I think it's but an ill heart that would desert hame and friends, and an auld man above three-score, for its ain will and pleasure. So Me'mar took it very sore to heart; he would not have her name named to him for years. And the next living creature in this world that he liked best, after his ungrateful daughter, was—laddies, you'll no' be surprised—just him that's gone from us—that everybody likit weel—just Norlaw."

There was a pause after this, the Mistress's displeasure melting into a sob of her permanent grief; and then the tale was resumed more gently, more slowly, as if she had sinned against the dead by the warmth and almost resentment of her first words.

"Me'mar lived to be an auld man," said the Mistress. "He aye lived on till Patie was about five years auld, and a' our bairns born. He was very good aye to me; mony's the present he sent me, when I was a young thing, and was more heeding for bonnie-dies, and took great notice of Huntley, and was kind to the whole house. It was said through a' the country-side that ye were to be his heirs, and truly so you might have been, but for one thing and anither; no' that I'm heeding—you'll be a' the better for making your way in the world yourselves."

"And the will, mother?" said Huntley, with a little eagerness.

"I'm coming to the will; have patience;" said the Mistress, who had not a great deal herself, to tell the truth. "Bairns, it's no' time yet for me to speak to you of your father; but he was aye a just man, with a tender heart for the unfortunate—you ken that as well as me. He wouldna take advantage of another man's weakness, or another man's ill-doing, far less of a poor silly lassie, that, maybe, didna ken what she was about. And when the old man made his will, Norlaw would not let him leave his lands beyond his ain flesh and blood. So the will was made, that Mary Huntley, if she ever came back, was to be heir of Melmar, and if she never came back, nor could be heard tell of, every thing was left to Patrick Livingstone, of Norlaw."

It was impossible to restrain the start of amazement with which Huntley, growing red and agitated, sprang to his feet, and the others stirred out of their quietness of listening. Their mother took no time to answer the eager questions in their eyes, nor to hear even the exclamations which burst from them unawares. She bent her head again, and drew through her fingers, rapidly, the hem of her apron. She did not see, nor seem to think of, her children. Her mind was busy about the heaviest epoch of her own life.

"When Melmar died, search was caused to be made every place for his daughter," said the Mistress, passing back and forwards through her hands this tight strip of her apron. "Your father thought of nothing else, night nor day; a' for justice, bairns, doubtless for justice—that nobody might think he would take an advantage of his kinswoman, though he could not approve of her ways! He went to Edinburgh himself, and from there to London. I was young then, and Cosmo little mair than an infant, and a' thing left in my hands. Aye this one and the other one coming to tell about Mary Huntley—and Norlaw away looking for her—and the very papers full of the heiress—and me my lane in the house, and little used to be left to mysel'. I mind every thing as if it had happened this very day."

The Mistress paused once more—it was only to draw a long breath of pain, ere she hurried on with the unwelcome tale, which now had a strange interest, even for herself. The boys could not tell what was the bitterness of the time which their mother indicated by these compressed and significant words; but it was impossible to hear even her voice without perceiving something of the long-past troubles, intense and vivid as her nature, which nothing in the world could have induced her to disclose.

"The upshot was, she could not be found," said the Mistress, abruptly; "either she never heard tell that she was sought for, or she took guilt to herself, and would not appear. They kept up the search as long as a year, but they never heard a word, or got a clue to where she was."

"And then?" cried Huntley, with extreme excitement.

"And then," said the Mistress—"was he a man to take another person's lands, when but a year had gane?" She spoke with a visible self-restraint, strong and bitter—the coercion which a mind of energy and power puts upon itself, determining not to think otherwise than with approbation of the acts of a weaker nature—and with something deeper underlying even this. "He said she would still come hame some day, as was most likely. He would not take up her rights, and her living, as he was persuaded in his mind. The will was proved in law, for her sake, but he would not take possession of the land, nor put forward his claims to it, because he said she lived, and would come hame. So, laddies, there's the tale. A Mr. Huntley, a writer, from the northcountry, a far-away friend, came in and claimed as next of kin. Mary of Melmar was lost and gane, and could not be found, and Norlaw would not put in his ain claim, though it was clear. He said it would be taking her rights, and that then she would never come back to claim her land. So the strange man got possession and kept it, and hated Norlaw. And from that day to this, what with having an enemy, and the thought of that unfortunate woman coming back, and the knowledge in his heart that he had let a wrongful heir step in—what with all that bairns, and more than that, another day of prosperity never came to this house of Norlaw."

"Then we are the heirs of Me'mar!" said Huntley; "we, and not my father's enemy! Mother, why did we never hear this before?"

"Na, lads," said the Mistress, with an indescribable bitterness in her tone; "it's her and her bairns that are the heirs—and they're to be found, and claim their inheritance, soon or syne."

"Then this is what I'll do," cried Cosmo, springing to his feet; "I'll go over all the world, but I'll find Mary of Melmar! I'm not so strong as Huntley, or as Patie, but I'm strong enough for this. I'll do what my father wished—if she should be in the furtherest corner of the earth, I'll bring her hame!"

To the extreme amazement of the boys, the Mistress laid a violent hand on Cosmo's shoulder, and, either with intention or unconsciously, shook the whole frame of the slender lad with her impetuous grasp.

"Will ye?" cried his mother, with a sharpness of suffering in her voice that confounded them. "Is it no' enough, all that's past? Am I to begin again? Am I to bring up *sons* for her service? Oh, patience, patience! it's more than a woman like me can bear!"

Amazed, grieved, disturbed by her words and her aspect, her sons gathered around her. She pushed them away impatiently, and rose up.

"Bairns, dinna anger me!—I'm no' meek enough," said the Mistress, her face flushing with a mixture of mortification and displeasure. "You've had your will, and heard the story—but I tell you this woman's been a vexation to me all my life—and it's no' your part, any one of you, to begin it a' over again."

CHAPTER XII

This story, which Mrs. Livingstone told with reluctance, and, in fact, did not tell half of, was, though the youths did not know it, the story of the very bitterest portion of their mother's life. The Mistress never told, either to them or to any one else, how, roused in her honest love and wifely sincerity into sympathy with her husband's generous efforts to preserve her own inheritance to his runaway cousin, she had very soon good reason to be sick of the very name of Mary of Me'mar; how she found out that, after years long of her faithful, warm-hearted, affectionate society, after the birth of children and consecration of time, after all the unfailing courage and exertions, by which her stout spirit had done much to set him right in the world, and, above all, in spite of the unfeigned and undivided love of a full heart like her own, the visionary heart of her husband had all this time been hankering after his first love.

Without preparation, and without softening, the Mistress found this out. He would not advantage his own family at the cost of Mary; he would seek for Mary through the whole world. These had been the words of Norlaw, ten years after Mary of Melmar's disappearance, and even years after he had become the father of Huntley. The unsuspecting wife thought no harm; then he went and came for a whole year seeking for his cousin; and during that time, left alone day after day, and month after month, the mistress of Norlaw found out the secret. It was a hard thing for her, with her strong personality and burning individual heart, to bear; but she did bear it with an indignant heroism, never saying a word to mortal ear. He himself never knew that she had discovered his prior love, or resented it. She would have scorned herself could she have reproached him or even made him conscious of her own feelings. Good fortune and strong affection at the bottom happily kept contempt out of the Mistress's indignation; but her heart continued sore for years with the discovery—sore, mortified, humiliated. To think that all her wifely, faithful regard had clung unwittingly to a man who, professing to cherish her, followed, with a wandering heart, a girl who had run away from him years before to be another man's wife! The Mistress had borne it steadily and soberly, so that no one knew of her discovery, but she had never got beyond this abiding mortification and injury; and it was not much wonder that she started with a sudden burst of exasperated feeling, when Cosmo, her own son, echoed his father's foolish words. Her youngest boy, her favorite and last nursling, the one bird that was to be left in the nest, could stir to this same mad search, when he had not yet ambition enough to stir for his own fortune. It was the last drop which made all this bitterness run over. No wonder that the Mistress lost command of herself for once, and going up to her own room in a gust of aggravated and angry emotions, thrust Cosmo away from her, and cried, "Am I to bring up sons for *her* service?" in the indignation of her heart.

Yes, it was a very pretty story for romance. The young girl running away, "all for love"—the faithful forsaken lover thinking of her in secret—rising up to defend her rights after ten long years—eagerly searching for her—and, with a jealous tenderness, refusing to do any thing which might compromise her title, while he alone still fondly believed in her return. A very pretty story, with love, and nothing else, for its theme. Yet, unfortunately, these pretty stories have a dark enough aspect often on the other side; and the Mistress, mortified, silent, indignant, cheated in her own perfect confidence and honest tenderness, when you saw her behind the scenes of the other pretty picture, took a great deal of the beauty out of that first-love and romantic constancy of Norlaw.

When Mrs. Livingstone went to her room, the sons, vexed and troubled, were a long time silent. Cosmo withdrew into a corner, and leaned his head on his mother's little table. He, too, was deeply mortified, and could not keep back the hot boyish tears from his eyes—he felt himself set aside like a child—he felt the shame of a sensitive temperament at perceiving how greatly his mother was disturbed. Somehow she seemed to have betrayed herself, and Cosmo, jealous for her perfect honor, was uneasy and abashed at this disturbance of it; while still his heart, young, eager, inexperienced, loving romance, secretly longed to hear more of this mystery, and secretly repeated his determination. Huntley, who was pacing up and down the room, lifting and replacing every thing in his way which could be lifted, was simply confounded and thunderstruck, which emotions Patie shared with his elder brother. Patie, however, was the most practical of the three, and it was he who first broke the silence.

"Somehow or other this vexes my mother," said Patie; "let us ask her no more questions about it; but, Huntley, you ought to know all the hiding-holes about the house. You should look up this will and put it in safe hands."

"In safe hands?—I'll act upon it forthwith! Are we to keep terms with Melmar after all that's past, and with power to turn him out of his seat?" cried Huntley; "no, surely; I'll put it into hands that will carry it into effect, and that without delay."

"They would want either this Mary, or proof that she was dead, before they would do any thing in it," said Patie, doubtfully; "and yet it's a shame!"

"She is not dead!" interrupted Cosmo; "why my mother should be angry, I can't tell; but I'll find out Mary of Melmar, I know I shall, though it should be twenty years!"

"Be quiet, Cosmo," said his elder brother, "and see that no one troubles my mother with another question; she does not like it, and I will not have her disturbed; but I'll tell you what I'll do. We know little about business, and we're not of a patient race. Me'mar had better not come near any of us just now, unless it were you, Patie, that can master yourself. I should like to knock him down, and my mother would do worse. I'll write to this friend of the minister's, this writer, and put it all in his hands—it's the best thing I can see. What do you say?"

Patie gave his assent readily; Cosmo did not say any thing. The boy began to feel his youth somewhat bitterly, and to think that they did not care for his opinion; so he went out, and swung himself up by an old elm tree into one of the vacant windows of the castle, a favorite seat of Cosmo, where, among the cool ivy, and hidden by the deep recess of the thick old wall, he could see the sunset, and watch how the shadows stole over the earth. The Eildons were at his right hand, paling gradually out of their royal purple against the pale sky in the east, and the last long rays of the sunset, too low to reach them, fell golden-yellow upon Tyne, and shed a pathetic light on the soft green bank before the door of Norlaw. The common sounds of life were not so subdued now about this lonely house; even the cackle of poultry and bark of dogs seemed louder since the shutters were opened and the curtains drawn back—and Marget went firmly forth upon her errands to the byre, and the hush and stealth of mourning had left the place already. Who would not escape somewhere into some personal refuge out of the oppressive shadow of grief, while youth remains to make that possible? Huntley had been startled to feel that there was such an escape for himself when Katie Logan took his hand in the fullness of her sympathy—and Huntley and Patie together were seeking a similar ease now in discussing the plans of their future life together. Cosmo was only a boy; he had no plans yet which could be called plans—and he was too young to be moved by the hand or the voice of any woman. So he sat among the ivy in the ledge of the deep old window, with his head uncovered, his fair hair falling over his long white hands, and those dark liquid eyes of his gazing forth upon as fair a landscape as ever entered into the dream of a poet.

If Cosmo was a poet he was not aware of it; yet his heart was easing itself after his fashion. He was too young to apprehend the position of his mother, and how it broke into the superficial romance of his father's life. He thought only of Mary of Melmar, of the girl, beautiful, young, and unfortunate, who ran away "for love," and had literally left all for her husband's sake; he thought of displacing his father's enemy and restoring his father's first love to her rights. In imagination he pursued her through all the storied countries to which a young fancy naturally turns. He saw himself delivering her out of dangers, suddenly appearing when she was in peril or poverty, dispersing her enemies like a champion of chivalry, and bringing her home in triumph. This was how, while his brothers comforted themselves with an earnest discussion of possibilities, and while his mother, differing from them as age differs from youth—and as personal bereavement, which nothing can ever make up, and which changes the whole current of a life, differs from a natural removal and separation—returned into the depths of the past and lived them over again—this is how Cosmo made his first personal escape out of his first grief.

CHAPTER XIII

"Oh! Patricia! Sinclair has been telling me such a story," cried a young girl, suddenly rushing upon another, in a narrow winding road through the woods which clothed a steep bank of Tyne; at this spot, for one exclusive mile, the rapid little river was "private property," the embellishment of a gentleman's grounds—shut out from vulgar admiration. Tyne, indifferent alike to admiration and exclusivism, was not less happy on that account; but foamed over his stony channel as brisk, as brown, and as clear, as when he ran in unrestricted freedom by the old castle walls of Norlaw. The path was slippery and irregular with great roots of trees, and one or two brooks, unseen, trickled down the brae below the underwood, only detected by the slender, half visible rivulet on the path which you had to step across, or the homely plank half penetrated by water, which bridged over Tyne's invisible tributary. They did not appear, these fairy springs, but they added each a tingle, like so many harp strings, to the many sounds of Nature. Through this winding road, or rather upon it, for she was not going anywhere, the elder of these two interlocutors had been for some time wandering. She was a delicate looking girl of seventeen, with blue eyes and pale golden hair, rather pretty, but very slight, and evidently not in strong health. The sudden plunge down upon her, which her younger sister made from the top of the brae, took away Patricia's breath, and made her drop the book which she had been reading. This was no very great matter, for the book was rather an indifferent production, being one of those books of poetry which one reads at seventeen, and never after—but it was rather more important that the color came violently into her pale cheek, and she clasped her hands upon her side, with a gasp which terrified the young hoiden.

"Oh, I forgot!" she cried, in sympathy, as eager as her onslaught had been. "Oh! have I hurt you? I did not mean it, you know."

"No, Joanna," said Patricia, faintly, "but you forget my nerves always—you never had any yourself."

Which was perfectly true, and not to be denied. These two, Patricia and Joanna Huntley, were the only daughters of their father's house—the only children, indeed, save one son, who was abroad. There were not many feminine family names in this branch of the house of Huntley, and invention in this matter being very sparely exercised in these parts, it came about that the girls were called after their uncles, and that the third girl, had there been such an unlucky little individual, following in the track of her sisters, would have turned out Jemima or Robina, according as the balance rose in favor of her father's brother or her mother's. Fortunately, Joanna was the last fruit of the household tree, which had blossomed sparely. She was only fifteen, tall, strong, red haired, and full of vigor—the greatest contrast imaginable to her pretty pale sister, whom Joanna devoutly believed in as a beauty, but secretly did somewhat grieve over as a fool. The younger sister was not in the least pretty, and knew it, but she was clever, and Joanna knew that also, which made an agreeable counterpoise. She was extremely honest, downright and straightforward, speaking the truth with less elegance than force, but speaking it always; and on the whole was a good girl, though not always a very pleasant one. At this present moment she was flushed, breathless, and eager, having run all the way from the house with something to tell. But Patricia's "nerves" could not bear the sudden announcement, though that delicate young lady loved a piece of news fully as well as her sister. Joanna, therefore, stood still, making hasty and awkward apologies, and eager to do something to amend her mistake, while her delicate companion recovered breath. There was something more than nerves in the young lady's discomposure. She was feeble by nature, the invalid of the family, which Joanna, knowing no sympathetic ailment in her own vigorous person, sometimes had the ill luck to forget.

"And my poor book!" said poor Patricia, picking up the unfortunate volume, which lay fluttering with open leaves on the very edge of that tiny current trickling over the brown path, which, save that it moved and caught an occasional sparkle of light, you could not have distinguished to be a burn. "Oh, Joanna, you are so thoughtless! what was all this haste about?"

"Oh, such a story!" cried Joanna, eagerly. "It's easy to speak about nerves—but when I heard it I could have run to papa and given him a good shake—I could! and he deserved it! for they say it was all his blame."

"I should like to hear what it was," said Patricia, with an exasperating and intolerable meekness, which usually quite overpowered the patience of her sister.

But Joanna was too much interested in the present instance.

"It was Mr. Livingstone of Norlaw," she said, sinking her voice; "he's dead, and his funeral was stopped because he was in debt, and it was papa that did it—and the three boys got up at midnight and carried him on their shoulders, with torches in their hands, to Dryburgh, and buried him there. Sinclair says it's true, every word; and I don't know whether Huntley did not swim over Tweed to get the boat. Oh, Patricia! I feel as if I could both greet and cry hurra, if I were to see them; and as for papa, he deserves—I don't know what he does not deserve!"

"I wish you would talk like a lady, Joanna," said her sister, without taking any notice of this unfilial sentiment; "greet! you could just as well say cry, or weep, for that matter—and it's only common people that say Tweed, as if they meant a person instead of a river; why don't you say *the* Tweed, as people of education say?"

"He's the truest person I know," cried Joanna. "Tweed and Tyne! you may say that they're just streams of water, if you like, but they're more to me; but the question is papa—I knew he was ill enough and hard-hearted, but I never, never thought he could have been so bad as that—and I mean to go this very moment and ask him how it was."

"I suppose papa knows better than we do," said Patricia, with a slight sigh; "but I wish he would not do things that make people talk. It is very annoying. I dare say everybody will know about this soon, if it's true. If it was all himself it would not so much matter, and you never go out anywhere, Joanna, so you don't feel it—but is very unpleasant to mamma and me."

"I was not thinking of either mamma or you; I was thinking of the Livingstones," cried Joanna, with a flush of shame on her cheeks; "and I mean to go in this very instant, and ask him what it means."

So saying, the impetuous girl rushed up the path, slowly followed by Patricia. It was one of the loveliest bits of woodland on the whole course of Tyne. Mosses and wild flowers, and the daintiest ferns known to Scotland, peeped out of every hollow—and overhead and around, stretching down half way across the river, and thrusting out, with Nature's rare faculty of composition, their most graceful curves of foliage against the sky, were trees, not too great or ancient to overshadow the younger growth; trees of all descriptions, birches and beeches and willows, the white-limbed ash, with its green bunches of fruit, and the tender lime, with its honey blossoms. You could have almost counted every separate flash of sunshine which burned through the leaves, misty with motes and dazzling bright with that limitation; and yet the shadow overhead trembled and fluctuated with such a constant interchange, that the spot which was in shade one moment was in the brightest light the very next. The light gleamed in Joanna's red hair, as she plunged along in her impetuous way towards the house, and fell in touches here and there upon the graceful little figure of her sister, in her close cottage bonnet and muslin gown, as Patricia came softly over the same road, book in hand. But we are bound to confess that neither of the two, perfectly accustomed and familiar as they were, found a moment's leisure among their other thoughts to pause upon this scene; they went towards the house, the one after the other—Patricia with a due regard to decorum as well as to her nerves and feebleness of frame—Joanna totally without regard for either the one or the other; and both occupied, to the entire neglect of every thing else, with thoughts of their own.

The house of Melmar was placed upon a level platform of land, of a considerably lower altitude than this brae. Pausing to look at it, as neither Joanna nor Patricia did, on the rustic bridge which crossed the Tyne, and led from this woodland path into the smooth lawn and properly arranged trees of "the private grounds," Melmar appeared only a large square house, pretentious, yet homely, built entirely for living in, and not for looking at. If Nature, with her trees, and grass, and bits of garden land, softening the angles and filling in the gaps, had done her best to make it seemly, the house was completely innocent of aiding in any such attempt. Yet, by sheer dint of persistence, having stood there for at least a hundred years, long enough to have patches of lichen here and there upon its walls, Melmar had gained that look of steadiness and security, and of belonging to the soil, which harmonizes even an ugly feature in a landscape. The door, which was sheltered by a little portico, with four tall pillars, in reality stone, but looking considerably like plaster, opened from without after the innocent fashion of the country. Running across the lawn, Joanna opened the door and plunged in, without further ado, into her father's study, which was at the end of a long passage looking out upon the other side of the house. He was not there—so the girl came rushing back again to the drawing-room, the door of which stood open, and once more encountering her sister there, did her best to disturb the delicate nerves a second time, and throw Patricia out of breath.

This papa, whom Joanna had no hesitation about bearding in his own den, could not surely be such an ogre after all. He was not an ogre. You could not have supposed, to look at him, that any exaltation of enmity, any heroic sentiment of revenge, could lodge within the breast of Mr. Huntley, of Melmar. He was a tall man, with a high, narrow head, and reddish grizzled hair. A man with plenty of forehead, making up in height for its want of breadth. He was rather jovial than otherwise in his manner, and carried about with him a little atmosphere of his own, a whiff of two distinct odors, not unusual attendants of elderly Scotsmen, twenty years ago, reminiscences of toddy and rappee. He looked around with a smile at the vehement entrance of Joanna. He permitted all kinds of rudenesses on the part of this girl, and took a certain pleasure in them. He was not in the slightest degree an exacting or punctilious father; but not all his indulgence, nor the practical jokes, banter, and teasing, which he administered to all children, his own, among the rest, when they were young enough—had secured him either fondness or respect at their hands. They got on very well on the whole. Patricia pouted at him, and Joanna took him to task roundly when they differed in opinion—but the affection they gave him was an affection of habit, and nothing more.

"I've come to speak to you, papa," cried Joanna. "I've just been hearing the whole story, every word—and oh, I think shame of you!—it's a disgrace, it's a sin—I wonder you dare look any of us in the face again!"

"Eh? what's all this?" said Melmar; "Joan in one of her tantrums already? Three times in a day! that's scarcely canny—I'll have to speak to your aunt Jean."

"Oh, papa!" cried Joanna, indignantly, "it's no fun—who do you think would carry *you* to Dryburgh if somebody stopped your funeral? not one! You would have to stay here in your coffin and never be buried—and I wouldna be sorry! You would deserve it, and nothing better—oh, I think shame on you!"

"What? in my coffin? that's a long look beforehand," said Melmar. "You may have time to think shame of me often enough before that time, Joan; but let's hear what's all this about Dryburgh and a funeral—who's been here?"

"Sinclair was here," cried Joanna, "and he heard it all at Kirkbride— every word—and he says you had better not be seen there, after all you've done at Norlaw."

"I am sure, papa, it's very hard," said Patricia. "You set everybody talking, and then people look strange at us. Mamma knows they do; and I could cry when I think that we're going out to-morrow, and it would have been such a nice party. But now everybody knows about this, and nobody will speak to us—it's too bad of you, papa."

"What is it, my darling?" cried Mrs. Huntley, from her easy chair.

"Eh, fat's this?" said Aunt Jean, wheeling round upon hers.

A popular commotion was rising; Melmar saw the premonitory tokens, and made his escape accordingly.

"Joan," he said, pulling her ear as he passed her, "you're an impudent monkey; but you may spare your wrath about Norlaw—I knew as little as you did that the man was dead—however, he is dead, and I don't break my heart; but you can tell Sinclair I'll tell him a word of my mind the next time I'm near Kirkbride."

"Sinclair doesna care!" said Joanna; but Melmar pulled a thick curl of her red hair, and betook himself to his study, leaving the rising gust of questions to wear itself out as it might.

CHAPTER XIV

The drawing-room of Melmar was a large room tolerably well furnished. Three long windows on one side of the apartment looked out upon the lawn before the house, carefully avoiding the view "up Tyne," which a little management might have made visible. The fire-place was at the upper end of the room, sparkling coldly with polished steel and brass, and decorated with a very elaborate construction of cut paper. The chairs were all covered with chintz in a large-flowered pattern, red and green—chintz which did not fit on well, and looked creasy and disorderly. A large crumb-cloth, spread over the bright-colored carpet, had the same disadvantage; one corner of it was constantly loose, folding up under the chairs and tripping unwary passengers. There was a round rose-wood table, sparely covered with books and ornaments, and another oblong one with a cover on it, which was meant for use.

By this last sat Mrs. Huntley, with some knitting in her lap, reclining in a cushioned chair, with her feet upon a high footstool. She was pale, with faint pink cheeks, and small, delicate features, a woman who had, to use her own expression, "enjoyed very bad health" all her life. She had very little character, not much animation, nothing very good nor very bad about her. It would scarcely have been true even to say that she loved her children; she was fond of them—particularly of Patricia—gave them a great many caresses and sweetmeats while they were young enough, and afterwards let them have their own will without restraint; but there did not seem enough of active life in her to deserve the title of any active sentiment. She was deeply learned in physic and invalid dietry, and liked to be petted and attended, to come down stairs at twelve o'clock, to lie on the sofa, to be led out for a little walk, carefully adapted to her weakness, and to receive all the little attentions proper to an invalid. Her exclusive pretensions in this respect had, it is true, been rather infringed upon of late years by Patricia, who sometimes threatened to be a more serious invalid than her mother, and who certainly assumed the character with almost equal satisfaction. However, Patricia was pretty well at the present moment, and Mrs. Huntley, supported by her maid, had only about half an hour ago come down stairs. She had a glass of toast-and-water on the table beside her, a smelling-bottle, an orange cut into quarters upon a china plate, a newspaper within reach of her hand, and her knitting in her lap. We beg Mrs. Huntley's pardon, it was not knitting, but netting—her industry consisted in making strange, shapeless caps, bags, and window-curtains, which became excessively yellow after they were washed, and were of no use to any creature; for the refined art of crotchet was not then invented, nor had fancy-work reached that perfection which belongs to it now.

In an arm-chair by one of the windows sat a very different person—an old woman, black-eyed, white-haired, wearing an old-fashioned black dress, with a snowy white muslin handkerchief pinned down to her waist in front and behind—a large muslin apron of the same spotless complexion, a cap of clear cambric trimmed with rich old-fashioned lace, and bound round with a broad black ribbon, which was tied in a bow on the top of her head. This was a relative of Mrs. Huntley, known as Aunt Jean in the house of Melmar. She was the last survivor of her family, and had a little annuity, just enough to keep her muslin kerchiefs and aprons and old-fashioned caps from wearing out. She was quite kindly used in this house where nobody paid any particular regard to her, but where long ago it had seemed very good fun to Melmar himself to get up a little delusion on the score of Aunt Jean's wealth, which, according to the inventor of it, was to be bequeathed to his daughter Joanna. This was a favorite joke of the head of the house; he was never tired of referring to Aunt Jean's fortune, or threatening Joanna with the chance of forfeiting it, which delicate and exquisite piece of fun was always followed by a loud laugh, equally delicate and characteristic. Aunt Jean, however, fortunately, was deaf, and never quite understood the wit of her nephew-in-law; she stuck quietly to her corner, made rather a pet of Joanna, persisted in horrifying Patricia by her dress and her dialect, which breathed somewhat strongly of Aberdeenshire, and by dint of keeping "thretty pennies," as she said, in the corner of her old-fashioned leather purse—pennies which were like the oil in the widow's cruse, often spent, yet always existing—and in her drawers in her own room an unfailing store of lace, and muslins, and ribbons, old dresses, quaint examples of forgotten fashion, and pieces of rich stuff, such as girls love to turn over and speculate on possible uses for—kept up an extensive popularity. Aunt Jean was not in the very slightest degree an invalid—the tap of her little foot, which wore high-heeled shoes, was almost the smartest in the house. She sat in winter by the fire, in summer by one of the windows, knitting endless pairs of stockings, mits, and those shapeless little gloves, with a separate stall for the thumb, and one little bag for all the fingers, in which the hapless hands of babies are wont to be imprisoned. It was from an occupation of this kind that Aunt Jean turned, when the din of Joanna's accusation penetrated faintly into her ears.

"Eh, fat's that?" said Aunt Jean; it was something about a debt and a funeral, two things which were not particularly likely to interest Joanna. Something remarkably out of the usual course must have happened, and the old lady had all the likings of an old woman in the country. Gossip was sweet to her soul.

"Oh, mamma, so vexatious!" cried Patricia, in a voice which could not by any possibility reach the ears of Aunt Jean; "papa has been doing something to Mr. Livingstone, of Norlaw—he's dead, and there's been something done that looks cruel—oh! I'm sure I don't know exactly what it is—Joanna knows;—but only think how the people will look at us to-morrow night."

"Perhaps I may not be able to go, my dear," said Mrs. Huntley, with a sigh.

"Not able to go? after promising so long! mamma, that is cruel!" cried Patricia; "but nobody cares for me. I never have what other people have. I am to be shut up in this miserable prison of a place all my life—not able to go! Oh, mamma! but you'll all be sorry when there's no poor Patricia to be shut up and made a victim of any more!"

"I do think you're very unreasonable, Patricia," said Mrs. Huntley; "I've gone out three times this last month to please you—a great sacrifice for a person in my weak health—and Dr. Tait does not think late hours proper for you; besides, if there is any thing disagreeable about your papa, as you say, I really don't think my nerves could stand it."

"Fat's all this about?" said Aunt Jean; "you ken just as well as me that I canna hear a word of fat you're saying. Joan, my bairn, come you here—fa's dun wrang? Fat's happened? Eh! there's Patricia ta'en to the tears—fat's wrang?"

Nothing loth, Joanna rushed forward, and shouted her story into the old woman's ears. It was received with great curiosity and interest by the new hearers. Aunt Jean lifted up her hands in dismay, shook her head, made all the telegraphic signs with eye and mouth which are common to people restrained from full communication with their companions. Mrs. Huntley, too, was roused.

"It's like a scene in a novel," she said, with some animation; "but after all, Mr. Livingstone should not have been in debt to papa, you know. What with Oswald abroad, and you two at home, you can tell Aunt Jean we need all our money, Joanna; and if people die when they're in debt, what can they expect? I don't see, really, in my poor health, that I'm called upon to interfere."

"Fat's this I hear?" said Aunt Jean; "Livingstone o' Norlaw? Na, Jeanie, if that's true, your good man's been sair left to himself. Eh, woman! Livingstone! fat's a'body's thinking of? I would sooner have cut off my little finger if I had been Me'mar; that man!"

"Oh, what about him, Aunt Jean?" cried Joanna.

"Ay, bairn, but I maun think," said the old woman. "I'm no' so clear it's my duty to tell you. Your father kens his ain concerns, and so does your mother, in a measure, and so do I myself. I canna tell onybody mair than my ain secret, Joan. Hout ay! I'll tell you, fun I was a young lass, fat happened to me."

"I want to hear about Norlaw," cried Joanna, screaming into the old woman's ear.

"Aunt Jean!" cried Mrs. Huntley, making a sudden step out of her chair. "If you do, Me'mar will kill me—oh! hold your tongues, children! Do you think I can bear one of papa's passions—a person in my poor health? Aunt Jean, if you do, I'll never speak to you again!"

Aunt Jean contemplated her niece, with her twinkling black eyes, making a *moue* of vivid contempt as she nodded her head impatiently.

"Fat for can ye no hold your peace for a fool-wife?" said Aunt Jean; "did ye think I had as little wit as you? What about Norlaw? You see the laird here and him were aye ill friends. Hout ay! mony a ane's ill friends with Me'mar. I mind the bairns just fun you were born, Joan. Twa toddling wee anes, and ane in the cradle. Pity me! I mind it because I was losing my hearing, and turning a cankered auld wife; and it was them that took and buried their father? Honest lads! I would like to do them a good turn."

"But I know there's something more about Norlaw," cried Joanna, "and I'll say you're a cankered auld wife till you tell me—I will! and you would have told me before now but for mamma. Do you hear, Aunt Jean?"

"Hout ay, I hear," said the old woman, who could manage her deafness like most people who possess that defect—(where it is not extreme, a little deafness is in its way quite a possession) "but I maun take time to think fat it was I promised to tell you. Something that happened when I was a young lass. Just that, Joan—I was staying at my married sister's, that was your grandmother, and Jeanie, there, your mamaw, was a bit little bairn—she was aye a sma' thing of her years, taking physic for a constancy. There was a poor gentleman there, ane of the Gordons, as good blood in his veins as ony man in the kingdom, and better than the king's ain, that was only a German lairdie—but ye see this lad was poor, and fat should save him but he got into debt, and fat should help him but he died. So the sheriff's officers came and stopped the funeral; and the lads rose, a' the friends that were at it, and all the men on the ground, and fat should ail them to crack the officers' crowns, and lay them up in a chamber; but I've heard say it was a sair sicht to see the hearse rattling away at a trot, and a' the black coaches afterhand, as if it was a bridal—oh fie!—nothing else was in everybody's mouth on our side of the water, a' the mair because the Gordon lad that died was of the English chapel, and behoved to have a service o'er his grave, and the English minister was faint-hearted and feared. It wasna done at nicht, but in broad daylicht, and by the strong hand—and that happened—I wouldna say but it was forty year ago; for I was a young lass and your mamaw there a little bairn."

"I daresay, mamma," said Patricia, who had dried her tears, "that people don't know of it yet; and at the worst it was all papa's fault—I don't think we should be afraid to go—it wasn't our blame, I'm sure."

"If I should be able, my dear," said Mrs. Huntley, with her languid sigh—whereupon Patricia exerted herself to arrange her mother's pillow, and render her sundry little attentions which pleased her.

Poor little Patricia loved "society;" she wanted to shine and to be admired "like other girls"—even the dull dinner-parties of the surrounding lairds excited the fragile little soul, who knew no better, and she spent the rest of the day, oblivious of her former terrors concerning public opinion, in coaxing Mrs. Huntley into betterness; while Joanna, for her part, persecuted Aunt Jean with an unavailing but violent pertinacity, vainly hoping to gain some insight into a family secret. Patricia was successful in her endeavors; but there never was a more signal failure than that attack upon Aunt Jean.

CHAPTER XV

"Bless me callants! what are ye doing here?" said Marget, looking in at the door of the mid-chamber, where Huntley and Patrick Livingstone were together.

It was a small apartment, originally intended for a dressing-room, and communicating by a door locked and barricaded on both sides with the east room, which was the guest-chamber of the house. Almost its sole piece of furniture was a large old-fashioned mahogany desk, standing upon a heavy frame of four tall legs, and filling half the space; it was not like the bureau of romance, with that secret drawer where some important document is always being discovered. The heavy lid was held open by Huntley's head, as he carried on his investigations. There were drawers enough, but they were all made by the hand of the joiner of Kirkbride, who knew nothing of secret contrivances—and these, as well as all the remaining space of the desk, were filled with the gatherings of Norlaw's life, trifles which some circumstance or other made important to him at the moment they were placed there, but which were now pathetic in their perfect insignificance and uselessness, closely connected as they were with the dead man's memory. Old letters, old receipts, old curiosities, a few coins and seals, and trifling memorials, and a heap of papers quite unintelligible and worthless, made up the store. In one drawer, however, Huntley had found what he wanted—the will— and along with it, carefully wrapped in at least a dozen different folds of paper, a little round curl of golden hair.

They were looking at this when Marget, whose question had not been answered, entered and closed the door. The lads were not aware of her presence till this sound startled them; when they heard it, Huntley hurriedly refolded the covers of this relic, which they had been looking at with a certain awe. Eye of stranger, even though it was this faithful old friend and servant, ought not to pry into their father's secret treasure. The Mistress's hair was of the darkest brown. It was not for love of their mother that Norlaw had kept so carefully this childish curl of gold.

"Laddies," said Marget, holding the door close behind her, and speaking low as she watched with a jealous eye the covering up of this secret, "some of ye's been minding the Mistress of auld troubles. I said to myself I would come and give you a good hearing—the haill three—what's Mary o' Melmar to you?"

"Did my mother tell you?" asked Huntley, with amazement.

"Her, laddies! na, it's little ye ken! *her* name the like o' that to the like o' me! But Cosmo behoved to ask about the story—he would part with his little finger to hear a story, that bairn—and 'deed I ken fine about it. What for could ye no' speak to me?"

"There was more than a story in Huntley's thoughts and in mine," said Patrick, shutting up the desk with some decision and authoritativeness.

"Hear him! my certy! that's setting up!" cried Marget; "I ken every thing about it for a' you're so grand. And I ken the paper in Huntley's hand is the will, and I ken I would run the risk o' firing the haill house, but I would have burnt it, afore he got sight o't, if it had been me."

"Why?" said Huntley, with a little impatience. It was not possible that the youth could read this bequest conferring Melmar, failing the natural heiress, on his father and himself, without a thrill of many emotions. He was ambitious, like every young man; he could not think of this fortune, which seemed almost to lie within his reach, without a stirring of the heart.

"It did nothing but harm to your father, and it can do nothing but mischief to you," said Marget, solemnly; "you're young and strong, and fit to make a fortune. But I tell you, Huntley Livingstone, if you attempt to seek this lass over the world, as your father did, you're a ruined man."

"Neither Huntley nor me believe in ruined men," said Patie; "we'll take care for that—go to your kye, and never mind."

"Don't be angry, Marget," said Huntley, who was more tender of the faithful retainer of the house; "trust us, as Patie says—besides, if she should never be found, Melmar's mine."

"Eh, whisht, lad! she'll come hame with half a dozen bairns before e'er your feet's across the door," cried Marget; "tell me to trust you, that are only callants, and dinna ken! Trust me, the twa of you! Gang and spend a' the best years of your life, if you like, seeking her, or witness that she's dead. If ye find her, ye're nane the better, if ye dinna find her, ye're aye deluded with the thought of a fortune ye canna claim—and if ye get word she's dead, there's still Melmar himself, that was bred a writer and kens a' the cheats of them, to fight the battle! They might say it was a false will—they might say,

Guid forgive them! that Norlaw had beguiled the auld man. There's evil in't but nae guid; Huntley, you're your father's son, you're to make his amends to her. Dinna vex the Mistress's life with Mary of Melmar ony mair!"

"The short and the long of it all, Marget," said Patrick, who was at once more talkative and more peremptory than usual—"is, that you must mind your own business and we'll mind ours. Huntley's not a knight in a story-book, seeking a distressed lady. Huntley's not in love with Mary of Melmar; but if she's to be found she shall be found; and if she's dead my brother's the heir."

"No' till you're done wi' a' her bairns," cried Marget; "say there's nae mair than three of them, like yoursels—and the present Me'mar's been firm in his seat this thirteen years. Weel, weel, I daur to say Patie's right—it's nae business o' mine; but I'd sooner see you a' working for your bread, if it was just like laboring men, and I warn ye baith, the day's coming when ye'll think upon what I say!"

Marget disappeared, solemnly shaking her head as she said these last words. For the moment, the two youths said nothing to each other. The desk was locked softly, the will placed in an old pocket-book, to be deposited elsewhere, and then, for the first time, the young men's eyes met.

"She's right," said Patie, with sudden emphasis; "if you seek her yourself, Huntley, you'll neither get Me'mar nor fortune—it's true."

Huntley paid little attention to his brother. He stood looking out from the window, where, in the distance, to the north, the banks of Tyne rose high among the woods of Melmar—opposite to him, fertile fields, rich in the glow of coming harvest, lay the wealthy lands of his father's enemy—those lands which perhaps now, if he but knew it, were indisputably his own. He stood fascinated, looking out, tracing with an unconscious eagerness the line of the horizon, the low hills, and trees, and ripening corn, which, as far as he could see before him, were still part of the same inheritance. He was not a dreamy boy like Cosmo—he thought little of his father's old love, or of the triumph of restoring her to her inheritance. The Mary of Norlaw's fancy was but a shadow upon the future of his own. He thought, with a glow of personal ambition, of the fair stretch of country lying before him. Generous, high-spirited, and incapable of meanness, Huntley still had the impulse of conquest strong within him. He could not but think, with a rising heart, of this visible fortune which lay at his feet and seemed to be almost within his grasp. He could not but think, with indignant satisfaction, of unseating the false heir whose enmity had pursued Norlaw to the very grave. All the excitement which had gathered into these few past weeks still throbbed in Huntley's heart and stirred his brain. He could not moderate the pace of his thoughts or subdue his mind at anybody's bidding. If it should be hard to get justice and a hearing for his claims, this very difficulty increased the attraction—for it was his claims he thought of while the others were thinking of Mary of Melmar. He was not selfish, but he was young, and had an ardent mind and a strong individual character. Mary of Melmar—a white ghost, unreal and invisible—faded from his mind entirely. He thought, instead, of the man who had arrested Norlaw's funeral, and of the inheritance of which he was the rightful heir.

With all these fumes in his brain it was quite impossible that Huntley could listen soberly to the sober counsels of Patie, or to the warnings of the old servant. *They* begged him not to think of a search for Mary. *He* thought of nothing of the kind. Mary had taken no position of romance in the young man's fancy. The romance which blossomed in his eyes was a much less disinterested one than that which Cosmo mused upon in the old window of the castle. He thought of himself, of his own family, of all the possibilities and powers of an extensive land-owner, and with the flush of youthful self-belief, of a great life. He had stood thus at the window a long time gazing out, and paying no attention to the occasional words of his sensible brother, when the sound of some one coming roused them both. It was the Mistress's firm footsteps ascending the stair—they both left the room immediately, agreed, at least, in one thing, to trouble their mother no more with recollections disagreeable to her. Then Patie went about his business, somewhat disturbed by the thought that Huntley meant to throw away a portion of his life in the same fruitless folly which had injured their father; while Huntley himself, remembering something that had to be done at Kirkbride, set off along the banks of Tyne at a great pace, which did not, however, overtake the swing of his thoughts. Marget, coming out to her kitchen door to look after him, held up her hands and exclaimed to herself, "The laddie's carried!" as she watched his rapid progress—which meaning, as it did, that Huntley was fairly lifted off his feet and possessed by a rapid and impetuous fancy, was perfectly correct—though the fancy itself was not such as Marget thought.

CHAPTER XVI

The village lay bright under the afternoon sun when Huntley Livingstone came in sight of it that day. It was perfectly quiet, as was its wont—some small children playing at the open doors, the elder ones, save here and there an elder daughter charged with the heavy responsibility of a baby, being for the most part safe at school. At the door of the Norlaw Arms an angler-visitor, with his rod over his shoulder, a single figure becalmed in the sunshine, stood lazily gazing about him—and in the shadow of the projecting gable of the inn, another stranger stood holding his horse before the door of the smithy, from whence big John Black, the smith, was about to issue to replace a lost shoe. John was the master of this important rural establishment, and was a big, soft-hearted giant, full of the good-humored obtuseness which so often accompanies great personal size and strength. Inside, in the fiery obscurity of the village Pandemonium, toiled a giant of quite a different order—a swarthy, thick-set little Cyclops, with a hump on his shoulder, and one eye. This was John's brother, the ruling spirit of mischief in Kirkbride, whom all the mothers of sons held in disgust and terror, and whom Dr. Logan himself could make no improvement in. Jacob, or Jaacob, as he was popularly called, was as strong as he was ugly, and, it was generally understood, as wicked as both. By natural consequence, his rustic neighbors found a considerable attraction in his society, and liked to repeat his sayings, which were not always funny, with explosions of laughter. Huntley's errand, as it happened, was with this individual, who was somewhat of a genius in his way, which was the way of agricultural implements. Jaacob had even taken out what he called a "paatent" for a new harrow of his own invention, and was, in right of this, the authority, on all such matters, of the country-side.

"Ye'll be carrying on the farm then?" said Jaacob. "A plow needs mair than a new coulter to drive it through a furrow—it'll be new work to you, Mr. Huntley, to gang atween the stilts yoursel'."

Huntley had descended suddenly out of the hurry of his fancies about Melmar, of which he already saw himself master. He came to the ground with rather a rude shock when he heard these words, and found himself on the hard earthen floor of the smithy, with the red sparks flying into the darkness over his head, and Jaacob's one eye twinkling at him in the fiery light. He was not the laird of Melmar to Jaacob, but only the son of the ruined Norlaw.

"What we want in the meantime is the plow," said Huntley, somewhat sharply, his face flushing in spite of himself; then he added, after a pause, all the humiliation of debt and poverty recurring to his mind, which had been defended for some time against that lesser pain by the excitement of grief, and to-day by the violent flush of ambitious hope. "I believe there is a bill—but if you'll send it up to the house I'll see to it without delay."

Bowed Jaacob was not ungenerous in his way, but he scorned to defend himself from any imputation of ungenerosity. He did not hasten, therefore, as might have been supposed, to say that the aforesaid bill was of no importance, and could wait. On the contrary, he proceeded, with sarcastic dryness in his tone:

"You'll find it hard work to get in your craps. How many acres have ye in wheat the year, Mr. Huntley? You'll no' ken? Houts, man! that's an ill beginning for a lad that farms his ain land."

In spite of himself, tears of mortification stole into Huntley's eyes. He turned his head away with a muttered exclamation.

"I don't know that we've half an acre safe!" cried Huntley, in the bitterness of his heart. His dream was broken. Me'mar, who was their chief creditor—Me'mar, whom he had not yet displaced—might be able to get into his hard worldly hands, for aught Huntley knew, every slope of Norlaw.

"Aweel, aweel, lad," said Jaacob, striking his hammer fiercely upon the glowing iron, "a' the better for you—you'll be your ain man—but I wouldna cheat myself with fancies if I was you. Make up your mind ae way or another, but dinna come here and speak to me about plows, as if that was what your mind was set on. I'm no' a Solomon, but if you mean to thrive, never delude yoursalf with a sham."

"What's a' that?" said big John, as his customer mounted the reshod horse, and trotted off in leisurely fashion as became the day; "has Jaacob won to his books, Mr. Huntley? but I reckon he has his match when he has you."

John, however, who was rather proud of his brother's intellectual powers, thought no such thing—neither did the little Cyclops himself.

"Mind your ain business," said Jaacob, briefly; "what do you think a man learns out of books, you haverel! Na, if I'm onything, I'm a man of observation; and take my word, lad, there never was a man trove yet till he saw distinck where he was, and ordered his ways according. There's mysel'—do you think I could ever make ony progress, ae way or another, if I minded what a' these stupid ideots say?"

"What do they say?" said Huntley, who was too much occupied with his own thoughts to perceive the drift of Jaacob's personal observations.

"Na, d'ye think I'm heeding?" said Jacob; "a man can rarely be more enlightened than his neighbors without suffering for't. A' this auld machinery of the world creaks like an auld bellows. There's naething but delusions on every side of ye. Ye canna be clear of a single thing that ye havena conquished for yoursel'."

Huntley, who had come out of the languid August afternoon, red in a glow of sunshine and heat, to which the very idea of long labor was alien, which accorded well enough with his own ambitious dreams and thoughts of sudden fortune—could not help feeling somehow as if Jaacob's hammer, beneath the strokes of which the sparks flew, struck himself as well as the iron. Melmar dissipated into thin air, in the ruddy atmosphere of the smithy. The two darkling giants, large and small, moving about in the fierce glow of the firelight, the puff of the bellows, plied by an attendant demon, and the ceaseless clank of the hammer, all combined to recall to reality and the present, the thoughts of the dreaming lad. In this atmosphere the long labors of the Australian emigrant looked much more reasonable and likely than any sudden enrichment; and with the unconscious self-reference of his age, Huntley took no pains to find out what Jaacob meant, but immediately applied the counsel to his own case.

"I suppose you're very right, Jacob," said Huntley; "but it's hard work making a fortune; maybe it's safer in the end than what comes to you from another man's labors; but still, to spend a life in gathering money, is no very great thing to look forward to."

"Money!" said Jaacob, contemptuously. "Na, lad; if that's your thought, you're no' in my way. Did you ever hear of a rich philosopher? ne'er a are have I heard tell o', though I ken the maist of that fraternity. Money! na! it's ideas, and no that sordid trash, that tempts me."

"And the mair fuil you!" said big John, half in chagrin, half in admiration. "You might have made your fortune twenty times over, if it hadna been for your philosophy."

"Whew!" whistled bowed Jaacob, with magnificent disdain; "what's a' the siller in the world and a' its delichts—grand houses, grand leddies, and a' the rest of thae vanities—to the purshuit of truth? That's what I'm saying, callant—take every thing on trust because you've heard sae a' your days, and your faither believed it before ye, gin ye please; but as for me, I'm no' the man for sham—I set my fit, if a' the world should come against me, on ideas I've won and battled for mysel'."

"When they're as reasonable as the harrow, I've nae objection," said big John; "but ilka man canna write his idies in wud and iron, Mr. Huntley. The like o' that may be a' very well for *him*, but it doesna answer you and me. Eh, man, but it's warm! If it wasna that philosophy's an awfu' drouthy thing—and the wife comes down on me like murder when I get a gill—I wouldna say but it's the best kind of wark for this weather. Ye'll be goin' up bye to the manse, Mr. Huntley. I hear they're aye very well pleased to see onybody out of Norlaw; but ye maunna say ye've been here, for Jaacob and the minister, they're at daggers drawn."

"Pish! nae such thing," cried Jaacob, with complacency; "the like of a man like yon shouldna mell with a man like me. It's no' a fair battle—I aye say sae—I can tak his measure fast enough, but he can nae mair tak mine than he can flee. Eh, lad! have you ta'en the gate? and no' a word mair about the plow?"

"I'll take your advice, Jacob," said Huntley; "the plow can stand till we see what use we'll have for it; but as for going between the stilts myself, if I do you'll see me draw as fair a furrow as any plowman about Kirkbride."

"Hurray!" said Jaacob; "the lad has some speerit after a'; never you mind—we'll send down somebody to see to the plow."

With this assurance, Huntley left the smithy; but not till Jaacob had begun to sing in the most singular of cracked and elvish voices, beating time with emphatic strokes of his hammer, "The Flaxen-headed Cowboy," a rustic and ancient ditty, much in favor in the country-side. Whether it was the gestures of the gnome which called them forth, or a ludicrous application of the song to himself, Huntley could not tell; but big John and the boy accompanied the chant with audible, yet restrained explosions of laughter. Huntley grew very red in spite of himself, as he hurried along to the little bridge. What a change from the fancy which possessed him as he came up the village street half an hour ago! He could not have believed that his hypothetical inheritance could have vanished so utterly; somehow he could not even recall that evanescent splendor. It was no longer the heir of Melmar who ascended the brae of Tyne, through the trees and scattered cottages towards the white-gabled manse. It was the same Huntley Livingstone who had buried his father at midnight, who had set his face against the evil fortune which seemed ready to overwhelm his house, and who had pledged himself to win in a new country a new and stable fortune for the race of Norlaw.

But the young man was by no means contented to part so lightly with his magnificent vision. He did all he could by dint of thinking to bring it back to his mind; but even when he paused at the top of the little hill and surveyed once more the fair fields of Melmar, he could not recover the enthusiasm and fervor of his former thoughts. Bowed Jaacob, with the odd philosophy which perceived other people's mistakes, but could not see its own ludicrous pretensions—big John, who believed in his brother—and the ruddy darkness of the smithy, where reality made a rude assault upon his vision—had disenchanted Huntley. He stood on the brae of Tyne, seeing every thing with practical and undazzled eyes, feeling himself to have a certain claim, difficult and doubtful, yet real, upon the lands before him; but seeing all the obstacles which lay in its way. And, distinct from this, far apart and separate, with a world between, lay the fortune far more secure and certain which Huntley had to make with his own hands.

It was with these thoughts that he entered the manse of Kirkbride.

CHAPTER XVII

Dr. Logan was in his study writing his sermon—Katie was alone in the manse parlor. It was a cheerful room, looking over the little front garden and down the brae to the roofs of the village from its front window, and peeping out through a flush of foliage upon Tyne and the Melmar woods from the other. The furniture was very simple, the carpet old, the walls painted of an ash-green, which was just one degree better than the drab-colored complexion of the Norlaw dining-room; but notwithstanding, the room was perfect and could not have been improved upon. There was only one easy-chair, and that was sacred to the minister; the others were of the ancient fashion of drawing-room chairs, once elaborately painted and gilded, but now much dimmed of their pristine splendor. Katie's own hands had made all the pretty chintz covers, which fitted without a wrinkle, and the result was extremely satisfactory—very much more agreeable to look upon than the crumpled covers of the Melmar drawing-room. There was a wonderful screen of needle work, in a very slim ebony frame in one corner, an old-fashioned work table, with a crimson bag and inlaid top, which could answer as a chess-board, in another—and a low bookcase, full of books, between the door and the end window. On the table, at this present moment, stood a basket, of goodly dimensions, full of stockings—and by the side of that a little pile of freshly-mangled linen, pinafores and other small garments in want of strings and buttons. It was Friday, very near the end of the week—so the minister, too wise to leave his preparations to the latest day, made ready for his weekly duty in the study, while Katie did her weekly mendings on the same principle in her own domain.

"You may go to the study if you please Huntley—my father will be glad to see you," said the young mistress of the manse, once more drawing Johnnie's sock over her hand after she had welcomed her visitor. Huntley did not avail himself of the privilege so soon as he might have done, considering that he had come with the intention of asking advice from the minister. It was pleasant to sit down in that quiet, bright, home-like room, which looked as though nothing could disturb its cheerful composure, and see that careful little woman among her family labors, so fresh, and bright, and young, yet so perfectly in her place among these pleasant cares.

Huntley, whose mind was in a tumult of unaccustomed anxieties, and who felt himself oppressed with a burden of responsibility, and the new necessity of deciding for himself, sank into a chair opposite Katie, with a sensation of rest and relief which he had not felt for weeks before. She looked up to him brightly with those smiling brown eyes which were so young and yet so full of elder-sisterly thoughtfulness. She saw in a moment the shadow on Huntley's face, and proceeded to minister to it as if it had been a cloud upon the boyish horizon of one of her own young brothers. Katie could not help being half maternal even to Huntley.

"Something ails you," said the little woman—"are you tired, Huntley? Oh, I mind when grief was here, what hard, hard work it was keeping up a smile. Never mind me; look sorrowful, if you like, and take a rest. It makes me think how I felt myself when dear mamma died, to see you keeping up a face like that."

"Oh, Katie, I wish we had you at Norlaw!" cried the lad, with sudden earnestness.

"Yes," said Katie, simply, "if you had only had a sister, Huntley!—but Mrs. Livingstone does not care for strangers. And mothers are sometimes fondest of their sons—everybody says so; but I know you're the eldest, and every thing comes on you."

"Patie is the wisest," said Huntley, with a momentary smile; "I think he could manage better without me—and, Katie, I'll have to go away."

She looked up at him with a question in her eyes. She asked nothing audibly, but merely suspended her work, and turned, with a friendly anxiety, her steady, kind gaze upon Huntley's face. The young man was not "in love"—he was still too familiar with this sisterly face, and too much occupied with all the sudden troubles in which he had himself been plunged, to think of any such thing; but, unconsciously, Huntley paused before answering—paused to take the peaceful scene, the home apartment, the bright serious eyes into his memory, a picture of strange influence and tenderness never to fade.

"I thought of going to Australia," he said; "they say a man with a will to work and some knowledge, especially of cattle, is sure to thrive there. It matters but little, I think, Katie, whether I'm a hundred or a thousand miles away, so long as I *am* away; and I think the best place for me is there."

"But Australia is many a thousand miles away," said Katie, "at the other end of the world; and you can not come home to see your friends as you might do from a nearer place. If you go there, Huntley, we'll never see you again."

"I'll go there, that I may come back," said Huntley, eagerly; then he began to play with the ball of cotton which Katie was mending her children's stockings with; then he looked round the room wistfully once more. "And when I do come home," said the lad, "Katie, I wonder, I wonder, what changes I'll see here?"

"Oh, whisht!" cried Katie, with a little overflow of tears; "papa's not young, but he's no' very old; and if it's God's will, we'll aye be the same."

"It might be ten—fifteen years," said Huntley; "and I was not thinking of the minister; I was thinking of—other things."

Katie did not ask what these other things might be. The color rose in her cheek a little, but not enough to confuse her.

"The little ones will be all grown up," she said, with a quiet laugh; "perhaps some of them away too, Huntley, into the battle; and me an old Katie with a cap, keeping house for papa."

She glanced across the table for her cotton as she spoke, and, meeting Huntley's eye, blushed a little more, yet was not discomposed. The young man's heart beat louder, he could not very well tell why. Some confused words came rushing into his mind, but none of them were fit to say. His own face flushed with a hasty flood of unaccustomed and unascertained emotions; he rose up hastily, scarcely knowing how it was that the repose of the manse parlor was broken, yet feeling it. Dr. Logan called Katie from his study, and Huntley answered the call. He gave back the ball of cotton, and said hurriedly:—

"Dinna forget me, Katie, when *that* time comes;" and so went away.

That time! what time? Huntley could have given no explanation of what he meant; neither could Katie, who put up her hand softly to her eyes, and smiled a very faint smile, and said, "Poor boy!" with a little sigh as the door closed upon him. But perhaps explanations would have done but little good, and every thing answered perfectly well as it was.

Huntley came with a blush into the presence of the innocent and unconscious minister, who had forgotten his own youth many a long day ago, and had never yet been roused into consciousness that his little Katie might be something else than a good child and elder sister, in the perverse imaginations of other people. He looked up from his desk and his manuscript, and pushed up his spectacles on his forehead when the young man entered.

"Huntley! is that you? What's wrong, my man?" said Dr. Logan. He thought the lad could not have seen Katie, or he must have become more composed by this time; and the excellent pastor thought of nothing else than some new accident or coil at Norlaw.

"Nothing's wrong," said Huntley, who only blushed the more in shamefaced self-consciousness, "but I wanted to ask your advice."

Dr. Logan laid down his pen with resignation; it was a new pen, sharply nibbed, such as the minister loved, and he had just got a capital idea for the third head of his sermon, an idea which might be nowhere before Huntley had half stated his case. The minister paused a moment, trying very hard to connect his idea with something in the room which might recall it to him when his visitor was gone. He tried the inkstand, the pretty paper-weight on the table, and even his large red and green pocket-handkerchief, in vain. At last he thought he had secured it on the knob of the glass door of his bookcase; he nodded ruefully to Huntley and made a knot on his handkerchief.

"Now, Huntley, proceed, my boy," said the minister with a sigh; he held the knot on the handkerchief in his hand, and fixed his eyes on the bookcase. Certainly he had it safe now.

Huntley, glad to get out of his embarrassment so, plunged at once into his tale. He could not quite make out how it was that the excellent doctor looked so steadily at the bookcase, and gave himself such divided and wandering answers. However, at last the minister forgot his idea, and threw away the handkerchief in despair.

"Eh? what was that you were saying, Huntley?" said Dr. Logan. The story had to be gone over again. But, to Huntley's surprise, his friend knew all about it, more about it indeed than he did himself, and shook his head when Huntley vehemently declared his conviction that he was the true heir of Melmar.

"I make no doubt," said the minister, "that if *she* could be found, the will would stand—but I mind the writer laying it down very clear to me and Norlaw at the time that ye behoved to produce her alive or dead—that is, by evidence in the last case, no doubt—before your case could stand. It might be well worth a man's while that had enough to keep him, and nothing else to do—but I would not advise *you* to put off your time seeking Mary Huntley. You're the eldest son and the prop of your family. I would not advise it, Huntley, my man."

"Nor do I mean it," said Huntley, with a blush at his own wild fancies; "and if I had known that you knew it so well, I should not even have troubled you. No, doctor, I've written to your friend in Edinburgh—I want him to take all our affairs in hand, and save, if it is possible, Norlaw itself for my mother. What we'll have to begin upon after, I can't very well tell—but Cosmo is the only one of us too young to set out for himself. I will leave the other matter with Mr. Cassilis, and he can do what he thinks best."

"Very wise, Huntley, very wise," said the minister, whose mind was still fumbling after his idea; "and you're thinking of going abroad yourself, they tell me?—I don't doubt it's a shock to your mother, but I would say it was the best thing you could do. Charlie Cassilis, no doubt, will be coming here. He's aye very willing to come to the manse. I'll make Katie write him a line to-day, to say we'll expect him—and any thing I can do to further the business, you know you can rely upon—eh? what was that you said?"

"Nothing," said Huntley, "except that there's little time to lose, and I am interrupting you. Good-bye, Dr. Logan—I'll see you again before I go away."

"Before he goes away," said the minister, with perplexity, half rising to follow Huntley, as he hurried from the room; "what does the callant mean?" But just then Dr. Logan's eye returned to the knob of the bookcase, which no longer recalled that precious lost idea. "Poor human nature!" said the good man, with a sigh. He thought it rather selfish of Huntley to have disturbed his studies just at that particular moment—and it was the young man's human nature over which he sighed.

Huntley, meanwhile, went back again to Norlaw in a greater tumult of mind than that which had brought him forth. But he no longer thought of Melmar as he had done in that sudden golden vision of fortune and conquest. His heart leaped within him like one on the verge of a new world. These three scenes through which he had passed:—bowed Jaacob's odd philosophy and startling groundwork—"Trust in nothing that you have not conquered for yourself;" Katie's quiet home-parlor, her blush and glance of kindness, which perhaps understood his unspoken and sudden fervor as well as he did himself; and, beyond these, the sober, calm every-day minister, giving only an outside and momentary attention to those matters in which this young life had all its hopes at stake, minding his sermon, and only kindly indifferent to Huntley, had brought the youth on a long way in the education of his life. He could not have put it all into words, or explained it to the satisfaction of the philosopher; yet the shock of reality and actual life which brought him back to himself in the little smithy of Kirkbride—the warm light of Katie's eyes which had stirred, with something of personal and distinct identity, separate from family interests, and individual in the world, the young man's heart and spirit—and not least, though very different, the composed friendliness of the minister, pre-occupied with his sermon, who had only a very spare amount of attention to bestow upon Huntley, and showed him that the world in general was not likely to be much absorbed by his interests, or startled by his hopes—were all very real, practical and permanent lessons. They sent him back to Norlaw an older man.

CHAPTER XVIII

Mr. Cassilis came to the manse in answer to Katie's invitation and the business of Huntley. He was young and did not particularly commend himself to the liking of the young master of Norlaw; but as he pleased all the other people very tolerably well, there were, perhaps, various reasons for the less friendly sentiment of Huntley. He was, however, a brisk man of business, and not sufficiently over-burdened with occupation to prevent him entering heartily into the concerns of the half-ruined family.

All this time Patrick Livingstone had been quietly busy, collecting and arranging all his father's memoranda which seemed to throw any light upon their circumstances; among these were many hurried, and only half intelligible notes of transactions with the former Huntley of Melmar, from which it very shortly appeared that Norlaw's debts had all been contracted to his old kinsman, and had only come into possession of "the present Melmar," when he took possession of the house and property, as heir-at-law, on the old man's death. They had suspected this before, for it seemed very unlikely that one man should borrow of another, whose claims were so entirely antagonistic to his own—but these were their only real evidence—for Norlaw had been so irregular and unsystematic that it was impossible to tell what money might or might not have passed through his hands.

The lawyer took all these scratchy memorandums out of Patrick's hands, and examined them carefully in presence of the lads. They were in the east room, in the midst of a pile of old papers from which these had been selected. Patie had not completed his task—he was going over his father's letters, to see whether they threw any light on these forgotten transactions. It was no small task; for Norlaw, like most other men of trifling habits and unimportant correspondence, kept every thing that everybody wrote to him, and even scrawls of his own letters. Some of these scrawls were curious enough—among them were one or two anxious and elaborate epistles to people abroad, whom his search for his lost love had brought him into contact with; some, dating still further back, were intimations of the birth of his children, and other family events of importance to his wife's relations. They were all composed with considerable care, and in somewhat pompous diction; they threw wonderful light upon the weaknesses and vanities of this departed life, and indifferent people might have laughed at them—but Huntley and Patie blushed instead of laughing, or folded the scrawls away hurriedly with tears in their eyes. To them these memorials were still pathetic, tender, full of a touching appeal to their affection, too sacred to meet the common eye.

Presently, however, Patie caught a glimpse of a handwriting still more scratchy than his father's—the trembling characters of old age. It was a letter from old Melmar, the most important they had yet lighted upon—and ran thus:—

"Dear Patrick,

"Touching the matter that was under discussion betwixt us the last time I saw you, I have just this to say, namely, that I hold your receipts and acknowledgments for money in the interests of your wife and family, and not in my own. I know well what would happen if you knew yourself free to incur more responsibility; so, mind you, though you'll get them all at my death, and most likely Melmar to the boot, I'll take care, as long as I'm to the fore, to keep my hand over you for your good. You can let the Mistress see this if you please, and I'll wager a bodle she agrees with me. I can not give you them back—but unless you behave all the worse, they'll never leave my hands until they return to your own.

"H. Huntley."

"Eh! what's that?" said Mr. Cassilis, looking up from his little lot of papers, as he saw the two brothers pass this letter between them.

They were half reluctant to show it; and when Huntley at last handed it across the table it was with a proud apology.

"My father was generous and liberal to the extreme. I suppose he was not what people call prudent; few understood him," said Huntley.

The lawyer took the paper with a half perceptible smile. He knew already what other people said of Norlaw.

However, he added old Melmar's letter with care to his own heap of scribbled memoranda.

"It's not very much good," he said, "but it shows intention. Unquestionably, neither the giver nor the receiver had any thought of payment for these loans. I had better see the present man to-morrow. What with the will and these he ought to come to reason."

"Me'mar?" cried Huntley—"no, I can have no appeal made to him on our behalf. Do you know how he persecuted my father?"

"I'm not much of an appealing man," said Cassilis, "but I had better see him. Don't be afraid—I'll not compromise you. You did not know much of the matter yourself, I understand, till recently. Be charitable—suppose he were as ignorant as you?"

"Stop!" cried Patie, "never mind personal feelings—is that all the value of the will?—to bring him to reason?"

"Not if I find Mary Huntley," said the young lawyer.

If *I* find. The young men exchanged glances—not quite sure that they were pleased with this transference of their interests.

"If she's to be found alive—or if she's dead, and we can prove it, every thing, of course, becomes as clear as daylight," said the minister's nephew, "and many a man would tell you that in these days either the one thing or the other is certain; but I've had some experience. I know there have been cases in which every effort was baffled; and failing either, I don't see at this moment what's to be done. You expect me to say, go to law, of course, but who's to pay the piper? Law's a very expensive luxury. Wait till you're rich, and then come down upon him—that is to say, if this search fails."

"But it is at least worth while to make the search," said Huntley, hastily, "and if it is so, it is too soon to treat with Melmar. Friendship is out of the question. Let us deal with him honestly. I can not accept a favor from a man one day and commence a lawsuit against him the next; it is not possible."

"In the meantime," said Cassilis, coolly sweeping all his papers up into a pocket-book, "you've committed your affairs into my hands, and I mean to do my best for my client, begging your pardon, whether my client perceives my tactics or no. Don't be offended. I'll claim these said acknowledgments as your right, and not as a favor. I want to see what kind of an animal this is that we're to fight; and to let you see what I mean, I may as well say that I've heard all the history of the last few weeks, and that I understand your feelings; but feelings, Livingstone, recollect, as your brother says, have little to do with the law."

Huntley could make very little further opposition; but he did not respond by any means to his new agent's friendliness; he received it even with a little *hauteur* and surliness, like a ridiculous young hero, finding out condescension and superiority, and sundry other of those agreeable figments of the jealous imagination, in the natural frankness of the young lawyer. If he had been fifty, or had known nothing of the manse, possibly Mr. Charles Cassilis, W. S., would have made a more favorable impression upon Huntley Livingstone.

CHAPTER XIX

"Do I look like a fool?"

The speaker was Huntley of Melmar, seated at that moment in his large leathern easy-chair at his own study-table; this was a long dim room, lined with dusty-looking bookcases, and lighted faintly by one window, from which nothing could be seen but a funereal yew-tree, which kept the room in perpetual shade. The whole apartment had a stifled, unventilated look, as if fresh air never entered it, as sunshine certainly never did; even in winter no fire could be coaxed into a blaze in Melmar's study—every thing was dusty, choked, and breathless, partaking in the general want of order visible through the house, with private additions of cheerlessness peculiarly its own.

And there could not well be a greater contrast than the two people in this room; Cassilis was young, good-looking, rather careless in manner, shrewd and quick, as became his profession, but by no means formal, as might have become it. He was not the solemn bearer of a legal challenge—a messenger of heroical enmity or hereditary dislike; he was only a morning visitor in a morning coat, quite as ready to talk of the last change of ministry or the ensuing election as of the immediate business which brought him here. Melmar sat watching him like an old cat, stealthy and absorbed. In *his* day business was managed in a different manner; and the old Aberdeen attorney watched with a chuckle of professional contempt and private satisfaction the informal proceedings of his younger brother and adversary. Mr. Huntley thought himself much too "deep" for the fathoming of this careless neophyte, while his visitor, on the other hand, found equal satisfaction in setting down the Laird of Melmar as one of the old school.

"Not exactly," said Cassilis, "but it's odd how often a fool and a man of sense are convertible terms. A man does a thing from a generous motive, and that's ridiculous, eh, Mr. Huntley? absurd to men of the world like you and me, who don't recognize the principle; but mind you, there *might* be circumstances which *might* induce the most sagacious of us, out of pure self-regard and prudence, to do the very same thing as the blockhead did out of generosity; the result would be the same, you know, in both cases—and who is to judge whether it is done by a wise man or a fool?"

"Aye, man, you're ironical, are you?" said Melmar, "very good practice, but it does not do with me—I'm too old for inuendoes; come, to the point. You've got a foolish case by the hand, though, of course, as an older man and member of the profession, I think it perfectly right of you not to seem conscious of that—*perfectly* proper. I highly approve of your demeanor in a professional point of view, my young friend."

"Which is very kind of you," said Cassilis, laughing; "I think it all the more so because I can't agree with you. Do you know, I hear everywhere about the country that there could not be a greater difference than between young Livingstone and his father?—quite a different man, I understand."

"Eh? and what's that to me?" asked Melmar, sharply.

"Well, you know, between ourselves as professional men," said Cassilis, laughing and speaking with the most delightful frankness, "if this Norlaw had been a man of spirit and energy, like his son, or indeed worth his salt, as people say, you know just as well as I do—possibly far better, for I bow to your experience—that you could not have had a chance of reigning here as you have done for so many years."

"What the deevil do you mean, sir?" cried Melmar, growing red and half rising from his chair; "is this language to hold to me, in my own house?"

"Nay, I was only appealing to your professional knowledge," said the young man, carelessly. "When you speak to me of the profession, of course I necessarily conclude that you are, at least, as well-informed as I am—and this is clear to anybody with half an eye. Mind you, I don't mean to say that young Livingstone's claim is weaker than his father's—you know it is not. I feel indeed that the whole matter is immensely simplified by having a professional man like yourself to deal with—for I don't presume to suppose that I am telling you any thing that you don't know already; but possibly—I can't tell—the young man may not feel it for his interest to push his claims at this moment. It's for *my* interest that he should, of course, for it will be a capital case—but we can both wait; however, under the circumstances, I am perfectly justified in asking you to consider whether the little restitution I suggested to you would be the act of a fool or of a wise man."

Melmar had been gazing with a kind of hazy, speechless wrath at the speaker, who passed so jauntily and lightly over this subject, and took his own perfect acquaintance with its right and wrong, for granted, with so much coolness. When Cassilis came to this pause, however, no explosion followed. The florid face grew redder with a bursting fiery fullness, in which even the grizzled red fringes of hair sympathized—but, in spite of himself, Melmar was afraid. His "young friend," whom he had patronized and despised, seemed somehow to have got him completely in his power—

seemed to see into the very thoughts of the old worldling, who thought himself so much wiser than his adversary. He made a pause of consideration, and felt much the reverse of comfortable. The unconcerned air of his visitor, which had relieved him at first, seemed somehow to give greater weight to his words now. If these downright blows were given in play, what should the serious strokes of the same hand be? and Melmar knew very well that the strength of his opponent's case lay in plain right and justice, while his was only to be held by art and stratagem. While he pondered, a sudden thought struck him—he rose, went to the window, glanced out there for a moment—then to the door, opened it and glanced along the long passage to make sure there were no listeners—then he returned to his chair, and bent towards the young lawyer, who had been watching all his proceedings with a half amused curiosity.

"To make an end of all this," said Melmar, with a very good imitation of impatience, "and because they are relatives of the old family, and friends, and all the rest of it—and to prove that I'm sorry for what took place at Norlaw's funeral—I'll tell you what I'll consent to do—"

"Well?" said Cassilis, quietly.

"I'll consent," continued Melmar, "because I'm not a man to have a will, or a bill, or any thing of the sort stuck into my face every moment of my life—I'll consent to give up all Norlaw's papers, every one of them, as a matter of favor, on condition that this document, that you've all made so much work about, shall be placed in my hands. After which I'll be able to look after my kinswoman's interests in the proper way—for, as for the fiction about those Livingstones, who have no more claim to Melmar than you have, *that's* quite beneath any notice from me. But on that condition, and to be done with the business, I'll consent to give up all my claims against Norlaw; and a more liberal offer never was made."

The young man looked steadily, and with a smile, into the old man's face—indeed, Mr. Cassilis went a step further, and did what is sometimes extremely impertinent, and always embarrassing. He looked into Melmar's eyes with a keen, yet laughing gaze, which his companion could by no means bear, and which made the florid face once more fiery red with a troubled and apprehensive rage.

"Would you advise me to accept this offer as one professional man might advise another?" said Cassilis, quietly, with his smile. That smile, and that look, and that question, silenced Melmar a thousand times more effectually than a vehement refusal of his proposition. This man was sometimes bold, but he was never brave. He saw himself found out in the laughing eyes of his young antagonist. He thought he had committed himself and exposed his weak point—somehow he seemed to stand self-betrayed and unvailed before this stranger, whose gaze was intolerable, and whose question he should have liked to answer with a curse, proper man as he was, if he had dared. But he did not dare, though the self-restraining effort brought the perspiration to his forehead. He scattered some papers on the table with an irrestrainable movement, a little safety-valve for his secret fury.

"Do as you please, you'll get no better," he said, hoarsely, gathering them up again, and turning his face from his young adversary, who did not now seem quite an opponent to be despised.

"I tell you frankly," said Mr. Cassilis, with that engaging candor of his, "that it's very much for my interest that young Livingstone should carry on his suit at once. It's for my interest, in short, to protract the whole business to my utmost ability; and a highly attractive case I have no doubt we should make of it—especially, Mr. Huntley, *especially* permit me to say, after the proposal you have just made. However, we understand all that, both you and I, and I must ask you again to consider what I said at first; here is this old man's letter, proving his intentions pretty distinctly; on our part we will not pay a penny under less than compulsion. I leave it entirely in your own hands—what will you do?"

Patricia Huntley was all alone in the drawing-room. She knew when Mr. Cassilis entered; she knew he had been shut up with papa for a very considerable time. She did not know any thing of the questions which were being put in the study, or how hard they were to answer. Though she read poetry-books, this poor little creature had very little to occupy her, save her bad health and her limited imagination—a visitor was an event to Patricia— especially when the visitor was young, rather handsome, and newly come from Edinburgh. She thought she might as well take an accidental stroll into the garden, and see what the gentlemen were about in the study. Accordingly, with her poetry-book in her hand, Patricia stole behind the yew-tree just at this particular moment and crisis of the conversation. She could see them both through the dim window, papa tumbling about his papers, and looking very stormy, Mr. Cassilis, smiling and genial as he always was. Perhaps the younger face of the two, being much the pleasanter, was, spite of filial veneration, the most attractive to Patricia. She thought Mr. Cassilis, who had been so long a time in the study, must surely have some very pleasant news to tell—but at the same time, with sincere and disinterested concern, felt that he must be dreadfully bored by so long an interview with papa. With a generous impulse she approached the window, and knocked on the glass playfully with her fingers.

"Papa, when do you mean to come to luncheon?" cried Patricia.

Melmar started up, opened the window, cried "Get away, you little fool!—who wanted you?" and shook his fist at her menacingly. Poor Patricia sprang back in terror, and lost her breath immediately. She did not know, and perhaps if she had known, would not have appreciated, the great relief which this little ebullition was to Melmar. He went back quite refreshed to finish his fight; but his poor little daughter, who did not understand it, first fell a-crying, and then, drying her eyes, proceeded to revenge herself. She sought out Joanna immediately, and informed that heroine of something extraordinary and mysterious going on in the study—and of the unaccountable and inexcusable affront to herself, "before Mr. Cassilis!" which Patricia could not forgive. Luncheon was ordered immediately, half an hour before its time, and Joanna herself went off to the study like a gale of wind, to order papa into the dining-room. But the scene had changed by this time in Melmar's private apartment. Mr. Cassilis was writing when Joanna entered, while her father stood by him holding some papers, and looking, stealthily watchful, over the young man's shoulder, so like an old brindled big cat in the most feline concentration of vigilance, that Joanna's irreverent imagination was tickled with the resemblance.

"Eh, papa," cried the girl, with a sudden laugh, "I would not like to be a mouse in your way!—but Mr. Cassilis is too big for a mouse," added Joanna; "come to luncheon, it's ready—but I don't believe Patricia will ever speak to you again—what are these?"

"No business of yours, you gipsy!" said Melmar, as she pulled at his papers.

"Eh, but it is—I can see Norlaw's name!" cried Joanna; "Mr. Cassilis, tell Mrs. Livingstone that we know—and that I think shame of papa!—and if it was not that I could not help it, I never, never, would have spoken to him again! What are *you* getting all these papers for? If it's to hurt the boys you shanna take them out of Melmar! You sha'n't, whatever he may say!"

"Softly—Mr. Huntley of Melmar will hurt the Livingstones no more," said Cassilis.

Meanwhile Melmar read the young lawyer's receipt for these precious bits of paper with no very pleasant face. It was a great deal too carefully worded to be of any ulterior service. Even the pettifogging ingenuity of the "old school" did not see at present any capabilities in it.

CHAPTER XX

On the afternoon of the same day the young lawyer dropped in quietly, with a smile on his lace, to Norlaw.

Huntley was busy in the out-buildings of the farm. He was taking an inventory of all their stock and belongings, and making such an estimate as he could, which was a very correct one on the whole, of the value of this primitive property. Every thing about the house was going on very much as usual. The Mistress was seated at the end window of the dining-room, in a position which not only commanded the kitchen door and all its comings and goings, but was likewise a good post of observation for the farm-yard in which Huntley was. The stillness and heat of summer brooded over the old castle walls, and even over the farm-yard, where the very poultry drowsed in their afternoon siesta. The apples were growing ruddy on the Norlaw trees, and the slope of the hill brightened in russet gold towards the harvest. An Irish "shearer," with his sickle over his shoulder, waited at a humble distance, till the young master was ready to hear his application for work; the weather was unusually favorable and the season early. In another week or ten days everybody prophesied the harvest would begin.

Huntley Livingstone, however, was not thinking of the harvest. His mind was busy with thoughts of the wild bush far away, the savage young colonies then but little advanced in their progress, and the long years of solitary labor which lay before him. He was not by any means in high spirits. Melmar had faded out of his fancy like a dream. He thought he perceived just what degree of probability there was in that vision of fortune, and turning his back upon it, he set his face towards the sober, homely, real future which must begin by the serious and solitary toil of so many years.

So that Huntley was by no means delighted to be interrupted in the midst of his task by the salutation of the young lawyer. He turned round immediately and put down his memorandum-book, but not with much cordiality. Cassilis was smiling—he always smiled; on the whole, this rather aggravated Huntley.

"I've got something for you," said the lawyer, holding up the same pocket-book into which he had put Norlaw's memoranda. He spoke with real glee and triumph. Independent altogether of the interests of the family, he felt he had made quite a professional success, and enjoyed it accordingly.

"What?" said Huntley—he was half unwilling to perceive that this was some advantage gained over the enemy. He had made up his mind in a different direction, and did not want to be moved back again by any new shift of fortune. But when the pocket-book was opened and its contents disclosed—when Huntley saw before him, safe and certain, those old yellow bonds and obligations signed with his father's name, the young man was startled—and the first idea of his unfriendliness was, that they had been purchased by some concession.

"You have given up our interests in the more important matter!" cried Huntley; "I warn you I will not adopt any such bargain; better ruin now than any sacrifice either of right or of honor."

"For what do you take me, Mr. Livingstone?" said the other, coldly; but as he was too good-natured and much too triumphant to keep malice, he continued, after a moment, in his usual tone:—"Don't be foolish; take these affairs and burn them—they're better out of harm's way; and go in, gather the family together, and hold a council of war. Now I've seen the man and understand the question, I'm ready to fight it out. We can but take our chance. *You* have every thing in your favor—he nothing but blood and possession. You are not ruined, Livingstone, you have enough to begin with—I am inclined to change my advice; if I were you, I should wait no longer, but put it to the touch. The chances are ten to one in your favor."

"This is quite different from your former opinion," said Huntley, in amazement.

"Not opinion, say advice," said Cassilis, who was now somewhat excited; "I believed, begging your pardon, Livingstone, that you were likely to need for your own immediate uses every penny you could scrape together; I thought your father had seriously injured your cause by taking no steps in the matter, and that the other side might think themselves justified in saying that he knew this will either to be unfairly got or invalid. But my visit to Melmar has dispelled these doubts. I think the course is quite clear if you choose to try."

This sudden suggestion took away Huntley's breath; the color mounted in his cheek in spite of himself—it was impossible to think of such a prospect unmoved—for Melmar, with its moderate rank and easy fortune, was very much more agreeable to think of than the bush and all its peradventures of hardship and solitude. He listened with only a half-attention while Cassilis explained to him how Mr. Huntley had been induced to relinquish these valuable scraps of paper. The whole sum represented by them was not very considerable, but it made all the difference between bare, absolute stripped poverty, and the enough which would satisfy everybody's demands, and leave a little over for themselves. There were still heavy mortgages upon the little property of Norlaw, but when Huntley took his father's canceled bonds in his hand, he knew there was no longer cause to apprehend a forced and ruinous sale of all their stock and crop and little possessions. He heard the lawyer speak of Melmar's fears, his proposal about the will—his gradual and growing apprehensions; but all that appeared visible to Huntley was the fact of their changed circumstances, and the new position in which the family stood. His companion perceived after a while that the young man was absorbed in his own thoughts, and paid no attention to what he said, and Cassilis wisely left him, once more bidding him hold a council of war. When he was alone, Huntley put aside his memorandum-book, drew his cap over his eyes, and set off on a rapid walk to the top of the hill. He scarcely drew breath till he had reached the summit of that fertile slope from whence he could just see in the distance the gray towers of Melrose and the silvery gleam of Tweed shining in the hazy golden sunshine beyond the purple Eildons. The broad country shone before him in all its tints of color and glow of summer light, wide, great, and silent as the life upon whose brink he stood—and at his feet lay Norlaw, with its humble homestead and its ruined castle, where sat this lad's mother, who was a widow. He stood there perfectly silent, full of thought, turning over half unconsciously in his mind the words of his adviser.

> "He either fears his fate too much,
> Or his deserts are small,
> Who dares not put it to the touch,
> To gain or lose it all."

Somehow these lines floated in upon Huntley's mind as he stood gazing upon the summer landscape. To win Melmar with all its wealth and influence, or to lose what remained of Norlaw, with all the associations and hereditary bonds that belonged to that home of his race—should he put it to the touch? A conflict, not less stormy that it was entirely unexpressed, rose within the young, ambitious, eager mind, gazing over those fields and hills. A certain personification and individuality came to the struggling powers within him. On either side stood a woman, one a pale, unknown shadow, hovering upon the chances of his triumph, ready to take the prize, when it was won, out of his hands—the other his own well-beloved, home-dwelling mother, whose comfort and certain habitation it was in Huntley's power at once to secure. Should he put it to the touch? should he risk all that he might win all?—and the tempters that assailed Huntley suddenly vailed over to his eyes all that sunny home landscape, and spread before him the savage solitudes of the far country, the flocks and the herds which should be his sole companions—the hut in the strange woods; oh beautiful home valleys, glorious hills, dear gleams of water-springs! oh, love hiding sweet among the trees, whispering ere it comes!—oh tender friends and bonds of youth!—shall he put it to the touch? The council of war held its debate among the dust and din of battle, though the summer sunshine shone all the time in an undisturbed and peaceful glory upon the slope of Norlaw.

CHAPTER XXI

"Do you think *I* could bear the thought—me!" cried the Mistress energetically; "have ye kent me all your days, Huntley Livingstone, and do ye dare to think your mother would baulk your fortune for ease to hersel'? is it like me? would any mortal even me with the like, but your ainsel'?"

The Mistress stood by herself in the middle of the room, with her hand on the table—her eyes shone with a mortified and grieved fire through unshed tears—her heightened color—her frame, which seemed to vibrate with a visible pang—the pain of unappreciated love, which looked like anger in her face—showed how little congenial to her mind was Huntley's self-abnegation. There was no sacrifice in the world which she herself could not and would not have made for her children; but to feel herself the person for whom a sacrifice was needed, a hindrance to her son's prospects, a person to be provided for, struck with intense and bitter mortification the high spirit of the Mistress. She could not be content with this subordinate and passive position. Poverty, labor, want itself, would have come easier to her proud, tender motherhood, than thus to feel herself a bar upon the prospects of her boy.

When Huntley looked into his mother's face, he thanked God silently within himself, that he had held his council of war upon the hill-side, and not in the Norlaw dining-parlor. It was the first time in his life that the young man had made an arbitrary personal decision, taking counsel with none; he had been naturally somewhat doubtful in his statement of it, being unused to such independent action—but now he rejoiced that he had made his conclusion alone. He came to his mother with tenderness, which perhaps if it touched her secretly, made her displeasure only the greater so far as appearance went—for the mother of this house, who was not born of a dependent nature, was still too young and vigorous in her own person, and too little accustomed to think of her sons as men, to be able to receive with patience the new idea that their relative positions were so far changed, and that it was now her children's part to provide for her, instead of hers to provide for them.

"Mother, suppose we were to fail—which is as likely as success," said Huntley, "and I had to go away—after all, should you like me to leave no home to think of—no home to return to?—is that not reason enough to make you content with Norlaw?"

"Hold your peace!" cried the Mistress—"hame! do you mean to tell me that I couldna make a cothouse in Kirkbride, or a lodging in a town look like hame to my own bairns, if Providence ordained it sae, and their hearts were the same? What's four walls here or there?—till you've firesides of your ain, your mother's your hame wherever she may be. Am I a weak auld wife to be maintained at the ingleside with my son's toil—or to have comfort, or fortune, or hope sacrificed to me? Eh, laddie, Guid forgive ye!—me that would shear in the harvest field, or guide the kye, or do any day's work in this mortal world, with a cheerful heart, if it was needful, for the sake of you!"

"Ay, mother," cried Cosmo, suddenly springing up from the table where he had been sitting stooping over a book in his usual attitude, without any apparent notice of the conversation. "Ay, mother," cried the boy, "you could break your heart, and wear out your life for us, because it's in your nature—but you're too proud to think that it's our nature as well, and that all you would do for your sons, your sons have a right to do for you!"

The boy's pale face shone, and his eyes sparkled; his slender, tall, overgrown boyish figure, his long arms stretching out of the narrow sleeves of his jacket, his long slender hands, and long hair, the entire and extreme youthfulness of his whole appearance, so distinct from the fuller strength and manhood of his brothers, and animated by the touch of a delicate spirit, less sober and more fervid than theirs, struck strangely and suddenly upon the two who had hitherto held this discussion alone. An instantaneous change came over the Mistress's face; the fire in her eyes melted into a tender effusion of love and sorrow, the yearning of the mother who was a widow. Those tears, which her proud temper and independent spirit had drawn into her eyes, fell with a softness which their original cause was quite incapable of. She could not keep to her first emotions; she could not restrain the expansion of her heart toward the boy who was still only a boy, and his father's son.

"My bairn!" cried the Mistress, with a short sob. He was the youngest, the tenderest, the most like him who was gone—and Cosmo's words had an unspeakable pathos in their enthusiasm—the heroism of a child!

After this the mother dropped into her chair, altogether softened, while Huntley spoke to her low and earnestly.

"Melmar is nothing to me," said her eldest son, in the half-whispered forcible words which Cosmo did not hear, but in which his mother recognized the distinct resolution of a nature as firm as her own; "nothing at least except a chance of wealth and fortune—only a chance which can wait; but Norlaw is every thing—house, family, ancestors, every thing that makes me proud of my name. Norlaw and the Livingstones must never be disconnected while we can prevent it—and, mother, for Cosmo's sake!"

"Eh, Huntley, God forgive me if I set more weight upon him than I should set!" said the Mistress, with tears; "no' to your detriment, my own son; but look at the bairn! is he not *his* very image that's gane?"

Not a single shadow of envy or displeasure crossed Huntley's face; he stood looking at his young brother with a love almost as tender as their mother's, with besides an unconscious swell of manhood and power in his own frame. He was the eldest brother, the head of the house, and the purest saint on earth could not have condemned the generous pride which rose in Huntley's breast. It was not a weak effusion of sentimental self-sacrifice— his own hopes, his own heart, his own life, were strong with an individual identity in the young man's nature. But the tender son of this house for the first time had made his own authoritative and masterly decision. To set aside his ambition and let it wait—to postpone fortune to labor—to do the first duty of a man on his own sole and unadvised responsibility—to provide for those of his own house, and set them above the anxieties of poverty. He was proud, when he thought of it, to feel the strength in his own arm, the vigor of his own step—but the pride was such as almost an angel might have shared.

When Huntley left the room, the Mistress called Cosmo to her side. She had resumed her seat by the corner window, and they could see him going out, disappearing behind the old castle walls, in the glory of the autumn sunset.

"Do you see him, Cosmo?" said the Mistress, with renewed tears, which this time were of mingled pride and tenderness; "I resisted, but I never wronged his thoughts. Do ye see your brother? Yonder he is, a young lad, proud, and bold, and masterful—he's no' like you—he has it in his heart to seek power, and riches, and honors, and to take pleasure in them—and he's that daring that the chance of a battle would be more pleasant to Huntley than any thing in this world that was secure. Yet—do you hear me, laddie? he's put them all aside, every ane, for the sake of this hame and name, and for you and me!"

And the color rose high upon the Mistress's cheek in a flush of triumph; the necessity and blessing of women came upon her in a sudden flood—she could not be heroic herself, though she might covet the glory—but with a higher, tenderer, more delicious pride, she could rejoice and triumph in the courage of her boy. Her voice rose even in those restrained and moderate words of common speech as if in a song; there was an indescribable something in her tone which reminded one involuntarily of the old songs of Scripture, the old triumphant Hebrew parallelisms of Miriam and Deborah. She grasped Cosmo's shoulder with an emphatic pressure, and pointed with the other hand to the retiring figure of Huntley, passing slowly and with a thoughtful step by the wall of the old castle. Cosmo leaned out beside her, catching a flush upon his delicate cheek from hers, but gazing upon the scene with a different eye. Insensibly the poetic glance of the boy left his brother, to dwell upon the other features of this picture before him. Those stern old walls with their windowless sockets, through which once the sunshine shone and the summer breezes entered to former generations of their name—that sweet evening glory of sunshine, pouring aslant in a lingering tender flood upon the world and the day, which it seemed sad to leave—that sunshine which never grew old—insensibly his own romance stole back into Cosmo's mind. He forgot, with the inadvertence of his years, that it was not a romance agreeable to his mother, or that, even if it had been, she was not of a temper to bear the intrusion of other subjects when her mind was so fully occupied with concerns of her own.

"Mother, Huntley is right," cried Cosmo; "Melmar can not be his if *she* is alive—it would not become him to seek *it* till he has sought her—and as Huntley can not seek her, for her sake and for my father's, *I* will, though it should take the half of my life!"

Once more the Mistress's face changed; a glance of fiery impatience flashed from her eyes, her cheek grew violently red, the tears dried as if by a spell, and she put Cosmo away hastily with the same arm which had held him.

"Get away to your plays, bairn—dinna trouble me!" cried the Mistress, with a harsh contempt, which was as strong as it was unjust; "to think I should open my heart to you that thinks of nothing but your romances and story books! Go! I've different things to think of—dinna trouble me!"

And she rose with a murmur of indignation and anger, and went hurriedly, with a flushed cheek, to seek her usual work, and take refuge in occupation. If the lost heiress had been her dearest friend, she would still have resented urgently the introduction of an intruder into her sudden burst of mother-pride. As it was, it overturned temper and patience entirely. She brushed past Cosmo with a hasty contempt, which humiliated and mortified the boy beyond expression. He did not attempt to justify himself—perhaps a kindred spark of resentment, and the bitterness with which youth appreciates injustice, helped to silence him—but when his mother resumed her seat and worked on hurriedly in a disdainful and angry silence, Cosmo withdrew out of the room and out of the house with a swelling heart. Too proud to betray how much he was wounded, he stole round behind the farm offices to his favorite perch among the ruins, where the lad brooded in mournful mood, sinking into the despairing despondency of his years and temperament, feeling himself misunderstood and unappreciated, and meditating a hundred melancholy heroisms. Mary of Melmar, so far, seemed as little propitious to Norlaw's son as she had once been to Norlaw.

CHAPTER XXII

"Go wherever you like, bairns, or travel straight on, if you please—I canna see a step before me, for my part—it's you and no' me that must take the lead," said the Mistress, with a heavy sigh. These words were said as the little party, Huntley, Patrick and herself, were left standing by a little pile of luggage, in the dusk of a harvest evening, in front of the coach office on the Edinburgh pavement. They were on their way to Liverpool, from which place Huntley was to sail in an emigrant ship for Port Philip. Princes Street was full of the open-air and street-loving crowd which gives to that splendid promenade, on summer nights, so much of a continental aspect. The dusk of the twilight fell softly in the valley which lay behind, the lights in the high houses on the other side hung softly midway in the air, the voices of the passengers, and sounds of the city, though doubtless many of these were sad enough, mingled in the soft-shadowed air to a harmonious hum of pleasant sound, which echoed with a mocking gayety into the heavy heart of the mother who was about to part with her boys. She was bewildered for the moment with her journey, with the unknown place and unusual animation around her, and it was only very slowly and by degrees that her mind regained its usual self-possession. She stood gazing blankly round her, while the boys made arrangements about their superfluous packages, which were to be left at the coach office, and finally came up to her, carrying between them the little trunk which contained the necessaries for their journey. Cabs were not in those days, and the Mistress would have been horrified into perfect self-possession by the preposterous idea of "a noddy." When they were thus far ready, she turned with them briskly enough, leading the way without any uncertainty, for, in spite of her exclamation, it had been already arranged where they were to go, and the Mistress had been at school in Edinburgh in her young days, and was by no means unacquainted with the town. They went along in this order—Mrs. Livingstone carrying a considerable bag on her own arm, and the young men with a trunk between them—across the North Bridge towards the old town, that scene of magic to every stranger; the valley, the hill, the dim gray turrets of Holyrood, the soft darkness of the night full of sounds, lying beneath them—the rugged outline, picturesque and noble, of the lofty old street before—the lights shining here and there like fairy stars in irregular specks among the high windows, and everywhere the half-seen, unrecognizable throng of wayfarers, and the world of subdued sound on every side made but small impression upon the absorbed minds of the little party. They knew it all before, and their thoughts were otherwise occupied; yet involuntarily that noble landscape, which no one could look upon with absolute indifference, soothed them all, in spite of themselves. Their destination was the High Street, where, in one of the more respectable closes, and at the top of an interminable ascent of stairs, there lived a native of Kirkbride, who was in the habit of letting lodgings to students, and with whom they were to find accommodation for the night. Mrs. Purdie gave to the Mistress a little room boasting a "concealed bed," that is to say, a recess shut in by folding-doors, and just large enough to contain a bedstead, and to the lads a bed-closet, with a borrowed light, both of which inventions specially belong to the economy of flats and great subdivided houses, and are the most unfavorable features in the same. But the window of Mrs. Livingstone's room, where they had tea, looked abroad over that great panorama, bounded by the gleam of the Firth, and the low green line of the Fife hills, which makes it worth while to ascend stairs and watch at lofty windows in Edinburgh. The yellow harvest moon had risen ere they had finished the simple meal, which none of them had any heart for, and Huntley drew his mother to the window to bid her look at the wonderful broad moonlight lying white upon the long line of street below, and thrusting out all the monuments of the little hill into bold and striking relief against the luminous sky. The Mistress turned away from the window, with big tears in her eyes.

"Eh, Huntley, laddie, what do I care? if it was the grandest view that ever was, do you think I could see it?" cried his mother, "when I ken that I'll never see the light of the moon mair without weary thoughts and yearning to where my bairns are, hundreds and thousands of miles away from me!"

"But, mother, only till we come home," said Huntley, with his arm round his mother, speaking low in her ear.

The Mistress only turned towards the dim little table, with its dim candles, hurriedly wiping the tears from her eyes. This was endurable—but the night and the calm, and the glory of the heavens and the earth, were too much for the mother. If she had remained there looking out, it almost seemed to her as if she must have wept her very heart dry.

The next morning they set out once more upon their journey—another day's travel by the canal to Glasgow. The canal was not to be despised in those days; it was cheaper, and it was not a great deal slower than the coach; and if the errand had been happier, the mode of traveling, in that lovely harvest weather, with its gradual glide and noiseless progress, was by no means an unpleasant one. Glasgow itself, a strange, unknown, smoky Babel, where, after Huntley was gone, the Mistress was to part with her second son, bewildered her mind completely with its first aspect; she could make nothing of it as they pursued their way from the canal to the river, through a maze of perplexing and noisy streets, where she felt assured hundreds of people might lose themselves, never to be found again. And, with a feeling half of awe and half of disgust, Mrs. Livingstone contemplated the place, so unlike the only other large town she knew, where Patie was to pass the next half dozen years of his life. Instinctively she caught closer hold of him, forgetting Huntley for the moment—Huntley's dangers would be those of nature, the sea and the wilderness—but temptation! ill-doing! The Mistress grasped her son's sleeve with tenacious fingers, and looked into his face with half an entreaty, half a defiance.

"If I should ever see the like of that in a bairn of mine!" she cried aloud, as they passed a corner where stood some of those precocious men, haggard and aged beyond double their years, whom it is the misfortune of a great town sometimes to produce. The idea struck her with an impatient dread which overcame even her half-apprehensive curiosity about the voyage they were going to undertake; and she had scarcely overcome this sudden alarm, when they embarked in the snorting steamer which was to convey them to Liverpool. Standing on the deck, surrounded by the pile of boxes which formed Huntley's equipment, and looking with startled and disapproving eyes upon the arriving passengers, and the crowded sheds of the Broomielaw, the Mistress saw the same moon rising above the masts, and housetops, and smoke of Glasgow, without any thing like the same feelings which had moved her on the previous night. Her mind was excited, her active spirit stirred, her very nerves, steady as they were, influenced a little by the entirely new anticipation of the voyage; a night at sea!—it seemed almost as great looking forward to it as Huntley's journey, though that was to the other end of the world.

And so they glided down the beautiful Clyde, the breeze freshening about them, as hills began to rise black in the moonlight, and little towns to glimmer on the water's edge. The mother and the sons walked about the deck together, talking earnestly, and when the vessel rose upon the bigger waves, as they stole out to sea, and every thing but the water and the sky, and the moonlight, gradually sank out of sight, the Mistress, with a little thrill of danger and adventure at her heart, forgot for the moment how, presently, she should return alone by the same road, and almost could suppose that she was setting out with Huntley. The fancy restored her to herself: she was not much of an advice giver. Her very cautions and counsels, perhaps, were arbitrary and slightly impatient, like her nature; but she was their true mother, heart and soul; and the lads did not forget for long years after what the Mistress said as she paced about the deck between them, with a firm, yet sometimes uncertain foot, as the midnight glided into morning, and the river disappeared in the bigger waters of the sea.

CHAPTER XXIII

The voyage, as it happened, was a very favorable one—even the Mistress's inland terrors were scarcely aroused by the swell of that summer sea; and Huntley himself, though his ideas expanded to a much longer journey, unconsciously took it as a good omen that his first night at sea should be so calm and fair. They came into the great seaport late on another summer evening. It was not nearly so extensive then as it is now, but still the masts were in forests, the ships in navies; and their inexperienced eyes, unenlightened by the hasty and darkling glimpse of the Clyde, and knowing nothing greater or busier than the Forth, with its great bosom diversified by an island and a sail, the one scarcely more plentiful than the other, opened wide with amazement at the fleet of vessels in the Mersey. Insensibly to herself, the Mistress drew a certain comfort from the fact, as the Glasgow steamer went gliding up the river, in the late summer sunset. Ships were moored in the deep calm and shadow of the banks; ships were coming and going in the midwaters of the river, and lines of spars and masts, indistinguishable and without number, fringed the whole water edge, from which the smoke of the town, reddened by a last ray of sunshine, rose inland, out of sight, in a great overhanging cloud. The sight of such a throng brought a momentary comfort to the heart of Huntley's mother. The very sea, it almost seemed, could not be so lonely, when all these big wayfarers, and thousands more, were tracking its waters day by day.

"Mony a mother's son is there," she said to herself softly, as she stood gazing about her—and even the community of hardship had a solace in it. As the steamboat puffed and snorted to its destination, a big ship, crowded with pensive faces, bare of sails, and tugged along by a little steamer, came lumbering silently along through the peaceful evening light, going out to sea. Two or three voices round announced it "an emigrant ship," and the Mistress gazed into it and after it, clasping her son's arm with a thrill at her heart. Evening; the sweet daylight fading into a charmed and tender twilight—the sky growing pale with very calm; the houses and churches and piles of buildings beginning to stand out black against the colorless, mysterious light which casts no shadows; the water gleaming in long, still ripples, as pale as the sky—every thing softening and darkening into natural rest—yet, through all, the great ship departing silently, with her throng of travelers, beginning to unfold the sails of her wayfaring, beginning to vibrate to the quickening wave, as she neared the sea.

"God go with them!" said the Mistress, with a sob out of her full heart. "Oh, Huntley, laddie! mony a mother's son is there!"

The landing, when they came to it; the rush of porters and vagabonds from the pier; the half light, in which it seemed doubly necessary to the Mistress, roused into prompt and vigorous self-defense, to keep the most vigilant watch on the luggage—and the confusion with which both mother and sons contemplated the screaming, shouting crowd who surrounded them with offers of service, and bawled to them from the shore, made altogether a very serious business of the arrival. The Mistress never knew how she came through that ordeal; the "English tongue," which had a decidedly Irish brogue in that scene, and under these circumstances, deafened the rural Scottish woman. The crowd of spectators, and the foray upon everybody's luggage made by some scores of ragged fellows, whom her uncharitable imagination set down as robbers or madmen, filled her with indignation and a strong propensity to resistance; and it was not till she found herself safely deposited in an odd little sitting-room of a little inn, close to the docks, with all her packages safe and undiminished, that a measure of calmness returned to the ruffled bosom of Mrs. Livingstone. Then, after they had rested and refreshed themselves, Huntley and Patrick went out with natural curiosity to see the new scene and the new country— for the whole party fully considered that it was "England," not Liverpool, in which they now found themselves—and the Mistress was left alone. She sat in the little parlor under the unfamiliar gas-light, looking round with forlorn eyes upon the room. There was a little model of a ship upon the mantel-piece in front of the little mirror, and another upon a small side-table under the barometer; other odd little ornaments, such as sailors bring home, shells and curious boxes, and little painted glass cups of Dutch art, gave a very nautical aspect to the shabby apartment, which, further, bore traces of having recently been smoked in, which disgusted the Mistress. Then all the noises of a noisy and not very well-behaved quarter seemed to rise up to her window, mingled with a jar of music from a big blazing drinking-place, almost next door—and the private tumult of the inn itself, voices and footsteps, shutting of doors and ringing of bells, still further oppressed the solitary stranger.

"Mercy on me! is that what they ca' speaking English?" cried the Mistress to herself, disturbed, lonely, sick at heart, and almost offended with her sons for leaving her. She put her hands to her ears with a gesture of disdain; the unfamiliar accent was quite an aggravation and insult to her solitude—and then her thoughts settled down upon the circumstances which brought her here. But a day or two more, and she might never see Huntley again.

Meanwhile the boys were straying through the mean, noisy streets, blazing with light, which only showed their squalor the more, where a whole disreputable population seemed to be exerting all its arts for the fascination of the sailors, who were the patrons and support of all this quarter. It was quite a new phase of life to the lads, fresh from their rural solitudes, and all the proprieties of a respectable Scottish family—but the novelty beguiled them on, though it disgusted them. They went wandering about, curious, astonished, revolted, till they found themselves among dark mazes of warehouses from which it was not easy to find their way back. When they did get back it was late, though the noise remained undiminished, and the Mistress's temper was not improved, if truth must be told, by her solitude. She had been trying to look out from the window, where opposite there was nothing but the high brick walls of the docks, and beneath, upon the lighted pavement, only such scenes as horrified the soul of the Mistress within her.

"It's a marvel to me what pleasure even thoughtless laddies could find wandering about a place like that," said the Mistress; "England, quotha! I thought mysel' there must be something worth seeing in a place that folk make such a wark about; but instead of that, it's waur than the Cowgate; pity me! and sharp tongues that gang through my head like a bell!"

"But Liverpool is not England," said Huntley, coming to a slow perception of that fact, and laughing at himself as he said it.

"And maybe this is not Liverpool," said Patie, with still greater enlightenment.

"Hold your peace, bairns," cried the Mistress, peremptorily; "what can you ken, twa laddies that have no more insight into life than babes unborn—how can the like of you tell? Do I no' see sin outbye there with a painted face, and sounds of fiddling and laughing, and light enough to burn up the haill town? Eh, bairns, if ever ye touch such dirt with but the ends of your fingers, the mother that bore ye will think shame of ye—burning shame! It sounds like pleasure—do ye hear?—but it's no pleasure, it's destruction!— and I canna tell, for my ain part, how a decent woman can daur to close her e'en, kenning what evil's nigh. But I'm no' meaning that for you," added the Mistress, changing her tone; "the like of you young things need sleep and rest, and though I canna tell where we're to get the things we want in a miserable place like this, we'll have to be stirring early the morn."

"And we'll find a better place," said Huntley; "don't be afraid, mother— but for that and all the rest that we have to do and to bear, you must try to rest yourself."

"Aye, laddie," said the Mistress, hurriedly wiping her eyes, "but I canna get my thoughts out of that ship that's on the sea this nicht! and maybe mony a lone woman sitting still with nae sons to come in to her—and whiles I canna but mind what's coming to mysel'."

"I am only twenty, mother, and Patie but eighteen," said Huntley; "would you like us to remain as we are, knowing nothing of life, as you say? or are you afraid to trust your sons in the battle, like other men?"

"Na! no' me!" cried the Mistress; "you're baith right, and I approve in my mind—but only just this, bairns;—I'm your mother—and yon ship is sailing in the dark before my very e'en, as plain as if I saw her now!"

And whether it was thinking of that ship, or of the sons of other mothers who were errant in her, or of her own boy, so soon to join their journey, the Mistress heard the last sound that disturbed the house that night, and the earliest in the morning. Her eyes were dry and sore when she got up to see the daylight aspect of the unknown and unlovely world around her; and the lads were still fast asleep in their privilege of youth, while their mother stood once more wistfully looking out upon the high black wall of the dock, and the masts appearing over it. She could not see the river, or any thing more gracious than this seaman-tempting street. There was nothing either within or without to divert her from her own thoughts; and as she watched the early sunshine brighten upon a scene so different from that of her own hills and streams, these thoughts were forlorn enough.

During the day, the little party went out to make some last purchases for Huntley. The young man was to carry with him, in the securest form which they could think of, a little fortune of a hundred pounds, on which he was to make his start in the world, nothing doubting to find in it a nucleus of wealth; and the Mistress, spite of the natural economy of her ideas, and her long habit of frugality, was extravagant and lavish in her anxiety to get every thing for Huntley that he could or might require. When they came into the region of shops, she began to drop behind, anxiously studying the windows, tempted by many a possible convenience, which, if she had acted on her first impulse and purchased each incontinently, would have made Huntley's outfit an unbelievable accumulation of peddlery.

As it was, his mother's care and inexperience freighted the young man with a considerable burden of elaborate conveniences—cumbrous machines of various forms, warranted invaluable for the voyage or for the bush, which Huntley lugged about with many a year after, and tried to use for his mother's sake. When they got back to their inn, the Mistress had suffered herself to be convinced that the noisy street outside the docks was not Liverpool, much less England. But the "English tongue," which "rang through her head like a knife," to vary the image—the mean brick houses at which the triumphant Scotchwoman pointed her finger with unspeakable contempt, the narrow streets, and noise and dust of the great commercial town, filled her patriotic spirit with a disdainful complacency.

"Weel, laddies," said Mrs. Livingstone, when they reached the inn, very tired, that night; and the Mistress spoke with the natural satisfaction of a traveled person; "I have aye heard a great wark made about England—but I'm very sure, now that we've been in it, and seen for ourselves, none of us desires to gang any further. Bits of brick houses that you can mostly see through!—streets that neighbors could shake hands across!—and for my part, ilka time I hear them speak, I think they're flyting. Eh, bairns, such sharp tongues! I wouldna gie Melrose though it's wee-er and hasna sae mony shops, for twenty of this place—and as for Edinburgh—!"

But the contrast was unspeakable, and took away the Mistress's breath.

CHAPTER XXIV

They were detained for some days waiting the sailing of the ship, which already the little party had gone over, the Mistress with awe and solemnity, the brothers with eager interest and excitement, more than once. The bark Flora, Captain Gardner master, bound for Port Philip—through those days and nights of suspense, when they hoped and feared every morning to hear that this was the last day, this name might have been heard even among the dreams of Huntley's mother. Yet this procrastination of the parting was not good even for her. She said her farewell a hundred times in the bitterness of imagination before the real moment came, and as they all went down every morning early to one of the piers, opposite to which in the river the Flora lay, and made a mournful, anxious promenade up and down, gazing at the anchored ship, with her bare cordage, the emigrant encampments on her big deck, and the fresh vegetables strung in her bows, noting with sharp and solicitous eyes any signs of preparation there, the pain of parting was indefinitely repeated, though always with a pang of joy at the end—another day. However, even emigrant ships have to make up their minds some time. At last came the last night, when they all sat together, looking into each other's faces, knowing that, after to-morrow, they might never meet again. The Mistress had not a great deal to say on that last night; what she did say was of no one continuous tone. She could not make sermons to her boys—it might be that there was abruptness and impatience even in her motherly warnings. The grief of this farewell did not change her character, though it pierced to her heart.

"Try and get a decent house to live in—dinna be about inns or such like places," said the Mistress; "I ken by mysel', just the time we've been here, Huntley—and if it's unsettling to the like of me, what should it be to a young lad?—but dinna be owre great friends either with them that put you up—I'm no fond of friendship out of folks' ain degree, though I ken weel that nobody that's kind to my bairn will find an ungrateful thought in me; but mind aye what ye are, and wha ye are, and a' that's looked for at your hands."

"A poor emigrant, mother," said Huntley, with rather a tremulous smile.

"Hold your peace, laddie, dinna be unthankful," said the Mistress; "a lad with a good house and lands at hame, and a hundred pound clear in his pocket, no' to say how many conveniences and handy things in his boxes, and a' the comforts that ye can carry. Dinna sin your mercies, Huntley, before me."

"It would not become me," said Huntley, "for I might have had few comforts but for you, mother, that thought of every thing; as every thing I have, if I needed reminding, would make me think of home and you."

"Whisht, whisht, bairn!" said the Mistress, with a broken voice and a sob, two big tears falling out of her eyes upon her trembling hands, which she wiped off hurriedly, almost with a gesture of shame; "and ye'll no' forget your duty, Huntley," she added with agitated haste; "mind what the minister said; if there be nae kirk, as there might not be, seeing it's a savage place, never let the Sabbath day slip out of your hand, as if there was na difference. Kirks and ministers are a comfort, whiles—but, Huntley, mind God's aye nigh at hand. I bid ye baith mind that—I'm no' what I should be—I canna say a' that's in my heart—but, oh, laddies, mind if you should never hear another word out of your mother's lips! They speak about ships and letters that make far-away friends nigh each other, but, bairns, the Lord Himsel' is the nighest link between you and me—as He's the only link between us a' and him that's gane."

There was a long pause after this burst out of the desolate heart of Norlaw's widow and Huntley's mother; a pause in which words would have been vain, even if any one of them could have found any words to say, and in which the fatherless sons, and the mother who was a widow, turned their faces from each other, shedding those hurried, irrestrainable tears, which they dared not indulge. It was the Mistress who found composure first, but she did not prolong the emotion of the little party by continuing the same strain. Like herself, she had no sooner found her voice, than, shy of revealing the depths of her heart, even to her children, she resumed on a totally different theme.

"If ye gang up into the country, Huntley, dinna bide aye among the beasts," said the Mistress, abruptly; "mind, it's no' that I put very much faith in this lad Cassilis, but still, whatever's possible shouldna be forgotten. You might be Melmar, with a great estate, before mony years were past, and, at any rate, you're master of your ain land, and have as good a name to bear as ever came of *that* house. It's my hope to see you back at the head of your household, a man respected—so dinna you sink into a solitary, Huntley, or dwell your lane ower lang. I've nothing to say against the making of siller—folk canna live without it in this world—but a fortune's no equal to a man—and if ye canna make the ane without partly sacrificing the other, come hame."

"I will, mother," said Huntley, seriously.

"And there's just one thing mair," added the Mistress, not without a look of uneasiness, "be aye particular about the kind of folk you make friends o'—and specially—weel, weel, you're both young lads. I canna keep ye bairns—you'll soon be thinking of the like of that yoursel'. I'm no fond of strangers, Huntley Livingstone, I dinna understand their ways; dinna bring me a daughter of that land to vex me as the fremd women vexed Rebecca. No' that I'm meaning to put bondage on you—na—I wouldna have it said I was jealous of my sons—but you're young, and young lads are easily beguiled; wait till you come hame."

"I give you my word for that, mother!" cried Huntley, eagerly, the blood rushing over his face, as he grasped the Mistress's hand with a quite unnecessary degree of fervor.

Perhaps his mother found him rather more in earnest than the vague nature of her advice seemed to justify. She looked at him with a startled glance of suspicion and dawning displeasure.

"Ay, laddie!" cried the Mistress; "ane would think you had made up your mind!" and she turned her eyes upon the glow and brightening of Huntley's face, with a little spark of impatience. But at that moment the clock below stairs began to strike twelve; it startled them all as they sat listening— and gradually, as stroke followed stroke with that inevitable regularity, the heart of Huntley's mother sank within her. She took the hand, which she had been half angry to find grasping hers in confirmation of his earnestness, tenderly between her own—she stroked the strong young fingers with that hand of hers, somewhat large, somewhat wrinkled, without an ornament upon it save its worn wedding-ring, the slow, fond, loving touch of which brought hot tears to Huntley's eyes. The Mistress did not look up, because her own face was moved with a grief and tenderness unspeakable and beyond the reach of words—she could not say any thing—she could only sit silent, keeping down the sob in her throat, the water that gathered in her eyes, fondly holding her son's hand, caressing it with an indescribable pathetic gesture, more touching than the wildest passionate embrace.

Then they all stood up together to say good-night.

"Laddies, it's no more night!—it's morning, and Huntley sails this day," said the Mistress; "oh, my bairns!—and I canna speak; dinna say a word to me!—but gang and lie down and take your rest, and the Lord send sleep to us a' and make us ready for what's to come."

It was with this good-night, and no more, that they parted, but the sleep and rest for which she had prayed did not come to the mother. She was up by daybreak, once more looking over the last box which Huntley was to take with him on board, to see if any thing could be added to its stores.

She stole into her sons' room to look at them in their sleep, but would not suffer any one to wake them, though the lads slept long, worn out by excitement and emotion. Then the Mistress put on her bonnet, and went out by herself to try if she could not get something for their breakfast, more delicate and dainty than usual, and, when she returned, arranged the table with her own hands, pausing often to wipe away, not tears, but a sad moisture with which her eyes were always full. But she was perfectly composed, and went about all these homely offices of love with a smile more touching than grief. The emergency had come at last, and the Mistress was not a woman to break down or lose the comfort of this last day. Time enough to break her heart when Huntley was gone.

And the inevitable hours went on, as hours do before one of those life-partings—slow, yet with a flow and current in their gradual progress, which seemed to carry them forward more forcibly than the quickest tide of pleasure. And at last it was time to embark. They went down to the river together, saying very little; then on the river, in a boat, to reach the ship.

It was a glorious harvest-day, warm, sunny, overflowing with happiness and light. The opposite bank of the river had never looked so green, the villages by its side had never detached themselves so brightly from the fields behind and the sands before. The very water swelling under their boat rippled past with a heave and swell of enjoyment, palpitating under the sunshine; and the commonest boatman and hardest-laboring sailor on these rejoicing waters looked like a man whose life was holiday. People on the pier, ignorant bystanders, smiled even upon this little party as their boat floated off into the midway of the sun-bright stream, as if it was a party of pleasure. Instinctively the Mistress put down her thick, black vail, worked with big, unearthly flowers, which made so many blots upon the sunshine, and said to Huntley, from behind its shelter:—

"What a pleasure it was to see such a day for the beginning of his voyage!"

They all repeated the same thing over mechanically at different times, and that was almost the whole substance of what they said until they reached the ship.

And presently, the same little boat glided back again over the same gleaming, golden waters, with Patie, very pale and very red by turns, in one end of it, and the Mistress, with her black vail over her face, sitting all alone on one side, with her hands rigidly clasped in her lap, and her head turned towards the ship. When the Flora began to move from her place, this silent figure gave a convulsive start and a cry, and so Huntley was gone.

He was leaning over the bulwark of the ship, looking out at this speck in the water—seeing before him, clearer than eyes ever saw, the faces of his mother, his brothers, his dead father—perhaps even of others still—with a pang at his heart, which was less for himself than for the widow who could no longer look upon her son; his heart rising, his heart sinking, as his own voyage hence, and her voyage home, rose upon his imagination—living through the past, the present, and the future—the leave-taking to which his mind vibrated—the home-coming which now seemed almost as near and certain—the unknown years of absence, which fled before him like a dream.

He, too, started when the vessel moved upon the sunny river—started with a swell of rising enterprise and courage. The daring of his nature, and the gay wind blowing down the river; fresh and favorable, dried the tears in Huntley's eyes; but did not dry that perpetual moisture from the pained eyelids of the Mistress, as she turned to Patie at last, with faltering lips, to repeat that dreary congratulation:—

"Eh, Patie! what a blessing, if we could but think upon it, to see such a day as this for a guid beginning on the sea!"

CHAPTER XXV

It was very well for the Mistress's spirit, though scarcely for her purse, that she was roused the next day to horror and indignation, scarcely restrainable, by the supposed exorbitant bill of the inn. She thought it the most monstrous imposition which ever had been practiced, and could scarcely be persuaded to depart from her first resolution of seeking out a "decent writer," "if there is such a person in this wicked town," as she added, scornfully—to arbitrate between her and the iniquitous publican. At last, however, Patie succeeded in getting his mother safely once more within the Glasgow steamer.

It was a melancholy voyage, for every breath of wind that blew, agitated Huntley's mother with questions of his safety; and she had no better prospect than to part with Patie at this journey's end. They reached their destination in the afternoon, when the great, smoky, dingy Glasgow, looked almost hotter and more stifled than the other great seaport they had left. From the Broomielaw, they went upon their weary way, through the town, to a humble lodging recommended by Dr. Logan, whose letter to the manager of one of the founderies Patie carried in his pocket. The house which the travelers sought was up three long flights of stairs, in a dark-complexioned close, where each flat was divided into two houses. The "land," or block of buildings in which it was placed, formed one side of a little street, just behind the place where Patie was to work; and the windows of their lodging looked across the black yard and big buildings of this great, noisy foundery, to a troubled, smoky glimpse of the Clyde, and Glasgow Green upon the other side.

After he had seen his mother safely arrived in this shelter, Patie had to set out immediately to deliver his letter. The Mistress was left once more by herself to examine her new resting-place. It was a little room, with a little bed in the corner, hung with dark, unlined chintz. It was also what is called in these regions "coomcieled," which is to say, the roof sloped on one side, being close under the leads. A piece of carpet in the centre, a little table in the centre of that, three chairs, a chest of drawers, and a washing stand, completed the equipment of the room. Was this to be Patie's room—the boy's only substitute for home?

The Mistress went to the window, to see if any comfort was to be found there; but there was only the foundery—the immense, black, coaly, smoky yard into which these windows looked; and, a little to the right, a great cotton factory, whence, at the sound of a big bell, troops of girls came crowding out, with their uncovered heads shining in the evening sun. The Mistress turned abruptly in again, much discomposed by the prospect. With their colored petticoats and short gowns, and shining, uncovered hair, the Glasgow mill girls were—at this distance at least—rather a pretty sight; and a perfectly uninterested person might have thought it quite seemly and natural that the black moleskin giants of the foundery, issuing from their own cavernous portals at the same time, should have exchanged sundry jokes and rough encounters of badinage with their female neighbors.

But the Mistress, whose son was to be left at this same foundery, awoke in a horror of injured pride and aristocracy to contemplate an unimagined danger.

"A barefooted lassie from a mill!—a bairn of mine!" cried the Mistress, with looks aghast; and she drew a chair carefully out of reach of the window, and sat down at the table to consider the matter.

But when she looked round upon the bare, mean room, and thought of the solitary lad, who knew nobody in Glasgow, who had been used to the kindly cares of home all his life, and who was only a boy, although a "bairn of mine!" it is not very wonderful, perhaps, that the Mistress should have done even the staid and sensible Patie the injustice of supposing him captivated by some one of that crowd of dumpy daughters of St. Mungo, who were so far beneath the dignity of a son of Norlaw. Even Huntley, far away at sea, disappeared, for the moment, from her anxious sight. Worse dangers than those of sea or storm might be here.

Patie, meanwhile, thinking of no womankind in the world, not even of his mother, was explaining very forcibly and plainly to Dr. Logan's friend, the manager, his own wishes and intentions; railways were a very recent invention in those days, and steamboats not an old one—it was the bright day of engineering, while there still lingered a certain romance about those wondrous creations of steel and steam, with which the world had not yet grown too familiar—gentlemen apprentices were not uncommon in those great Cyclopean workshops—but Patrick Livingstone did not mean to be a gentleman apprentice. He wanted to put himself to school for a couple of years, to learn his craft like a man, without privilege of gentility, he was too old for the regular trade apprenticeship, but he desired nothing more than a lessening of the time of that probation—and whatever circumstances might lead him to do at the end of it, Patie was not afraid of being found wanting in needful skill or knowledge. Dr. Logan had given a most flattering description of his family and "station," partly stimulated thereto by the zeal with which his nephew Cassilis took up the cause of the Livingstones—and Mr. Crawford, the Glasgow manager, was very civil to the lad, who was the son of a landed proprietor, and whose brother might, in a few years, be one of the first gentlemen in the county of Melrose; the interview on the whole was a very satisfactory one, and Patie plodded his way back to the little room where he had left his mother, engaged to return next day with her, to conclude the arrangement by which he should enter the foundery; the lad was satisfied, even exhilarated, in his sober fashion, to find himself thus upon the threshold of a more serious life. Though he observed perfectly the locality and appearances around him, they had not so much effect upon Patie as they might have had on a more imaginative temper. His calmer and more practical mind, paradox though it seems to say so, was less affected by external circumstances than either his mother or Huntley, and a thousand times less than Cosmo would have been. He did not concern himself about his surroundings—*they* had little debasing or depressing influence upon his thoughts—he scarcely noticed them indeed, if they were sufficient for his necessities. Patie could very well contrive to live without beauty, and could manage to get on with a very moderate degree of comfort, so long as his own vigorous mind approved his life, and he had plenty to do.

In consequence of which it happened that Patie scarcely comprehended his mother's dissatisfaction with the room; if he remained here, it was the only room the mistress of the house could give her lodger. He thought it very well, and quite as much as he required, and apprehended no particular cheerlessness in consequence of its poverty.

"It is not home, of course," he said, with great nonchalance, "but, granting that, mother, I don't see what difference it makes to me. It's all well enough. I don't want any thing more—it's near the work, and it's in a decent house—that should be enough to please you."

"Hold your peace, Patie—do you think I'm careless of my bairn's comfort?" cried the Mistress, with a half tone of anger; "and wha' was ever used to a place like this, coming out of Norlaw?"

"But there can not be two Norlaws," said Patie, "nor two homes. I want but one, for my part. I have no desire at present to like a second place as well."

"Eh, laddie, if you can but keep that thought, and be true!" cried the Mistress, "I wouldna heed, save for your ain comfort, where you were then."

"Do you doubt me, mother? what are you feared for? tell me, and I'll know what to do," said Patie, coming close to her, with his look of plain, unmistakable sincerity.

"I'm no' feared," said the Mistress, those ever-rising, never-falling tears dimming her eyes again, while yet a little secondary emotion, half shame of her own suspicions, half petulance, rose to her voice; "but it's a poor place for a laddie like you, bred up at hame—and it's a great town, full of temptations—and night and day in a place like this, ilka street is full of evil—and naething but bare bed and board instead of hame. Oh! Patie if I was feared, it was because I knew mony a dreary story of lads that meant as well as yoursel'!"

"Perhaps I was presumptuous, mother," said Patie; "I will not say there's no fear;—but there's a difference between one man and another, and time and your own judgment will prove what's temptation to me. Now, come, if you have rested enough—the air will do you more good than sitting here."

The Mistress was persuaded, and went out accordingly with her son, feeling strangely forlorn and solitary in the crowded thoroughfares, where she was struck with the common surprise of country people, to meet so many and to know no one. Still there was a certain solace in the calm summer evening, through which the moon was rising in that pale sky so far away and clear, above the hanging smoke of the town—and in Patie's arm, which seemed to support her with more pride and tenderness now that Huntley was gone. The soft moon shining down upon the river, which here was not the commercial Clyde, of ships and steamers, the many half-distinguishable figures upon the Green opposite, from which color and light were fading, and the tranquillity of the night even here, bore back the thoughts of the mother into a tenderer channel. She put up her hand to her eyes to clear them.

"Eh Patie! I think I see my son on the sea, looking up at that very sky," said the Mistress, with a low sob; "how will I look at it from Norlaw, where Cosmo and me will be our lane?—and now but another day more, and I'll lose you!"

CHAPTER XXVI

The Mistress traveled home once more by the slow canal to Edinburgh, and from thence by the stage-coach to Kirkbride. She had left Patie, at last, with some degree of confidence, having seen Mr. Crawford, the manager of the foundery, and commended her son specially to his care; and having, besides, done what she could to improve the comfort of Patie's little apartment, and to warn him against the temptations of Glasgow. It was rather heavy work afterward, gliding silently home alone by the monotonous motion of that canal, seeing the red-tiled cottages, the green slopes, the stubble-fields move past like a dream, and remembering how she had left her boys behind, one on the sea, and one among strangers, both embarked upon the current of their life. She sat still in the little cabin of the boat by one of the windows, moving nothing but her fingers, which clasped and unclasped mechanically. Her big black vail hung over her bonnet, but did not shroud her face; there was always moisture in her eyes, but very seldom tears that came the length of falling; and her mind was very busy, and with life in its musings—for it was not alone of the past she was thinking, but also of the future—of her own life at home, where Huntley's self-denial had purchased comfort for his mother, and where his mother, not to be outdone, silently determined upon the course of those days, which she did not mean to be days of leisure. This Melmar, which had been a bugbear to the Mistress all her days, gradually changed its aspect now. It no longer reminded her of the great bitterness of her life—it was her son's possible inheritance, and might be the triumphant occasion of Huntley's return.

It was late on a September afternoon, when she descended from the coach at the door of the Norlaw Arms, and found Cosmo and Marget waiting there to welcome her. The evening sunshine streamed full in their faces, falling in a tender glory from the opposite brae of Tyne, where the white manse at the summit, and the cottages among the trees, shone in the tranquil light, with their kindliest look of home. The Mistress turned hurriedly from the familiar prospect, to repose her tired and wet eyes on the shadowed corner of the village street, where the gable of the little inn kept out the sunshine, and where the ostler had lifted down her trunk. She grasped Cosmo's hand hastily, and scarcely ventured to look the boy in the face; it was dreary coming home alone; as she descended, bowed Jaacob at the smithy door took off his cowl in token of respect, and eyed her grimly with his twinkling eye. Jaacob, who was a moral philosopher, was rather satisfied, on the whole, with the demeanor of the family of Norlaw under their troubles, and testified his approbation by a slightly authoritative approval. The Mistress gave him a very hasty nod, but could not look even at Jaacob; a break-down, or public exhibition of emotion, being the thing of all others most nervously avoided by respectable matrons of her country and temper, a characteristic very usual among Scotchwomen, of middle age and sober mind. She would have "thought shame" to have been seen crying or "giving way," "in the middle of the town," as, even now, enlightened by the sight of Edinburgh, Glasgow, and Liverpool, the Mistress still called the village street of Kirkbride; another hasty nod acknowledged the sympathetic courtesy of the widow who kept the village mangle, and whose little boy had wept at the door of Norlaw when its master was dying; and then Cosmo and Marget took the trunk between them, and the Mistress drew down her vail, and the little party set out, across the foot-bridge, through the tender slanting sunshine going home.

Then, at last, between the intervals of question and answer as to the common matters of country life, which had occurred during her absence, the Mistress's lips were opened. Marget and Cosmo went on before, along the narrow pathway by the river, and she followed. Cosmo had spent half of his time at the manse, it appeared, and all the neighbors had sent to make kindly inquiry when his mother was expected home.

"It's my hope you didna gang oftener than you were welcome, laddie," said the Mistress, with a characteristic doubt; "but I'll no deny the minister's aye very kind, and Katie too. You should not call her Katie now, Cosmo, she's woman grown. I said the very same to Huntley no' a week ago, but *he's* no like to offend onybody, poor lad, for many a day to come. And I left him very weel on the whole—oh, yes, very weel, in a grand ship for size, and mony mair in her—and they say they'll soon be out of our northerly seas, and win to grand weather, and whiles I think, if there was *great* danger, fewer folk would gang—no' to say that the Almighty's no' a bit nigher by land than he is by sea."

"Eh! and that's true!" cried Marget, in an involuntary amen.

The Mistress was not perfectly pleased by the interruption. This tender mother could not help being imperative even in her tenderest affections; and even the faithful servant could not share her mother-anxieties without risk of an occasional outbreak.

"How's a' the kye?" said the Mistress with a momentary sharpness. "I've never been an unthrifty woman, I'm bauld to say; but every mutchkin of milk maun double itself now, for my bairns' sakes."

"Na, mem," said Marget, touched on her honor, "it canna weel do that; but you ken yoursel', if you had ta'en my advice, the byre might have been mair profit years ago. Better milkers are no' in a' the Lowdens; and if you sell Crummie's cauf, as I aye advised—"

"You're aye very ready with your advice, my woman. I never meant any other thing," said the Mistress, with some impatience; "but after this, the house of Norlaw maun even get a puir name, if it must be so; for I warn ye baith, my thoughts are upon making siller; and when I put my mind to a thing, I canna do it by halves."

"Then, mother, you must, in the first place, do something with me," said Cosmo. "I'm the only useless person in the house."

"Useless, laddie!—hold you peace!" said the Mistress. "You're but a bairn, and you're tender, and you maunna make a profitless beginning till you win to your strength. Huntley and Patie—blessings on them!—were both strong callants in their nature, and got good time to grow; and I'll no' let my youngest laddie lose his youth. Eh, Cosmo, my man! if you were a lassie, instead of their brother, thae twa laddies that are away could not be mair tender of you in their hearts!"

A flush came over Cosmo's face, partly gratified affection, partly a certain shame.

"But I'll soon be a man," he said, in a low and half excited tone; "and I can not be content to wait quietly at home when my brothers are working. I have a right to work as well."

"Bless the bairn!" cried Marget, once more involuntarily.

"Dinna speak nonsense," said the Mistress. "There's a time for every thing; and because I'm bereaved of twa, is that a reason my last bairn should leave me? Fie, laddie! Patie's eighteen—he's come the length of a man—there's a year and mair between him and you. But what I was speaking of was the kye. There's nae such stock in the country as the beasts that are reared at Tyneside; and I mean to take a leaf out of Mr. Blackadder's book, if I'm spared, and see what we can do at Norlaw."

"Eh, Mistress, Mr. Blackadder's a man in his prime!" cried Marget.

"Weel, you silly haverel, what am I? Do you think a man that's laboring just for good name and fame, and because he likes it, and that has nae kin in the world but a far-away cousin, should be stronger for his wark than a widow woman striving for her bairns?" cried the Mistress, with a hasty tear in her eye, and a quick flush on her cheek; "but I'll let you a' see different things, if I'm spared, in Norlaw."

While she spoke with this flush of resolution, they came in sight of their home; but it was not possible to see the westerly sunshine breaking through those blank eyes of the old castle, and the low, modern house standing peacefully below, those unchanged witnesses of all the great scenes of all their lives, without a strain of heart and courage, which was too much for all of them. To enter in, remembering where the father took his rest, and how the sons began their battle—to have it once more pierced into the depths of her heart, that, of all the family once circling her, there remained only Cosmo, overpowered the Mistress, even in the midst of her new purpose, with a returning agony. She went in silent, pressing her hand upon her heart. It was a sad coming home.

CHAPTER XXVII

"And so you're the only ane of them left at hame?" said bowed Jaacob, looking up at Cosmo from under his bushy brows, and pushing up his red cowl off his forehead.

And there could not have been a more remarkable contrast of appearance than between this slight, tall, fair boy, and the swart little demon, who considered him with a scientific curiosity, keen, yet not unkindly, from the red twilight of the blacksmith's shop.

"I should be very glad not to be left at home," said Cosmo, with a boyish flush of shame; "and it will not be for long, if I can help it."

"Weel, I'll no' say but ye a' show a good spirit—a very good spirit, considering your up-bringing," said Jaacob, "which was owre tender for laddies. I've little broo, for my ain part, of women's sons. We're a' that, more or less, doubtless, but the less the better, lad. I kent little about mothers and such like when I was young mysel'."

"They say," said Cosmo, who, in spite of his sentiment, had a quick perception of humor, and was high in favor with the little Cyclops, "they say you were a fairy, and frightened everybody from your cradle, Jacob, and that your mother fainted with fear when she saw you first—is it true?"

"True!—aye, just as true as a' the rest," said Jaacob. "They'll say whatever ye like that's marvellous, if ye'll but listen to them. A man o' sense is an awfu' phenomenon in a place like this. He's no' to be accounted for by the common laws o' nature; that's the philosophy of the matter. *You're* owre young yet to rouse them; but they'll make their story, or a's one—take my word for it—of a lad of genius like yoursel'."

"Genius, Jacob!"

The boy's face grew red with a sudden, violent flush; and an intense, sudden light shone in his dark eyes. He did not laugh at the compliment—it awoke some powerful sentiment of vanity or self-consciousness in his own mind. The lighting-up of his eyes was like a sudden gleam upon a dark water—a revelation of a hundred unknown shadows and reflections which had been there unrevealed for many a day before.

"Aye, genius. I ken the true metal when I hear it ring," said Jaacob. "Like draws to like, as ony fool can tell."

And then the boy turned away with a sudden laugh—a perfectly mirthful, pure utterance of the half-fun, half-shame, and wholly ludicrous impression which this climax made upon him.

Strangely enough, Jaacob was not offended. He went on, moving about the red gloom of his workshop, without the slightest appearance of displeasure. He had no idea that the lad whom he patronized could laugh at him.

"I can not say but I'm surprised at your brother for a' that," said Jaacob. "Huntley's a lad of spirit; but he should have stood up to Me'mar like a man."

"Do you know about Me'mar, too?" cried Cosmo, in some surprise.

"I reckon I do; and maist things else," said Jaacob, dryly. "I'm no' vindictive mysel', but when a man does me an ill turn, I've a real good disposition to pay him back. He aye had a grudge against the late Norlaw, this Aberdeenawa' man; and if I had been your faither, Cosmo, lad, I'd have fought the haill affair to the last, though it cost me every bodle I had; for wha does a' the land and the rights belong to, after all?—to *her*, and no' to him!"

"Did you know her?" asked Cosmo, breathlessly, not perceiving, in his eager curiosity, how limited Jaacob's real knowledge of the case was.

"Aye," said Jaacob; and the ugly little demon paused, and breathed from his capacious lungs a sigh, which disturbed the atmosphere of the smithy with a sudden convulsion. Then he added, quietly, and in an undertone, "I had a great notion of her mysel'."

"You!" said Cosmo.

The boy did not know whether to fall upon his companion with sudden indignation, and give him a hearty shake by his deformed shoulders, or to retire with an angry laugh of ridicule and resentment. Both the more violent feelings, however, merged into the unmitigated amazement with which Cosmo at last gazed at the swarthy hunchback, who had ventured to lift his eyes to Norlaw's love.

"And what for no' me?" said Jaacob, sturdily; "do ye think it's good looks and naught else that takes a woman's e'e? do you think I havena had them in my offer as weel favored as Mary Huntley? Na, I'll do them this justice; a woman, if she's no' a downright haverel, kens a man of sense when she sees him. Mony a wiselike woman has cast her e'e in at this very smiddy; but I'm no' a marrying man."

"You would have made many discontented, and one ungrateful," said the boy, laughing. "Is that what kept you back, Jacob?"

"Just that," said the philosopher, with a grim smile; "but I had a great notion of Miss Mary Huntley; she was aulder than me; that's aye the way with callants; ye'll be setting your heart on a woman o' twenty yoursel'. I'd have gane twenty miles a-foot, wet or dry, just to shoe her powny; and I wouldna have let her cause gang to the wa', as your father did, if it had been me."

"Was she beautiful? what like was she, Jacob?" cried Cosmo, eagerly.

"I can not undertake to tell you just what she was like, a callant like you," said Jaacob; then the dark hobgoblin made a pause, drawing himself half into his furnace, as the boy could suppose. "She was like a man's first fancy," continued the little giant, abruptly, drawing forth a red-hot bar of iron, which made a fiery flash in the air, and lighted up his own swart face for the moment; "she was like the woman a lad sets his heart on, afore he kens the cheats of this world," he added, at another interval, with a great blow of his hammer, which made the sparks fly; and through the din and the flicker no further words came. Cosmo's imagination filled up the ideal. The image of Mary of Melmar rose angel-like out of the boy's stimulated fancy, and there was not even a single glimmer of the grotesque light of this scene to diminish the romantic halo which rose around his father's first love.

"As for me, if you think the like of me presumed in lifting his e'en," said Jaacob, "I'll warn you to change your ideas, my man, without delay; a' that auld trash canna stand the dint of good discussion and opinion in days like these. Speak about your glorious revolutions! I tell you, callant, we're on the eve of the real glorious revolution, the time when every man shall have respect for his neighbors—save when his neighbor's a fool; nane o' your oligarchies for a free country; we're men, and we'll have our birthright; and do you think I'm heeding what a coof's ancestors were, when I ken I'm worth twa o' him—ay, or ten o' him!—as a' your bits o' lords and gentlemen will find as soon as we've The Bill."

"An honorable ancestor is an honor to any man," said Cosmo, firing with the pride of birth. "I would not take the half of the county, if it was offered me, in place of the old castle at Norlaw."

"Well," said Jaacob, with a softening glance, "it's no' an ill sentiment that, I'll allow, so far as the auld castle gangs; but ony man that thinks he's of better flesh and bluid than me, no' to say intellect and spirit, on the strength of four old wa's, or the old rascals that thieved in them—I'll tell ye, Cosmo, my lad, I think he's a fool, and that's just the short and the long o' the affair."

"Better flesh and blood, or better intellect and spirit!" said the boy, with a half-meditative, half-mirthful smile. "Homer was a beggar, and so was Belisarius, and so was Blind Harry, of Wallace's time."

This highly characteristic, school-boyish, and national confusion of heroes, moved the blacksmith-philosopher with no sensation of the absurd. Homer and Blind Harry were by no means unfit companions in the patriotic conception of bowed Jaacob, who, nevertheless, knew Pope's Homer very tolerably, and was by no means ignorant of the pretensions of the "blind old man of Scio's rocky isle."

"A feesical disqualification, Cosmo, is quite a different matter," said Jaacob; "nae man could make greater allowance for the like of that than me, that might have been supposed at one time to be on the verge of it mysel'."

And as he spoke, his one bright eye twinkled in Jaacob's head with positive scintillations, as if Nature had endowed it with double power to make up for its solitude.

"The like of Homer and Blind Harry, however, belong to a primitive age," said Jaacob; "the minstrel crew were aye vagrants—no' to say it was little better than a kind of a servile occupation at the best, praises of the great. But the world's wiser by this time. I would not say I would make the Bill final, mysel', but let's aince get it, laddie, and ye'll see a change. We'll hae nae mair o' your lordlings in the high places—we'll hae naething but *men*."

"Did you ever hear any thing, Jacob," said Cosmo, somewhat abruptly—for the romantic story of his kinswoman was more attractive to the boy's mind than politics—"of where the young lady of Me'mar went to, or who it was she married? I suppose not, since she was searched for so long."

"No man ever speered at me before, so far as I can mind," said Jaacob, with a little bitterness; "your father behoved to manage the haill business himsel', and he was na great hand. I'm no' fond of writers when folk can do without them, but they're of a certain use, nae doubt, like a' other vermin; a sharp ane o' them would have found Mary Huntley, ye may take my word for that. I was aince in France mysel'."

"In France?" cried Cosmo, with, undeniable respect and excitement.

"Ay, just that," said Jaacob, dryly; "it's nae such great thing, though folk make a speech about it. I wasna far inower. I was at a bit seaport place on the coast; Dieppe they ca' it, and deep it was to an innocent lad like what I was at the time—though I could haud my ain with maist men, both then and at this day."

"And you saw there?"—cried Cosmo, who became very much interested.

"Plenty of fools," said Jaacob, "and every wean in the streets jabbering French, which took me mair aback than onything else I heard or saw; but there was ae day a lady passed me by. I didna see her face at first, but I saw the bairn she had in her hand, and I thought to mysel' I could not but ken the foot, that had a ring upon the path like siller bells. I gaed round about, and round about, till I met her in the face, but whether it was her or no I canna tell; I stood straight afore her in the midroad, and she passed me by with a glance, as if she kent nae me."

The tone in which the little hunchback uttered these words was one of indescribable yet suppressed bitterness. He was too proud to acknowledge his mortification; yet it was clear enough, even to Cosmo, that this pride had not only prevented him from mentioning his chance meeting at the proper time, but that even now he would willingly persuade himself that the ungrateful beauty, who did not recognize him, could not be the lady of his visionary admiration.

"Do you think it was the Lady of Melmar?" asked the boy, anxiously, for Jaacob's "feelings," though they had no small force of human emotion in them, were, for the moment, rather a secondary matter to Cosmo.

"If it had been her, she would have kent *me*," said Vulcan, with emphasis, and he turned to his hammering with vehemence doubly emphatic. Jaacob had no inclination to be convinced that Mary of Melmar might forget him, who remembered her so well. He returned to the Bill, which was more or less in most people's thoughts in those days, and which was by no means generally uninteresting to Cosmo—but the boy's thoughts were too much excited to be amused by Jaacob's politics; and Cosmo went home with visions in his mind of the quaint little Norman town, where Mary of Melmar had been seen by actual vision, and which henceforth became a region of dreams and fancy to her young knight and champion, who meant to seek her over all the world.

CHAPTER XXVIII

Ere the winter had fully arrived, visible changes had taken place in the house and steading of Norlaw. As soon as all the operations of the harvest were over, the Mistress dismissed all the men-servants of the farm, save two, and let, at Martinmas, all the richer portion of the land, which was in good condition, and brought a good rent. Closely following upon the plowmen went Janet, the younger maidservant, who obtained, to her great pride, but doubtful advantage, a place in a great house in the neighborhood.

The Norlaw byres were enlarged and improved—the Norlaw cattle increased in number by certain choice and valuable specimens of "stock," milch-kine, sleek and fair, and balmy-breathed. Some few fields of turnips and mangelwurzel, and the rich pasture lands on the side of Tyne behind the castle, were all that the Mistress retained in her own hands, and with Marget for her factotum, and Willie Noble, the same man who had assisted in Norlaw's midnight funeral, for her chief manager and representative out of doors, Mrs. Livingstone began her new undertaking.

She was neither dainty of her own hands, nor tolerant of any languid labor on the part of others. Not even in her youth, when the hopes and prospects of Norlaw were better than the reality ever became, had the Mistress shown the smallest propensity to adopt the small pomp of a landed lady. She was always herself, proud, high-spirited, somewhat arbitrary, by no means deficient in a sense of personal importance, yet angrily fastidious as to any false pretensions in her house, and perceiving truly her real position, which, with all the added dignity of proprietorship, was still in fact that of a farmer's wife. All the activity and energy with which she had toiled all her life against her thriftless husband's unsteady grasp of his own affairs, and against the discouraging and perpetual unprosperity of many a year, were intensified now by the consciousness of having all her purposes within her own hand and dependent on herself. Naked and empty as the house looked to the eyes which had been accustomed to so many faces, now vanished from it, there began to grow an intention and will about all its daily work, which even strangers observed. Though the Mistress sat, as usual, by the corner window with her work in the afternoon, and the dining-parlor was as homelike as ever, and the neighbors saw no change, except the change of dress which marked her widowhood, Marget, half ashamed of the derogation, half proud of the ability, and between shame and pride keeping the secret of these labors, knew of the Mistress's early toils, which even Cosmo knew very imperfectly; her brisk morning hours of superintendence and help in the kitchen and in the dairy, which, with all its new appliances and vigorous working, became "just a picture," as Marget thought, and the pride of her own heart. Out of the produce of those carefully tended precious "kye," out of the sweet butter, smelling of Tyne gowans, and the rich, yellow curds of cheese, and the young, staggering, long-limbed calves which Willie Noble had in training, the Mistress, fired with a mother's ambition, meant to return tenfold to Huntley his youthful self-denial, and even to lay up something for her younger sons.

It was still only fourteen years since the death of the old Laird of Melmar, the father of the lost Mary; and there was yet abundant time for the necessary proceedings to claim her inheritance, without fear of the limiting law, which ultimately might confirm the present possessor beyond reach of attack. The last arrangement made by Huntley had accordingly been, that all these proceedings should be postponed for three or four years, during which time the lost heiress might reappear, or, more probable still, the sanguine lad thought, his own fortunes prosper so well, that he could bear the expense of the litigation without touching upon the little patrimony sacred to his mother. After so long an interval, a few years more or less would not harm the cause, and in the meantime every exertion was to be made by Cassilis, as Huntley's agent, for the discovery of Mary of Melmar. This was the only remaining circumstance of pain in the whole case to the Mistress. She could not help resenting everybody's interest about this heiress, who had only made herself interesting by her desertion of that "home and friends," which, to the Mistress herself, were next to God in their all-commanding, all-engrossing claim. She was angry even with the young lawyer, but above all, angry that her own boys should be concerned for the rights of the woman who had forsaken all her duties so violently, and with so little appearance of penitence; and if sometimes a thought of despondency and bitterness crossed the mind of the Mistress at night, as she sat sewing by the solitary candle, which made one bright speck of light, and no more, in the dim dining-room of Norlaw, the aggrieved feeling found but one expression. "I would not say now, but what after we've a' done our best—me among the beasts, and my laddie ower the seas, and the writers afore the Fifteen," were the words, never spoken, but often conceived, which rose in the Mistress's heart; "I would not wonder but then, when the land's gained and a's done, she'll come hame. It would be just like a' the rest!" And let nobody condemn the Mistress. Many a hardly-laboring soul, full of generous plans and motives, has seen a stranger enter into its labors, or feared to see it, and felt the same.

In the meantime, Cosmo, who had got all that the parish schoolmaster of Kirkbride—no contemptible teacher—could give him, had been drawing upon Dr. Logan's rusty Latin and Greek, rather to the satisfaction of the good minister than to his own particular improvement, and tired of reading every thing that could be picked up in the shape of reading from the old parchment volumes of second-rate Latin divinity, which the excellent minister never opened, but had a certain respect for, down to the *Gentle Shepherd* and the floating ballad literature of the country-side, began to grow more and more anxious to emulate his brothers, and set out upon the world. The winter nights came on, growing longer and longer, and Cosmo scorched his fair hair and stooped his slight shoulders, reading by the fire-light, while his mother worked by the table, and while the November winds began to sound in the echoing depths of the old castle. The house was very still of nights, and missed the absent sorely, and both the Mistress and her faithful servant were fain to shut up the house and go to rest as soon as it was seemly, a practice to which their early habits in the morning gave abundant excuse, though its real reason lay deeper.

"Ane can bear mony a thing in good daylight, when a' the work's in hand," Marget said; "but womenfolk think lang at night, when there's nae blythe step sounding ower the door, nor tired man coming hame." And though she never said the same words, the same thought was in the Mistress's heart.

One of these slow nights was coming tardily to a close, when Cosmo, who had been gathering up his courage, having finished his book on the hearth-rug, where the boy half sat and half reclined, rose suddenly and came to his mother at the table. Perhaps some similar thoughts of her own had prepared the Mistress to anticipate what he was about to say. She did not love to be forestalled, and, before Cosmo spoke, answered with some impatience to the purpose in his eye.

"I ken very well what you're going to say. Weel, I wot the night's lang, and the house is quiet—mair folk than you can see that," said the Mistress, "and you're a restless spirit, though I did not think it of you. Cosmo, do you ken what *I* would like you to do?"

"I could guess, mother," said the boy.

"Ay, 'deed, and ye could object. I might have learned that," said his mother.

"I've got little of my ain will a' my life, though a fremd person would tell you I was a positive woman. Most things I've set my heart on have come to naught. Norlaw's near out of our hands, and Huntley and Patie are in the ends of the earth, and I'm a widow woman, desolate of my bairns; weel, weel, I'm no complaining—but when I saw you first in your cradle, Cosmo—you were the bonniest of a' my bairns—I put my hands on your head, and I said to myself—'I'll make him my offering to the Lord, because he's the fairest lamb of a'.' Na, laddie—never mind, I'm no heeding. You needna put your arms round me. It's near seventeen year ago, and mony a weary day since then, but I've aye thought upon my vow."

"Mother, if I can, I'll fulfill it!" cried Cosmo; "but how could I know your heart was in it, when you never spoke of it before?"

"Na," said the Mistress, restraining herself with an effort. "I've done my best to bring you up in the fear of the Lord, and it's no written that you maun be a minister, before you can serve Him. I'll no' put a burden on your conscience; but just I was a witless woman, and didna mind when I saw the bairn in the cradle that before it came that length, it would have a will of its own."

"Send me to college, mother!" said Cosmo, with tears in his eyes. "I have made no plans, and if I had I could change them—and at the worst, if we find I can not be a minister, I will never forget your vow—put your hands on my head and say it over again."

But when the boy knelt down at her side with the enthusiasm of his temper, and lifted his glowing, youthful face, full of a generous young emotion, which was only too generous and ready to be swayed by the influences of love, the Mistress could only bend over him with a silent burst of tenderness.

"God bless my dearest bairn!" she said at last, with her broken voice. "But no, no!—I've learned wisdom. The Lord make ye a' His ain servants— every ane—I can say nae mair."

CHAPTER XXIX

It was accordingly but a very short time after these occurrences when Cosmo, with his wardrobe carefully over-looked, his "new blacks" supplemented by a coarser every-day suit, which took the place of the jacket which the lad had outgrown, and a splendid stock of linen, home-made, snow-white and bleached on the gowans—took his way to Edinburgh in all the budding glory of a student. In those days few people had begun to speculate whether the Scotch Universities were or were not as good as the English ones, or what might be the characteristic differences of the two. The academic glories of Edinburgh still existed in the fresh glories of tradition, if they had begun to decline in reality—and chairs were still held in the northern college by men at whose feet statesmen had learned philosophy.

The manner in which Cosmo Livingstone went to college was not one, however, in which anybody goes to Maudlin or Trinity. The lad went to take up his humble lodging at Mrs. Purdie's in the High Street, and from thence dropped shyly to the college, paid his fees and matriculated, and there was an end of it. There were no rooms to look after, no tutors to see, no "men" to be made acquainted with. He had a letter in his pocket to one of the professors, and one to the minister of one of the lesser city churches. His abode was to be the same little room with the "concealed bed" and window overlooking the town, in which his mother had rested as she passed through Edinburgh, and the honest Kirkbride woman, who was his landlady, had been already engaged at a moderate weekly rate to procure all that he wanted for him.

After which fashion—feeling very shy and lonely, somewhat embarrassed by the new coat which his mother called a surtoo and regarded with respect, dismayed by the necessity of entering shops and making purchases for himself, and standing a little in awe of the other students and of the breakfast to which the professor had invited him—Cosmo began the battle of his life.

He was now nearly seventeen, young enough to be left by himself in that little lantern and watch-house hanging high over the picturesque heights and hollows of the beautiful old town, where the lad sat at his window in the winter evenings, watching the gorgeous frosty sunset, how it purpled with royal gleams and shadows all the low hills of Fife, and shed a distant golden glow—sometimes a glow redder and fiercer than gold—upon the chilly glories of the Firth. Then, as the light faded from the western horizon, and Inchkeith and Inchcolm no longer stood out in vivid relief against the illuminated waters, how the lights of the town, scarcely less fairy-like, began to steal along the streets and to sparkle out in the windows, hanging in irregular lines from the many-storied houses at the other side of the North Bridge, and gleaming like glow-worms in the dark little valley between.

Cosmo sat at his window with a book in his hand, but did not read much—perhaps the lad was not thinking much either, as he sat in the silent little room, listening to all the voices of all the population beneath him, which rose in a softened swell of sound to his high window; sometimes mournful, sometimes joyful, sometimes with a sharp cry in it like an appeal to God, sometimes full of distinct tones, inarticulate yet individual, sometimes sweet with the hum of children—a great, full, murmuring chorus never entirely silenced, in which the heart of humanity seemed, somehow, to betray itself, and reveal unawares the unspeakable blending of emotions which no one man can ever confess for himself.

Cosmo, who had spent a due portion of his time in his class-room, had taken notes of the lectures, and been, if not a remarkably devoted, at least a moderately conscientious student, often found himself very unwilling to light the candle, and sometimes even let his fire go out, in the charmed idleness of his window-seat, which was so strangely different from his old meditative haunt in the old castle, yet which absorbed him even more— and then Mrs. Purdie would come in with brisk good-humor, and rate him soundly for sitting in the dark, and make up the much-enduring northern coals into a blaze for him, and sweep the hearth, and light the candle, and bring in the little tray with its little tea-pot and blue and white cup and saucer, and the bread and butter—which Cosmo did full justice to, in spite of his dreams. When she came to remove the things again, Mrs. Purdie would stand with one arm a-kimbo to have a little talk with her young lodger; perhaps to tell him that she had seen the Melrose courier, or met somebody newly arrived by the coach from Kirkbride, or encountered an old neighbor, who "speered very kindly" for his mother; or, on the other hand, to confide to him her fear that the lad from the Highlants in her little garret overhead, who provided himsel', would perish with cauld in this frosty weather, and was just as like as no' to starve himsel', and didna keep up a decent outside, puir callant, without mony a sair pinch that naebody kent onything about; or that her other lodger, who was also a student, was in a very ill way, coming in at a' the hours of the night, and spending hard-won siller, and that she would be very glad to let his father and mother ken, but it didna become her to tell tales.

These, and a great many other communications of the same kind, Mrs. Purdie relieved her mind by making to Cosmo, whose youth and good-looks and local claims upon her regard, made him a great favorite with the kind-hearted, childless woman, who compounded "scones" for his tea, and even occasionally undertook the trouble of a pudding, "a great fash and fyke," as she said to herself, puddings being little in favor with humble Scotchwomen of her class.

Under the care of this motherly attendant, Cosmo got on very well in his little Edinburgh lodging, and even in some degree enjoyed the solitude which was so new and so strange to the home-bred boy. He used to sally out early in the morning, perhaps to climb as far as St. Anthony's Chapel, or mount the iron ribs of the Crags, to watch the early mists breaking over the lovely country, and old Edinburgh rising out of the cloud like a queen—or perhaps only to hasten along the cheerful length of Princes Street, when the same mists parted from the crags of the Castle, or lay white in the valley. The boy knew nothing about his own sentiments, what manner of fancies they were, and did not pause to inquire whether any one else thought like him. He hurried in thereafter to breakfast, fresh and blooming, and then with his books to college, encountering often enough that grave, gaunt Highlander in the garret, who had no time for poetic wanderings, and perhaps not much capacity, but who struggled on towards his own aim, with a desperate fortitude and courage, which no man of his name ever surpassed in a forlorn hope, or on a battle-field. The Highland student was nearly thirty, a man full grown and labor-hardened, working his way through his "humanity" and Divinity classes, looking forward, as the goal of his ambition, to some little Gaelic-speaking parish in the far north, where some day, perhaps, the burning Celtic fervor, imprisoned under his slow English speech and impenetrable demeanor, might make him the prophet of his district; and as he entered day by day at the same academic gates, side-by-side with the seventeen-year-old boy, a strange tenderness for the lad came into the man's heart. They grew friends shyly yet warmly, unlike as they were, though Cosmo never was admitted to any of those secrets of his friend's *menage*, which Mrs. Purdie guessed at, but which Cameron would never have forgiven any one for finding out; and next to the household of

Norlaw, and the strange, half-perceived knowledge that came stealing to his mind, like a fairy, in his vigils by his window, Cameron was Cosmo's first experience of what he was to meet in life.

The Highlander lived in his garret, you could not believe or understand how, gentleman-commoner—and would have tossed, not only your shoes, but you out of his high window, had you tried to be benevolent to him, as you tried it once to that clumsy sizar of Pembroke; notwithstanding, he was no ignoble beginning for a boy's friendship, a fact which Cosmo Livingstone had it in him to perceive.

CHAPTER XXX

"I mean to call on Miss Logan at the manse to-day," said Patricia Huntley, as she took her place with great dignity in "the carriage," which she had previously employed Joanna to bully Melmar into ordering for her conveyance. Mrs. Huntley was too great an invalid to make calls, and Aunt Jean was perfectly impracticable as a companion, so Patricia armed herself with her mother's card-case, and set out alone.

Alone, save for the society of Joanna, who was glad enough of a little locomotion, but did not much enjoy the call-making portion of the enterprise. Joanna, whom no pains, it was agreed, could persuade into looking genteel, had her red hair put up in bows under her big bonnet, and a large fur tippet on her shoulders. Her brown merino frock was short, as Joanna's frocks invariably became after a few weeks' wearing; and the abundant display of ankle appearing under it said more for the strength than the elegance of its proprietor. Patricia, for her part, wore a colored silk cloak, perfectly shapeless, and as long as her dress, with holes for her arms, and a tippet of ermine to complete it. It was a dress which was very much admired, and "quite the fashion" in those days; when the benighted individuals who wore such vestments actually supposed themselves as well-dressed as *we* have the comfort of knowing ourselves now.

"For I am sure," said Patricia, as they drove along towards Kirkbride, "that there is some mystery going on. I am quite sure of it. I never will forget how shamefully papa treated me that day Mr. Cassilis was at Melmar—before a stranger and a gentleman too! and you know as well as I do, Joanna, how often that poor creature, Whitelaw, from Melrose, has been at our house since then."

"Yes, I know," said Joanna, carelessly. "I wonder what Katie Logan will say when she knows I'm going to school?"

"What a selfish thing you are, always thinking about your own concerns," said Patricia; "do you hear what I say? I think there's a mystery—I'm sure there's a secret—either papa is not the right proprietor, or somebody else has a claim, or there's something wrong. He is always making us uncomfortable some way or other; wouldn't it be dreadful if we were all ruined and brought to poverty at the end?"

"Ruined and brought to poverty? it would be very good fun to see what mamma and you would do," cried the irreverent Joanna. "*I* could do plenty things; but I'm no' feared—it's you, that's always reading story-books."

"It's not a story-book; I almost heard papa say it," said Patricia, reddening slightly.

"Then you've been listening!" cried her bolder sister. "I would scorn to do that. I would ask him like a man what it was, if it was me, but I wouldna go stealing about the passages like a thief. I wouldna do it for twice Melmar—nor for all the secrets in the world!"

"I wish you would not be so violent, Joanna! my poor nerves can not stand it," said Patricia; "a thoughtless creature like you never looks for any information, but I'm older, and I know we've no fortunes but what papa can give us, and we need to think of ourselves. Think, Joanna, if you can think. If anybody were to take Melmar from papa, what would become of you and me?"

"You and me!" the girl cried, in great excitement. "I would think of Oswald and papa himsel', if it was true. Me! I could nurse bairns, or keep a school, or go to Australia, like Huntley Livingstone. I'm no' feared! and it would be fun to watch *you*, what you would do. But if papa had cheated anybody and was found out—oh, Patricia! could you think of yourself instead of thinking on that?"

"When a man does wrong, and ruins his family, he has no right to look for any thing else," said Patricia.

"I would hate him," cried Joanna, vehemently, "but I wouldna forsake him—but it's all havers; we've been at Melmar almost as long as I can mind, and never any one heard tell of it before."

"I mean to hear what Katie Logan says—for Mr. Cassilis is her cousin," said Patricia, "and just look, there she is, on the road, tying little Isabel's bonnet. She's just as sure to be an old maid as can be—look how prim she is! and never once looking to see what carriage it is, as if carriages were common at the manse. Don't call her Katie, Joanna; call her Miss Logan; I mean to show her that there is a difference between us and the minister's daughter at Kirkbride."

"And I mean no such thing," cried Joanna, with her head half out at the window; "she's worth the whole of us put together, except Oswald and Auntie Jean. Katie! Katie Logan! we're going to the manse to see you—oh don't run away!"

The day was February, cold but sunny, and the manse parlor was almost as bright in this wintry weather as it had been in summer. The fire sparkled and crackled with an exhilaration in the sound as well as the warmth and glow it made, and the sunshine shone in at the end window, through the leafless branches, with a ruddy wintry cheerfulness, which brightened one's thoughts like good news or a positive pleasure. There were no stockings or pinafores to be mended, but instead, a pretty covered basket, holding all Katie's needles and thread, and scraps of work in safe and orderly retirement, and at the bright window, in an old-fashioned china flower-pot, a little group of snow-drops, the earliest possibility of blossom, hung their pale heads in the light. Joanna Huntley threw herself into the minister's own easy-chair with a riotous expression of pleasure.

"Fires never burn as if they liked to burn in Melmar," cried Joanna; "oh, Katie Logan, what do you do to yours? for every thing looks as if something pleasant happened here every day."

"Something pleasant is always happening," said Katie, with a smile.

"It depends upon what people think pleasure," said Patricia. "I am sure you that have so much to do, and all your little brothers and sisters to look after, and no society, should be worse off than me and Joanna; but it's very seldom that any thing pleasant happens to us."

"Never mind her, Katie. Listen to me. I'm going to Edinburgh to school," cried Joanna. "I don't know whether to like it or to be angry. What would you do, if you were me?"

"I don't think I could fancy myself you, Joanna," said Katie, laughing; "but I should have liked it when I was younger, and had less to do. I'm to go in with papa if he goes to the Assembly this May. We have friends in Edinburgh, and I like it for that—besides the Assembly and all the things country folk see there."

"But Edinburgh is a very poor place after being in London," said Patricia; "if you could only see Clapham, where I was at school! But Mr. Cassilis is a cousin of yours—is he not? I suppose he told you how papa behaved to me when he was last at Melmar."

"No, indeed—he did not," said Katie, with some curiosity.

"Oh! I thought perhaps he noticed it, being a stranger," said Patricia; "do you know what was his business with papa?"

"No."

"You might tell us—for we ought to hear, if it is any thing important," said Patricia; "and as for papa, he never lets us know any thing till everybody else has heard it first. I am sure it was some business, and business which made papa as cross as possible; do tell us what it was."

"I don't know any thing about it," said Katie. "My cousin staid here only two or three days, and he never spoke of business to me."

"Oh! but you know what he came here about," insisted Patricia.

"He came to see us, and also—oh, yes—to manage something for the Livingstones, of Norlaw," said Katie, with a slight increase of color.

For the moment she had actually forgotten this last and more important reason for the visit of the young lawyer, having a rather uncomfortable impression that "to see us" was a more urgent inducement to Cousin Charlie than it had better be. She paused accordingly with a slight embarrassment, and began to busy herself opening her work basket. Patricia Huntley was not a person of the liveliest intelligence in general, but she was quick-sighted enough to see that Katie stumbled in her statement, and drew up her small shoulders instantly with two distinct sentiments of jealous offense and disapproval, the first relating to the presumption of the minister's daughter in appropriating the visit of Cassilis to herself, and the second to a suggestion of the possible rivalry, which could affect the house of Melmar in the family of Norlaw.

"I think we are never to be done with these Livingstones," cried Patricia, "and all because the old man owed papa a quantity of money. We can't help it when people owe us money, and I am sure I am very much surprised at Mr. Cassilis, if he came to annoy papa about a thing like that. I thought he was a gentleman! I thought it must be something important he came to say."

"Perhaps it might be," said Katie, quietly, coloring rather more, but losing her embarrassment; "and the more important it was, the less likely is it that my cousin would tell it to any one whom it did not concern. Mr. Huntley could answer your questions better than I."

"Oh, I see you're quite offended. I see you're quite offended. I am sure I did not know Mr. Cassilis was any particular kind of cousin," said Patricia, spitefully. "If I had known I should have taken care how I spoke; but if my papa was like yours, and was not very able to afford a housekeeper, it would need to be another sort of a man from Mr. Cassilis who could make *me* go away and leave my home."

"Katie, you should flyte upon her," said Joanna. "She does not understand any thing else—never mind her—talk to me—are all the Livingstones away but Cosmo? Patricia thinks there's a mystery and papa's wronged somebody. If he has, it's Norlaw."

"I don't think any thing of the sort—hold your tongue, Joanna," said her sister.

"Eh, what else?" cried the young lady, roused to recrimination. "Katie, do you think Mrs. Livingstone knows? for I would go and ask her in a minute. I would not forsake papa if he was poor, but if he's wronged anybody, I'll no' stand it—for it would be my blame as well as his the moment I knew!"

"I don't think you have any thing to do with it," said Katie, with spirit, "nor Patricia either. Girls were not set up to keep watch over their fathers and mothers; are you the constable at Melmar, Joanna, to keep everybody in order? I wish you were at the manse sometimes when the boys have a holiday. Our Johnnie would be a match for you. The Livingstones are all away,—Cosmo, too; he's gone to college in Edinburgh, and some day, perhaps, you'll hear him preach in Kirkbride."

"I am quite sure papa would not give him the presentation; he's promised it to a cousin of our own," said Patricia, eagerly.

Katie grew very red, and then very pale.

"My father is minister of Kirkbride," she said, with a great deal of simple dignity; "there is no presentation in anybody's power just now."

"Katie, I wish you would not speak to her, she's a cat!" cried Joanna, with intense disgust, turning her back upon her sister; "oh I wish you would write Cosmo to come and see me! I'll be just the same as at college, too; and I'm sure I'll like him a great deal better than any of the girls. Or, never mind; if that's not right, I'll be sure to meet him in the street. I'm to go next week, Katie, and there's a French governess and a German master, and an Italian master, and nothing but vexation and trouble. It's quite true, and we're not even to speak our own tongue, but jabber away at French from morning to night. English is far better—I know I'll quarrel with them a'."

"Do you call your language English, Joanna?" said her sister, with contempt.

"If it's no' English it's Scotch, and that's far better," cried Joanna, with an angry blush; "wha cares for English? They never say their r's and their h's, except when they shouldna say them, and they never win the day except by guile, and they canna do a thing out of their own head till Scotsmen show them how! and it's a' true, and I'd rather be a servant-maid in Melmar, than one of your Clapham fine ladies, so you needna speak your English either to Katie or me."

And it must be confessed that Katie, sensible as she was, laughed and applauded, and that poor little Patricia, who could find nothing heroical to say on behalf of Clapham, was very much disposed to cry with vexation, and only covered her defeat by a retreat to the carriage, where Joanna followed, only after a few minutes' additional conversation with Katie, who was by no means disposed to aid the elder sister. When they were gone, however, Katie Logan shook her wise little elder-sisterly head over the pair of them. She thought if Charlie (which diminutive in the manse meant Charlotte) and Isabel grew up like Patricia and Joanna, she would "break her heart;" and the little mistress of the manse went into the kitchen to oversee the progress of a birthday cake and give her homely orders, without once thinking of the superior grandeur of the carriage, as it rolled down the slope of the brae and through the village, the scene of a continued and not very temperate quarrel between the two daughters of Melmar, which was only finished at last by the sudden giving way of Patricia's nerves and breath, to the most uncomfortable triumph of Joanna. Joanna kept sulkily in her corner, and refused to alight while the other calls were made. On the whole, it was not a very delightful drive.

CHAPTER XXXI

Three months later, in the early sweetness of May, Cosmo Livingstone stood upon an "outside stair," one of those little flights of stone steps, clearing the half-cellar shops of the lowest story, which are not unfrequent in the High Street of Edinburgh, and which make a handy platform when any thing is to be seen, or place of refuge when any thing is to be escaped from. A little further down, opposite to him, was the Tron Church, with its tall steeple striking up into the sunny mid-day heavens; and above, at a little distance, the fleecy white clouds hung over the open crown of St. Giles's, with the freshness of recent rain. Many bystanders stood on the other "stair-heads," and groups of heads looked out from almost every window of the high houses on every side. The High Street of Edinburgh, lined with expectant lookers-on, darkening downwards towards the picturesque slope of the Canongate, with its two varied and noble lines of lofty old houses, black with time, between which the sunshine breaks down in a moted and streamy glory, as into a well, is no contemptible object among street sights; and the population of Edinburgh loves its streets as perhaps only the populations of places rich in natural beauty can love them. A man who has seen a crowd in the High Street might almost be tempted to doubt, indeed, whether the Scottish people were really so reserved and grave and self-restraining as common report pronounces them. The women on the landings of the stairs shrilly claiming here and there a Tam or a Sandy, or else discussing in chorus the event of the moment; the groups of men promenading up and down upon the pavement with firm-set mouth and gleaming eyes—the mutter of forcible popular sentiment saying rather more than it means, and saying that in the plainest and most emphatic words; and the stir of general excitement in a scene which has already various recollections of tumults which are historical, make altogether a picturesque and striking combination, which is neither like a Parisian mob nor a London one, yet is quite as characteristic as either. It was not, however, a mob on this day, when Cosmo Livingstone stood on the stair-head in front of a little bookseller's shop, the owner of which, in high excitement, came every minute or two to the door, uttering vehement little sentences to the little crowd on his steps:—

"We'll have it oot o' them if we have to gang to St. Stephen's very doors for't!" cried the shopkeeper. "King William had better mind his crown than mind his wife. We're no' to lose the Bill for a German whimsey. Hey, laddies! dinna make so muckle clatter—they're coming! do ye hear them?"

They were coming, as the increased hum and cluster of the bystanders told clearly enough—an extraordinary procession of its kind. Without a note of music, without a tint of color, with a tramp which was not the steady tramp of trained footsteps, but only the sound of a slowly advancing crowd, to which immense excitement gave a kind of solemnity—a long line of men in their common dress, unornamented, unattended, keeping a mysterious silence, and carrying a few flags, black, and with ominous devices, which only the strain of a great climax of national feeling could have suffered to pass without that ridicule which is more fatal than state prosecutions. Nobody laughed, so far as we are aware, at the skulls and cross-bones of this voiceless procession; and the tramp of that multitude of men, timed and cheered by no music, broken by no shouts, lightened by no gleam of weapons, or glitter of emblems, or variety of color, and only accompanied by the agitated hum of the bystanders, had a very remarkable and somewhat "gruesome" impressiveness. The people who were looking on grew silent gradually, and held their breath as the long train went slowly past. It might not be a formidable band. *Punch*—if *Punch* had been in those days—might very likely have found a comfortable amount of laughter in the grim looks of the processionists, who were not likely to do much in justification of their deadly-looking flags. But the occasion was a remarkable occasion in the national history; the excitement was such—so general and overpowering—as no subsequent agitation has been able to equal. The real force of popular emotion in it covered even its own mock-heroics, which is no small thing to say; and there was something solemn in the unanimity of so many sober persons, who were not under the immediate sway and leadership of any demagogue, nor could be supposed to look for personal advantages, and whose extreme fervor and excitement at the same time were not revolutionary, but simply political. The "Bill," on which the popular hope had fixed itself, had just met with one of its failures, and this was the exaggerated, yet expressive way in which the Edinburgh crowd demonstrated the popular sentiment of the day.

These things can not be judged in cold blood; at that time everybody was excited. Cosmo Livingstone, white with boyish fervor, watched and counted them as they passed, with irresistible exclamations—"twenty, forty, sixty, eighty, a hundred!" the boy cried aloud with triumph, as score after score went past; and the women on the lower steps of the stair began to share his calculations and exult in them. The very children beneath, who were looking on with restless and excited curiosity, knew something about the "Bill," which day by day, as the coach from the south, with the London mails, came in, they had been sent to learn tidings of; and the bookseller in the little shop could not restrain himself.

"There will be news of this!" he cried, as the last detachment passed; "when the men of Edinburgh take up a matter, nothing can stand before them. There ne'er was a march like it that I ever heard o' in a' my reading. Kings, Lords, and Commons—I defy them to stand against it—how many?— hurra for Auld Reekie! Our lads, when they do a thing, never make a fool o't. Hark to the tramp of them! man, it's grand!"

"I've seen the sodgers out for far less in my day," said an old woman.

"A snuff for the sodgers!" cried the excited shopkeeper, snapping his fingers; "'a wheen mercenaries, selling their bluid for a trade. They daur nae mair face a band like that than I dare face Munch Meg."

"Oh, Cosmo—Cosmo Livingstone!" cried a voice from below; "it's me—look this way!—do you no' mind me?—I'm Joanna; come down this moment and tell us how we're to get home."

Cosmo looked down through the railings, close to the bottom of which the owner of the voice had been pressed by the crowd. She had a little silk umbrella in her hand, with the end of which, thrust between the rails, she was impatiently, and by no means lightly, beating upon his foot.

An elderly person, looking very much frightened, clung close to her arm, and a girl somewhat younger stood a little apart, looking with bright, vivacious eyes and parted lips after the disappearing procession.

The swarm of lads, of idle women and children, who followed in the wake of the Reformers, as of every other march, had overwhelmed for a moment this little group, which was not like them; and the tumult of voices, which rose when the sight was over, made it difficult to hear even Joanna, clear, loud, and unhesitating as her claim was.

"Miss Huntley!" cried Cosmo, with a momentary start—but it was not so much to witness his recognition as to save his foot from further chastisement.

"It's no' Miss Huntley—it's me!" cried Joanna; "we've lost our road— come and tell us how we're to go. Oh, madame, don't hold so fast to my arm!"

Cosmo made haste to swing himself down over the railings, when Joanna's elderly companion immediately addressed herself to him in a long and most animated speech, which, unfortunately, however, was in French, and entirely unintelligible to the poor boy. He blushed violently, and stood listening with a natural deference, but without the slightest hope of comprehending her—making now and then a faint attempt to interrupt the stream. Joanna in the meantime, who was not a great deal more enlightened than he was, vainly endeavored to stay the course of madame's eloquence by pulling her shawl and elbow.

"He does not understand you! he canna understand you!" cried Joanna, in words which, the Frenchwoman comprehended as little as Cosmo did *her* address.

During this little episode, the other girl stood by with an evident impulse to laughter, and a sparkle of amusement in her black eyes. At last she started forward with a rapid motion, said something to madame which succeeded better than the remonstrances of Joanna, and addressed Cosmo in her turn.

"Madame says," said the lively little stranger, "that she can not understand your countrymen—they are so grave, so impassionate, so sorrowful, she knows not if they march in *le corétge funêbre* or go to make the barricades. Madame says there is no music, no shouts, no voice. She demands what the *jeune Monsieur* thinks of a so grave procession."

"The men are displeased," said Cosmo, hastily; "they think that the government trifles with them, and they warn it how they feel. They don't mean to make a riot, or break the peace—we call it a demonstration here."

"A de-mon-stracion!" said the little Frenchwoman; "I shall look for it in my dictionary. They are angry with the king—*eh bien!*—why do not they fight?"

"Fight! they could fight the whole world if they liked!" cried Joanna; "but they would scorn to fight for every thing like people that have nothing else to do. Desirée and I wanted to see it, Cosmo, and madame did not know in the least where we were bringing her to—and so we got into the crowd, and I don't know how to get back to Moray Place, unless you'll show us the way."

"Madame says," said the other girl laughing, after receiving another vehement communication from the governess, "that *ce jeune Monsieur* is to go with us only to Princes Street—then we shall find our own way. He is not to go with you, *belle* Joanna; and madame demands to know what all the people say."

"What all the people say!—they're gossiping, and scolding, and speaking about the procession, and about us, and about their own concerns, and about every thing," said Joanna; "and how can I tell her? Oh, Cosmo, I've looked everywhere for you! but you never walk where we walk; and I saw your mother at the church, and I saw Katie Logan, and I told Katie to write you word to come and see me—but everybody teazes us to death about being proper; however, come along, and I'll tell you all about everybody—wasn't it grand to see the procession? Papa's a terrible Tory, and says it'll destroy the country—so I hope they'll get it. Are you for the Reform?"

"Yes," said Cosmo, but the truth was, the boy felt considerably embarrassed walking onward by the side of Joanna, with the governess and the little Frenchwoman behind, talking in their own language with a rapidity which made Cosmo dizzy, interrupted by occasional bursts of laughter from the girl, which he, being still very young and inexperienced, and highly self-conscious, could not help suspecting to be excited by himself—an idea which made him excessively awkward. However, Joanna trudged along, with her umbrella in one hand, and with the other holding up the skirt of her dress, which, however, was neither very long nor very wide. Joanna's tall figure might possibly be handsome some day—but it certainly wanted filling up and rounding in the meantime—and was not remarkably elegant at present, either in garb or gait.

But her young companion was of a very different aspect. She was little, graceful, light, with a step which, even in the High Street, reminded Cosmo of Jaacob's bit of sentiment—"a foot that rang on the path like siller bells"—with sparkling black eyes, a piquant rosy mouth, and so bright and arch a look, that the boy forgave her for laughing at himself, as he supposed she was doing. Desirée!—there was a charm too in the strange foreign name which he could not help saying over to himself—and if Joanna had been less entirely occupied with talking to him, she could not have failed to notice how little he answered, and how gravely he conducted the party to Princes Street, from whence the governess knew her way. Joanna shook hands with Cosmo heartily at parting, and told him she should write to Katie Logan to say she had seen him—while Desirée made him a pretty parting salutation, half a curtsey, with a mischievous glance out of her bright eyes, and madame made him thanks in excellent French, which the lad did not appreciate.

By that time, as he turned homeward, Cosmo had forgotten all about the procession, we are grieved to say, and was utterly indifferent to the fate of the "Bill."

He was quite confused in his thoughts, poor boy, as he betook himself to his little room and his high window. This half frolic, half adventure, which gave the two girls a little private incident to talk of, such as girls delight in, buzzed about Cosmo's brain with embarrassing pleasure. He felt half disposed to begin learning French on the instant—not that he might have a better chance of improving his acquaintance with Desirée—by no means—but only that he might never feel so awkward and so mortified again as he did to-day, when he found himself addressed in a language which he did not know.

CHAPTER XXXII

Cosmo saw nothing more of Joanna Huntley, nor of her bright-eyed companion for a long time. He fell back into his old loneliness, with his high window, and his landlady, and the Highland student for society. Cameron, whom the boy made theories about, and wistfully contemplated on the uncomprehended heights of his maturer age, knew a good deal by this time of the history of the Livingstones, a great deal more than Cosmo was aware of having told him, and had heard all about the adventure in the High Street, about Desirée's laugh and the old French grammar which Cosmo had secretly bought at a book-stall.

"If she had only taken to Latin, as the philosophers used to do at the Reformation time," cried Cosmo, with a little fun and a great deal of seriousness, "but women never learn Latin now-a-days. Why shouldn't they?"

"Does it do *us* so much good?" said Cameron, brushing a little dust carefully from the sleeve of that black coat of his, which it went to his heart to see growing rustier every day, and casting a momentary glance of almost envy at the workmen in their comfortable fustian jackets. Cameron was on his way to knock the "Rudiments" into the heads of three little boys, in whose service the gaunt Highlander tasted the sweets of "private tuition," so that at the moment he had less appreciation than usual of the learning after which he had toiled all his life.

"If any one loves scholarship, you should!" cried Cosmo, with a little enthusiasm.

"Why?" said the elder man, turning round upon him with a momentary gleam of proud offense in his eye. The Highlander wanted no applause for the martyrdoms of his life. On the contrary, it galled him to think that his privations should be taken into account by any one as proofs of his love of learning. His strong, absolute, self-denying temper wanted that last touch of frankness and candor which raises the character above detraction and above narrowness. He could not acknowledge his poverty, and take his stand upon it boldly. It was a necessity of his nature to conceal what he could manfully endure. But the glance which rested on Cosmo softened.

"Letters may be humane and humanizing, Cosmo," said the Highland student, with a little humor; "but I doubt if men feel this particular influence of them in teaching little callants. I don't think, in a general way, that either my genteel boys in Fette's Row, or my little territorial villains in St. Mary's Wynd, improve *my* humanity."

"Yet the last, at least, is purely a voluntary office and labor of love," said Cosmo, earnestly.

Cameron smiled.

"I'm but a limited man," he said; "love takes but narrow bounds with the like of me. Two or three at the most are as many as my heart can hold. Are you horrified to hear it, Cosmo? I'll do my neighbor a good turn if I can, and I'll not think ill of him if I can help it; but love, laddie, love!—that's for one friend—for a mother or—a wife—not for every common man or every bairn I see in the street and have compassion on. No! Love is a different concern."

"Is it duty, then?" said Cosmo, with a small shrug of his boyish shoulders.

"Hush! If I can not love every man I see, I can love Him who loves all!" said the Highlander, raising his high head with an unconscious loftiness and elevation of gesture. Cosmo made no answer and no comment—he was awed for the moment with the personal reality of that heavenly affection which made this limited earthly man, strong in his own characteristic individualities, and finding it impossible to abound in universal tenderness, still to do with fervor those works of the Evangelist which were for love of One who loved the all, whom he himself had not a heart expansive enough to love.

When Cameron arrived at the house of his pupils, Cosmo wandered back again toward the region of his friend's unrewarded labors;—ah! those young champions of Maudlin and Trinity!—what a difference between this picture and that. Let us confess that the chances are that Cameron, at the height of his hardly-earned scholarship, would still be a world behind a double-first; and it is likely, unless sheer strength had done it, that nothing earthly could have made a stroke-oar of the Highlandman. If any one could have watched him through the course of one of his laborious days, getting up to eat his rude and scanty breakfast, going out to his lecture and classes, from thence to one quarter and another to his pupils—little boys in the "Rudiments;" from thence to St. Mary's Wynd to do the rough pioneer evangelist work of a degraded district—work which perhaps his Divinity professor, perhaps the minister of his church urged upon him as the best preparation for his future office—then home to his garret to a meal which he would not have liked any one to see or share, to labor over his notes, to read, to get up his college work for the next day, to push forward, steadily, stoutly, silently, through almost every kind of self-denial possible to man.

Then, when the toilsome session was over, perhaps the weary man went home—not to Switzerland or Wales with a reading party—not to shoot, nor to fish, nor to travel, nor to give himself up to the pure delights of uninterrupted study—perhaps, instead, to return to weary days of manual labor, to the toils of the field, or the trials of the schoolmaster; or perhaps finding the expense of the journey too much for him, or thinking it inexpedient to risk his present pupils, lingered through the summer in Edinburgh, teaching, reading, pinching, refreshing himself by his work in St. Mary's Wynd. The result of all this was not an elegant divine, nor an accomplished man of the world—very possibly it might be an arbitrary optimist, a one-sided Christian—but it was neither an idle nor a useless man.

Some thoughts of this kind passed through the mind of Cosmo Livingstone as he went through the same St. Mary's Wynd, pondering the occupations and motives of his friend—the only comparison which he made, thinking of Cameron, was with himself; forgetting the difference of their age entirely, as such a boy was likely to do, Cosmo could not be sufficiently disgusted and discontented with his own dependence and worthlessness. Then he had, at the present moment, no particular vocation for the church. St. Mary's Wynd, so far from attracting him, even failed at this moment to convey to the visionary lad the sentiment which it wrote with words of fire upon the less sensitive mind of Cameron. Love for the inhabitants of those wretched closes—for the miserable squalid forms coming and going through those high, dark, narrow, winding stairs, down which sometimes a stray sunbeam, piercing through a dusty window, threw a violent glory into the darkness, like a Rembrandt or an indignant angel, seemed something impossible. He believed in the universal love of the Lord, but it only filled him with awe and wonder—he did not understand it as Cameron did—and Cosmo could not see how reaching ultimately into the position of teaching, preaching, laboring, wearing out, for the benefit of such a population, was worth the terrible struggle of preparation which at present taxed all the energies of his friend. He repeated to himself dutifully what he had heard— that to save a soul was better than to win a kingdom—but such words were still only of the letter, and not of the spirit, for Cosmo. And he was glad at last to escape from the subject, and hasten to the fresh and breezy solitude of the hill, which was not a mile from this den of misery, yet seemed as far away as another world.

It was spring, and the air was full of that invigorating hopefulness, which was none the worse to Cosmo for coming on a somewhat chilly breeze. The glory of the broad, blue Firth, with its islands and its bays, and the world of bright, keen, sunny air in which its few sails shone with a dazzling indescribable whiteness, like nothing but themselves—the round white clouds ranging themselves in lines and fantastic groups over the whole low varied line of the opposite coast—and the intoxication of that free, unbroken breeze, coming fresh over miles of country and leagues of sea, lifted Cosmo out of his former thoughts, only to rouse in him a vague heroical excitement—a longing after something, he knew not what, which any tangible shaping would but have vulgarized. The boy spread out his arms with an involuntary enthusiasm, drinking in that wine of youth. What would he do?—he stood upon the height of the hill like a young Mercury, ready to fly over all the world on the errands of the gods—but even the voice of Jupiter, speaking out of the clouds, would only have been prose and bathos to the unconscious, unexplainable poetic elevation of the lad, who neither knew himself nor the world.

A word of any kind, even the sublimest, would have brought him to his feet and to a vague sense of shame and self-ridicule in a moment—which consummation happened to him before he was aware.

The word was a name—a name which he had only heard once before—and the voice that spoke it was at some distance, for the sound came ringing to him, faint yet clear, brightened into a cry of pleasure by the breath of the hills on which it came. "Desirée!" The boy started, blushed at himself in the awaking of his dream, and pausing only a moment, rushed down the slope of Arthur's Seat toward Duddingstone, where, on the first practicable road which he approached, he perceived a solemn procession of young ladies, two-and-two, duly officered and governed, and behaving themselves irreproachably. Cosmo did not make a rush down through their seemly and proper ranks, to find out Desirée or Joanna; instead, the lad watched them for a moment, and then turned round laughing, and went back to his lodging—laughing the shamefaced rosy laugh of his years, when one can feel one has been a little ridiculous without feeling one's self much the worse for it, and when it strikes rather comically than painfully to find how different one's high-flown fancies are, to all the sober arrangements of the every-day world.

CHAPTER XXXIII

The end of the season arrived, Cosmo came home, leaving his fellow-student, who would not even accept an invitation to Norlaw, behind him in Edinburgh. Cameron thought it half a weakness on his part, the sudden affection to which the boy had moved him, but he would not yield so much to it as to lay himself under "an obligation," nor suffer any one to suppose that any motive whatever, save pure liking, mingled in the unlikely friendship he had permitted himself to form. Inveterate poverty teaches its victims a strange suspiciousness; he was half afraid that some one might think he wanted to share the comforts of Cosmo's home; so, as he was not going home himself, he remained in Edinburgh, working and sparing as usual, and once more expanding a little with the idea, so often proved vain hitherto, of getting so much additional work as to provide for his next session, leaving it free to its own proper studies; and Cosmo returned to rejoice the hearts of the women in Norlaw.

Who found him grown and altered, and "mair manlike," and stronger, and every way improved, to their hearts' content. The Mistress was not given to caresses or demonstrations of affection—but when the lad got home, and saw his mother's eye brighten, and her brow clear every time she looked at him, he felt, with a compunction for his own discontented thoughts, of how much importance he was to the widow, and tried hard to restrain the instinct of wandering, which many circumstances had combined to strengthen in his mind, although he had never spoken of it. Discontent with his present destination for one thing; the example of Huntley and Patrick; the perpetual spur to his energy which had been before him during all his stay in Edinburgh, in the person of Cameron; his eager visionary desire to seek Mary of Melmar, whom the boy had a strong fancy that *he* was destined to find; and, above and beyond all, a certain vague ambition, which he could not have described to any one, but which lured him with a hundred fanciful charms—moved him to the new world and the unknown places, which charmed chiefly because they were new and unknown. Cosmo had written verses secretly for a year or two, and lately had sent some to an Edinburgh paper, which, miracle of fortune! published them. He was not quite assured that he was a poet, but he thought he could be something if he might but reach that big, glorious world which all young fancies long for, and the locality of which dazzling impossible vision, is so oddly and so often placed in London. Cosmo was not sure that it was in London—but he rather thought it was not in Edinburgh, and he was very confident it could not be in Norlaw.

About the same time, Joanna Huntley came home for the long summer holidays. Joanna had persuaded her father into giving her a pony, on which she trotted about everywhere unattended, to the terror of her mother and the disgust of Patricia, who was too timid for any such impropriety. Pony and girl together, on their rambles, were perpetually falling in with Cosmo Livingstone, whom Joanna rather meant to make a friend of, and to whom she could speak on one subject which occupied, at the present time, two thirds of her disorderly thoughts, and deafened, with perpetual repetition, the indifferent household of Melmar.

This was Desirée. The first of first loves for a girl is generally another girl, or young woman, a little older than herself; and nothing can surpass the devotion of the worshiper.

Desirée was only a year older than Joanna, but she was almost every thing which Joanna was not; and she was French, and had been in Paris and London, and was of a womanly and orderly temper, which increased the difference in years. She was, for the time being, Joanna's supreme mistress, queen, and lady-love.

"I'm very glad you saw her, Cosmo," cried the girl, in one of their encounters, "because now you'll know that what I say is true. They laugh at me at Melmar; and Patricia (she's a cat!) goes on about her Clapham school, and says Desirée is only a little French governess—as if I did not know better than that!"

"Is she a governess?" asked Cosmo.

"She's a lady!" said Joanna, reddening suddenly; "but she does not pay as much as we do; and she talks French with the girls, and sometimes she helps the little ones on with their music, and—but as for a governess like madame, or like Miss Trimmer, or even Mrs. Payne herself—she is no more like one of them than you are. Cosmo. I think Desirée would like you!"

"Do you think so?" said Cosmo, with a boyish blush and laugh.

Joanna, however, was far too much occupied to notice his shamefacedness.

"I'll tell you just what I would like," she said, as they went on together, the pony rambling along at its own will, with the reins lying on its neck, while Cosmo, half-attracted, half-reluctant, walked by its side. "I don't think I should tell you either," said Joanna, "for I don't suppose you care about us. Cosmo Livingstone, I am sure, if I were you, I would hate papa; but you'll no' tell—I would like Desirée to come here and marry my brother Oswald, and be lady of Melmar. I would not care a bit what became of *me*. Though she's French, there's nobody like her; and that's just what I would choose, if I could choose for myself. Would it not be grand? But you don't know Oswald—he's been away nearly as long as I can mind; but he writes me letters sometimes, and I like him better than anybody else in the world."

"Where is he?" said Cosmo.

"He's in Italy. Whiles he writes about the places, whiles about Melmar; but he never seems to care for coming home," said Joanna. "However, I mean to write him to tell him he *must* come this summer. Your Huntley is away too. Isn't it strange to live at home always the same, and have so near a friend as a brother far, far away, and never, be able to know what he is doing? Oswald might be ill just now for any thing we know; but I mean to write and tell him he must come to see Desirée, for that is what I have set my heart upon since I knew her first."

Joanna, for sheer want of breath, came to a pause; and Cosmo made no reply. He walked on, rather puzzled by the confidence she gave him, rather troubled by this other side of the picture—the young man in Italy, who very likely thought himself the unquestionable heir, perfectly entitled to marry and bring home a lady of Melmar. The whole matter embarrassed Cosmo. Even his acquaintance with Joanna, which was not of his seeking, seemed quite out of place and inappropriate. But the girl was as totally unconscious as the pony of the things called improprieties, and had taken a friendship for Cosmo as she had taken a love for Desirée—partly because the house of Norlaw bore a certain romance to her fancy—partly because "papa would be mad"—and partly because, in all honesty, she liked the boy, who was not much older, and was certainly more refined and gentle than herself. Joanna was not remarkably amiable in her present development, but she could appreciate excellence in others.

"And she's beautiful, too—don't you think so?" said Joanna; "not pretty, like Patricia, nor bonnie, like Katie Logan—but beautiful. I wish I could bring her to Melmar—I wish Oswald could see her—and I'll do any thing in the world rather than let Desirée go to anybody's house like any other governess. Isn't it a shame? A delicate little lady like her has to go and teach little brats of children, and me that am strong and big, and could do lots of things—I never have any thing to do! I don't understand it—they say it's providence. I would not make things be like that if it was me. What do you think? You never say a word. I suppose you just listen, and laugh at me because I speak every thing out. What for do you not speak like a man?"

"A man sometimes has nothing to say, Miss Huntley," said Cosmo, with a rather whimsical shyness, which he was half-inclined himself to laugh at.

"Miss Huntley!—I'm Joanna!" cried the girl, with contempt. "I would like to be friends with you, Cosmo, because papa behaved like a wretch to your father; and many a time I think I would like to come and help Mrs. Livingstone, or do any thing for any of you. I canna keep in Melmar in a corner, and never say a word to vex folk, like Patricia, and I canna be good, like Katie Logan. Do you want to go away and no' to speak to me? You can if you like—I don't care! I know I'm no' like a lady in a ballad; but neither are you like one of the old knights of Norlaw!"

"Not if you think me rude, or dull, or ungrateful for your frankness!" cried Cosmo, touched by Joanna's appeal, and eager to make amends; but the girl pulled up the pony's reins, and darted away from him in mighty dudgeon, with the slightest touch of womanish mortification and shame heightening her childish wrath. Perhaps this was the first time it had really occurred to Joanna that, after all, there was a certain soul of truth in the proprieties which she hated, and that it might not be perfectly seemly to bestow her confidence, unasked, upon Cosmo—a confidence which was received so coldly.

She comforted herself by starting off at a pace as near a gallop as she and her steed were equal to, leaving Cosmo rather disconcerted in his turn, and not feeling particularly pleased with himself, but with many thoughts in his mind, which were not there when he left Norlaw.

CHAPTER XXXIV

Day by day, the summer went over Cosmo's head, leaving his thoughts in the same glow and tumult of uncertainty, for which, now and then, the lad blamed himself bitterly, but which, on the whole, he found very bearable. Every thing went on briskly at Norlaw. The Mistress, thoroughly occupied, and feeling herself, at last, after so many unprosperous years, really making some forward progress, daily recovered heart and spirit, and her constant supervision kept every thing alive and moving in the house. Here Cosmo filled the place of natural privilege accorded to him alike as the youngest child and the scholar-son. Though the Mistress's heart yearned over the boys who were away, she expected to be most tenderly proud of Cosmo, whose kirk and manse she could already see in prospect.

It is not a very great thing to be a minister of the Church of Scotland, but, in former days, at least, when the Church was less divided than it is now, the people of Scotland regarded with a particular tenderness of imagination the parish pastor. He was less elevated above his flock than the English rector, and sprang very seldom from the higher classes; but even among wealthy yeomen families in the country, the manse was still a kind of *beau ideal* of modest dignity and comfort, the pride and favorite fancy of the people. It was essentially so to the Mistress, whose very highest desire it had been to move her boy in this direction, and whose project of romance now, in which her imagination amused itself, was, above all other things, the future home and establishment of Cosmo. She had no idea to what extent her favorite idea was threatened in secret.

For the moment, however, Melmar and their connection with that house seemed to have died out of everybody's mind save Cosmo's. It never could quite pass from his so long as he took his place at sunset in that vacant window of the old castle, where the ivy tendrils waved about him, and where the romance of Norlaw's life seemed to have taken up its dwelling. The boy could not help wandering over the new ground which Joanna had opened to him—could not help associating that Mary of Melmar, long lost in some unknown country, with Oswald Huntley, a stranger from home for years; and the boy started with a jealous pang of pain to think how likely it was that these two might meet, and that another than his father's son should restore the inheritance to its true heir. This idea was galling in the extreme to Cosmo. He had never sympathized much in the thought that Melmar was Huntley's, nor been interested in any proceedings by which his brother's rights were to be established; but he had always reserved for himself or for Huntley the prerogative of finding and reinstating the true lady of the land, and Cosmo was human enough to regard "the present Melmar" with any thing but amiable feelings. He could not bear the idea of being left out entirely in the management of the concern, or of one of the Huntleys exercising this champion's office, and covering the old usurpation with a vail of new generosity. It was a most uncomfortable view of the subject to Cosmo, and when his cogitations came to that point, the lad generally swung himself down from his window-seat and went off somewhere in high excitement, scarcely able to repress the instant impulse to sling a bundle over his shoulder and set off upon his journey. But he never could rouse his courage to the point of reopening this subject with his mother, little witting, foolish boy, that this admirable idea of his about Oswald Huntley was the very inducement necessary to make the Mistress as anxious about the recovery of Mary of Melmar as he himself was—and the only thing in the world which could have done so.

It happened on one of these summer evenings, about this time, when his own mind was exceedingly restless and unsettled, that Cosmo, passing through Kirkbride as the evening fell, encountered bowed Jaacob just out of the village, on the Melrose road. The village street was full of little groups in earnest and eager discussion. It was still daylight, but the sun was down, and lights began to sparkle in some of the projecting gable windows of the Norlaw Arms, beneath which, in the corner where the glow of the smithy generally warmed the air, a little knot of men stood together, fringed round with smaller clusters of women. A little bit of a moon, scarcely so big as the evening star which led her, was already high in the scarcely shadowed skies. Every thing was still—save the roll of the widow's mangle and the restless feet of the children, so many of them as at this hour were out of bed—and most of the cottage doors stood open, revealing each its red gleam of fire, and many their jugs of milk, and bowls set ready on the table for the porridge or potatoes which made the evening meal. On the opposite brae of Tyne was visible the minister, walking home with an indescribable consciousness and disapproval, not in his face, for it was impossible to see that in the darkness, but in his figure and bearing, as he turned his back upon his excited parishioners, which was irresistibly ludicrous when one knew what it meant. Beyond the village, at the opposite extremity, was Jaacob, in his evening trim, with a black coat and hat, which considerably changed the little dwarf's appearance, without greatly improving it. He had his face to the south, and was pushing on steadily, clenching and opening, as he walked, the great brown fist which came so oddly out of the narrow cuff of his black coat. Cosmo, who was quite ready to give up his own vague fancies for the general excitement, came up to Jaacob quite eagerly, and fell into his pace without being aware of it.

"Are you going to Melrose for news? I'll go with you," said Cosmo.

The road was by no means lonely; there were already both men and boys before them on the way.

"We should hear to-night, as you ken without me telling you," said Jaacob. "I'm gaun to meet the coach; you may come if you like—but what matter is't to the like o' you?"

"To me! as much as to any man in Scotland," cried Cosmo, growing red; he thought the dignity of his years was impugned.

"Pish! you're a blackcoat, going to be," said Jaacob; "there's your friend the minister there, gaun up the brae. I sent *him* hame wi' a flea in his lug. What the deevil business has the like of him to meddle in our concerns? The country's coming to ruin, forsooth! because the franchise is coming to a man like me! Get away with you, callant! as soon as you come to man's estate you'll be like a' the rest! But ye may just as weel take an honest man's, advice, Cosmo. If we dinna get it we'll tak it, and that'll be seen before the world afore mony days are past."

"What do you think the news will be?" asked Cosmo.

"Think! I'm past thinking," cried Jaacob, thrusting some imaginary person away; "haud your tongue—can a man think when he's wound up the length of taking swurd in hand, if need should be? If we dinna get it, we'll tak it—do ye hear?—that's a' I'm thinking in these days."

And Jaacob swung along the road, working his long arms rather more than he did his feet, so that their action seemed part of his locomotive power. It was astonishing, too, to see how swiftly, how steadily, and with what a "way" upon him, the little giant strode onward, swinging the immense brown hands, knotted and sinewy, which it was hard to suppose could ever have been thrust through the narrow cuffs of his coat, like balancing weights on either side of him. Before them was the long line of dusty summer road disappearing down a slope, and cut off, not by the sky, but by the Eildons, which began to blacken in the fading light—behind them the lights of the village—above, in a pale, warm sky, the one big dilating star and the morsel of moon; but the thoughts of Jaacob, and even of Cosmo, were on a lesser luminary—the red lantern of the coach, which was not yet to be seen by the keenest eyes advancing through the summer dimness from the south.

"Hang the lairds and the ministers!" cried Jaacob, after a pause, "it's easy to see what a puir grip they have, and how well they ken it. Free institutions dinna agree with the like of primogeniture and thae inventions of the deevil. Let's but hae a reformed Parliament, and we'll learn them better manners. There's your grand Me'mar setting up for a leader amang the crew, presenting an address, confound his impudence! as if he wasna next hand to a swindler himself."

"Jacob, do you know any thing about his son?" asked Cosmo, eagerly.

"He's a virtuoso—he's a dilettawnti; I ken nae ill of him," said Jaacob, who pronounced these titles with a little contempt, yet secretly had a respect for them; "he hasna been seen in this country, so far as I've heard tell of, for mony a day. A lad's no aye to blame for his father and his mother; it's a thing folk in general have nae choice in—but he's useless to his ain race, either as friend or foe."

"Is he a good fellow, then? or is he like Me'mar?" cried Cosmo.

"Tush! dinna afflict me about thae creatures in bad health," said Jaacob; "what's the use o' them, lads or lasses, is mair than I can tell—can they no' dee and be done wi't? I tell you, a docken on the roadside is mair guid to a country than the like of Me'mar's son!"

"Is he in bad health?" asked the persistent Cosmo.

"They're a' in bad health," said Jaacob, contemptuously, "as any auld wife could tell you; a' but that red-haired lassie, that Joan. Speak o' your changelings! how do ye account to me, you that's a philosopher, for the like of an honest spirit such as that, cast into the form of a lassie, and the midst of a hatching o' sparrows like Me'mar? If she had but been a lad, she would have turned them a' out like a cuckoo in the nest."

"And Oswald Huntley is ill—an invalid?" said Cosmo, softly returning to the thread of his own thoughts.

Jaacob once more thrust with contempt some imaginary opponent out of the way.

"Get away with you down Tyne or into the woods wi' your Oswald Huntleys!" cried Jaacob, indignantly—"do you think I'm heeding about ane of the name? Whisht! what's that? Did you hear onything?—haud your tongue for your life!"

Cosmo grew almost as excited as Jaacob—he seized upon the lowest bough of a big ash tree, and swung himself up, with the facility of a country boy, among the fragrant dark foliage which rustled about him as he stood high among the branches as on a tower.

"D'ye see onything?" cried Jaacob, who could have cuffed the boy for the noise he made, even while he pushed him up from beneath.

"Hurra! here she comes—I can see the light!" shouted Cosmo.

The lad stood breathless among the rustling leaves, which hummed about him like a tremulous chorus. Far down at the foot of the slope, nothing else perceptible to mask its progress, came rushing on the fiery eye of light, red, fierce, and silent, like some mysterious giant of the night. It was impossible to hear either hoofs or wheels in the distance, still more to see the vehicle itself, for the evening by this time was considerably advanced, and the shadow of the three mystic hills lay heavy upon the road.

"She's late," said Jaacob, between his set teeth. The little Cyclops held tight by the great waving bough of the ash, and set his foot in a hollow of its trunk, crushing beneath him the crackling underwood. Here the boy and he kept together breathless, Cosmo standing high above, and his companion thrusting his weird, unshaven face over the great branch on which he leaned. "She's up to Plover ha'—she's at the toll—she's stopped. What's that! listen!" cried Cosmo, as some faint, far-off sound, which might have been the cry of a child, came on the soft evening air towards them.

Jaacob made an imperative gesture of silence with one hand, and grasped at the branch with the other till it shook under the pressure.

"She's coming on again—she's up to the Black ford—she's over the bridge—another halt—hark again!—that's not for passengers—they're hurraing—hark, Jaacob! hurra! she's coming—they've won the day!"

Jaacob, with the great branch swinging under his hands like a willow bough, bade the boy hold his peace, with a muttered oath through his set teeth. Now sounds became audible, the rattle of the hoofs upon the road, the ring of the wheels, the hum of exclamations and excited voices, under the influence of which the horses "took the brae" gallantly, with a half-human intoxication. As they drew gradually nearer, and the noise increased, and the faint moonlight fell upon the flags and ribbons and dusty branches, with which the coach was ornamented, Cosmo, unable to contain himself, came rolling down on his hands and feet over the top of Jaacob, and descended with a bold leap in the middle of the road. Jaacob, muttering fiercely, stumbled after him, just in time to drag the excited boy out of the way of the coach, which was making up for lost time by furious speed, and on which coachman, guard, and outside passengers, too much excited to be perfectly sober, kept up their unanimous murmurs of jubilee, with only a very secondary regard to the road or any obstructions which might be upon it.

"Wha's there? get out o' my road, every soul o' ye! I'll drive the gait blindfold, night or day, but I'll no' undertake the consequence if ye rin among my wheels," cried the driver.

"Hurra! lads! the Bill's passed—we've won! Hurra!" shouted another voice from the roof of the vehicle, accompanying the shout with a slightly unsteady wave of a flag, while, with a little swell of sympathetic cheers, and a triumphant flourish of trumpet from the guard, the jubilant vehicle dashed on, rejoicing as never mail-coach rejoiced before.

Jaacob took off his hat, tossed it into the air, crushed it between his hands as it came down, and broke into an extraordinary shout, bellow, or groan, which it was impossible to interpret; then, turning sharp round, pursued the coach with a fierce speed, like the run of a little tiger, setting all his energies to it, swinging his long arms on either side of him, and raising about as much dust as the mail which he followed. Cosmo, left behind, followed more gently, laughing in spite of himself, and in spite of the heroics of the day, which included every national benefit and necessity within the compass of "the Bill," at the grotesque little figure disappearing before him, twisting its great feet, and swinging its arms in that extraordinary race. When the boy reached Kirkbride, the coach was just leaving the village amid a chorus of cheers and shouts of triumph. No one could think of any thing else, or speak of any thing else; everybody was shaking hands with everybody, and in the hum of amateur speechifying, half a dozen together, Cosmo had hard work to recall even that sober personage, the postmaster, who felt himself to some extent a representative of government and natural moderator of the general excitement, to some sense of his duties. Cosmo's exertions, however, were rewarded by the sight of three letters, with which he hastened home.

CHAPTER XXXV

"The Reform Bill's passed, mother! we've won the day!" cried Cosmo, rushing into the Norlaw dining-parlor with an additional hurra! of exultation. After all the din and excitement out of doors, the summer twilight of the room, with one candle lighted and one unlit upon the table, and the widow seated by herself at work, the only one living object in the apartment, looked somewhat dreary—but she looked up with a brightening face, and lighted the second candle immediately on her son's return.

"Eh, laddie, that's news!" cried the Mistress; "are you sure it's true? I didna think, for my part, the Lords had as much sense. Passed! come to be law!—eh, my Huntley! to think he's at the other end of the world and canna hear."

"He'll hear in time," said Cosmo, with a little agitation, producing his budget of letters. "Mother, I've more news than about the Bill. I've a letter here."

His mother rose and advanced upon him with characteristic vehemence:—

"Do you dare to play with your mother, you silly bairn? Give it to me," said the Mistress, whom Cosmo's hurried, breathless, joyful face had already enlightened; "do you think I canna bear gladness, me that never fainted with sorrow? Eh Huntley, my bairn!"

And in spite of her indignation, Huntley's mother sank into the nearest chair, and let her tears fall on his letter as she opened it. It did not, however, prove to be the intimation of his arrival, which they hoped for. It was written at sea, three months after his departure, when he was still not above half way on his journey; for it was a more serious business getting to Australia in those days than it is now. Huntley wrote out of his little berth in the middle of the big ocean, with all the strange creaks of the ship and voices of his fellow-passengers to bear him company, with a heart which was still at Norlaw. The Mistress tried very hard to read his letter aloud; she drew first one and then the other candle close to her, exclaiming against the dimness of the light; she stopped in the middle of a sentence, with something very like a sob, to bid Cosmo sharply be quiet and no' interrupt her, like a restless bairn, while she read his brother's letter; but at last the Mistress broke down and tried no further. It was about ten months since she bade him farewell, and this was the first token of Huntley's real person and existence which for all that lingering and weary time had come to his mother, who had never missed him out of her sight for a week at a time, all his life before.

There was not a very great deal in it even now, for letter-writing had been a science little practiced at Norlaw, and Huntley had still nothing to tell but the spare details of a long sea voyage; there was, however, in it, what there is not in all letters, nor in many—even much more affectionate and effusive epistles than this—Huntley himself. When the Mistress had come to the end, which was but slowly, in consideration of the dimness of the candles or her eyes, she gave it to Cosmo, and waited rather impatiently for his perusal of the precious letter. Then she went over it again, making hasty excuse, as she did so; for "one part I didna make out," and finally, unable to refrain, got up and went to the kitchen, where Marget was still busy, to communicate the good news.

The kitchen door was open; there was neither blind nor shutter upon the kitchen-window, and the soft summer stars, now peeping out in half visible hosts like cherubs, might look in upon Marget, passing back and forward through the fire light, as much and as often as they pleased. From the open door a soft evening breath of wind, with the fragrance of new growth and vegetation upon it, which is almost as sweet as positive odors, came pleasantly into the ruddy apartment, where the light found a hundred bright points to sparkle in, from the "brass pan" and copper kettle on the shelf to the thick yolks of glass in one or two of the window-panes. It was not quite easy to tell what Marget was doing; she was generally busy, moving about with a little hum of song, setting every thing in order for the night.

"Marget, my woman, you'll be pleased to hear—I've heard from my son," said the Mistress, with unusual graciousness. She came and stood in front of the fire, waiting to be questioned, and the fire light still shone with a very prismatic radiance through the Mistress's eyelashes, careful though she had been, before she entered, to remove the dew from her eyes.

"You're no' meaning Mr. Huntley? Eh! bless him! has he won there?" cried Marget, letting down her kilted gown, and hastening forward.

And then the Mistress was tempted to draw forth her letter, and read "a bit here and a bit there," which the faithful servant received with sobs and exclamations.

"Bless the laddie, he minds every single thing at Norlaw—even the like of me!" cried Marget; upon which the Mistress rose again from the seat she had taken, with a little start of impatience:—

"Wherefore should he no' mind you?—you've been about the house a' his life; and I hope I'll never live to see the day when a bairn of mine forgets his hame and auld friends! It's time to bar the door, and put up the shutter. You should have had a' done, and your fire gathered by this time; but it's a bonnie night!"

"'Deed, ay!" said Marget to herself, when Huntley's mother had once more joined Cosmo in the dining-room; "the bonniest night that's been to her this mony a month, though she'll no' let on—as if I didna ken how her heart yearns to that laddie on the sea, blessings on him! Eh, sirs! to think o' thae very stars shining on the auld castle and the young laird, though the world itsel's between the twa—and the guid hand of Providence ower a'— God be thanked!—to bring the bairn hame!"

When the Mistress returned to the dining-parlor, she found Cosmo quite absorbed with another letter. The lad's face was flushed with half-abashed pleasure, and a smile, shy, but triumphant, was on his lip. It was not Patie's periodical letter, which still lay unopened before her own chair, where it had been left in the overpowering interest of Huntley's. The Mistress was not perfectly pleased. To care for what anybody else might write—"one of his student lads, nae doubt, or some other fremd person," in presence of the first letter from Huntley, was almost a slight to her first-born.

"You're strange creatures, you laddies," said the Mistress. "I dinna understand you, for my part. There are you, Cosmo Livingstone, as pleased about your nonsense letter, whatever it may be, as if there was no such person as my Huntley in the world—him that aye made such a wark about you!"

"This is not a nonsense letter—will you read it, mother?" said Cosmo.

"Me!—I havena lookit at Patie's letter yet!" cried the Mistress, indignantly. "Do you think I'm a person to be diverted with what one callant writes to another? Hold your peace, bairn, and let me see what my son says."

The Mistress accordingly betook herself to Patrick's letter with great seriousness and diligence, keeping her eyes steadily upon it, and away from Cosmo, whom, nevertheless, she could still perceive holding *his* letter, his own especial correspondence, with the same look of shy pleasure, in his hand. Patie's epistle had nothing of remarkable interest in it, as it happened, and the Mistress could not quite resist a momentary and troubled speculation, Who was Cosmo's correspondent, who pleased him so much, yet made him blush? Could it be a woman? The idea made her quite angry in spite of herself—at his age!

"Now, mother, read this," said Cosmo, with the same smile.

"If it's any kind of bairn's nonsense, dinna offer it to me," said the Mistress, impatiently. "Am I prying into wha writes you letters? I tell you I've had letters enough for ae night. Peter Todhunter!—wha in the world is he?"

"Read it, mother," repeated Cosmo.

The Mistress read in much amazement; and the epistle was as follows:

"North British Courant Office,
"Edinburgh.

"Dear Sir,

"Hearing that you are the C. L. N. who have favored the *North British Courant* from time to time with poetical effusions which seem to show a good deal of talent, I write to ask whether you have ever done any thing in the way of prose romance, or essays of a humorous character in the style of Sterne, or narrative poetry. I am just about to start (with a good staff of well-known contributors) a new monthly, to be called the *Auld Reekie Magazine,* a miscellany of general literature; and should be glad to receive and give my best consideration to any articles from your pen. The rates of remuneration I can scarcely speak decisively about until the success of this new undertaking is in some degree established; but this I may say—that they shall be *liberal* and *satisfactory,* and I trust may be the means of inaugurating a new and better system of mutual support between publishers and authors—the accomplishment of which has long been a great object of my life.

"Your obedient servant,
"Peter Todhunter."

"The *North British Courant!* poetry! writing for a magazine!—what does it a' mean?" cried the Mistress. "Do you mean to tell me you're an author, Cosmo Livingstone?—and me never kent—a bairn like you!"

"Nothing but some—verses, mother," said the boy, with a blush and a laugh, though he was not insensible to the importance of Mr. Todhunter's communication. Cosmo's vanity was not sufficiently rampant to say poems. "I did not send them with my name. I wanted to do something better before I showed them to you."

"And here they're wanting the callant for a magazine!" cried the Mistress. "Naething but a bairn—the youngest! a laddie that was never out of Norlaw till within six months time! And I warrant they ken what's for their ain profit, and what kind of a lad they're seeking after—and me this very night thinking him nae better than a bairn!"

And the Mistress laughed in the mood of exquisite pride at its highest point of gratification, and followed up her laugh by tears of the same. The boy was pleased, but his mother was intoxicated. The *North British Courant* and the *Auld Reekie Magazine* were glorious in her eyes as celestial messengers of fame, and she could not but follow the movements of her boy with the amazed observation of a sudden discovery. He who was "naething but a bairn" had already proved himself a genius, and Literature urgent called him to her aid. He might be a Scott—he might turn out a Shakespeare. The Mistress looked at him with no limit to her wonder, and for the moment none in her faith.

"And just as good a laddie as he aye was," she murmured to herself, stroking his hair fondly—"though mony a ane's head would have been clean turned to see themsels in a printed paper—no' to say in a book. Eh, bairn! and to think how little I kent, that am your mother, what God had put among my very bairns!"

"Mother, it may turn out poor enough, after all," cried Cosmo, half ashamed—"I don't know yet myself what I can do."

"I daresay no'," said the Mistress, proudly, "but you may take my word this decent man does, Cosmo, seeing his ain interest is concerned. Na, laddie, *I* ken, if you dinna, the ways of this world, and I wouldna say but they think they've got just a prize in my bairn. Eh! if the laddies were but here and kent!—and oh, Cosmo! what *he* would have thought of it that's gone!"

When the Mistress had dried her eyes, she managed to draw from the boy a gradual confession that the *North British Courant,* sundry numbers of it, were snugly hid in his own trunk up stairs, from which concealment they were brought forth with much shamefacedness by Cosmo, and read with the greatest triumph by his mother. The Mistress had no mind to go to rest that night—she staid up looking at him—wondering over him; and Cosmo confessed to some of his hitherto secret fancies—how he would like to go abroad to see new countries, and to hear strange tongues, and how he had longed to labor for himself.

"Whisht! laddie—I would have been angry but for this," said the Mistress. "The like of you has nae call to work; but I canna say onything mair, Cosmo, now that Providence has taken it out of my hand. And I dinna wonder you would like to travel—the like of you canna be fed on common bread like common folk—and you'll hae to see every thing if you're to be an author. Na, laddie, no' for the comfort of seeing you and hearing you would I put bars on your road. I aye thought I would live to be proud of my sons, but I didna ken I was to be overwhelmed in a moment, and you naething but a bairn!"

CHAPTER XXXVI

The result of this conversation was that Cosmo made a little private visit to Edinburgh to determine his own entrance into the republic of letters, and to see the enterprising projector of the *Auld Reekie Magazine* through whom this was to take place. The boy went modestly, half abashed by his good fortune and dawning dream of fame, yet full of a flush of youthful hope, sadly out of proportion to any possible pretensions of the new periodical. He saw it advertised in the newspaper which one of his fellow-passengers on the coach read on the way. He saw a little printed hand-bill with its illustrious name in the window of the first bookseller's shop he looked into on his arrival in Edinburgh, and Cosmo marched over the North Bridge with his carpet-bag in his hand, with a swell of visionary glory. He could not help half wondering what the indifferent people round him would think, if they knew—and then could not but blush at himself for the fancy. Altogether the lad was in a tumult of delightful excitement, hope, and pleasure, such as perhaps only falls to the lot of boys who hope themselves poets, and think at eighteen that they are already appreciated and on the highway to fame.

As he ascended the stairs to Mrs. Purdie's, he met Cameron coming down. There was a very warm greeting between them—a greeting which surprise startled into unusual affectionateness on the part of the Highlander. Cameron forgot his own business altogether to return with Cosmo, and needed very little persuasion to enter the little parlor, which no other lodger had turned up to occupy, and share the refreshment which the overjoyed landlady made haste to prepare for her young guest. This was so very unusual a yielding on Cameron's part, that Cosmo almost forgot his own preoccupation in observing his friend, who altogether looked brightened and smoothed out, and younger than when they parted. The elder and soberer man, who knew a little more of life and the world than Cosmo, though very little more of literature, could not help a half-perceptible smile at the exuberance of Cosmo's hopes. Not that Cameron despised the *Auld Reekie Magazine*; far from that, the Divinity student had all the reverence for literature common to those who know little about it, which reverence, alas! grows smaller and smaller in this too-knowing age. But at thirty years old people know better than at eighteen how the sublimest undertakings break down, and how sometimes even "the highest talent" can not float its venture. So the man found it hard not to smile at the boy's shy triumph and undoubting hope, yet could not help but be proud, notwithstanding, with a tenderness almost feminine, of the unknown gifts of the lad, whose youth, he could not quite tell how, had found out the womanish corner of his own reserved heart, in which, as he said himself, only two or three could find room at any time.

"But you never told me of these poetical effusions, Cosmo," said his friend, as he put up the bookseller's note.

"Don't laugh at Mr. Todhunter. *I* only call them verses," said Cosmo, with that indescribable blending of vanity and humility which belongs to his age; "and I knew you would not care for them; they were not worth showing to you."

"I'm not a poetical man," said Cameron, "but I might care for *your* verses in spite of that; and now Cosmo, laddie, while you have been thinking of fame, what novel visitor should you suppose had come to me?"

"Who?—what?" cried Cosmo, with eager interest.

"What?" echoed Cameron, "either temptation or good fortune—it's hard to say which—only I incline to the first. Satan's an active chield, and thinks little of trouble; but I doubt if the other one would have taken the pains to climb my stair. I've had an offer of a tutorship, Cosmo—to go abroad for six months or so with a callant like yourself."

"To go abroad!" Cosmo's eyes lighted up with instant excitement, and he stretched his hand across the table to his friend, with a vehemence which Cameron did not understand, though he returned the grasp.

"An odd enough thing for me," said the Highlandman, "but the man's an eccentric man, and something has possessed him that his son would be in safe hands; as in safe hands he might be," added the student in an undertone, "seeing I would be sorry to lead any lad into evil—but as for *fit* hands, that's to be seen, and I'm far from confident it would be right for me."

"Go, and I'll go with you," said Cosmo, eagerly. "I've set my heart upon it for years."

"More temptation!" said the Highlandman. "Carnal inclinations and pleasures of this world—and I've little time to lose. I can not afford a session—whisht! Comfort and ease to the flesh, and pleasure to the mind, are hard enough to fight with by themselves without help from you."

It was almost the first time he had made the slightest allusion to his own hard life and prolonged struggle, and Cosmo was silent out of respect and partially in the belief that if Cameron's mind had not been very near made up in favor of this new proposal, he would not have suffered himself to refer to it. The two friends sat up late together that night. Cosmo pouring out all his maze of half-formed plans and indistinct intentions into Cameron's ears—his projects of authorship, his plan for a tragedy of which Wallace wight should be the hero; of a pastoral poem and narrative, something between Colin Clout and the Gentle Shepherd—and of essays and philosophies without end; while Cameron on his part smiled, as he could not but smile by right of his thirty years, yet somehow began to believe, like the Mistress, in the enthusiastic boy, with all that youthful flush and fervor in the face which his triumph and inspiration of hope made beautiful. The elder man could not give his own confidence so freely as Cosmo did, but he opened himself as far as it was his nature to do, in droppings of shy frankness—a little now and a little then—which were in reality the very highest compliment which such a man could pay to his companion. When they separated, Cameron, it is true, knew all about Cosmo, while Cosmo did not know all about Cameron; but the difference was not even so much a matter of temperament as of years, and the lad, without hearing many particulars, or having a great deal of actual confidence given to him, knew the man better at the end of this long evening than ever he had done before.

In the morning Cosmo got up full of pleasurable excitement, and set out early to call on Mr. Todhunter. The *North British Courant* office was in one of the short streets which run between Princes Street and George Street, and in the back premises, a long way back, through a succession of rooms, Cosmo was ushered into the especial little den of the publisher. Mr. Todhunter was of a yellow complexion, with loose, thick lips, and wiry black hair. The lips were the most noticeable feature in his face, from the circumstance that when he spoke his mouth seemed uncomfortably full of moisture, which gave also a peculiar character to his voice. He was surrounded by a mass of papers, and had paste and scissors—those palladiums of the weekly press—by his side. If there was one thing more than another on which the *North British Courant* prided itself, it was on the admirable collection of other people's opinions which everybody might find in its columns. Mr. Todhunter made no very great stand upon politics. What he prized was a reputation which he thought "literary," and a skill almost amounting to genius for making what he called "excerpts."

"Very glad to make your personal acquaintance, Mr. Livingstone," said the projector of the *Auld Reekie Magazine*, "and still more to receive your assurances of support. I've set my heart on making this a real, impartial, literary enterprise, sir—no' one of your close boroughs, as they say now-a-days, for a dozen or a score of favored contributors, but open to genius, sir—genius wherever it may be—rich or poor."

Cosmo did not know precisely what to answer, so he filled in the pause with a little murmur of assent.

"Ye see the relations of every thing's changing," said Mr. Todhunter; "old arrangements will not do—wull not answer, sir, in an advancing age. I have always held high opinions as to the claims of literary men, myself—it's against my nature to treat a man of genius like a shopkeeper; and my principle, in the *Auld Reekie Magazine*, is just this—first-rate talent to make the thing pay, and first-rate pay to secure the talent. That's my rule, and I think it's a very safe guide for a plain man like me."

"And it's sure to succeed," said Cosmo, with enthusiasm.

"I think it wull, sir—upon my conscience, if you ask me, I think it wull," said Mr. Todhunter; "and I have little doubt young talent will rally round the *Auld Reekie Magazine*. I'm aware it's an experiment, but nothing shall ever make me give in to an ungenerous principle. Men of genius must be protected, sir; and how are they protected in your old-established periodicals? There's one old fogy for this department, and another old fogy for that department; and as for a genial recognition of young talent, take my word for't, there's no such thing."

"I know," said Cosmo, "it is the hardest thing in the world to get in. Poor Chatterton, and Keats, and—"

"Just that," said Mr. Todhunter. "It's for the Keatses and the Chattertons of this day, sir, that I mean to interpose; and no lad of genius shall go to the grave with a pistol in his hand henceforward if I can help it. I admire your effusions very much, Mr. Livingstone—there's real heart and talent in them, sir—in especial the one to Mary, which, I must say, gave me the impression of an older man."

"I am pretty old in practice—I have been writing a great many years," said Cosmo, with that delightful, ingenuous, single-minded, youthful vanity, which it did one's heart good to see. Even Mr. Todhunter, over his paste and scissors, was somehow illumined by it, and looked up at the lad with the ghost of a smile upon his watery lips.

"And what do you mean to provide us for the opening of the feast?" said the bookseller, "which must be ready by the 15th, at the very latest, and be the very cream of your inspiration. It's no small occasion, sir. Have you made up your mind what is to be your *deboo*?"

"It depends greatly upon what you think best," said Cosmo, candid and impartial; "and as you know what articles you have secured already, I should be very glad of any hint from you."

"A very sensible remark," said Mr. Todhunter. "Well, I would say, a good narrative now, in fine, stirring, ballad verse—a narrative always pleases the public fancy—or a spirited dramatic sketch, or a historical tale, to be completed, say, in the next number. I should say, sir, any one of these would answer the *Auld Reekie*;—only be on your mettle. I consider there's good stuff in you—real good stuff—but, at the same time, many prudent persons would tell me I was putting too much reliance on so young a man."

"I will not disappoint you," said Cosmo, with a little pride; "but, supposing this first beginning over, could it do any good to the magazine, do you think, to have a contributor—letters from abroad—I had some thoughts—I—I wished very much to know—"

"Were you thinking of going abroad?" said the bookseller, benignantly.

"I can scarcely say *think*—but, there was an opportunity," said Cosmo, with a blush; "that is, if it did not stand in the way of—"

"*Auld Reekie?* Certainly not—on the contrary, I know nothing I would like better," said Mr. Todhunter. "Some fine Italian legends, now, or a few stories from the Rhine, with a pleasant introduction, and a little romantic incident, to show how you heard them—capital! but I must see you at my house before you go. And as for the remuneration, we can scarcely fix on that, perhaps, till the periodical's launched—but ye know my principle, and I may say, sir, with confidence, no man was left in the lurch that put reliance upon me. I'm a plain man, as you see me, but I appreciate the claims of genius, and young talent shall not want its platform in this city of Edinburgh; or, if it does, it shall be no fault of mine."

With a murmured applause of this sentiment, and in a renewed tumult of pleasure, Cosmo left his new friend, and went home lingering over the delightful thought of Italian legends and stories of the Rhine, told in the very scenes of the same. The idea intoxicated him almost out of remembrance of Mary of Melmar, and if the boy's head was not turned, it seemed in a very fair way of being so, for the sentiments of Mr. Todhunter—a publisher!—a practical man!—one who knew the real value of authorship! filled the lad with a vague glory in his new craft. A London newspaper proprietor, who spoke like the possessor of the *North British Courant*, would have been, the chances are, a conscious humbug, and perhaps so might an Edinburgh bookseller of the present time, who expressed the same sentiments. Mr. Todhunter, however, was not a humbug. He was like one of those dabblers in science who come at some simple mechanical principle by chance, and in all the flush of their discovery, claim as original and their own what was well known a hundred years since. He was perfectly honest in the rude yet simple vanity with which he patronized "young talent," and in his vulgar, homely fashion, felt that he had quite seized upon a new idea in his *Auld Reekie Magazine*—an idea too original and notable to yield precedence even to the *Edinburgh Review*.

CHAPTER XXXVII

The pace of events began to quicken with Cosmo. When he encountered his fellow-lodger in the evening, he found that Cameron had been permitting his temptation to gain more and more ground upon him. The Highlander, humbly born and cottage bred as he was, and till very recently bounded by the straitest prospects as to the future, had still a deep reserve of imaginative feeling, far away down where no one could get at it—under the deposit left by the slow toil and vulgar privations of many years. Unconsciously to himself, the presence and society of Cosmo Livingstone had recalled his own boyhood to the laboring man, in the midst of that sweat of his brow in which he ate his scanty bread in the Edinburgh garret. Where was there ever boyhood which had not visions of adventure and dreams of strange countries? All that last winter, through which his boy companion stole into his heart, recollections used to come suddenly upon the uncommunicating Highlander of hours and fancies in his own life, which he supposed he had long ago forgotten—hours among his own hills, herding sheep, when he lay looking up at the skies, and entranced by the heroic lore with which he was most familiar, thinking of David's well at Bethlehem, and the wine-press where Gideon thrashed his wheat, and the desert waters where Moses led his people, and of all the glorious unknown world beside, through which his path must lie to the Holy Land. Want, and labor, and the steady, desperate aim, with which he pushed through every obstacle towards the one goal of his ambition, had obscured these visions in his mind, but Cosmo's fresh boyhood woke them by degrees, and the unusual and unexpected proposal lately made to him, had thrilled the cooled blood in Cameron's veins as he did not suppose it could be thrilled. Ease, luxury (to him), and gratification in the meantime, with a reserve fund great enough to carry him through a session without any extra labor. Why did he hesitate? He hesitated simply because it might put off for six months—possibly for a year—the accomplishment of his own studies and the gaining of that end, which was not a certain living, however humble, but merely a license to preach, and his chance with a hundred others of a presentation to some poor rural parish, or a call from some chapel of ease. But he did hesitate long and painfully. He feared, in his austere self-judgment, to prefer his own pleasure to the work of God, and it was only when his boy-favorite came back again and threw all his fervid youthful influence into the scale, that Nature triumphed with Cameron, and that he began to permit himself to remember that, toilworn as he was, he was still young, and that the six months' holiday might, after all, be well expended. The very morning after Cosmo's arrival, after lying awake thinking of it half the night, he had gone to the father of his would-be-pupil to explain the condition on which he would accept the charge, which was, that Cosmo might be permitted to join the little party. Cameron's patron was a Highlander, like himself—obstinate, one-sided, and imperious. He did not refuse the application. He only issued instant orders that Cosmo should be presented to him without delay, that he might judge of his fitness as a traveling companion—and Cameron left him, pledged, if his decision should be favorable, to accept the office.

The next day was a great day in Edinburgh—an almost universal holiday, full of flags, processions, and all manner of political rejoicings— the Reform Jubilee. Cosmo plunged into the midst of it with all the zeal of a young politician and all the zest of a school-boy, and was whirled about by the crowd through all its moods and phases, through the heat, and the dust, and the sunshine, through the shouts and groans, the applauses and the denunciations, to his heart's content. He came in breathless somewhere about midday, as he supposed, though in reality it was late in the afternoon, to snatch a hurried morsel of the dinner which Mrs. Purdie had vainly endeavored to keep warm for him, and to leave a message for Cameron to be ready for him in the evening, to go out and see the illumination. When Cosmo reappeared again, flushed, tired, excited, yet perfectly ready to begin once more, it was already darkening towards night. Cameron was ready, and the boy was not to be persuaded to lose the night and "the fun," which already began to look rather like mischief. The two companions, so unlike each other, made haste to the Calton Hill, where a great many people had already preceded them. Oh, dwellers on the plains! oh, cockney citizens!—spite of your gas stars and your transparencies—your royal initials and festoons of lamps, don't suppose that you know any thing about an illumination; you should have seen the lines of light stealing from slope to slope along the rugged glory of that antique Edinburgh—the irregular gleams descending into the valley, the golden threads, here and there broken, that intersected the regular lines of the new town. Yonder tall houses, seven stories high, where every man is a Reformer, and where the lights come out in every window, star by star, in a flicker and glow, as if the very weakness of those humble candles gave them the animation and humanness of a breathing triumph—swelling higher towards the dark Castle, over whose unlighted head the little moon looks down, a serene spectator of all this human flutter and commotion—undulating down in rugged breaks towards lowly Holyrood, sometimes only a thin line visible beneath the roof—sometimes a whole house aglow. The people went and came, in excited groups, upon the fragrant grass of the Calton Hill; sometimes turning to the other side of the landscape, to see the more sparely lighted streets of gentility, or the independent little sparkle which stout little Leith in the distance threw out upon the Firth—but always returning with unfailing fascination to this scene of magic—the old town shining with its lamps and jewels, like a city in a dream.

But it was not destined to be a perfectly calm summer evening's spectacle. The hum of the full streets grew riotous even to the spectators on the hill. Voices rose above the hum, louder than peaceful voices ever rise. The triumph was a popular triumph, and like every other such, had its attendant mob of mischief. Shouts of rising clamor and a noise of rushing footsteps ran through the busy streets—then came a sharp rattle and peal like a discharge of musketry. What was it? The crowd on the hill poured down the descent, in fright, in excitement, in precaution—some into the mischief, some eager to escape out of it. "It's the sodgers," "it's the police," "it's the Tories," shouted the chorus of the crowd—one suggestion after another raising the fury of some and the terror of others; again a rattling, dropping, continued report—one after another, with rushes of the crowd between, and perpetual changes of locality in the sound, which at last indicated its nature beyond mistake. It was no interference of authority—no firing of "the sodgers." It was a sound less tragic, yet full of mischief—the crash of unilluminated windows, the bloodless yet violent revenge of the excited mob.

The sound—the swell—the clamor—the tramp of feet—the shouts—the reiterated volleys, now here, now there, in constant change and progress, the silent flicker and glow of the now neglected lights, the hasty new ones thrust into exposed windows, telling their story of sudden alarm and reluctance, and above all the pale, serene sky, against which the bold outline of Arthur's Seat stood out as clear as in the daylight, and the calm, unimpassioned shining of the little moon, catching the windows of the Castle and church beneath with a glimmer of silver, made altogether a scene of the most singular excitement and impressiveness. But Cosmo Livingstone had forgotten that he was a poet—he was only a boy—a desperate, red-hot Radical—a friend of the people. Despite all Cameron's efforts, the boy dragged him into the crowd, and hurried him along to the scene of action. The rioters by this time were spreading everywhere, out of the greater streets into the calm of the highest respectability, where not one window in a dozen was lighted, and where many had closed their shutters in defiance—far to the west in the moonlight, where the illuminations of the old town were invisible, and where wealth and conservatism dwelt together. Breathless, yet dragging his grave companion after him, Cosmo rushed along one of the dimmest and stateliest of these streets. The lad leaped back again into the heart of a momentary fancy, which was already old and forgotten, though it had been extremely interesting a month ago. He cried "Desirée!" to himself, as he rushed in the wake of the rioters through Moray Place. He did not know which was the house, yet followed vaguely with an instinct of defense and protection. In one of the houses some women appeared, timidly putting forward candles in the highest line of windows; perhaps out of exasperation at this cowardice, perhaps from mere accident, some one among the crowd discharged a volley of stones against one of the lower range. There was a moment's pause, and it remained doubtful whether this lead was to be followed, when suddenly the door of the house was thrown open, and a girl appeared upon the threshold, distinctly visible against the strong light from the hall. Though Cosmo sprang forward with a bound, he could not hear what she said, but she rushed down on the broad step, and made a vehement address to the rioters, with lively motions of her hands, and a voice that pierced through their rough voices like a note of music. This lasted only a moment; in another the door had closed behind her with a loud echo, and all was dark again. Where was she? Cosmo pushed through the crowd in violent excitement, thrusting them away on every side with double strength. Yes, there she stood upon the step, indignant, vehement, with her little white hands clasped together, and her eyes flashing, from the rioters before her to the closed door behind.

"You English!—you are cowards!" cried the violent little heroine; "you do not fight like men, with balls and swords—you throw pebbles, like children—you wound women—and when one dares to go to speak to the madmen, she is shut out into the crowd!"

"We're no' English, missie, and naebody meant to hurt you; chap at the door for her, yin o' you lads—and let the poor thing alone—she's a very good spirit of her ain. I'm saying, open the door," cried one of the rioters, changing his soothing tone to a loud demand, as he shook the closed door violently. By this time Cosmo was by the little Frenchwoman's side.

"I know her," cried Cosmo, "they'll open when you're past—pass on— it's a school—a housefull of women—do you mean to say you would break a lady's windows that has nothing to do with it?—pass on!—is that sense, or honor, or courage? is that a credit to the Bill, or to the country? I'll take care of the young lady. Do you not see they think you robbers, or worse? They'll not open till you pass on."

"He's in the right of it there—what are ye a' waiting for?" cried some one in advance. The throng moved on, leaving a single group about the door, but this little incident was enough to damp them. Moray Place escaped with much less sacrifice of glass and temper than might have been looked for—while poor little Desirée, subsiding out of her passion, leaned against the pillar of the inhospitable door, crying bitterly, and sobbing little exclamations of despair in her own tongue, which sounded sweet to Cosmo's ear, though he did not know what they were.

"Mademoiselle Desirée, don't be afraid," cried the boy, blushing in the dark. "I saw you once with Joanna Huntley—I'm a friend. Nobody will meddle with you. When they see these fellows gone, they'll open the door."

"And I despise them!" cried Desirée, suddenly suspending her crying; "they will shut me out in the crowd for fear of themselves. I despise them! and see here!"

A stone had struck her on the temple; it was no great wound, but Desirée was shocked and excited, and in a heroic mood.

"And they will leave me here," cried the little Frenchwoman, pathetically, with renewed tears; "though it is my mother's country, and I meant to love it, they shut me out among strangers, and no one cares. Ah, they would not do so in France! there they do not throw stones at women— they kill men!"

Cosmo was horrified by the blow, and deeply impressed by the heroics. The boy blushed with the utmost shame for his townsmen and co-politicians. He thought the girl a little Joan of Arc affronted by a mob.

"But it was accident; and every man would be overpowered with shame," cried Cosmo, while meanwhile Cameron, who had followed him, knocked soberly and without speaking, at the door.

After a little interval, the door was opened by the mistress of the school, a lady of grave age and still graver looks; a couple of women-servants in the hall were defending themselves eagerly.

"I was up stairs, and never heard a word of it, mum," said one. "Eh, it wasna me!" cried another; "the French Miss flew out upon the steps, and the door just clashed behind her; it was naebody's blame but her ain."

In the midst of these self-exculpatory addresses, the mistress of the house held the door open.

"Come in, Mademoiselle Desirée," she said gravely.

The excited little Frenchwoman was not disposed to yield so quietly.

"Madame, I have been wounded, I have been shut out, I have been left alone in the crowd!" cried Desirée; "I demand of you to do me justice—see, I bleed! One of the *vauriens* struck me through the window with a stone, and the door has been closed upon me. I have stood before all the crowd alone!"

"I am sorry for it, my dear," said the lady, coldly; "come in—you ought never to have gone to the door, or exposed yourself; young ladies do not do so in this country. Pray come in, Mademoiselle Desirée. I am sorry you are hurt—and, gentlemen, we are much obliged to you—good night."

For the girl, half-reluctantly, half-indignantly, had obeyed her superior, and the door was calmly closed in the faces of Cosmo and Cameron, who stood together on the steps. Cosmo was highly incensed and wrathful. He could have had the heart to plunge into that cold, proper, lighted hall, to snatch the little heroine forth, and carry her off like a knight of romance.

"Do you hear how that woman speaks to her?" he cried, indignantly.

Cameron grasped his arm and drew him away.

"She's French!" said the elder man, laconically, and without any enthusiasm; "and not to anger you, Cosmo, the lady is perfectly right."

CHAPTER XXXVIII

Cosmo went home that evening much excited by his night's adventures. Mrs. Payne, of Moray Place, was an ogre in the boy's eyes, the Giantess Despair, holding bewitched princesses in vile durance and subjection—and Desirée, with the red mark upon her pretty forehead, with her little white hands clasped together, and her black eyes sparkling, was nothing less than a heroine. Cosmo could not forget the pretty attitude, the face glowing with resentment and girlish boldness; nor the cold gravity of the voice which bade her enter, and the unsympathetic disapproval in the lady's face. He could not rest for thinking of it when he got home. In his new feeling of importance and influence as a person privileged to address the public, his first idea was to call upon Mrs. Payne in the morning, by way of protector to Desirée, to explain how the whole matter occurred; but on further thoughts Cosmo resolved to write a very grave and serious letter on the subject, vindicating the girl, and pointing out, in a benevolent way, the danger of repressing her high spirit harshly.

As soon as he was alone, he set about carrying out this idea in an epistle worthy the pages of the *Auld Reekie Magazine*, and written with a solemn authority which would have become an adviser of eighty instead of eighteen. He wrote it out in his best hand, put it up carefully, and resolved to leave it himself in the morning, lest the post (letters were dear in those days) might miscarry with so important a document. But Cosmo, who was much worn out, slept late in the morning, so late that Cameron came into his room, and saw the letter before he was up. It excited the curiosity of the Highlander, and Cosmo, somewhat shyly, admitted him to the privilege of reading it. It proved too much, however, for the gravity of his friend; and, vexed and ashamed at last, though by no means convinced the lad tore it in bits, and threw it into the fire-place. Cameron kept him occupied all day, breaking out, nevertheless, into secret chuckles of amusement now and then, which it was very difficult to find a due occasion for; and Cosmo was not even left to himself long enough to pass the door of the house in Moray Place, or to ask after the "wound" of his little heroine. He did the only thing which remained possible to him, he made the incident into a copy of verses, which he sent to the *North British Courant*, and which duly appeared in that enlightened newspaper—though whether it ever reached the eyes of Desirée, or touched the conscience of the schoolmistress by those allusions which, though delicately vailed, were still, Cosmo flattered himself, perfectly unmistakable by the chief actors in the scene, the boy could not tell.

These days of holiday flew, however, as holidays will fly. Cameron's Highland patron had Cosmo introduced to him, and consented that his son should travel in the company of the son of "Mrs. Livingstone, of Norlaw," and the lad went home, full of plans for his journey, to which the Mistress as yet had given only a very vague and general consent, and of which she scarcely still understood the necessity. When Cosmo came home, he had the mid-chamber allotted to him as a study, and went to work with devotion. The difficulty was rather how to choose between the narrative in ballad verse, the spirited dramatic sketch, and the historical tale, than how to execute them, for Cosmo had that facility of language, and even of idea, which many very youthful people, with a "literary turn," (they were very much less common in those days) often possess, to the half-amusement, half-admiration of their seniors and their own intense confusion in maturer days. Literature was not then what it is now, the common resource of most well-educated young men, who do not know what else to do with themselves. It was still a rare glory in that rural district where the mantle of Sir Walter lay only over the great novelist's grave, and had descended upon nobody's shoulders; and as Cosmo went on with his venture, the Mistress, glowing with mother-pride and ambition, hearing the little bits of the "sketch"—eighteen is always dramatical—which seemed, to her loving ears, melodious, and noble, and life-like, almost above comparison, became perfectly willing to consent to any thing which was likely to perfect this gift of magic. "Though I canna weel see what better they could have," she said to herself, as she went down from Cosmo's study, wiping her eyes. Cosmo's muse had sprung, fully equipped, like Minerva, into a glorious existence—at least, so his mother, and so, too, if he had permitted himself to know his own sentiments—perhaps also Cosmo thought.

The arrangement was concluded, at last, on the completion of Cosmo's article. Cameron and his young pupil were to start in August; and the Mistress herself went into Edinburgh to buy her boy-author the handiest of portmanteaus, and every thing else which her limited experience thought needful for him; the whole country-side heard of his intended travels, and was stirred with wonder and no small amount of derision. The farmers' wives wondered what the world was coming to, and their husbands shook their heads over the folly of the widow, who would ruin her son for work all his days. The news was soon carried to Melmar, where Mr. Huntley by no means liked to hear it, where Patricia turned up her little nose with disgust, and where Joanna wished loudly that she was going too, and announced her determination to intrust Cosmo with a letter to Oswald. Even in the manse, the intelligence created a little ferment. Dr. Logan connected it vaguely—he could not quite tell how—with the "Bill," which the excellent minister feared would revolutionize every thing throughout the country, and confound all the ranks and degrees of social life; and shook his head over the idea of Cosmo Livingstone, who had only been one session at college, and was but eighteen, writing in a magazine.

"Depend upon it, Katie, my dear, it's an unnatural state of things," said the Doctor, whose literature was the literature of the previous century, and who thought Cosmo's pretensions unsafe for the stability of the country.

And sensible Katie, though she smiled, felt still a little doubtful herself, and, in her secret heart, thought of Huntley gone away to labor at the other end of the world, while his boy-brother tasted the sweets of luxury and idleness in an indulgence so unusual to his station.

"Poor Huntley!" said Katie to herself, with a gentle recollection of that last scene in the manse parlor, when she mended her children's stockings and smiled at the young emigrant, as he wondered what changes there might be there when he came back. Katie put up her hand very softly to her eyes, and stood a long time in the garden looking down the brae into the village—perhaps only looking at little Colin, who was visible amid some cottage boys on the green bank of Tyne—perhaps thinking of Cosmo, who was going "to the Continent,"—perhaps traveling still further in her thoughts, over a big solitary sea; but Katie said "nothing to nobody," and was as blythe and busy in the manse parlor when the minister rejoined her, as though she had not entered with a little sigh.

All this time Cosmo never said a word to his mother of Mary of Melmar; but he leaped up into the old window of the castle every evening to dream his dream, and a hundred times, in fancy, saw a visionary figure, pale, and lovely, and tender, coming home with him to claim her own. He, too, looked over the woods of Melmar as his brother had done, but with feelings very different—for no impulse of acquisition quickened in the breast of Cosmo. He thought of them as the burden of a romance, the chorus of a ballad—the inheritance to which the long lost Mary must return; and while the Mistress stocked his new portmanteau, and made ready his traveling wardrobe, the lad was hunting everywhere with ungrateful pertinacity for scraps of information to guide him in this search which his mother had not the most distant idea was the real motive of his journey. If she had known it, scarcely even the discovery of her husband's longing after his lost love could have affected the Mistress with more overpowering bitterness and disgust. Marget shut the door when Cosmo came to question her on the subject, and made a vehement address to him under her breath.

"Seek her, if you please," said Marget, in a violent whisper; "but if your mother ever kens this—sending out her son into the world with a' this pride and pains for *her* sake—I'd rather the auld castle fell on our heads, Cosmo Livingstone, and crushed every ane of us under a different stane!"

"Hush, Marget! my mother is not unjust," said Cosmo, with some displeasure.

"She's no' unjust; but she'll no' be second to a stranger woman that has been the vexation of her life," said Marget, "spier where you like, laddie. Ye dinna ken, the like of you, how things sink into folks' hearts, and bide for years. I ken naething about Mary of Melmar—neither her married name nor naught else—spier where ye like, but dinna spier at me."

But it did not make very much matter where Cosmo made inquiry. Never was disappearance more entire and complete than that of Mary of Melmar. He gathered various vague descriptions of her, not quite so poetical in sentiment as Jaacob's, but quite as confusing. She was "a great toast among a' the lads, and the bonniest woman in the country-side"— she was "as sweet as a May morning"—she was "neither big nor little, but just the best woman's size"—she was, in short, every thing that was pretty, indefinite, and perplexing. And with no clue but this, Cosmo set out, on a windy August morning, on his travels, to improve his mind, and write for the *Auld Reekie Magazine*, as his mother thought—and to seek for the lost heir of the Huntleys, as he himself and the Laird of Melmar knew.

CHAPTER XXXIX

"Oh, papa," cried Joanna Huntley, bursting into Melmar's study like a whirlwind, "they're ill-using Desirée! they shut her out at the door among a crowd, and they threw stones at her, and she might have been killed but for Cosmo Livingstone. I'll no' stand it! I'll rather go and take up a school and work for her mysel'."

"What's all this?" said Melmar, looking up in amazement from his newspaper; "another freak about this Frenchwoman—what is she to you?"

"She's my friend," said Joanna, "I never had a friend before, and I never want to have another. You never saw anybody like her in all your life; Melmar's no' good enough for her, if she could get it for her very own—but I think she would come here for me."

"That would be kind," said Mr. Huntley, taking a somewhat noisy pinch of snuff; "but if that's all you have to tell me, it'll keep. Go away and bother your mother; I'm busy to-day."

"You know perfectly well that mamma's no' up," said Joanna, "and if she was up, what's the use of bothering *her*? Now, papa, I'll tell you—I often think you're a very, very ill man—and Patricia says you have a secret, and I know what keeps Oswald year after year away—but I'll forgive you every thing if you'll send for Desirée here."

"You little monkey!" cried Melmar, swinging his arm through the air with a menaced blow. It did not fall on Joanna's cheek, however, and perhaps was not meant to fall—which was all the better for the peace of the household—though feelings of honor or delicacy were not so transcendentally high in Melmar as to have made a parental chastisement a deadly affront to the young lady, even had it been inflicted. "You little brat!" repeated the incensed papa, growing red in the face, "how dare you come to me with such a speech—how dare you bother me with a couple of fools like Oswald and Patricia?—begone this moment, or I'll—" "No, you will not, papa," interrupted Joanna. "Oswald's no' a fool—and I'm no' a monkey nor a brat, nor little either—and if any thing was to happen I would never forsake you, whatever you had done—but I like Desirée better than ever I liked any one—and she knows every thing—and she could teach me better than all the masters and mistresses in Edinburgh—and if you don't send for her here to be my governess, I may go to school, but I'll never learn a single thing again!"

Melmar was perfectly accustomed to be bullied by his youngest child; he had no ideal of feminine excellence to be shocked by Joanna's rudeness, and in general rather enjoyed it, and took a certain pleasure in the disrespectful straightforwardness of the girl, who in reality was the only member of his family who had any love for him. His momentary passion soon evaporated—he laughed and shook his closed hand at her, no longer threateningly.

"If you like to grow up a dunce, Joan," he said, with a chuckle, "what the deevil matter is't to me?"

"Oh, yes, but it is, though," said Joanna. "I know better—you like people to come to Melmar as well as Patricia does—and Patricia never can be very good for any thing. She canna draw, though she pretends—and she canna play, and she canna sing, and I could even dance better myself. It's aye like lessons to see her and hear her—and nobody cares to come to see mamma—it's no' her fault, for she's always in bed or on the sofa; but if *I* like to learn—do you hear, papa?—and I would like if Desirée was here—*I* know what Melmar might be!"

It was rather odd to look at Joanna, with her long, angular, girl's figure, her red hair, and her bearing which promised nothing so little as the furthest off approach to elegance, and to listen to the confidence and boldness of this self-assertion—even her father laughed—but, perhaps because he was her father, did not fully perceive the grotesque contrast between her appearance and her words; on the contrary, Melmar was considerably impressed with these last, and put faith in them, a great deal more faith than he had ever put in Patricia's prettiness and gentility, cultivated as these had been in the refined atmosphere of the Clapham school.

"You are a vain little blockhead, Joan," said Mr. Huntley, "which I scarcely looked for—but it's in the nature of woman. When Aunt Jean leaves you her fortune, we'll see what a grand figure you'll make in the country. A French governess, forsooth! the bairn's crazy. I'll get her to teach *me*."

"She could teach you a great many things, papa," said Joanna, with gravity, "so you need not laugh. I'm going to write to her this moment, and say she's to come here—and you're to write to Mrs. Payne and tell her what you'll give, and how she's to come, and every thing. Desirée is not pleased with Mrs. Payne."

"What a pity!" said Melmar, laughing; "and possibly, Joan—you ought to consider—Desirée might not be pleased with me."

"You are kind whiles—when you like, papa," said Joanna, taking this possibility into serious consideration, and fixing her sharp black eyes upon her father, with half an entreaty, half a defiance.

Somehow this appeal, which he did not expect, was quite a stroke of victory, and silenced Melmar. He laughed once more in his loud and not very mirthful fashion, and the end of the odd colloquy was, that Joanna conquered, and that, to the utter amazement of mother, sister, and Aunt Jean, the approaching advent of a French governess for Joanna became a recognized event in the house. Patricia spent one good long summer afternoon crying over it.

"No one ever thought of getting a governess for me!" sobbed Patricia, through a deluge of spiteful tears.

And Aunt Jean put up her spectacles from her eyes, and listened to the news which Joanna shouted into her ear, and shook her head.

"If she's a Papist it's a tempting of Providence," said Aunt Jean, "and they're a' Papists, if they're no' infidels. She may be nice enough and bonnie enough, but I canna approve of it, Joan. I never had any broo of foreigners a' my days. Deseery? fhat ca' you her name? I like names to be Christian-like, for my part. Did ever ye hear that, or the like o' that, in the Scriptures? Na, Joan, it's very far from likely she should please me."

"Her name is *Desirée*, and it means desired; it's like a Bible name for that," cried Joanna. "My name means nothing at all that ever I heard of—it's just a copy of a boy's—and I would not have copied a man if anybody had asked me."

"What's that the bairn says?" said Aunt Jean. "I like old-fashioned plain names, for my part, but that's to be looked for in an old woman; but I can tell you, Joan, I'm never easy in my mind about French folk—and never can tell fha they may turn out to be; and 'deed in this house, it's no canny; and I never have ony comfort in my mind about your brother Oswald, kenning faur he was."

"Why is it not canny in this house, Aunt Jean?" asked Joanna.

"Eh, fhat's that?" said the old woman, who heard perfectly, "fhat's no canny? just the Pope o' Rome, Joan, and a' his devilries; and they're as fu' o' wiles, every ane, as if ilka bairn was bred up a priest. Oh, fie, na! you ma ca' her desired, if you like, but she's no' desired by me."

"Desired!" cried Patricia; "a little creature of a governess, that is sure always to be scheming and trying to be taken notice of, and making herself as good as we are. It's just a great shame! it's nothing else! no one ever *thought* of a governess for me. But it's strange how I always get slighted, whatever happens. I don't think any one in the world cares for me!"

"Fhat's Patricia greeting about?" said Aunt Jean, "eh, bairns! if I were as young as you I would save up a' my tears for real troubles. You've never kent but good fortune a' your days, but that's no' to say ill fortune can never come. Whisht then, ye silly thing! I can see you, though I canna hear you. Fhat's she greeting for, Joan? eh! speak louder, I canna hear."

"Because Desirée is coming," shouted Joan.

"Aweel, aweel, maybe I'm little better mysel'," said the old woman. "I'm just a prejudiced auld wife, I like my ain country best—but's no malice and envie with me; fhat ails Patricia at her for a stranger she doesna ken? She's keen enough about strangers when they come in her ain way. You're a wild lassie, Joan, you're no' just fhat I would like to see you—but there's nae malice in *you*, so far as I ken."

"Oh, Auntie Jean," cried Joanna, with enthusiasm, "wait till you see what I shall be when Desirée comes!"

CHAPTER XL

After a little time Desirée came to Melmar. She had been placed in charge of Mrs. Payne by an English lady, who had brought her from her home in France with the intention of making a nursery governess of the little girl, but who, finding her either insufficiently trained or not tractable enough, had transferred her, with the consent of her mother, to the Edinburgh boarding-school as half pupil, half teacher. When Melmar's proposal came, Desirée, still indignant at her present ruler, accepted it eagerly, declared herself quite competent to act independently, and would not hear of anybody being consulted upon the matter. She herself, the little heroine said, with some state, would inform her mother, and she made her journey accordingly half in spite of Mrs. Payne, who, however, was by no means ill pleased to transfer so difficult a charge into other hands. Desirée arrived alone on an August afternoon, by the coach, in Kirkbride. The homely little Scotch village, so unlike any thing she had seen before, yet so pretty, dwelling on the banks of its little brown stream, pleased the girl's fanciful imagination mightily. Two or three people—among them the servant from Melmar who had come to meet her—stood indolently in the sultry sunshine about the Norlaw Arms. In the shadow of the corner, bowed Jaacob's weird figure toiled in the glow of the smithy. One or two women were at the door of the cottage which contained the widow's mangle, and the opposite bank lay fair beneath the light, with that white gable of the manse beaming down among its trees like a smile. The wayward, excitable little Frenchwoman had a tender little heart beneath all her vivacity and caprices. Somehow her eyes sought instinctively that white house on the brae, and instinctively the little girl thought of her mother and sister. Ah, yes, this surely, and not Edinburgh, was her mother's country! She had never seen it before, yet it seemed familiar to her; they could be at home here. And thoughts of acquiring that same white house, and bringing her mother to it in triumph, entered the wild little imagination. Women make fortunes in France now and then; she did not know any better, and she was a child. She vowed to herself to buy the white house on the brae and bring mamma there.

Melmar pleased Desirée, but not so much; she thought it a great deal too square and like a prison; and Patricia did not please her at all, as she was not very slow to intimate.

"Mademoiselle does not love me, Joanna," she said to her pupil as they wandered about the banks of Tyne together, "to see every thing," as Joanna said before they began their lessons; "and I never can love any one who does not love me."

"Patricia does not love anybody," cried Joanna, "unless maybe herself, and not herself either—right; but never mind, Desirée, *I* love you, and by-and-by so will Aunt Jean; and oh! if Oswald would only come home!"

"I hope he will not while I am here," said Desirée, with a little frown; "see! how pretty the sun streams among the trees; but I do not like Melmar so well as that white house at the village; I should like to live there."

"At the manse?" cried Joanna.

"What is the manse? it is not a great house; would they sell it?" said Desirée.

"Sell it!" Joanna laughed aloud in the contempt of superior knowledge; "but it's only because you don't know; they could as well sell the church as the manse."

"I don't want the church, however—it's ugly," said Desirée; "but if I had money I should buy that white house, and bring mamma and Maria there."

"Eh, Desirée! your mamma is English—I heard you say so," cried Joanna.

"*Eh bien!* did I ever tell you otherwise?" said the little Frenchwoman, impatiently; "she would love that white house on the hill."

"Did *she* teach you to speak English?" asked Joanna, "because everybody says you speak so well for a Frenchwoman—and I think so myself; and papa said you looked quite English to him, and he thought he knew some one like you, and you were not like a foreigner at all."

The pretty little shoulders gave an immediate shrug, which demonstrated their nationality with emphasis.

"Every one must think what every one pleases," said Desirée. "Who, then, lives in that white house? I remember mamma once spoke of such a house, with a white gable and a great tree. Mamma loves rivers and trees. I think, when she was a child, she must have been here."

"Why?" asked Joanna, opening her eyes wide.

"I know not why," said Desirée, still with a little impatience, as she glanced hurriedly round with a sudden look of half-confused consideration; "but either some one has told me of this place, or I have been here in a dream."

It was the loveliest dell of Tyne. The banks rose so high on either side, and were so richly dotted with trees, that it was only here and there, through breaks in the foliage, that you could catch a momentary glimpse of the brown river, foaming over a chance rock, or sparkling under some dropping line of sunshine which reached it, by sweet caprice and artifice of nature, through an avenue of divided branches. The path where the two girls stood together was at a considerable height above the stream; and close by them, in a miniature ravine, thickly fringed with shrubs, poured down a tiny, dazzling waterfall, white as foam against the background of dark soil and rocks, the special feature of the scene. Desirée stood looking at it with her little French hands clasped together, and the chiming of the water woke strange fancies in her mind. Had she seen it somewhere, in fairy-land or in dreams?—or had she heard of it in that time which was as good as either—when she was a child? She stood quite silent, saying nothing to Joanna, who soon grew weary of this pause, complimentary as it might be. Desirée was confused and did not know what to make of it. She said no more of the white house, and not much more of her own friends, and kept wondering to herself as she went back, answering Joanna's questions and talking of their future lessons, what strange sentiment of recollection could have moved her in sight of that waterfall. It was very hard to make it out.

And no doubt it was because Desirée's mother was English that Aunt Jane could not keep up her prejudice against the foreigner, but gradually lapsed to Joanna's opinion, and day by day fell in love with the little stranger. She was not a very, very good girl—she was rather the reverse, if truth must be told. She had no small amount of pretty little French affectations, and when she was naughty fell back upon her own language, especially with Patricia, whose Clapham French was not much different from the French of Stratford-atte-Bowe, and who began with vigor and reality to entertain, not a feeble prejudice but a hearty dislike, to the invader. Neither did she do what good governesses are so like to do, at least in novels—she did not take the place of her negligent daughters with the invalid Mrs. Huntley, nor remodel the disorderly household. Sometimes, indeed, out of pure hatred to things ugly, Desirée put a sofa-cover straight, or spread down a corner of the crumb-cloth; but she did not captivate the servants, and charm the young ladies into good order and good behavior; she exercised no very astonishing influence in that way over even Joanna. She was by no means a model young lady in herself, and had no special authority, so far as she was aware of. She taught her pupil, who was one half bigger than herself, to speak French very tolerably, and to practice a certain time every day. She took charge of Joanna's big hands, and twisted, and coaxed, and pinched them into a less clumsy thump, upon the trembling keys of the piano. She mollified her companion's manners even unconsciously, and suggested improvements in the red hair and brown merino frock; but having done this, Desirée was not aware of having any special charge of the general morals and well-being of the family; she was rather a critic of the same, indeed, but she was not a Mentor nor a reformer. She obeyed what rules there were in the sloven house—she shrugged her little French shoulders at the discomforts and quarrels. She sometimes pouted, or curled her little disdainful upper lip; but she took nobody's part save Joanna's, whom she always defended manfully. It was not a particularly brilliant or entertaining life for Desirée. Melmar himself, with his grizzled red hair, and heated face; Mrs. Huntley, who sometimes never left her room all day, and who, when she did, lay on a sofa; Patricia, who was spiteful, and did her utmost to shut out both Joanna and Desirée when any visitors came to break the tedium—were not remarkably delightful companions; and as the winter closed in, and there were long evenings, and less pleasure out of doors—winter, when all the fires looked half choked, and would not burn, and when a perennial fog seemed to lie over Melmar, did not increase the comforts of the house. Yet it happened that Desirée was by no means unhappy; perhaps at sixteen it is hard to be really unhappy, even when one feels one ought, unless one has some very positive reason for it. Joanna and she sat together at the scrambling breakfast, which Patricia was always too late for; then they went to the music lesson, which tried Joanna's patience grievously, but which Desirée managed to get some fun out of, and endured with great philosophy. Then they read together, and the unfortunate Joanna inked her fingers over her French exercise. In the afternoon they walked—save when Joanna was compelled to accompany her sister "in the carriage," a state ceremonial in which the little governess was never privileged to share; and after their return from their walk, Desirée taught her pupil all manner of fine needleworks, in which she was herself more than usually learned, and which branch of knowledge was highly prized by Aunt Jean, and even by Mrs. Huntley. Such was the course of study pursued by Joanna under the charge of her little governess of sixteen.

CHAPTER XLI

"A French governess!—she is not French, though she might be born in France. Anybody might be born in France," said Patricia, with some scorn; "but her mother was Scotch—no, not English, Joanna, I know better—just some Scotchwoman from the country; I should not wonder if she was a little impostor, after all."

"You had better take care," cried Joanna, "I'm easier affronted than Desirée; you had better not say much more to me."

"It is true though," said Patricia, with triumph; "she took quite a fancy to Kirkbride, when she came first, and was sure she had heard of the Kelpie waterfall. *I* expect it will turn out some poor family from this quarter that have gone to France and changed their name. Joanna may be as foolish about her as she likes, but *I* know she never was a true Frenchwoman by her look. I have seen French people many a time in England."

"Yet you always look as if you would like to eat Desirée when she speaks to you in French," said Joanna, with a spice of malice; "if you knew French people, you should like the language."

"Low people don't pronounce as ladies do," said Patricia. "Perhaps she was not even born in France, for all she says—and I am *quite* sure her mother was some country girl from near Kirkbride."

"What is that you say?" said Melmar, who was present, and whose attention had at last been caught by the discussion.

"I say Joanna's French governess is not French, papa. Her mother was a Scotchwoman and came from this country," cried Patricia, eagerly. "I think she belongs to some poor family who have gone abroad and changed their name—perhaps her father was a poacher, or something, and had to run away."

"And that is all because Desirée thinks she must have heard her mamma speak of the Kelpie waterfall," said Joanna; "because she thought she knew it as soon as she saw it—that is all!—did you ever hear the like, papa?"

Melmar's face grew redder, as was its wont when he was at all disturbed. He laid down his paper.

"She thought she knew the Kelpie, did she?—hum! and her mother is a Scotchwoman—for that matter, so is yours. What is to be made of that, eh, Patricia?"

"*I* never denied where I belonged to," said Patricia, reddening with querulous anger; "and I did not speak to you, papa, so you need not take the trouble to answer. But her mother *was* Scotch—and I do not believe she is a proper Frenchwoman at all. I never did think so; and as for a governess, Joanna could learn as much from mamma's maid."

Joanna burst out immediately into a loud defense, and denunciation of her sister. Melmar took no notice what, ever of their quarrel, but he still grew redder in the face, twisted about his newspaper, got up and walked to the window, and displayed a general uneasiness. He was perfectly indifferent as to the tone and bearing of his daughters, but he was not indifferent to what they said in this quarrel, which was all about Desirée. Presently, however, both the voices ceased with some abruptness. Melmar looked round with curiosity. Desirée herself had entered the room, and what his presence had not even checked, her presence put an end to. Desirée wore a brown merino frock, like Joanna, with a little band and buckle round the waist, and sleeves which were puffed out at the shoulders, and plain at the wrists, according to the fashion of the time. It had no ornament whatever except a narrow binding of velvet at the neck and sleeves, and was not so long as to hide the handsome little feet, which were not in velvet slippers, but in stout little shoes of patent leather, more suitable a great deal for Melmar, and the place she held there. The said little feet came in lightly, yet not noiselessly, and both the sisters turned with an immediate acknowledgment of the stranger's entrance. Patricia's delicate pink cheeks were flushed with anger, and Joanna looked eager and defiant, but quarrels were so very common between them that Desirée took no notice of this one. She came to a table near which Melmar was standing, and opened a drawer in it to get Joanna's needlework.

"You promised to have—oh, such an impossible piece, done to-day!" said Desirée, "and look, you naughty Joanna!—look here."

She shook out a delicate piece of embroidery as she spoke, with a merry laugh. It was a highly-instructive bit of work, done in a regular succession of the most delicate perfection and the utmost bungling, to wit, Desirée's own performance and the performance of her pupil. As the little governess clapped her hands over it, Joanna drew near and put her arms round the waist of her young teacher, overtopping her by all her own red head and half her big shoulders.

"I'll never do it like you, Desirée," said the girl, half in real affection, half with the benevolent purpose of aggravating her sister. "I'll never do any thing so well as you, if I live to be as old as Aunt Jean."

"Ah, then, you will need no governess," said Desirée, "and if you did it as well as I, now, you should not want me, Joanna. I shall leave it for you there—and now it is time to come for one little half hour to the music. Will mademoiselle do us the honor to come and listen? It shall be only one little half hour."

"No, thank you! I don't care to hear girls at their lessons—and Joanna's time is always so bad," said the fretful Patricia. "Oh, I can't help having an ear! I can hear only too well, thank you, where I am."

Desirée made a very slight smiling curtsey to her opponent, and pressed Joanna's arm lightly with her fingers to keep down the retort which trembled on that young lady's lips. Then they went away together to the little supplementary musical lesson. Melmar had never turned round, nor taken the slightest notice, but he observed, notwithstanding, not only all that was done, but all that was looked and said, and it struck him, perhaps for the first time, that the English of Desirée was perfectly familiar and harmonious English, and that she never either paused for a word nor translated the idiom of one tongue into the speech of another. Uneasy suspicions began to play about his mind: he could scarcely say what he feared, yet he feared something. The little governess was French undeniably and emphatically— and yet she was not French, either, yet bore an unexplainable something of familiarity and home-likeness which had won for her the heart of Aunt Jean, and had startled himself unawares from her first introduction to Melmar. He stood at the window, looking out upon the blank, winterly landscape, the leafless trees in the distance, the damp grass and evergreens near the door, as the cheerful notes of Joanna's music came stealing through the cold passages. The music was not in bad time, and it was in good taste, for Joanna was ambitious, and Desirée, though not an extraordinary musician herself, kept her pupil to this study with the most tenacious perseverance. As Melmar listened, vague thoughts, almost of fear, stole over him. He had been a lawyer, and a lawyer of a low class, smart in schemes and trickeries.

He was ready to suspect everybody of cunning and the mean cleverness of deceit. Perhaps this was a little spy whom he fostered in his house. Perhaps her presence in the Edinburgh school was a trick to attract Joanna, and her presence here a successful plot to undermine and find out himself. His face grew redder still as he "put things together;" and by the time the music ceased, Melmar had concocted and found out (it is so easy to find out what one has concocted one's own self,) a very pretty little conspiracy. He *had* found it out, he was persuaded, and it should go no further—trust him for that!

Accordingly, when his daughter and her governess returned, Melmar paid them a compliment upon their music, and was disposed to be friendly, as it appeared. Finally, after he had exhausted such subjects of chat as occurred to him, he got up, looking at Desirée, who was now busy with her embroidery.

"I rather think, mademoiselle, you have been more than three months here," said Melmar, "and I have been inconsiderate and ungallant enough to forget the time. I'll speak with you about that in my study, if you'll favor me by coming there. I never speak of business but in my own room—eh, Joan? You got your thrashings there when you were young enough. Where does mademoiselle give you them now?"

"Don't be foolish, papa," said Joanna, jerking her head aside as he pinched her ear. "What do you want of Desirée? if it's for Patricia, and you're going to teaze her, I'll not let her go, whatever you say."

"And it is not quite three months, yet," said Desirée, looking up with a smile. "Monsieur is too kind, but it still wants a week of the time."

"Then, lest I should forget again when the week was over, we'll settle it now, mademoiselle," said Melmar. Desirée rose immediately to follow him. They went away through the long passage, he leading, suspicious and stealthy, she going after him, with the little feet which rang frankly upon the stones. Desirée thought the study miserable when she went into it. She longed to throw open the window, to clear out the choked fire—she did not wonder that her pupil's papa had a heated face, even before dinner; the wonder seemed how any one could breathe here.

They had a conference of some duration, which gradually diverged from Desirée's little salary, which was a matter easily settled. Mr. Huntley took an interest in her family. He asked a great many questions, which the girl answered with a certain frankness and a certain reserve, the frankness being her own, and the reserve attributable to a letter which Desirée kept in her pocket, and beyond the instructions of which nothing could have tempted her to pass. Mr. Huntley learned a great deal during that interview, though not exactly what he expected and intended to learn. The afternoon was darkening, and as he sat in the dubious light, with the window and the yew-tree on the other side of him, he became more and more like the big, brindled, watchful cat, which he had so great a tendency to resemble. Then he dismissed "mademoiselle" with a kindly caution. He thought she had better not mention—not even to any one in the house, that her mother was a Scotchwoman—as she was French herself, he thought the less said about that the better—he would not even speak of it much to Joanna, he thought, if she would take his advice—it might injure her prospects in life—and with this fatherly advice he sent Desirée away.

When she was gone, he looked out stealthily for some one else, though he had taken previous precautions to make sure that no one could listen. It was Patricia for whom her father looked, poor little delicate Patricia, who *would* steal about those stone-cold passages, and linger in all manner of draughts at half-closed doors, to gain a little clandestine information. When Melmar had watched a few minutes, he discovered her stealing out of a little store-room close by, and pounced upon the poor little stealthy, chilly figure. He did not care that the grasp of his fingers hurt her delicate shoulders, and that her teeth chattered with cold; he drew her roughly into the dusk of the study, where the pale window and the black yew were by no means counterbalanced by any light from the fire. Once here, Patricia began to vindicate herself, and upbraid papa's cruelty. Her father silenced her with a threatening gesture.

"At it again!" said Melmar; "what the deevil business have you with my affairs? let me but catch you prying when there is any thing to learn, and for all your airs, I'll punish you! you little cankered elf! hold your tongue, and hear what I have to say to you. If I hear another word against that governess, French or no French—or if you try your hand at aggravating her, as I know you have done, I'll turn you out of this house!"

For once in her life Patricia was speechless; she made no answer, but stood shivering in his grasp, with a hundred terrified malicious fancies in her mind, not one of which would come to utterance. Melmar proceeded:—

"If anybody asks you who she is, or what she is, you can tell them *I* know—which is more than you know, or she either—and if you let any mortal suppose she's slighted at Melmar, or give her ground to take offense, or are the means of making her wish to leave this place—if it should be midnight, or the depths of winter, I'll turn you out of doors that moment! Do you hear?"

Patricia did hear, with sullen terror and wicked passion, but she did not answer; and when she was released, fled to her own room, ready, out of the mere impotence of her revengeful ill-humor to harm herself, since she could not harm Desirée, and with all kinds of vile suspicions in her mind— suspicions further from the reality than Melmar's had been, and still more miserable. When she came to herself a little, she cried and made her eyes red, and got a headache, and the supernumerary maid was dispatched up stairs to nurse her, and be tormented for the evening. Suffering is very often vicarious in this world, and poor Jenny Shaw bore the brunt which Desirée was not permitted to bear.

CHAPTER XLII

"I should like to live here," said Desirée, looking out of the window of the manse parlor, with a little sigh.

Katie Logan looked up at her with some little doubt. She had come by herself to the manse, in advance of Joanna, who had been detained to accompany her sister. The two girls had been invited some time before to "take tea" at the manse—and Desirée had been very curious and interested about her first visit to her white house on the hill. Now that she had accomplished it, however, it subdued her spirit a little, and gave the little Frenchwoman for once a considerable inclination to get "low," and cry. The house and the room were very unlike any house she had ever known— yet they were so homelike that Desirée's thoughts grew tender. And Katie Logan looked at her doubtfully. Desirée's impulsive little heart had clung to Katie every time she saw her. She was so sweet and neat—so modest and natural—so unlike Patricia and Joanna, and all the womankind of that sloven house of Melmar. The girl, who had a mother and an elder sister, and was far from home, yearned to Katie—but the little mistress of the manse looked with doubt upon the French governess—principally, to tell the truth, because she was French, and Katie Logan, with all her good sense, was only a country girl, and had but a very, very small experience of any world beyond Kirkbride.

"Mamma came from this country," said Desirée, again, softly. She had a letter in her pocket—rather a sentimental letter—from mamma, which perhaps a wiser person might have smiled at a little—but it made Desirée's heart expand toward the places which mamma too had seen in her youth, and remembered still.

"Indeed! then you are a little bit Scotch, you are not all French," said Katie, brightening a little; "is it very long since your mamma went away?— is she in France now? Is she likely to come back again?"

Desirée shook her head.

"I should like to be rich, and buy this house, and bring her here—I love this house," cried the girl.

A little cloud came upon Katie's face. She was jealous of any inference that some time or other the manse might change hands. She could not bear to think of that—principally because Katie had begun to find out with painful anxiety and fear, that her father was growing old, that he felt the opening chill of winter a great deal more than he used to do—and that the old people in the village shook their heads, and said to themselves that the minister was "failing" every time he passed their doors.

"This house can never be sold," said Katie, briefly—even so briefly as though the words were rather hard to say.

"It is not like Melmar," said Desirée. "I want the air and the sun to come into that great house—it can not breathe—and how the people breathe in it I do not know."

"But they are very kind people," said Katie, quickly.

Desirée lifted her black eyes and looked full at her—but Katie was working and did not meet the look.

"Joanna is fond of you," said Desirée, "and I like her—and I am fond of the old lady whom they call Aunt Jean."

This distinct summary of the amount of her affection for the household amused Katie, who was half afraid of a governess-complaint against her employers.

"Do you like to be so far from home?" she said.

"Like!" Desirée became suddenly vehement. "I should like to live with mamma—but," cried the girl, "how could you ask me?—do not *you* know?"

"I have no mother," said Katie, very quietly; "boys are always eager to leave home—girls might sometimes wish it too. Do you know Cosmo Livingstone, whom you saw in Edinburgh, has gone abroad for no reason at all that I know—and his brothers have both gone to work, and make their fortunes if they can—and my little brothers speak already of what they are going to do when they grow men—they will all go away."

"In this country, people always talk of making fortunes. I should like to make a fortune too," said Desirée, "but I do not know what to do."

"Girls never make fortunes," said Katie, with a smile.

"Why?" cried the little governess, "but I wish it—yes, very much—though I do not know how to do it; here I have just twenty pounds a year. What should you do if you had no papa, and had to work for yourself."

Katie rose from her chair in trouble and excitement.

"Don't speak so—you frighten me!" she cried, with an involuntary pang. "I have all the children. You do not understand it—you must not speak of *that*."

"Of what?" asked Desirée, with a little astonishment. But she changed the subject with ready tact when she saw the painful color on Katie's face. "I should like mamma to see you," she said in a vein of perfectly natural and sincere flattery. "When I tell her what kind of people I live among, I do not speak of mademoiselle at Melmar, or even of Joanna—I tell her of you, and then she is happy—she thinks poor little Desirée is very well where she is with such as these."

"I am afraid you are too good to me," said Katie, with a half conscious laugh—"you don't know me well enough yet—is it Patricia whom you call mademoiselle?"

Desirée shrugged her little shoulders slightly; she gave no other answer, but once more looked out from the window down the pretty brae of Tyne, where all the cottages were so much the clearer from the winterly brown aspect of the trees, stripped of their foliage. It was not like any other scene familiar to Desirée, still it did seem familiar to her—she could not tell how—as if she had known it all her life.

"Does Cosmo Livingstone, whom you spoke of, live near?" asked Desirée, "and will you tell me of *his* mother? Is she by herself, now that all her boys are gone?—is she a lady? Are they great people or are they poor? Joanna speaks of a great old castle, and I think I saw it from the road. They must be great people if they lived there."

"They are not great people now," said Katie, the color warming in her cheek—"yet the castle belonged to them once, and they were different. But they are good people still."

"I should like to hear about them," said Desirée, suddenly coming up to Katie, and sitting down on a stool by her feet. Katie Logan was slightly flattered, in spite of herself. She thought it very foolish, but she could not help it. Once more a lively crimson kindled in her cheek. She bent over her work with great earnestness, and never turned her eyes toward the questioning face of the girl.

"I could not describe the Mistress if I were to try all day," said Katie at last, in a little burst, after having deliberated. Desirée looked up at her very steadily, with grave curiosity.

"And that is what I want most," said the little Frenchwoman. "What! can you not tell if she has black eyes or blue ones, light hair or dark hair?—

was she pretty before she grew old—and does she love her boys—and did her husband love her? I want to know all that."

Desirée spoke in the tone of one who had received all these questions from another person, and who asked them with a point-blank quietness and gravity, for the satisfaction of some other curiosity than her own; but the investigation was half amusing, half irritating to Katie. She shook her head slightly, with a gesture expressing much the same sentiment as the movement of her hand, which drew away the skirts on which Desirée almost leaned. Her doubt changed into a more positive feeling. Katie rather feared Desirée was about to fulfill all her unfavorable anticipations as to the quality of French governesses.

"Don't go away," said Desirée, laying her little white hand upon the dress which Katie withdrew from her touch. "I like to sit by you—I like to be near you—and I want to hear; not for me. Tell me only what you please, but let me sit here till Joanna comes."

There was a little pause. Katie was moved slightly, but did not know what to say, and Desirée, too, sat silent, whether waiting for her answer or thinking, Katie could not tell. At last she spoke again with emotion, grasping Katie's dress.

"I like Joanna," said Desirée, with tears upon her eyelashes—"but I am older than she is—a great deal older—and no one else cares for me. You do not care for me—it is not likely; but let me sit here and forget all that house and every thing till Joanna comes. Ah, let me! I am far away from home—I am a little beggar girl, begging at your window—not for crumbs, or for sous, but for love. I am so lonely. I do not think of it always—but I have thought so long and so often of coming here."

"You must come oftener then," said Katie, who, unused to any demonstration, did not quite know what to say.

"I can not come often," said Desirée, softly, "but let me sit by you and forget all the others—only for a very, very little time—only till Joanna comes. Ah, she is here!"

And the little Frenchwoman shrugged her shoulders, and ran to the window to look out, and came back with a swift gliding motion to take Katie's hand out of her work and kiss it. Katie was surprised, startled, moved. She did not half understand it, and she blushed, though the lips which touched her hand were only those of a girl; but almost before she could speak, Desirée had sprung up again, and stood before her with a smile, winking her pretty long eyelashes to clear them of those wayward April tears. She was very pretty, very young, with her little foreign graces.

Katie did not understand the rapid little girl, who darted from one thought to another, so quickly, yet with such evident truthfulness—but her heart was touched and surprised. Joanna came in immediately, to put an end to any further confidences. Joanna, loudly indignant at Patricia's selfishness, and making most audible and uncompromising comparisons between Melmar and the manse, which Desirée skillfully diverted, soothed, and gradually reduced to silence, to Katie's much amazement. On the whole, it was a very pleasant little tea-party to everybody concerned; but Katie Logan, when she stood at the door in the clear frosty moonlight, looking after her young guests, driving away in the double gig which had been sent for them, still doubted and wondered about Desirée, though with a kindly instead of an unfavorable sentiment. What could the capricious little foreigner mean, for instance, by such close questions about Norlaw?

CHAPTER XLIII

At Norlaw every thing was very quiet, very still, in this early winter. The "beasts" were thriving, the dairy was prosperous, the Mistress's surplus fund—spite of the fifty pounds which had been given out of it to Cosmo—grew at the bank. Willie Noble, the factotum, lived in his cosy cottage at a little distance, and throve—but no one knew very well how the Mistress and Marget lived by themselves in that deserted house. No one could have told any external difference in the house, save for its quietness. It was cheerful to look upon in the ruddy winter sunshine, when the glimmer of the fire shone in the windows of the dining-parlor, and through the open door of Marget's kitchen; and not even the close pressure of the widow's cap could bring decay or melancholy to the living looks of the Mistress, who still was not old, and had much to do yet in the world where her three boys were wandering. But it was impossible to deny that both Mistress and servant had a little dread of the long evenings. They preferred getting up hours before daylight, when, though it was dark, it was morning, and the labors of the day could be begun—they took no pleasure in the night.

It was a habitual custom with the minister, and had been for years, to "take tea" occasionally, now and then, without previous invitation, at Norlaw. When Dr. Logan was new in his pastorate, he thought this device of dropping in to take tea the most admirable plan ever invented for "becoming acquainted with his people," and winning their affections; and what was commenced as a famous piece of wisdom, had fallen years ago into natural use and wont, a great improvement upon policy. From the same astute reasoning, it had been the fancy of the excellent minister, whose schemes were all very transparent, and, indeed, unconcealable, to take Katie with him in these domestic visitations. "It pleased the people," Dr. Logan thought, and increased the influence of the ecclesiastical establishment. The good man was rather complacent about the manner in which he had conquered the affections of his parish. It was done by the most elaborate statesmanship, if you believed Dr. Logan, and he told the young pastors, with great satisfaction, the history of his simple devices, little witting that his devices were as harmless as they were transparent, and that it was himself, and not his wisdom, which took the hearts of his people. But in the meantime, those plans of his had come to be the course of nature, and so it was that Katie Logan found herself seated with her work in the Norlaw dining-parlor at sunset of a wintry afternoon, which was not exactly the day that either she or the Mistress would have chosen for her visit there.

For that day the Mistress had heard from her eldest son. Huntley had reached Australia—had made his beginning of life—had written a long, full-detailed letter to his mother, rich in such particulars as mothers love to know; and on that very afternoon Katie Logan came with her father to Norlaw. Now in her heart the Mistress liked Katie as well, perhaps better, than she liked any other stranger out of the narrow magic circle of her own blood and family—but the Mistress was warm of temper and a little unreasonable. She could not admit the slightest right on Katie's part, or on the part of any "fremd person," to share in the communication of her son. She resented the visit which interrupted her in the midst of her happiness and excitement with a suggestion of some one else who might claim a share in Huntley. She knew they were not lovers, she knew that not the shadow of an engagement bound these two, she believed that they had never spoken a word to each other which all the world might not have heard—yet, notwithstanding all these certainties, the Mistress was clear-sighted, and had the prevision of love in her eyes, and with the wildest unreasonableness she resented the coming of Katie, of all other days in the year, upon that day.

"She needna have been in such an awfu' hurry; she might have waited a while, if it had only been for the thought of what folk might say," muttered the Mistress to herself, very well knowing all the time, though she would not acknowledge it to herself, that Katie Logan had no means whatever of knowing what precious missive had come in the Kirkbride letter-bag that day.

And when the Mistress intimated the fact with a little heat and excitement, Katie blushed and felt uncomfortable. She was conscious, too; she did not like to ask a natural question about Huntley. She sat embarrassed at the homely tea-table, looking at the cream scones which Marget had made in honor of the minister, while Dr. Logan and the Mistress kept up the conversation between them—and when her father rose after tea to go out, as was his custom, to call at the nearest cottages, Katie would fain have gone too, had that not been too great an invasion of established rule and custom, to pass without immediate notice. She sat still accordingly by the table with her work, the Mistress sitting opposite with *her* work also, and her mind intent upon Huntley's letter. The room was very still and dim, with its long background of shade, sometimes invaded by a red glimmer of fire, but scarcely influenced by the steady light of the two candles, illuminating those two faces by the table; and the Mistress and her visitor sat in silence without any sound but the motion of their hands, and the little rustle of their elbows as they worked. This silence became very embarrassing after a few minutes, and Katie broke it at last by an inquiry after Cosmo—where was he when his mother heard last?

"The laddie is a complete wanderer," said the Mistress, not without a little complacence. "I could not undertake to mind, for my part, all the places he's been in—though they're a' names you see in books—he's been in Eetaly, and he's been in Germany, and now he's back again in France; but I canna say he forgets hame either," she added, with a tender pride, "only the like of him must improve his mind; and foreign travel, folk say, is good for that—though I canna say I ever had much to do with foreigners, or likit them mysel'."

"Did you ever hear of any one from this country marrying a Frenchman, Mrs. Livingstone?" asked Katie.

"Marrying a Frenchman? I'll warrant have I—it's no' such a great wonder, but the like of me might hear tell of it in a lifetime," said the Mistress, with a little offense, "but marriage is no' aye running in everybody's head, Miss Katie, and there's little fear of my Cosmo bringing me hame a French wife."

"No, I did not think of that," said Katie, with a smile, "I was thinking of the little French governess at Melmar, whose mother, they say, came from this quarter, or near it. She is an odd little girl and yet I like her—Cosmo saw her in Edinburgh, and she was very anxious, when she came to the manse, to hear about Norlaw. I thought perhaps you might have known who her mother was."

The Mistress was slightly startled—she looked up at Katie quickly, with a sparkle of impatience in her eye, and a rising color.

"Me!" said the Mistress. "How should I ken? There might have been a hundred young women in the countryside married upon Frenchmen for any thing I could tell. 'This quarter' is a wide word. I ken nae mair about Melrose and what happens there, wha's married or wha dies, than if it was a thousand miles away. And many a person has heard tell of Norlaw that I ken naething about, and that never heard tell of me."

Katie paused to consider after this. She knew and understood so much of the Mistress's character that she neither took offense nor wished to excite it. This had not been a quite successful essay at conversation, and Katie took a little time to think before she began again.

But while Katie's thoughts left this subject, those of the Mistress held to it. Silence fell upon them again, disturbed only by the rustle of their sleeves as they worked, and the crackle of the fire, which burned brightly, when suddenly the Mistress asked:—

"What like is she?" with an abruptness which took away Katie's breath.

"She?"—it required an effort to remember that this was Desirée of whom they had been speaking—"the little girl at Melmar?" asked Katie. "She is little and bright, and pretty, with very dark eyes and dark hair, a quick little creature, like a bird or a fairy. I confess I was half afraid of her, because she was French," admitted the little mistress of the manse with a blush and a laugh, "but she is a very sweet, winning little girl, with pretty red lips, and white teeth, and black eyes—very little—less than me."

The Mistress drew a long breath and looked relieved.

"I do not know any thing about her," she said slowly; and it seemed quite a comfort to the Mistress to be able to say so, distinctly and impartially. "And so she's at Melmar—a governess—what is that for, Katie? The oldest is woman grown, and the youngest is more like a laddie than a lassie. What are they wanting with a governess? I canna say I ken much of the present family mysel', though my Huntley, if he had but sought his ain, as he might have done—but you'll hear a' that through your cousin, without me."

"No," said Katie.

"Ah, Katie Logan! you speak softly and fairly, and you're a good lassie, and a comfort to the house you belong to," cried the Mistress. "I ken a' that, and I never denied it a' your days! But my Huntley, do you ken what that laddie did before he went away? He had a grand laird-ship within his hand if he would gang to the law and fight it out, as the very writer, your ain cousin, advised him to do. But my son said, 'No; I'll leave my mother her house and her comfort, though they're a' mine,' said my Huntley. 'I'll gang and make the siller first to fight the battle with.' And yonder he is, away at the end of the world, amang his beasts and his toils. He wouldna listen to me. I would have lived in a cothouse or one room, or worked for my bread rather than stand in the way of my son's fortune; but Huntley's a man grown, and maun have his way; and the proud callant had that in his heart that he would make his mother as safe as a queen in her ain house before he would think of either fortune or comfort for himsel'."

The Mistress's voice was broken with her mother-grief, and pride, and triumph. It was, perhaps, the first time she had opened her heart so far— and it was to Katie, whose visit she had resented, and whose secret hold on Huntley's heart was no particular delight to his mother. But even in the midst of the angry impatience with which the Mistress refused to admit a share in her son's affections, she could not resist the charm of sympathy, the grateful fascination of having some one beside her to whom every thing concerning Huntley was almost as interesting as to herself. Huntley's uncommunicated letter was very near running over out of her full heart, and that half-apologetic, half-defiant burst of feeling was the first opening of the tide. Katie's eyes were wet—she could not help it—and they were shining and glowing behind their tears, abashed, proud, joyous, tender, saying what lips can not say—she glanced up, with all her heart in them, at the Mistress, and said something which broke down in a half sob, half laugh, half sigh, and was wholly and entirely inarticulate, though not so unintelligible as one might have supposed. It was a great deal better than words, so far as the Mistress was concerned—it expressed what was inexpressible—the sweet, generous tumult in the girl's heart—too shy even to name Huntley's name, too delicate to approve, yet proud and touched to its depths with an emotion beyond telling. The two women did not rush into each other's arms after this spontaneous burst of mutual confidence. On the contrary, they sat each at her work—the Mistress hurriedly wiping off her tears, and Katie trying to keep her's from falling, if that were possible, and keeping her eyes upon the little glancing needle, which flashed in all manner of colors through the sweet moisture which filled them. Ah! that dim, silent dining-parlor, which now there was neither father nor children to fill and bless!—perhaps by the solitary fireside, where she had sat for so many hours of silent night, alone commanding her heart, a new, tender, soothing, unlooked for relationship suddenly surprised the thoughts of the Mistress. She had not desired it, she had not sought it, yet all at once, almost against her will, a freshness came to her heart like the freshness after showers. Something had happened to Huntley's mother—she had an additional comfort in the world after to-night.

But when Dr. Logan returned, after seeing Willie Noble, the good minister, with pleasant consciousness of having done his duty, was not disturbed by any revelation on the part of the Mistress, or confession from his daughter. He heard a great many extracts read from Huntley's letter, feeling it perfectly natural and proper that he should hear them, and expressing his interest with great friendliness and good pleasure; and then Marget was called in, and the minister conducted family worship, and prayed with fervor for the widow's absent sons, like a patriarch. "The Angel which redeemed me from all evil bless the lads," said the minister in his prayer; and then he craved a special blessing on the first-born, that he might return with joy, and see the face of his mother, and comfort her declining years. Then the excellent pastor rose from his knees placidly, and shook the Mistress's hand, and wended his quiet way down Tyne through the frosty moonlight, with his daughter on his arm. He thought the Mistress was pleased to see them, and that Katie had been a comfort to her to-night. He thought it was a very fine night, and a beautiful moon, and there were Orion, Katie, and the Plow; and so Dr. Logan went peacefully home, and thought he had spent a very profitable night.

CHAPTER XLIV

It was frost, and Tyne was "bearing" at Kirkbride, where the village held a carnival of sliding and skating, and where even the national winter sport, the yearly curling matches, began to be talked of. There was, however, no one at Melmar to tempt Tyne to "bear," even had it been easy to reach his glassy surface through the slippery whitened trees, every twig of which was white and stiff with congealed dew. The Kelpie fell scantily, with a drowsy tinkle, over its little ravine, reduced to the slenderest thread, while all the branches near it were hung with mocking icicles. The sun was high in the blue, frosty midday skies, but had only power enough to clear here and there an exposed branch, and to moisten the path where some little burn crept half frozen under a crust of ice. It was a clear, bracing, invigorating day, and Joanna and Desirée, spite of the frost, were on Tyne-side among the frozen woods.

When standing close together, investigating a bit of moss, both simultaneously heard a crackling footstep among the underwood, and turning round at the same moment, saw some one approaching from the house. He was one of her own countrymen, Desirée thought, with a little flutter at her heart. He wore a large blue cloak, with an immense fur collar, a very French hat, a moustache, and long black hair; Desirée gazed at him with her heart in her eyes, and her white little French hands clasped together. No doubt he brought some message from mamma. But Desirée's hopes were brought to an abrupt conclusion when Joanna sprang forward, exclaiming:

"Oh, Oswald, Oswald! have you really come home? I am so glad you have come home!" with a plunge of welcome which the stranger looked half annoyed, half pleased to encounter. He made a brotherly response to it by stooping to kiss Joanna, a salutation which the girl underwent with a heightened color, and a half-ashamed look; she had meant to shake both his hands violently; any thing in the shape of an embrace being much out of Joanna's way—but Oswald's hands were occupied with his cloak, which he could not permit to fall from his shoulders in the fervor of his brotherly pleasure. Holding it fast, he had only half a hand to give, which Joanna straightway possessed herself of, repeating as she did so her cry of pleasure: "Oh, Oswald, how glad I am! I have wished for such a long time that you would come home!"

"It was very kind of my little sister—or should I say my big sister," said the stranger, looking gallant and courtier-like, "but why, may I ask, were you so anxious for me now? that was a sudden thought, Joanna."

Joanna grew very red as she looked up in his face—then unconsciously she looked at Desirée. Mr. Oswald Huntley was a man of the world, and understood the ways and fancies of young ladies—at least he thought so. He followed Joanna's glance, and a comical smile came to his lips. He took off his hat with an air half mocking, half reverential.

"May I hope to be introduced to your friend, Joanna?" said the new-found brother. With great haste, heat, and perturbation, blushing fiery red, and feeling very uncomfortable, Joanna stumbled through this ceremony, longing for some private means of informing the new-comer who "her friend" was, ere accident or Patricia made him unfavorably aware of it. He was a little amazed evidently by the half-pronounced, half-intelligible name.

"Mademoiselle Desirée?" he repeated after Joanna, with an evident uncertainty, and an air of great surprise.

"Oh, Oswald, you have never got my last letter," cried Joanna; "did you really not know that Desirée was here?"

"I am the governess," cried Desirée, with immense pride and dignity, elevating her little head and drawing up her small figure. Patricia had done her best during these three months to annoy and humiliate the little Frenchwoman—but her pride had never been really touched until to-day.

Oswald's countenance cleared immediately into suavity and good-humor—he smiled, but he bowed, and looked with great graciousness upon the two girls. He could see at a glance how pretty and graceful was this addition to the household of Melmar—and Oswald Huntley was a dilettanti. He liked a pretty person as well as a pretty picture. He begged to know how they could find any pleasure out of doors in this ferocious climate on such a day—and with a glance, and a shrug and a shiver at the frosty languor of the diminished Kelpie, drew his cloak close round him, and turned towards the house, whither, Joanna eagerly, and Desirée with great reluctance and annoyance, the girls were constrained to follow. He walked between them, inclining his ear to his sister, who overwhelmed him with questions, yet addressing now and then a courteous observation to Desirée which gradually mollified that little lady. He was a great deal more agreeable than Melmar or than Patricia—he was something new in the house at least—he knew her own country, perhaps her own very town and house. Desirée became much softened as they drew near the house, and she found herself able to withdraw and leave the brother and sister together. To know the real value of a new face and a new voice, one needs to live for a long winter in a country house like Melmar, whose hospitality was not very greatly prized in the country-side. Desirée had quite got over her anger by the time she reached her own apartment. She made rather a pretty toilet for the evening, and was pleased, in spite of herself, that there would be some one else to talk to besides Melmar, and Aunt Jean and Joanna. The whole house, indeed, was moved with excitement. A dark Italian servant, whom he had brought with him, was regulating with a thermometer, to the dismay and wonder of all the maids, the temperature of Mr. Oswald's room, where these unscientific functionaries had put on a great, uncomfortable fire, piled half-way up the chimney. Patricia had entered among them to peer over her brother's locked trunks, and see if there was any thing discoverable by curiosity. Mrs. Huntley was getting up in haste to see her son, and even Aunt Jean trotted up and down stairs on her nimble little feet, on errands of investigation and assistance. It made no small commotion in the house when the only son of Melmar came home.

Oswald Huntley, but for his dark hair, was like his sister Patricia. He was tall, but of a delicate form, and had small features, and a faint color which said little for his strength. When they all met together in the evening, the traveled son was by much the most elegant member of the household circle. His dainty, varnished boots, his delicate white hands, his fine embroidered linen, filled Joanna with a sentiment which was half impatience and half admiration. Joanna would rather have had Oswald despise these delicacies of apparel, which did not suit with her ideal of manhood. At the same time she had never seen any thing like them, and they dazzled her. As for Patricia, she looked from her brother to herself, and colored red with envious displeasure. One of Oswald's rings would have purchased every thing in the shape of jewelry which Patricia ever had or hoped for—his valet, his dress, his "style," at once awed and irritated his unfortunate sister. If papa could afford to keep Oswald thus, was it not a disgrace to confine "me!" within the tedious bounds of this country house? Poor little Patricia could have cried with envy and self pity.

In the meantime, Oswald made himself very agreeable, and drew the little party together as they seldom were drawn. His mother sat up in her easy chair, looking almost pretty with her pink cheeks, and for once without any invalid accompaniments of barley-water or cut oranges. Melmar himself staid in the drawing-room all the evening, displaying his satisfaction by some occasional rude fun with Joanna and jokes at "Mademoiselle," and listening to his son very complacently though he seldom addressed him. Aunt Jean had drawn her chair close to Mrs. Huntley, and seriously inclined, not her ear only, which was but a dull medium, but the lively black eyes with which she seemed almost able to hear as well as see. Joanna hung upon her mother's footstool, eagerly and perpetually asking questions. The only one out of the family group was Desirée, who kept apart, working at her embroidery, but whom Mr. Oswald by no means neglected. The new comer had good taste. He thought the little table which held the governess's thread and scissors, and little crimson work-bag, and the little chair close by, where the little governess herself sat working with her pretty white hands, her graceful girlish dress, her dark hair in which the light shone, and her well-formed, well-poised head bending over her embroidery, was the prettiest bit in the room, and well worth looking at. He looked at it accordingly as he talked, distributing his favors impartially among the family, and wondered a little who this little girl might be, and what brought her here. When Oswald stooped forward to say something politely to the little Frenchwoman—when he brought a flush to her cheek by addressing her in her own language, though Desirée's own good sense taught her that it was best to reply in English—when he pronounced himself a connoisseur in embroidery, and inspected the pretty work in her hands—his ailing mother and his deaf aunt, as well as the spiteful Patricia, simultaneously perceived something alarming in the courtesy. Desirée was very young and very pretty, and Oswald was capricious, fanciful, and the heir of Melmar. What if the little governess, sixteen years old, should captivate the son, who was only five-and-twenty? The fear sprang from one feminine mind to another, of all save Joanna, who had already given her thoughts to this catastrophe as the most desirable thing in the world. Oswald's experience and knowledge of the world, on which he prided himself, went for nothing in the estimation of his female relatives. They thought Desirée, at sixteen, more than a match for him, as they would have thought any other girl in the same circumstances. People say women have no *esprit du corps*, but they certainly have the most perfect contempt for any man's powers of resistance before the imagined wiles and fascinations of "a designing girl." These ladies almost gave Oswald over, as he stood, graceful and self-satisfied, in the midst of them—a monarch of all he surveyed—extending his lordly courtesies to the poor little governess. Had he but known! but he did not know any thing about it, and said to himself compassionately, "Poor little thing—how pretty she is!—what could bring her here?" as he threw himself back upon the pillow in that room of which Antonio had regulated the temperature, and thought no more about Desirée; whereas poor little Desirée, charmed with the new voice, and the new grace, and the unusual kindness, dreamed of him all night.

CHAPTER XLV

"Am I to understand that our title is somehow endangered? I do not quite comprehend your last letter," said Oswald, addressing his father somewhat haughtily. They were in Melmar's study, where everybody went to discuss this business, and where the son sat daintily upon a chair which he had selected from the others for his own use, leaning the points of his elbows upon the table, and looking elaborately uncomfortable—so much so, that some faint idea that this study, after all, could not be a very pleasant apartment, entered, for the first time, the mind of Melmar.

"Come nearer to the fire, Oswald," said Mr. Huntley, suddenly. He was really solicitous about the health and comfort of his son.

"Thank you; I can scarcely breathe *here*," said the young man, ungratefully. "Was I right, sir, in supposing *that* to be your reason for writing me such a letter as your last?"

"You were right in supposing that I wanted to see you," said the father, with some natural displeasure. "You live a fine life in foreign parts, my lad; you've little to put you about; but what could you do for yourself if the funds at Melmar were to fail?"

"Really the idea is disagreeable," said Oswald, laughing. "I had rather not take it into consideration, unless it is absolutely necessary."

"If it were so," said Melmar, with a little bitterness, "which of you could I depend upon—which of you would stretch out a helping hand to help me?"

"To help *you*? Upon my word, sir, I begin to think you must be in earnest," said his son. "What does this mean? Is there really any other claimant for the estate? Have we any real grounds for fear? Were not you the heir-at-law?"

"I was the heir-at-law; and there is no other claimant," said Melmar, dryly; "but there is a certain person in existence, Oswald Huntley, who, if she but turns up soon enough—and there's two or three years yet to come and go upon—can turn both you and me to the door, and ruin us with arrears of income to the boot."

Oswald grew rather pale. "Is this a new discovery?" he said, "or why did I, who am, next to yourself, the person most concerned, never hear of it before?"

"You were a boy, in the first place; and in the second place, a head-strong, self-willed lad; nextly, delicate," said Melmar, still with a little sarcasm; "and it remains to be seen yet whether you're a reasonable man."

"Oh, hang reason!" cried the young man with excitement. "I understand all that. What's to be done? that seems the main thing. Who is this certain person that has a better right to Melmar than we?"

"Tell me first what you would do if you knew," said Mr. Huntley, bending his red gray eyes intently upon his son. Melmar knew that there were generous young fools in the world, who would not hesitate to throw fortune and living to the winds for the sake of something called honor and justice. He had but little acquaintance with his son; he did not know what stuff Oswald was made of. He thought it just possible that the spirit of such Quixotes might animate this elegant mass of good breeding and dillettanteism; for which reason he sat watching under his grizzled, bushy eyebrows, with the intensest looks of those fiery eyes.

"Pshaw! do? You don't suppose *I* would be likely to yield to any one without a struggle. Who is it?" said Oswald; "let me know plainly what you mean."

"It is the late Me'mar's daughter and only child; a woman with children; a woman in poor circumstances," replied Mr. Huntley, still with a certain dry sarcasm in his voice.

"But she was disinherited?" said Oswald, eagerly.

"Her father left a will in her favor," said Melmar, "reinstating her fully in her natural rights; that will is in the hands of our enemies, whom the old fool left his heirs, failing his daughter: she and her children, and these young men, are ready to pounce upon the estate."

"But she was lost—did I not hear so?" cried Oswald, rising from his chair in overpowering excitement.

"Ay!" said his father, "but I know where she is."

"In Heaven's name, what do you mean?" cried the unfortunate young man; "is it to bewilder and overwhelm me that you tell me all this? Have we no chance? Are we mere impostors? Is all this certain and beyond dispute? What do you mean?"

"It is all certain," said Melmar, steadily; "her right is unquestionable; she has heirs of her own blood, and I know where she is—she can turn us out of house and home to-morrow—she can make me a poor writer, ruined past redemption, and you a useless fine gentleman, fit for nothing in this world that I know of, and your sisters servant-maids, for I don't know what else they're good for. All this she can do, Oswald Huntley, and more than this, the moment she makes her appearance—but she is as ignorant as you were half an hour ago. *I* know—but *she* does not know."

What will Oswald do?—he is pacing up and down the little study, no longer elegant, and calm, and self-possessed; the faint color on his cheeks grows crimson—the veins swell upon his forehead—a profuse cold moisture comes upon his face. Pacing about the narrow space of the study, thrusting the line of chairs out of his way, clenching his delicate hand involuntarily in the tumult of his thoughts, there could not have been a greater contrast than between Oswald at his entrance and Oswald now. His father sat and watched him under his bushy eyebrows—watched him with a steady, fixed, fascinating gaze, which the young man's firmness was not able to withstand. He burst out into uneasy, troubled exclamations.

"What are we to do, then?—must we go and seek her out, and humble ourselves before her?—must we bring her back in triumph to her inheritance? It is the only thing we can do with honor. What *are* we to do?"

"Remember, Oswald," said Melmar, significantly, "*she* does not know."

The young man threw himself into a chair, hid his face in his hands, and broke into low, muttered groans of vexation and despair, which sounded like curses, and perhaps were so. Then he turned towards his father violently and suddenly, with again that angry question, "What are we to do?"

He was not without honor, he was not without conscience; if he had there could have been little occasion for that burning color, or for the cold beads of moisture on his forehead. The sudden and startling intelligence had bewildered him for a moment—then he had undergone a fierce but brief struggle, and then Oswald Huntley sank into his chair, and into the hands of his father, with that melancholy confession of his weakness—a question when the matter was unquestionable—"what are we to do?"

"Nothing," said Melmar, grimly, regarding his son with a triumph which, perhaps, after all, had a little contempt in it. This, then, was all the advantage which his refinement and fine-gentlemanliness gave him—a moment's miserable, weakly hesitation, nothing more nor better. The father, with his coarse methods of thought, and unscrupulous motives, would not have hesitated: yet not a whit stronger, as it appeared, was the honor or courage of the son.

"Nothing!" said Melmar; "simply to keep quiet, and be prepared against emergencies, and if possible to stave off every proceeding for a few years more. They have a clever lad of a lawyer in their interests, which is against us, but you may trust me to keep him back if it is possible; a few years and we are safe—I ask nothing but time."

"And nothing from me?" said Oswald, rising with a sullen shame upon his face, which his father did not quite comprehend. The young man felt that he had no longer any standing ground of superiority; he was humiliated, abased, cast down. Such advantage as there was in moral obtuseness and strength of purpose lay altogether with Melmar. His son only knew better, without any will to do better. He was degraded in his own eyes, and angrily conscious of it, and a sullen resentment rose within him. If he could do nothing, why tell him of this to give him a guilty consciousness of the false position which he had not courage enough to abandon? Why drag him down from his airy height of mannerly and educated elevation to prove him clay as mean as the parent whom he despised? It gave an additional pang to the overthrow. There was nothing to be done—the misery was inflicted for nothing—only as a warning to guard against an emergency which, perhaps, had it come unguarded, might not have stripped Oswald so bare of self-esteem as this.

"We'll see that," said Melmar, slowly; then he rose and went to the door and investigated the passages. No one was there. When he returned, he said something in his son's ear, which once more brought a flush of uneasy shame to his cheek. The father made his suggestion lightly, with a chuckle. The young man heard it in silence, with an indescribable look of self-humiliation. Then they separated—Oswald to hurry out, with his cloak round him, to the grounds where he could be alone—Melmar to bite his pen in the study, and muse over his victory. What would come of it?—his own ingenuity and that last suggestion which he had breathed in Oswald's ear. Surely these were more than enough to baffle the foolish young Livingstones of Norlaw, and even their youthful agent? He thought so. The old Aberdonian felt secure in his own skill and cunning—he had no longer the opposition of his son to dread. What should he fear?

In the meantime, Patricia, who had seen her brother leave the house in great haste, like a man too late for an appointment, and who had spied a light little figure crossing the bridge over Tyne before, wrapped herself up, though it was a very cold day, and set out also to see what she could discover. Malice and curiosity together did more to keep her warm than the cloak and fur tippet, yet she almost repented when she found herself among the frozen, snow-sprinkled trees, with the faint tinkle of the Kelpie striking sharp, yet drowsy, like a little stream of metal through the frost-bound stillness, and no one visible on the path, where now and then her foot slid upon a treacherous bit of ice, inlaid in the hard brown soil. Could they have left the grounds of Melmar? Where could they have gone? If they had not met, one of them must certainly have appeared by this time; and Patricia still pushed on, though her cheeks were blue and her fingers red with cold, and though the intensity of the chill made her faint, and pierced to her poor little heart. At last she was rewarded by hearing voices before her. Yes, there they were. Desirée standing in the path, looking up at the trunk of a tree, from which Oswald was stripping a bit of velvet moss, with bells of a little white fungus, delicate and pure as flowers, growing upon it. As Patricia came up, her brother presented the prize to the little Frenchwoman, almost with the air of a lover. The breast of his poor little sister swelled with bitterness, dislike, and malicious triumph. She had found them out.

"Oswald! I thought you were quite afraid of taking cold," cried Patricia—"dear me, who could have supposed that you would have been in the woods on such a day! I am sure Mademoiselle ought to be very proud— you would not have come for any one else in the house."

"I am extremely indebted to you, Patricia, for letting Mademoiselle know so much," said Oswald. "One does not like to proclaim one's own merits. Was it on Mademoiselle's account that you, too, undertook the walk, poor child? Come, I will help you home."

"Oh, I'm sure she does not want *me*!" exclaimed Patricia, ready to cry in the height of her triumph. "Papa and you are much more in her way than I am—as long as she can make you gentlemen do what she pleases, she does not care any thing about your sisters. Oh, I know all about it!—I know papa is infatuated about her, and so are you, and she is a designing little creature, and does not care a bit for Joanna. You may say what you please, but I know I am right, and I will not stand it longer—I shall go this very moment and tell mamma!"

"Mademoiselle Huntley shall not have that trouble," cried Desirée, who had been standing by utterly amazed for the first few moments, with cheeks alternately burning red and snow pale. "*I* shall tell Mrs. Huntley; it concerns me most of any one. Mademoiselle may be unkind if she pleases—I am used to that—but no one shall dare," cried the little heroine, stamping her little foot, and clapping her hands in sudden passion, "to say insulting words to me! I thank you, Monsieur Oswald—but it is for me, it is not for you—let me pass—I shall tell Mrs. Huntley this moment, and I shall go!"

"Patricia is a little fool, Mademoiselle," said Oswald, vainly endeavoring to divert the seriousness of the incident. "Nay—come, we shall all go together—but every person of sense in the house will be deeply grieved if you take this absurdity to heart. Forget it; she shall beg your pardon. Patricia!" exclaimed the young man, in a deep undertone of passion, "you ridiculous little idiot! do you know what you have done?"

"Oh, I know! I've told the truth—I am too clear-sighted!" sobbed Patricia, "*I* can not help seeing that both papa and you are crazy about the governess—it will break poor mamma's heart!"

Though Desirée was much wounded, ashamed, and angry, furious rather, to tell the truth, she could not resist the ludicrous whimper of this mock sorrow. She laughed scornfully.

"I shall go by myself, please," she said, springing through a by-way, where Oswald was not agile enough or sufficiently acquainted with to follow. "I shall tell Mrs. Huntley, instantly, and she will not break her heart—but no one in the world shall dare to speak thus again to me."

So Desirée disappeared like a bird among the close network of frozen branches, and Patricia and her brother, admirable good friends, as one might suppose, together pursued their way home.

CHAPTER XLVI

A series of violent scenes in Melmar made a fitting climax to this little episode in the wood. Desirée demanded an interview with Mrs. Huntley, and obtained it in that lady's chamber, which interview was not over when Patricia appeared, and shortly after Melmar himself, and Oswald, who sent both the governess and her enemy away, and had a private conference with the unfortunate invalid, who was not unwilling to take up her daughter's suspicions, and condemn the little Frenchwoman as a designing girl, with schemes against the peace of the heir of Melmar. Somehow or other, the father and son together managed to still these suspicions, or to give them another direction; for, on the conclusion of this conference Desirée was sent for again to Mrs. Huntley's room; the little governess in the meanwhile had been busy in her own, putting her little possessions together with angry and mortified haste, her heart swelling high with a tumult of wounded pride and indignant feeling. Desirée obeyed with great stateliness. She found the mother of the house lying back upon her pillow, with a flush upon her pink cheeks, and angry tears gleaming in her weak blue eyes. Mrs. Huntley tried to be dignified, too, and to tell Desirée that she was perfectly satisfied, and there was not the slightest imputation upon her, the governess; but finding this not answer at all, and that the governess still stood in offended state, like a little queen before her, Mrs. Huntley took to her natural weapons—broke down, cried, and bemoaned herself over the trouble she had with her family, and the vexation which Patricia gave her. "And now, when I had just hoped to see Joanna improving, then comes this disturbance in the house, and my poor nerves are shattered to pieces, and my head like to burst, and you are going away!" sobbed Mrs. Huntley. Desirée was moved to compassion; she went up to the invalid, and arranged her cushions for her, and trusted all this annoyance would not make her ill. Mrs. Huntley seized the opportunity; she went on bewailing herself, which was a natural and congenial amusement, and she made Desirée various half-sincere compliments, with a skill which no one could have suspected her of possessing. The conclusion was, that the little Frenchwoman yielded, and gave up her determination to leave Melmar; instead of that she came and sat by Mrs. Huntley all day, reading to her, while Patricia was shut out; and a storm raged below over that exasperated and unhappy little girl. The next day there was calm weather. Patricia was confined to her room with a headache. Joanna was energetically affectionate to her governess, and Mrs. Huntley came down stairs on purpose to make Desirée feel comfortable. Poor little Desirée, who was so young, and in reality so simple-hearted, forgot all her resentment. Her heart was touched by the kindness which they all seemed so anxious to show her—impulses of affectionate response rose within herself—she read to Mrs. Huntley, she put her netting in order for her, she arranged her footstool as the invalid declared no one had ever been able to do it before; and Desirée blushed and went shyly away to her embroidery, when Oswald came to sit by his mother's little table. Oswald was very animated, and anxious to please everybody; he found a new story which nobody had seen, and read it aloud to them while the ladies worked. The day was quite an Elysian day after the troubles of the previous one; and Desirée, with a little tumult in her heart, found herself more warmly established in Melmar that evening than she had ever been hitherto; she did not quite comprehend it, to tell the truth. All this generous desire to make her comfortable, though the girl accepted it without question as real, and never suspected deceit in it, was, notwithstanding, alien to the character of the household, and puzzled her unconsciously. But Desirée did not inquire with herself what was the cause of it. If some fairy voice whispered a reason in her ear, she blushed and tried to forget it again. No, his father and mother were proud of Oswald; they were ambitious for him; they would think such a fancy the height of folly, could it even be possible that he entertained it. No, no, no! it could not be that.

Yet, next day, when Joanna and Desirée went out to walk, Oswald encountered them before they had gone far, and seemed greatly pleased to constitute himself the escort of his sister and her governess. If he talked to Joanna sometimes, it was to Desirée that his looks, his cares, his undertones of half-confidential conversation were addressed. He persuaded them out of "the grounds" to the sunny country road leading to Kirkbride, where the sun shone warmer; but where all the country might have seen him stooping to the low stature of his sister's governess. Desirée was only sixteen; she was not wise and fortified against the blandishments of man;—she yielded with a natural pleasure to the natural pride and shy delight of her position. She had never seen any one so agreeable; she had never received before that unspoken but intoxicating homage of the young man to the young woman, which puts an end to all secondary differences and degrees. She went forward with a natural expansion at her heart—a natural brightening in her eyes—a natural radiance of young life and beauty in her face. She could not help it. It was the first tender touch of a new sunshine upon her heart.

A woman stood by herself upon the road before them, looking out, as it seemed, for the entrance of a little by-way, which ran through the Melmar woods, and near the house, an immemorial road which no proprietor could shut up. Desirée observed Joanna run up to this bystander; observed the quick, lively, middle-aged features, the pleasant complexion and bright eyes, which turned for a moment to observe the party; yet would have passed on without further notice but for hearing the name of Cosmo. Cosmo! could this be his mother? Desirée had her own reasons for desiring to see the Mistress; she went forward with her lively French self-possession to ask if it was Mrs. Livingstone, and if she might thank her for her son's kindness in Edinburgh. The Mistress looked at her keenly, and she looked at the Mistress; both the glances were significant, and meant more than a common meeting; half a dozen words, graceful and proper on Desirée's part, and rather abrupt and embarrassed on that of the Mistress, passed between them, and then they went upon their several ways. The result of the interview, for the little Frenchwoman, was a bright and vivid little mental photograph of the Mistress, very clear in external features, and as entirely wrong in its guess at character as was to be expected from the long and far difference between the little portrait-painter and her subject. Desirée broke through her own pleasant maze of fancy for the moment to make her rapid notes upon the Mistress. She was more interested in her than there seemed any reason for; certainly much more than simply as the mother of Cosmo, whom she had seen but twice in her life, and was by no means concerned about.

"Who is that?" asked Oswald, when the Mistress had passed.

"It is Mrs. Livingstone, of Norlaw," said Joanna, "Cosmo's mother; Desirée knows; but I wonder if she's going up to Melmar? I think I'll run and ask her. I don't know why she should go to Melmar, for I'm sure she ought to hate papa."

"That will do; I am not particularly curious—you need not trouble yourself to ask on my account," said Oswald, putting out his hand to stop Joanna, "and, pray, how does Mademoiselle Desirée know? I should not suppose that ruddy countrywoman was much like a friend of *yours*."

"I have never seen her before," said Desirée.

"Ah, I might have trusted that to your own good taste," said Oswald, with a bow and a smile; "but you must pardon me for feeling that such a person was not an acquaintance meet for you."

Desirée made no answer. The look and the smile made her poor little heart beat—she did not ask herself why he was so interested in her friendships and acquaintances. She accepted it with downcast eyes and a sweet, rising color; he *did* concern himself about all the matters belonging to her—that was enough.

"Mrs. Livingstone of Norlaw is not a common person—she is as good as we are, if she is not as rich," cried Joanna. "*I* like her! I would rather see her than a dozen fine ladies, and, Desirée, you ought to stand up for her, too. If you think Norlaw is no' as good as Melmar, it's because you're not of this country and don't know—that is all."

Desirée, looking up, saw to her surprise an angry and menacing look upon the face, which a minute ago had been bent with such gallant courtesy towards her own, and which was now directed to Joanna.

"Norlaw may be as good as Melmar," said the gentle Oswald, with an emphasis which for the moment made him like Patricia; "but that is no reason why one of that family should be a worthy acquaintance for Mademoiselle Desirée, who is not much like you, Joanna, nor your friends."

Joanna loved Desirée with all her heart—but this was going too far even for her patience; she ended the conversation abruptly by a bewildered stare in her brother's face, and a burst of tears.

"Desirée used to be fond of me, till you came—*she* was my only friend!" cried poor Joanna, whom Desirée's kiss scarcely succeeded in comforting. She did not know what to do, this poor little governess—it seemed fated that Oswald's attentions were to embroil her with all his family—yet somehow one can not resent with very stern virtue the injustice which shows particular favor to one's self. Desirée still thought it was very kind of Oswald Huntley to concern himself that she should have proper friends.

CHAPTER XLVII

Katie Logan was by herself in the manse parlor. Though the room was as bright as ever, the little housekeeper did not look so bright. She was darning the little stockings which filled the basket, but she was not singing her quiet song, nor thinking pleasant thoughts. Katie's eyes were red, and her cheeks pale. She was beginning to go, dark and blindfold, into a future which it broke her heart to think of. Those children of the manse, what would become of them when they had neither guide nor guardian but Katie? This was question enough to oppress the elder sister, if every thing else had not been swallowed in the thought of her father's growing weakness, of the pallor and the trembling which every one observed, and of the exhaustion of old age into which the active minister visibly began to fall. Katie was full of these thoughts when she heard some one come to the door; she went immediately to look at herself in the mirror over the mantel-piece, and to do her best to look like her wont; but it was alike a wonder and a relief to Katie, looking round, to find the Mistress, a most unusual visitor, entering the room.

The Mistress was not much in the custom of paying visits—it embarrassed her a little when she did so, unless she had some distinct errand. She dropped into a chair near the door, and put back her vail upon her bonnet, and looked at Katie with a little air of fatigue and past excitement.

"No, no, thank ye," said the Mistress, "I've been walking, I'll no' come to the fire; it's cold, but it's a fine day outbye—I just thought I would take a walk up by Whittock's Gate."

"Were you at Mrs. Blackadder's?" asked Katie.

"No," said the Mistress, with a slightly confused expression. "I was no place, but just taking a walk. What for should I no' walk for pleasure as well as my neighbors? but indeed, to tell the truth, I had a very foolish reason, Katie," she added, after a little interval. "I've never had rest in my mind after what you said of the French lassie at Melmar. I did ken of a person that was lost and married long ago, and might just as well be in France as in ony other place. She was no friend of mine, but I kent of her, and I've seen her picture and heard what like she was, so, as I could not help but turn it over in my mind, I just took the gate up there, a wise errand, to see if I could get a look of this bairn. I meant to go through the Melmar footpath, though that house and them that belong to it are little pleasure to me; but as guid fortune was, I met them in the road."

"Joanna and the governess?" said Katie.

"And mair than them," answered the Mistress. "A lad that I would take to be the son that's been so long away. An antic with a muckle cloak, and a black beard, and a' the looks of a French fiddler; but Joanna called him by his name, so he bid to be her brother; and either he's deluding the other bit lassie, or she's ensnaring him."

Katie smiled, so faintly and unlike herself, that it was not difficult to perceive how little her heart was open to amusement. The Mistress, however, who apprehended every thing after her own fashion, took even this faint expression of mirth a little amiss.

"You needna laugh—there's little laughing matter in it," said the Mistress. "If a bairn of mine were to be led away after ony such fashion, do ye think I could find in my heart to smile? Na, they're nae friends of mine, the present family of Melmar; but I canna see a son of a decent house maybe beguiled by an artfu' foreign woman, however great an antic he may be himself, and take ony pleasure in it. It's aye sure to be a grief to them he belongs to, and maybe a destruction to the lad a' his life."

"But Desirée is only sixteen, and Oswald Huntley, if it was Oswald—is a very great deal older—he should be able to take care of himself," said Katie, repeating the offense. "You saw her, then? Do you think she was like the lady you knew?"

"I never said I knew any lady," said the Mistress, testily. "I kent of one that was lost mony a year ago. Na, na, this is naebody belonging to *her*. She was a fair, soft woman that, with blue e'en, and taller than me; but this is a bit elf of a thing, dark and little. I canna tell what put it into my head for a moment, for Melmar was the last house in the world to look for a bairn's of *hers* in; but folk canna help nonsense thoughts. Cosmo, you see, he's a very fanciful laddie, as indeed is no' to be wondered at, and he wrote me hame word about somebody he had seen—and then hearing of this bairn asking questions about me; but it was just havers, as I kent from the first—she is no more like her than she's like you or me. But I'm sorry about the lad. Naething but ill and mischief can come of the like, so far as I've seen. If he's deluding the bairn, he's a villain, Katie, and if she's leading him on—and ane can never tell what snares are in these Frenchwomen from their very cradle—I'm sorry for Melmar and his wife, though they're no friends to me."

"I think Oswald Huntley ought to be very well able to take care of himself," repeated Katie—"and to know French ways, too. I like Desirée, and I don't like him. I hope she will not have any thing to say to him. When is Cosmo coming home?"

The Mistress, however, looked a little troubled about Cosmo. She did not answer readily.

"He's a fanciful bairn," she said, half fondly, half angrily—"as indeed what else can you expect? He's ane of the real auld Livingstones of Norlaw— aye some grand wild plan in his head for other folks, and no' that care for himself that might be meet. He would have been a knight like what used to be in the ballads in my young days, if he hadna lived ower late for that."

Pausing here, the Mistress closed her lips with a certain emphatic movement, as though she had nothing more to say upon this subject, and was about proceeding to some other, when they were both startled by the noisy opening of a door, which Katie knew to be the study. The sound was that of some feeble hand, vainly attempting to turn the handle, and shaking the whole door with the effort which was at last successful; then came a strange, incoherent, half-pronounced "Katie!" Katie flew to the door, with a face like death itself. The Mistress rose and waited, breathless, yet too conscious of her own impatience of intrusion to follow. Then a heavy, slow fall, as of some one whose limbs failed under him, a cry from Katie, and the sudden terrified scream of one of the maids from the kitchen moved the Mistress beyond all thoughts but those of help. She ran into the little hall of the manse, throwing her cloak off her shoulders with an involuntary promise that she could not leave this house to-day. There she saw a melancholy sight, the minister, with a gray ashen paleness upon his face, lying on the threshold of his study, not insensible, but powerless, moving with a dreadful impotence those poor, pale, trembling lips, from which no sound would come. Katie knelt beside him, supporting his head, almost as pallid as he, aggravating, unawares, the conscious agony of his helplessness by anxious, tender questions, imploring him to speak to her—while the maid stood behind, wringing her hands, crying, and asking whether she should bring water? whether she should get some wine? what she should do?

"Flee this moment," cried the Mistress, pushing this latter to the door, "and bring in the first man you can meet to carry him to his bed—that's what *you're* to do—and, Katie, Katie, whisht, dinna vex him—he canna speak to you. Keep up your heart—we'll get him to his bed, and we'll get the doctor, and he'll come round."

The Laird Of Norlaw | 233

Katie lifted up her woeful white face to the Mistress—the poor girl did not say a word—did not even utter a sob or shed a tear. Her eyes said only, "it has come! it has come!" The blow which she had been trembling for had fallen at last. And the Mistress, who was not given to tokens of affection, stooped down in the deep pity of her heart and kissed Katie's forehead. There was nothing to be said. This sudden calamity was beyond the reach of speech.

They got the sufferer conveyed to his room and laid on his bed a few minutes after, and within a very short time the only medical aid which the neighborhood afforded was by the bed-side. But medical aid could do little for the minister—he was old, and had long been growing feeble, and nobody wondered to hear that he had suffered "a stroke," and that there was very, very little hope of his recovery. The old people in Kirkbride clustered together, speaking of it with that strange, calm curiosity of age, which always seems rather to congratulate itself that some one else is the present sufferer, yet is never without the consciousness that itself may be the next. A profound sympathy, reverence, and compassion was among all the villagers—passive towards Dr. Logan, active to Katie, the guardian and mother of the little household of orphans who soon were to have no other guardian. They said to each other, "God help her!" in her youth and loneliness—what was she to do?

As for the Mistress, she was not one of those benevolent neighbors who share in the vigils of every sick room, and have a natural faculty for nursing. To her own concentrated individual temper, the presence of strangers in any household calamity was so distasteful, that she could scarcely imagine it acceptable to others; and she never offered services which she would not have accepted. But there was neither offer nor acceptance now. The Mistress sent word at once to Marget, took off her bonnet, and without a word to any one, took her place in the afflicted house. Even now she was but little in the sick chamber.

"If he kens her, he'll like best to see Katie—and if he doesna ken her, it'll aye be a comfort to herself," said the Mistress. "I'll take the charge of every thing else—- but his ain bairn's place is there."

"I only fear," said the doctor, "that the poor thing will wear herself out."

"She's young, and she's a good bairn," said the Mistress, "and she'll have but one father, if she lives ever so long a life. I'm no feared. No, doctor, dinna hinder Katie; if she wears herself out, poor bairn, she'll have plenty of sad time to rest in. Na, I dinna grudge her watching; she doesna feel it now, and it'll be a comfort to her a' her life."

It was, perhaps, a new doctrine to the country doctor; but he acknowledged the truth of it, and the Mistress, wise in this, left Katie to that mournful, silent, sick room, where the patient lay motionless and passive in the torpor of paralysis, perhaps conscious, it was hard to know—but unable to communicate a word of all that might be in his heart. The children below, hushed and terror-stricken, had never been under such strict rule, yet never had known so many indulgences all their lives before; and the Mistress took *her* night's rest upon the sofa, wrapped in a shawl and morning gown, ready to start in an instant, should she be called; but she did not disturb the vigil of the daughter by her father's bed-side.

And Katie, absorbed by her own sorrows, hardly noticed—hardly knew—this characteristic delicacy. She sat watching him with an observation so intent, that she almost fancied she could see his breath, watching the dull, gray eyes, half closed and lustreless, to note if, perhaps, a wandering light of expression might kindle in them; watching the nerveless, impotent hands, if perhaps, motion might be restored to them; watching the lips, lest they should move, and she might lose the chance of guessing at some word. There was something terrible, fascinating, unearthly in the task; he was there upon the bed, and yet he was not there, confined in a dismal speechless prison, to which perhaps—they could not tell—their own words and movements might penetrate, but out of which nothing could come. His daughter sat beside him, looking forward with awe into the blank solemnity of the future. No mother, no father; only the little dependent children, who had but herself to look to. She went over and over again the very same ground. Orphans, and desolate; her thoughts stopped there, and went no further. She could not help contemplating the terrible necessity before her; but she could not make plans while her father lay there, speechless yet breathing, in her sight.

She was sitting thus, the fourth day after his seizure, gazing at him; the room was very still—the blinds were down—a little fire burned cheerfully in the grate—her eyes were fixed upon his eyes, watching them, and as she watched it seemed to Katie that her father's look turned towards a narrow, ruddy, golden arrow of sunshine, which streamed in at the side of the window. She rose hastily and went up to the bed. Then his lips began to move—she bent down breathlessly; God help her!—he spoke, and she was close to his faltering lips; but all Katie's strained and agonizing senses could not tell a word of what he meant to say. What matter? His eyes were not on her, but on the sunshine—the gleam of God's boundless light coming in to the chamber of mortality—his thoughts were not with her in her sore youthful trouble. He was as calm as an angel, lying there in the death of his old age and the chill of his faculties. But she—she was young, she was desolate, she was his child—her heart cried out in intolerable anguish, and would not be satisfied. Could it be possible? Would he pass away with those moving lips, with that faint movement of a smile, and she never know what he meant to say?

With the restlessness of extreme and almost unbearable suffering, Katie rang her bell—the doctor had desired to know whenever his patient showed any signs of returning consciousness. Perhaps the sound came to the ear of the dying man, perhaps only his thoughts changed. But when she turned again, Katie found the reverent infantine calm gone from his face, and his eyes bent upon her with a terrible struggle after speech, which wrung her very heart. She cried aloud involuntarily with an echo of the agony upon that ashen face. The sound of her voice, of her hasty step and of the bell, brought the Mistress to the room, and the terrified servants to the door. Katie did not see the Mistress; she saw nothing in the world but the pitiful struggle of those palsied lips to speak to her, the anguish of uncommunicable love in those opened eyes. She bent over him, putting her very ear to his mouth; when that failed, she tried, Heaven help her, to look as if she had heard him, to comfort his heart in his dying. The old man's eyes opened wider, dilating with the last effort—at last came a burst of incoherent sound—he had spoken—what was it? The Mistress turned her head away and bowed down upon her knees at the door, with an involuntary awe and pity, too deep for any expression, but Katie cried, "Yes, father, yes, I hear you!" with a cry that might have rent the skies. If she did, Heaven knows; she thought so—and so did he; the effort relaxed—the eyes closed—and word of human language the good minister uttered never more.

It was all over. Four little orphans sat below crying under their breath, unaware of what was their calamity—and Katie Logan above, at nineteen, desolate and unsupported, and with more cares than a mother, stood alone upon the threshold of the world.

CHAPTER XLVIII

While the peaceful Manse of Kirkbride was turned into a house of mourning, a strange little drama was being played at Melmar. The household there seemed gradually clustering, a strange chorus of observation, round Oswald and Desirée, the two principal figures in the scene. Melmar himself watched the little Frenchwoman with cat-like stealthiness, concentrating his regard upon her. Aunt Jean sat in her chair apart, troubled and unenlightened, perpetually calling Desirée to her, and inventing excuses to draw her out of the presence and society of Oswald. Patricia, when she was present in the family circle, directed a spiteful watch upon the two, with the vigilance of an ill-fairy; while even Joanna, a little shocked and startled by the diversion of Desirée's regard from herself, a result which she had not quite looked for, behaved very much like a jealous lover to the poor little governess, tormenting her by alternate sulks and violent outbursts of fondness. Oswald himself, though he was always at her side, though he gave her a quite undue share of his time and attention, and made quite fantastical exhibitions of devotion, was a lover, if lover he was, ill at ease, capricious and overstrained. He knew her pretty, he felt that she was full of mind, and spirit, and intelligence—but still she was a little girl to Oswald Huntley, who was not old enough to find in her fresh youth the charm which has subdued so many a man of the world—nor young enough to meet her on equal ground. Why he sought her at all, unless he had really "fallen in love" with her, it seemed very hard to find out. Aunt Jean, looking on with her sharp black eyes, could only shake her head in silent wonder, and doubt, and discomfort. He could have "nae motive"—but Aunt Jean thought that lovers looked differently in her days, and a vague suspicion disturbed the mind of the old woman. She used to call Desirée to her own side, to keep her there talking of her embroidery, or telling her old stories of which the girl began to tire, being occupied by other thoughts. The hero himself was unaware of, and totally indifferent to, Aunt Jean's scrutiny, but Melmar himself sometimes turned his fiery eyes to her corner, with a glance of doubt and apprehension. She was the only spectator in the house of whose inspection Mr. Huntley was at all afraid.

Meanwhile Desirée herself lived in a dream—the first dream of extreme youth, of a tender heart and gentle imagination, brought for the first time into personal contact with the grand enchantress and Armida of life. Desirée was not learned in the looks of lover's eyes—she had no "experience," poor child! to guide her in this early experiment and trembling delight of unfamiliar emotion. She knew she was poor, young, solitary, Joanna's little French governess, yet that it was she, the little dependent, whom Joanna's graceful brother, everybody else's superior, singled out for his regard. Her humble little heart responded with all a young girl's natural flutter of pride, of gratitude, of exquisite and tremulous pleasure. There could be but one reason in the world to induce this unaccustomed homage and devotion. She could not believe that Oswald admired or found any thing remarkable in herself, only—strange mystery, not to be thought of save with the blush of that profoundest humility which is born of affection!—only, by some unexplainable, unbelievable wonder, it must be love. Desirée did not enter into any questions on the subject; she yielded to the fascination; it made her proud, it made her humble, it filled her with the tenderest gratitude, it subdued her little fiery spirit like a spell. She was very, very young, she knew nothing of life or of the world, she lived in a little world of her own, where this grand figure was the centre of every thing; and it was a grand figure in the dewy, tender light of Desirée's young eyes—in the perfect globe of Desirée's maiden fancy—but it was not Oswald Huntley, deeply though the poor child believed it was.

So they all grouped around her, watching her, some of them perplexed, some of them scheming; and Oswald played his part, sometimes loathing it, but, for the most part, finding it quite agreeable to his vanity, while poor little Desirée went on in her dream, thinking she had fallen upon a charmed life, seeing every thing through the glamour in her own eyes, believing every thing was true.

"Dr. Logan is ill," said Melmar, on one of those fairy days, when they all met round the table at lunch; all but Mrs. Huntley, who had relapsed into her quiescent invalidism, and was made comfortable in her own room—"very ill—so ill that I may as well mind my promise to old Gordon of Ruchlaw for his minister-son."

"Oh, papa, don't be so hard-hearted!" cried Joanna—"he'll maybe get better yet. He's no' such a very old man, and he preached last Sabbath-day. Oh, poor Katie! but he has not been a week ill yet, and he'll get better again."

"Who is Gordon of Ruchlaw? and who is his minister-son?" asked Oswald.

Joanna made a volunteer answer.

"A nasty, snuffy, disagreeable man!" cried Joanna, with enthusiasm. "I am sure I would never enter the church again if he was there; but it's very cruel and hard-hearted, and just like papa, to speak of him. Dr. Logan is only ill. I would break my heart if I thought he was going to die."

"Gordon would be a very useful man to us," said Melmar—"a great deal more so than Logan ever was. I mean to write and ask him here, now that his time's coming. Be quiet, Joan, and let's have no more nonsense. I'll tell Auntie Jean. If you play your cards well, you might have a good chance of him yourself, you monkey, and with Aunt Jean's fortune to furnish the manse, you might do worse. Ha! ha! I wonder what Patricia would say?"

"Patricia would say it was quite good enough for Joanna," said that amiable young lady. "A poor Scotch minister! I am thankful I never had such low tastes. Nobody would speak of such a thing to me."

"Don't quarrel about the new man till the old man is dead, at least," said Oswald, laughing. "Mademoiselle Desirée quite agrees with me, I know. She is shocked to hear all this. Is it not so?"

"I thought of his daughter," said Desirée, who was very much shocked, and had tears in her eyes. "She will be an orphan now."

"And Desirée was very fond of Katie," said Joanna, looking half jealously, half fondly at the little governess, "and so am I too; and she has all the little ones to take care of. Oh, papa, I'll never believe that Dr. Logan is going to die."

"Fhat is all this, Joan? tell me," cried Aunt Jean, who had already shown signs of curiosity and impatience. This was the signal for breaking up the party. When Joanna put her lips close to the old woman's ear, and began to shout the required information, the others dispersed rapidly. Desirée went to her room to get her cloak and bonnet. It was her hour for walking with her pupil, and that walk was now an enchanted progress, a fairy road, leading ever further and further into her fairy land. As for Oswald, he stood in the window, looking out and shrugging his shoulders at the cold. His blood was not warm enough to bear the chill of the northern wind; the sight of the frost-bound paths and whitened branches made him shiver before he went out. He meant to attend the girls in their walk, in spite of his shiver; but the frosty path by the side of Tyne was not a fairy road to him.

Joanna had left them on some erratic expedition among the trees; they were alone together, Desirée walking by Oswald's side, very quiet and silent, with her eyes cast down, and a tremor at her heart. The poor little girl did not expect any thing particular, for they were often enough together thus—still she became silent in spite of herself, as she wandered on in her dream by Oswald's side, and, in spite of herself, cast down her eyes, and felt the color wavering on her cheek. Perhaps he saw it and was pleased—he liked such moments well enough. They had all the amusing, tantalizing, dramatic pleasure of moments which might be turned to admirable account, but never were so—moments full of expectation and possibility, of which nothing ever came.

At this particular moment Oswald was, as it happened, very tenderly gracious to Desirée. He was asking about her family, or rather her mother, whom, it appeared, he had heard of without hearing of any other relative, and Desirée, in answering, spoke of Marie—who was Marie? "Did I never, then, tell you of my sister?" said Desirée with a blush and smile.

"Your sister?—I was not aware—" stammered Oswald—and he looked at her so closely and coldly, and with such a scrutinizing air of suspicion, that Desirée stared at him, in return, with amazement and half-terror— "Perhaps Mademoiselle Desirée has brothers also," he said, in the same tone, still looking at her keenly. What if she had brothers? Would it have been wrong?

"No," said Desirée, quietly. The poor child was subdued by the dread of having wounded him. She thought it grieved him to have so little of her confidence; it could be nothing but that which made him look so cold and speak so harsh.

"Then Mademoiselle Marie is a little sister—a child?" said Oswald, softening slightly.

Desirée clapped her hands and laughed with sudden glee. "Oh, no, no," she cried merrily, "she is my elder sister; she is not even Mademoiselle; she is married! Poor Marie!" added the little girl, softly. "I wish she were here."

And for the moment Desirée did not see the look that regarded her. When she lifted her eyes again, she started and could not comprehend the change. Oswald's lip was blue with cold, with dismay, with contempt, with a mixture of feelings which his companion had no clue to, and could not understand. "Mademoiselle has, no doubt, a number of little nephews and nieces," he said, with a sinister curl of that blue lip over his white teeth. The look struck to Desirée's heart with a pang of amazement and terror—what did it mean?

"Oh, no, no, not any," she said, with a deep blush. She was startled and disturbed out of all her maiden fancies—was it a nervous, jealous irritation, to find that she had friends more than he knew. It was very strange—and when Joanna rejoined them shortly, Oswald made an excuse for himself, and left them. The girls followed him slowly, after a time, to the house; Desirée could scarcely answer Joanna's questions, or appear interested in her pupil's interests. What was the reason? She bewildered her poor little head asking this question; but no answer came.

CHAPTER XLIX

It was a kind of twilight in Aunt Jean's room, though it was still daylight out of doors; the sun, as it drew to the west, threw a ruddy glory upon this side of the house of Melmar, and coming in at Aunt Jean's window, had thrown its full force upon the fire-place half an hour ago. It was the old lady's belief that the sun put out the fire, so she had drawn down her blind, and the warm, domestic glimmer of the firelight played upon the high bed, with those heavy, dull, moreen curtains, which defied all brightness—upon the brighter toilet-glass on the table, and upon the old lofty chest of drawers, polished and black like ebony, which stood at the further side of the room. Aunt Jean herself sat in a high-backed arm-chair by the fire, where she loved to sit—and Desirée and Joanna, kneeling on the rug before her, were turning out the contents of a great basket, full of such scraps as Aunt Jean loved to accumulate, and girls have pleasure in turning over; there were bits of silk, bits of splendid old ribbon, long enough for "bows," in some cases, but in some only fit for pin-cushions and needle-books of unbelievable splendor, bits of lace, bits of old-fashioned embroidery, bits of almost every costly material belonging to a lady's wardrobe. It was a pretty scene; the basket on the rug, with its many-colored stores, the pretty little figure of Desirée, with the fire-light shining in her hair, the less graceful form of Joanna, which still was youthful, and honest, and eager, as she knelt opposite the fire, which flushed her face and reddened her hair at its will; and calmly seated in her elbow-chair, overseeing all, Aunt Jean, with her white neckerchief pinned over her gown, and her white apron warm in the fire-light, and the broad black ribbon bound round her old-fashioned cap, and the vivacious sparkle of those black eyes, which were not "hard of hearing," though their owner was. The pale daylight came in behind the old lady, faintly through the misty atmosphere and the closed blind—but the ruddier domestic light within went flickering and sparkling over the high-canopied bed, the old-fashioned furniture, and the group by the hearth. When Joanna went away, the picture was even improved perhaps, for Desirée still knelt half meditatively by the fire, turning over with one hand the things in the basket, listening to what the old lady said, and wistfully pondering upon her own thoughts.

"Some o' the things were here when I came," said Aunt Jean. "I was not so auld then as I am now—I laid them a' away, Deseery, for fear the real daughter of the house should ever come hame; for this present Melmar wasna heir by nature. If right had been right, there's ane before him in the succession to this house; but, poor misguided thing, fha was gaun to seek her; but I laid by the bits o' things; I thought they might 'mind her some time of the days o' her youth."

"Who was she?" said Desirée, softly: she did not ask so as to be heard by her companion—she did not ask as if she cared for an answer—she said it quietly, in a half whisper to herself; yet Aunt Jean heard Desirée's question with her lively eyes, which were fixed upon the girl's pretty figure, half kneeling, half reclining at her feet.

"Fha was she? She was the daughter of this house," said Aunt Jean, "and fhat's mair, the mistress of this house, Deseery, if she should ever come hame."

The little Frenchwoman looked up sharply, keenly, with an alarmed expression on her face. She did not ask any further question, but she met Aunt Jean's black eyes with eyes still brighter in their youthful lustre, yet dimmed with an indefinable cloud of suspicion and fear.

What was in the old woman's mind it was hard to tell. Whether she had any definite ground to go upon, or merely proceeded on an impulse of the vague anxiety in her mind.

"'Deed, ay," said Aunt Jean, nodding her lively little head, "I'll tell you a' her story, my dear, and you can tell me fhat you think when I'm done. She was the only bairn and heir of that silly auld man that was Laird of Melmar before this present lad, my niece's good-man—she was very bonnie, and muckle thought of, and she married and ran away, and that's all the folk ken of her, Deseery; but whisht, bairn, and I'll tell you mair."

Desirée had sunk lower on her knees, leaning back, with her head turned anxiously towards the story-teller. She was an interested listener at least.

"It's aye thought she was disinherited," said Aunt Jean, "and at the first, when she ran away, maybe so she was—but nature will speak. When this silly auld man, as I'm saying, died, he left a will setting up her rights, and left it in the hand of another silly haverel of a man, that was a bit sma' laird at Norlaw. This man was to be heir himsel' if she never was found— but he had a sma' spirit, Deseery, and he never could find her. She's never been found from that day to this—but it'll be a sore day for Melmar when she comes hame."

The Laird Of Norlaw | 243

"Why?" said Desirée, somewhat sharply and shrilly, with a voice which reached the old woman's ears, distant though they were.

"Fhat for?—because they'll have to give up all the lands, and all the siller, and all their living into her hand—that's fhat for," said Aunt Jean; "nae person in this country-side can tell if she's living, or fhaur she is; she's been away langer than you've been in this life, Deseery; and Melmar, the present laird—I canna blame him, he was the next of the blood after hersel', nae doubt he thought she was dead and gane, as a'body else did when he took possession—and his heart rose doubtless against the other person that was left heir, failing her, being neither a Huntley nor nigh in blood; but if aught should befall to bring her hame—ay, Deseery, it would be a sore day for this family, and every person in this house."

"Why?" asked Desirée again with a tremble—this time her voice did not reach the ear of Aunt Jean, but her troubled, downcast eyes, her disturbed look, touched the old woman's heart.

"If it was a story I was telling out of a book," said the old woman, "I would say they were a' in misery at keeping her out of her rights—or that the man was a villain that held her place—but you're no' to think that. I dinna doubt he heeds his ain business mair than he heeds her—it's but natural, fha would do otherwise? and then he takes comfort to his mind that she must be dead, or she would have turned up before now, and then he thinks upon his ain family, and considers his first duty is for them; and then—'deed ay, my dear, memory fails—I wouldna say but he often forgets that there was another person in the world but himsel' that had a right—that's nature, Deseery, just nature—folk learn to think the way it's their profit to think, and believe what suits them best, and they're sincere, too, except maybe just at the first; you may not think it, being a bairn, yet it's true."

"If it were me," cried Desirée, with a vehemence which penetrated Aunt Jean's infirmity, "the money would burn me, would scorch me, till I could give it back to the true heir!"

"Ay," said Aunt Jean, shaking her head, "I wouldna say I could be easy in my mind mysel'—but it's wonderful how weel the like of you and me, my dear, can settle ither folks' concerns. Melmar, you see, he's no' an ill man, he thinks otherwise, and I daur to say he's begun to forget a' about her, or just thinks she's dead and gane, as most folk think. I canna help aye an expectation to see her back before I die mysel'—but that's no' to say Me'mar has ony thought of the kind. Folk that are away for twenty years, and never seen, nor heard tell o', canna expect to be minded upon and waited upon. It's very like, upon the whole, that she *is* dead many a year syne—and fhat for should Melmar, that kens nothing about her—aye except that she could take his living away frae him—fhat for, I'm asking, should Melmar gang away upon his travels looking for her, like yon other haverel of a man?"

"What other man?" cried Desirée, eagerly.

"Oh, just Norlaw; he was aince a wooer himsel', poor haverel," said Aunt Jean; "he gaed roaming about a' the world, seeking after her, leaving his wife and his bonny bairns at hame; but fhat good did he?—just nought ava, Deseery, except waste his ain time, and lose his siller, and gie his wife a sair heart. She's made muckle mischief in her day, this Mary of Melmar. They say she was very bonnie, though I never saw her mysel'; and fhat for, think you, should the present lad, that kens nought about her, take up his staff and gang traveling the world to seek for her? Oh, fie, nae!—he has mair duty to his ain house and bairns, than to a strange woman that he kens not where to seek, and that would make him a beggar if he found her; I canna see she deserves ony such thing at his hand."

At first Desirée did not answer a word; her cheek was burning hot with excitement, her face shadowed with an angry cloud, her little hand clenched involuntarily, her brow knitted. She was thinking of something private to herself, which roused a passion of resentment within the breast of the girl. At last she started up and came close to Aunt Jean.

"But if you knew that she was living, and where she was?" cried Desirée, "what would you do?"

"Me! Oh, my bairn!" cried Aunt Jean, in sudden dismay. "Me! what have I to do with their concerns?—me! it's nane of my business. The Lord keep that and a' evil out of a poor auld woman's knowledge. I havena eaten his bread—I never would be beholden that far to any mortal—but I've sitten under his roof tree for mony a year. Me!—if I heard a word of such awfu' news, I would gang furth of this door this moment, that I mightna be a traitor in the man's very dwelling;—eh, the Lord help me, the thought's dreadful! for I behoved to let her ken!"

"And what if he knew?" asked Desirée, in a sharp whisper, gazing into Aunt Jean's eyes with a look that pierced like an arrow. The old woman's look fell, but it was not to escape this gaze of inquiry.

"The Lord help him!" said Aunt Jean, pitifully. "I can but hope he would do right, Deseery; but human nature's frail; I canna tell."

This reply softened for the moment the vehement, angry look of the little Frenchwoman. She came again to kneel before the fire, and was silent, thinking her own thoughts; then another and a new fancy seemed to rise like a mist over her face. She looked up dismayed to Aunt Jean, with an unexplained and terrified question, which the old woman could not interpret. Then she tried to command herself with an evident effort—but it was useless. She sprang up, and came close, with a shivering chill upon her, to put her lips to Aunt Jean's ear.

"Do they all know of this story?" she asked, in the low, sharp voice, strangely intent and passionate, which even deafness itself could not refuse to hear; and Desirée fixed her gaze upon the old woman's eyes, holding her fast with an eager scrutiny, as though she trembled to be put off with any thing less than the truth.

"Hout, no!" said Aunt Jean, disturbed a little, yet confident; "fha would tell the like of Patricia or Joan—fuils and bairns! and as for the like of my niece herself, she's muckle taken up with her ain bits of troubles; she might hear of it at the time, but she would forget the day after; naebody minds but me."

"And—Oswald?" cried Desirée, sharply, once again.

"Eh! ay—I wasna thinking upon him; he's the heir," said Aunt Jean, turning her eyes sharp and keen upon her young questioner. "I canna tell fhat for you ask me so earnest, bairn; you maunna think mair of Oswald Huntley than becomes baith him and you; ay, doubtless, you're right, whatever learned ye—*he* kens."

Desirée did not say another word, but she clasped her hands tightly together, sprang out of the room with the pace of a deer, and before Aunt Jean had roused herself from her amazement, had thrown her cloak over her shoulders, and rushed out into the gathering night.

CHAPTER L

The sunset glory of this January evening still shone over the tops of the trees upon the high bank of Tyne, leaving a red illumination among the winter clouds; but low upon the path the evening was gathering darkly and chilly, settling down upon the ice-cold branches, which pricked the hasty passenger like thorns, in the black dryness of the frost. The Kelpie itself was scarcely recognizable in the torpid and tiny stream which trickled down its little ravine; only the sharp sound of its monotone in the tingling air made you aware of its vicinity; and frozen Tyne no longer added his voice to make the silence musical. The silence was dry, hard, and harsh, the sounds were shrill, the air cut like a knife. No creature that could find shelter was out of doors; yet poor little Desirée, vehement, willful, and passionate, with her cloak over her shoulders, and her pretty uncovered head, exposed to all the chill of the unkindly air, went rushing out, with her light foot and little fairy figure, straight as an arrow over Tyne, and came up the frozen path, into the wood and the night.

One side of her face was still scorched and crimsoned with the fervor of Aunt Jean's fire, before which she had been bending; the other, in comparison, was already chilled and white. She ran along up the icy, chilly road, with the night-wind cutting her delicate little ears, and her rapid footsteps sliding upon the knots of roots in the path, straight up to that height where the Kelpie trickled, and the last red cloud melted into gray behind the trees. The dubious, failing twilight was wan among those branches, where never a bird stirred. There was not a sound of life anywhere, save in the metallic tinkle of that drowsing waterfall. Desirée rushed through the silence and the darkness, and threw herself down upon the hard path, on one of the hard knots, beneath a tree. She was not sorry, in her passionate *abandon*, to feel the air prick her cheek, to see the darkness closing over her, to know that the cold pierced to the bone, and that she was almost unprotected from its rigor. All this desolation was in keeping with the tumult which moved the willful heart of the little stranger. The prick of the wind neutralized somewhat the fiery prick in her heart.

Poor little Desirée! She had, indeed, enough to think of—from her morning's flush of happiness and dawning love to plunge into a cold profound of treachery, deceit, and falsehood like that which gaped at her feet, ready to swallow her up. For the moment it was anger alone, passionate and vivid as her nature, which burned within her. She, frank, child-like, and unsuspicious, had been degraded by a pretended love, a false friendship; had been warned, "for her own sake," by the treacherous host whom Desirée hated, in her passion, to say nothing of her descent or of her mother. For her own sake! and not a syllable of acknowledgment to confess how well the wily schemer knew who that mother was. Yet, alas, if that had but been all!—if there had been nothing to do but to confound Melmar, to renounce Joanna, to shake off the dust of her indignant feet against the house where they would have kept her in bondage!—if that had but been all! But Desirée clenched her little hands with a pang of angry and bitter resentment far more overpowering. To think that she should have been insulted with a false love! Bitter shame, quick, passionate anger, even the impulse of revenge, came like a flood over the breast of the girl, as she sat shivering with cold and passion at the foot of that tree, with the dark winter night closing over her. She could almost fancy she saw the curl of Oswald Huntley's lip as he heard to-day, on this very spot, that she had a sister; she could almost suppose, if he stood there now, that she had both strength and will to thrust him through the rustling bushes down to the crackling, frozen Tyne, to sink like a stone beneath the ice, which was less treacherous than himself. Poor little desolate, solitary stranger! She sat in the darkness and the cold, with the tears freezing in her eyes, but passion burning in her heart; she cried aloud in the silence with an irrepressible cry of fury and anguish—the voice of a young savage, the uncontrolled, unrestrained, absolute violence of a child. She was half crazed with the sudden downfall, the sudden injury; she could think of nothing but the sin that had been done against her, the vengeance, sharp and sudden as her passion, which she would inflict if she could.

But as poor little Desirée crouched beneath the tree, not even the vehemence of her resentment could preserve her from the influences of Nature. Her little feet seemed frozen to the path; her hands were numb and powerless, and ice-cold as the frozen water beneath. The chill stole to her heart with a sickening faintness, then a gradual languor crept over her passion; by degrees she felt nothing but the cold, the sharp rustle of the branches, the chill gloom of the night, the harsh wind that blew in at her uncovered ears. Her hair fell down on her neck, and her fingers were too powerless to put it up. She had no heart to return to the house from which she fled in so violent an excess of insulted feeling—it almost seemed that she had no place in the world to go to, poor child, but this desolate winter woodland, which in its summer beauty she had associated with her mother.

The night blinded her, and so did the growing sickness of extreme cold. Another moment, and poor little Desirée sank against the tree, passionless and fainting—the last thought in her heart a low outcry for her mother, who was hundreds of miles away and could not hear.

The cold was still growing sharper and keener as the last glimmer of daylight faded out of the skies. She might have slid down into the frozen Tyne, as she had imagined her enemy, or she might have perished in her favorite path, in the cold which was as sharp as an Arctic frost. But Providence does not desert those poor, suffering, wicked children who fly to death's door at the impulse of passion as Desirée did. A laborer, hastening home by the footpath through the Melmar woods, wandered out of his way, by chance, and stumbled over the poor little figure lying in the path. When the man had got over his first alarm, he lifted her up and carried her like a child—she was not much more—to Melmar, where he went to the side door and brought her in among the servants to that great kitchen, which was the most cheerful apartment in the house. The maids were kind-hearted, and liked the poor little governess—they chafed her hands and bathed her feet, and wrapped her in blankets, and, at last, brought Desirée to her senses. When she came alive again, the poor, naughty child looked round her bewildered, and did not know where she was—the place was strange to her—and it looked so bright and homely that Desirée's poor little heart was touched by a vague contrasting sense of misery.

"I should like to go to bed," she said, sadly, turning her face away from the light to a kind housemaid, who stood by her, and who could not tell what ailed "the French miss," whom all the servants had thought rather too well-used of late days, and whose look of misery seemed unaccountable.

"Eh, Missie, but ye maun wait until the fire's kindled," said the maid.

Desirée did not want a fire—she had no desire to be comforted and warmed, and made comfortable—she would almost rather have crept out again into the cold and the night. Notwithstanding, they carried her up stairs carefully, liking the stranger all the better for being sad and in trouble and dependent on them—and undressed her like a child, and laid her in bed in her little room, warm with firelight, and looking bright with comfort and kindness. Then the pretty housemaid, whom Patricia exercised her tempers on, brought Desirée a warm drink and exhorted her to go to sleep.

"What made ye rin out into the cauld night, Missie, without a thing on your head," said Jenny Shaw, compassionately; "but lie still and keep yoursel' warm—naebody kens yet but us in the kitchen, or Miss Joan would be here; but I thought you would like best to be quiet, and it would do you mair good."

"Oh, dear Jenny, don't let any one know—don't tell them—promise!" cried Desirée, half starting from her bed.

The maid did not know what to make of it, but she promised, to compose the poor little sufferer; and so Desirée was left by herself in the little room, with the warm fire light flickering about the walls, and her little hands and feet, which had been so cold, burning and prickling with a feverish heat, her limbs aching, her thoughts wandering, her heart lost in an ineffable, unspeakable melancholy. She could not return to her passion, to the bitter hurry and tumult of resentful fancies which had occupied her out of doors. She lay thinking, trying to think, vainly endeavoring to confine the wandering crowd of thoughts, which made her head ache, and which seemed to float over every subject under heaven. She tried to say her prayers, poor child, but lost them in an incoherent mist of fancy. She fell asleep, and awoke in a few minutes, thinking she had slept for hours—worse than that, she fell half asleep into a painful drowse, where waking thoughts and dreams mingled with and confused each other. Years of silence and unendurable solitude seemed to pass over her before Jenny Shaw came up stairs again to ask her how she was, and the last thing clear in Desirée's remembrance was that Jenny promised once more not to tell any one. Desirée did not know that the good-hearted Jenny half slept, half watched in her room all that night. The poor child knew nothing next day but that her limbs ached, and her head burned, and that a dull sense of pain was at her heart. She was very ill with all her exposure and suffering—she was ill for some time, making a strange commotion in the house. But no one had any idea of the cause of her illness, save perhaps Aunt Jean, who did not say a word to any one, but trotted about the sick-room, "cheering up" the little sick stranger and finding out her wants with strange skill in spite of her deafness. All the time of Desirée's illness Aunt Jean took not the slightest notice of Oswald Huntley—she was doubly deaf when he addressed her—she lost even her sharp and lively eyesight when she encountered him on the stair. Aunt Jean did not know what ailed Desirée besides the severe cold and fever which the doctor decided on, but the old woman remembered perfectly at what point of their conversation it was that the little girl rushed from her side and fled out of the house—and she guessed at many things with a keen and lively penetration which came very near the truth. And so Desirée was very ill, and got slowly well again, bringing with her out of her sickness a thing more hard to cure than fever—a sick heart.

CHAPTER LI

While all these new events and changes were disturbing the quiet life of the home district at Melmar, and Norlaw, and Kirkbride, Cosmo Livingstone wandered over classic ground with Cameron and his young pupil, and sent now and then, with modest pride, his contribution to the *Auld Reekie Magazine* which had now been afloat for four months, and on account of which Mr. Todhunter, in his turn, sent remittances—not remarkably liberal, yet meant to be so, in letters full of a rude, yet honest, vanity, which impressed the lad with great ideas of what the new periodical was to do for the literary world. So far, all was satisfactory with Cosmo. He was very well off also in his companions. Cameron, who had been shy of undertaking a manner of life which was so new to him, and whom all the innkeepers had fleeced unmercifully on the first commencement of their travels—for the very pride which made him starve in his garret at home, out of everybody's ken, made him, unused and inexperienced as he was, a lavish man abroad, where everybody was looking on, and where the thought of "meanness" troubled his spirit. But by this time, even Cameron had become used to the life of inns and journeys, and was no longer awed by the idea that landlords and waiters would suspect his former poverty, or that his pupil himself might complain of undue restraint. The said pupil, whose name was Macgregor, was good-natured and companionable, without being any thing more. They had been in Italy, in Switzerland, and in Germany. They had all acquired a traveler's smattering of all the three tongues familiar on their road—they had looked at churches, and pictures, and palaces, till those eyes which were unguided by *Murray*, and knew just as much, or rather as little, of art, as the bulk of their countrymen at the time, became fairly bewildered, and no longer recollected which was which. They were now in France, in chilly February weather, on their way home. Why they pitched upon this town of St. Ouen for their halt it would have been hard to explain. It was in Normandy, for one reason, and Cosmo felt rather romantically interested in that old cradle of the conquering race. It was within reach of various places, of historic interest. Finally, young Macgregor had picked up somewhere a little archaic lore, which was not a common accomplishment in those days, and St. Ouen was rich in old architecture. Thus they lingered, slow to leave the shores of France, which was not sunny France in that February, but had been the beginning and was about to be the end of their pleasant wandering, and where accordingly they were glad to rest for a little before returning home.

Though, to tell the truth, Cosmo would a great deal rather have tarried on the very edge of the country, at the little sea-port which bowed Jaacob called "Deep," and where that sentimental giant had seen, or fancied he had seen, the lady of his imagination. Cosmo had enjoyed his holiday heartily, as became his temperament and years, yet he was returning disappointed, and even a little chagrined and ashamed of himself. He had started with the full and strong idea that what his father could not succeed in doing, and what advertisements and legal search had failed in, he himself, by himself, could do—and he was now going home somewhat enlightened as to this first fallacy of youth. He had not succeeded, he had not had the merest gleam or prospect of success; Mary of Melmar was as far off, as totally lost, as though Cosmo Livingstone, who was to be her knight and champion, had never known the story of her wrongs, and Time was gliding away with silent, inevitable rapidity. A year and a half of the precious remaining interval was over. Huntley had been at his solitary work in Australia for nearly a whole year, and Huntley's heart was bent on returning to claim Melmar, if he could but make money enough to assert his right to it. This Cosmo knew from his brother's letters, those to himself, and those which his mother forwarded to him (in copy). He loved Huntley, but Cosmo thought he loved honor more—certainly he had more regard for the favorite dream of his own imagination, which was to restore the lost lady to her inheritance. But he had not found her, and now he was going home!

However, they were still in St. Ouen. Since Cameron recovered himself out of his first flutter of shy extravagance and fear lest he should be thought "mean," they had adopted an economical method of living when they staid long in any one place. Instead of living at the inn, they had taken rooms for themselves, a proceeding which Cameron flattered himself made them acquainted with the natives. On this principle they acted at St. Ouen. Their rooms were, two on the *premier étage* for Cameron and his pupil, and one *au troisième* for Cosmo. Cosmo's was a little room in a corner, opening by a slim, ill-hung door upon the common stair-case—where rapid French voices, and French feet, not very light, went up the echoing flight above to the *mansarde*, and made jokes, which Cosmo did not understand, upon the young Englishman's boots, standing in forlorn trustfulness outside his door, to be cleaned. Though Cosmo had lived in a close in the High Street, he was quite unused to the public traffic of this stair-case, and sometimes suddenly extinguished his candle with a boy's painful modesty, at the sudden fancy of some one looking through his keyhole, or got up in terror with the idea that a band of late revelers might pour in and find him in bed, in spite of the slender defense of lock and key. The room itself was very small, and had scarcely a feature in it, save the little clock on the mantel-piece, which always struck in direct and independent opposition to the great bell of St. Ouen. The window was in a corner, overshadowed by the deep projection of the next house, which struck off from Cosmo's wall in a right angle, and kept him obstinately out of the sunshine. Up in the corner, *au troisième*, with the next door neighbor's blank gable edging all his light away from him, you would not have thought there was any thing very attractive in Cosmo's window—yet it so happened that there was.

Not in the window itself, though that was near enough the clouds— but Cosmo, looking down, looked, as his good fortune was, into another window over the way, a pretty second floor, with white curtains and flowers to garnish it, and sunshine that loved to steal in for half the day. It was a pretty point of itself, with its little stand of early-blooming plants, and its white curtains looped up with ribbon. The plants were but early spring flowers, and did not at all screen the bright little window which Cosmo looked at, as though it had been a picture—and even when the evening lamp was lighted, no jealous blinds were drawn across the cheerful light. The lad was not impertinent nor curious, yet he sat in the dusk sometimes, looking down as into the heart of a little sacred picture. There were only two people ever in the room, and these were ladies, evidently a mother and daughter— one of them an invalid. That there was a sofa near the fire, on which some one nearly always lay—that once or twice in the day this recumbent figure was raised from the couch, and the two together paced slowly through the room—and that, perhaps once a week, a little carriage came to the door to take the sick lady out for a drive, was all that Cosmo knew of the second person in this interesting apartment; and the lad may have been supposed to be sufficiently disinterested in his curiosity, when we say that the only face which he ever fully saw at that bright window was the face of an *old* lady—a face as old as his mother's. It was she who watered the flowers and looped the curtains—it was she who worked within their slight shadow, always visible—and it was she who, sometimes looking up and catching his eye, smiled either at or to Cosmo, causing him to retreat precipitately for the moment, yet leaving no glance of reproach on his memory to forbid his return.

Beauty is not a common gift; it is especially rare to the fanciful, young imagination, which is very hard to please, save where it loves. This old lady, however, old though she was, caught Cosmo's poetic eye with all the glamour, somehow tenderer than if she had been young, of real loveliness. She must have been beautiful in her youth. She had soft, liquid, dark-blue eyes, full of a motherly and tender light now-a-days, and beautiful light-brown hair, in which, at this distance, it was not possible to see the silvery threads. She was tall, with a natural bend in her still pliant form, which Cosmo could not help comparing to the bend of a lily. He said to himself, as he sat at his window, that he had seen many pretty girls, but never any one so beautiful as this old lady. Her sweet eyes of age captivated Cosmo; he was never weary of watching her. He could have looked down upon her for an hour at a time, as she sat working with her white hands, while the sun shone upon her white lace cap, and on the sweet old cheek, with its lovely complexion, which was turned to the window; or when she half disappeared within to minister to the other half visible figure upon the sofa. Cosmo did not like to tell Cameron of his old lady, but he sat many an hour by himself in this little room, to the extreme wonderment of his friend, who supposed it was all for the benefit of the *Auld Reekie Magazine*, and smiled a little within himself at the lad's literary enthusiasm. For his part, Cosmo dreamed about his opposite neighbors, and made stories for them in his own secret imagination, wondering if he ever could come to know them, or if he left St. Ouen, whether they were ever likely to meet again. It certainly did not seem probable, and there was no photography in those days to enable Cosmo to take pictures of his beautiful old lady as she sat in the sunshine. He took them on his own mind instead, and he made them into copies of verses, which the beautiful old lady never would see, nor if she saw could read—verses for the *Auld Reekie Magazine* and the *North British Courant*.

CHAPTER LII

The house of Cosmo's residence was not a great enough house to boast a regular *portière* or *concierge*. A little cobbler, who lived in an odd little ever-open room, on the ground floor, was the real renter and landlord of the much-divided dwelling place. He and his old wife lived and labored without change or extension in this one apartment, which answered for all purposes, and in which Baptiste's scraps of leather contended for preëminence of odor over Margot's *pot au feu*; and it was here that the lodgers hung up the keys of their respective chambers, and where the letters and messages of the little community were left. Cameron and Cosmo were both very friendly with Baptiste. They understood him but imperfectly, and he, for his part, kept up a continual chuckle behind his sleeve over the blunders of *les Anglais*. But as they laughed at each other mutually, both were contented, and kept their complacence. Cosmo had found out by guess or inference, he could not quite tell how, that madame in the second floor opposite, with the invalid daughter, was the owner of Baptiste's house—a fact which made the cobbler's little room very attractive to the lad, as it was easy to invent questions, direct or indirect, about the beautiful old lady. One morning, Baptiste looked up, with a smirk, from his board, as he bid good-day to his young lodger. He had news to tell.

"You shall now have your wish," said Baptiste; "Madame has been asking Margot about the young Englishman. Madame takes interest in *les Anglais*. You shall go to present yourself, and make your homage when her poor daughter is better. She loves your country. Madame is *Anglais* herself."

"Is she?" cried Cosmo, eagerly; "but I am not English, unfortunately," added the lad, with a jealous nationality. "I am a Scotsman, Baptiste; madame will no longer wish to see me."

"Eh, bien!" said Baptiste, "I know not much of your differences, you islanders—but madame is *Ecossais*. Yes, I know it. It was so said when Monsieur Jean brought home his bride. Ah, was she not beautiful? too pretty for the peace of the young man and the ladies; they made poor Monsieur Jean jealous, and he took her away."

"Is that long ago?" asked Cosmo.

"It was the year that Margot's cousin, Camille, was drawn in the conscription," said Baptiste, smiling to himself at his own private recollections. "It is twenty years since. But madame was lovely! So poor Monsieur Jean became jealous and carried her away. They went, I know not where, to the end of the world. In the meantime the old gentleman died. He was of the old *régime*—he was of good blood—but he was poor—he had but this house here and that other to leave to his son—fragments, monsieur, fragments, crumbs out of the hands of the Revolution; and Monsieur Jean was gay and of a great spirit. He was not a *bourgeois* to go to become rich. The money dropped through his fine fingers. He came back, let me see, but three years ago. He was a gentleman, he was a noble, with but a thousand francs of rent. He did not do any thing. Madame sat at the window and worked, with her pretty white hands. Eh, bien! what shall you say then? she loved him—nothing was hard to her. He was made to be loved, this poor Monsieur Jean."

"It is easy to say so—but he could not have deserved such a wife," cried Cosmo, with a boy's indignation; "he ought to have toiled for her rather, night and day."

"Ah, monsieur is young," said Baptiste, with a half satirical smile and shrug of his stooping French shoulders. "We know better when we have been married twenty years. Monsieur Jean was not made to toil, neither night nor day; but he loved madame still, and was jealous of her—he was a *beau garçon* himself to his last days."

"Jealous!" Cosmo was horrified; "you speak very lightly, Baptiste," said the boy, angrily, "but that is worst of all—a lady so beautiful, so good—it is enough to see her to know how good she is—the man deserved to be shot!"

"Nay, nay," cried Baptiste, laughing, "monsieur does not understand the ways of women—it pleased madame—they love to know their power, and to hear other people know it; all the women are so. Madame loved him all the better for being a little—just a little afraid of her beauty. But he did not live long—poor Monsieur Jean!"

"I hope she was very glad to be rid of such a fellow," cried Cosmo, who was highly indignant at the deficient husband of his beautiful old lady. Baptiste rubbed the corner of his own eye rather hard with his knuckle. The cobbler had a little sentiment lingering in his ancient bosom for the admired of his youth.

"But he had an air noble—a great spirit," cried Baptiste. "But madame loved him! She wept—all St. Ouen wept, monsieur—and he was the last of an old race. Now there are only the women, and madame herself is a foreigner and a stranger, and knows not our traditions. Ah, it is a great change for the house of Roche de St. Martin! If you will believe it, monsieur, madame herself is called by the common people nothing but Madame Roche!"

"And that is very sad, Baptiste," said Cosmo, with a smile. Baptiste smiled too; the cobbler was not particularly sincere in his aristocratical regrets, but, with the mingled wit and sentiment of his country, was sufficiently ready to perceive either the ludicrous or the pathetic aspect of the decayed family.

Cosmo, however, changed his tone with the most capricious haste. Whether she was a plain Madame Roche, or a noble lady, it did not matter much to the stranger. She was at the present moment, in her lovely age and motherhood, the lady of Cosmo's dreams, and ridicule could not come near her. She was sacred to every idea that was most reverential and full of honor.

"And she is a widow, now, and has a sick daughter to take care of," said Cosmo, meditatively; "strange how some people in the world have always some burden upon them. Had she no one to take care of *her*?"

"If monsieur means *that*," said Baptiste, with a comical smile, "I do not doubt madame might have married again."

"Married—she! how dare you say so, Baptiste," cried the lad, coloring high in indignation; "it is profane!—it is sacrilege!—but she has only this invalid daughter to watch and labor for—nothing more?"

"Yes—it is but a sad life," said Baptiste; "many a laboring woman, as I tell Margot, has less to do with her hard fingers than has madame with those pretty white hands—one and another all her life to lean upon her, and now, alas! poor Mademoiselle Marie!"

The cobbler looked as if something more than mere compassion for her illness moved this last exclamation, but Cosmo was not very much interested about Mademoiselle Marie, who lay always on the sofa, and, hidden in the dimness of the chamber, looked older than her mother, as the lad fancied. He went away from Baptiste, however, with his mind very full of Madame Roche. For a homeborn youth like himself, so long accustomed to the family roof and his mother's rule and company, he had been a long time now totally out of domestic usages and female society—longer than he had ever been in his life before—he was flattered to think that his beautiful old lady had noticed him, and an affectionate chivalrous sentiment touched Cosmo's mind with unusual pleasure. He loved to imagine to himself the delicate womanly fireside, lighted up by a smile which might remind him of his mother's, yet would be more refined and captivating than the familiar looks of the Mistress. He thought of himself as something between a son and a champion, tenderly reverent and full of affectionate admiration. No idea of Mademoiselle Marie, nor of any other younger person with whom it might be possible to fall in love, brought Cosmo's imagination down to the vulgar level. He felt as a lad feels who has been brought up under the shadow of a mother heartily loved and honored. It was still a mother he was dreaming about; but the delicate old beauty of his old lady added an indefinable charm to the impulse of affectionate respect which animated Cosmo. It made him a great deal more pleased and proud to think she had noticed him, and to anticipate perhaps an invitation to her very presence. It made him think as much about her to-day as though she had been a girl, and he her lover. The sentiment warmed the lad's heart.

He was wandering around the noble old cathedral later in the day, when the February sun slanted upon all the fretted work of its pinnacles and niches, and playing in, with an ineffectual effort, was lost in the glorious gloom of the sculptured porch. Cosmo pleased himself straying about this place, not that he knew any thing about it, or was at all enlightened as to its peculiar beauties—but simply because it moved him with a sense of perfectness and glory, such as, perhaps, few other human works ever impress so deeply. As he went along, he came suddenly upon the object of his thoughts. Madame Roche—as Baptiste lamented to think the common people called her—was in an animated little discussion with a market-woman, then returning home, about a certain little bundle of sweet herbs which remained in her almost empty basket. Cosmo hurried past, shyly afraid to be supposed listening; but he could hear that there was something said about an omelette for Mademoiselle Marie, which decided the inclinations of his old lady. He could not help standing at the corner of the lane to watch her when she had passed. She put the herbs into her own little light basket, and was moving away towards her house, when something called her attention behind, and she looked back. She could not but perceive Cosmo, lingering shy and conscious at the corner, nor could she but guess that it was herself whom the lad had been looking at. She smiled to him, and made him a little courtesy, and waved her hand with a kindly, half-amused gesture of recognition, which completed the confusion of Cosmo, who had scarcely self-possession enough left to take off his hat. Then the old lady went on, and he remained watching her. What a step she had!—so simple, so straightforward, so unconscious, full of a natural grace which no training could have given. It occurred to Cosmo for a moment, that he had seen but one person walk like Madame Roche. Was it a gift universal to French women?—but then she was not a Frenchwoman—she was English—nay—

hurrah! better still—she was his own countrywoman. Cosmo had not taken time to think of this last particular before—his eye brightened with a still more affectionate sentiment, his imagination quickened with new ground to go upon. He could not help plunging into the unknown story with quite a zest and fascination. Perhaps the little romance which the lad wove incontinently, was not far from the truth. The young heir of the house of Roche de St. Martin, whom the Revolution left barely "lord of his presence and no land beside"—the stately old French father, perhaps an *emigré*—the young man wandering about the free British soil, captivated by the lovely Scottish face, bringing his bride here, only to carry her away again, a gay, volatile, mercurial, unreliable Frenchman. Then those wanderings over half the world, those distresses, and labors, and cares which had not been able to take the sweet bloom from her cheek, nor that elastic grace from her step—and now here she was, a poor widow with a sick daughter, bargaining under the shadow of St. Ouen for the sweet herbs for Marie's omelette. Cosmo's young heart rose against the incongruities of fortune. She who should have been a fairy princess, with all the world at her feet, how had she carried that beautiful face unwithered and unfaded, that smile undimmed, that step unburthened, through all the years and the sorrows of her heavy life?

It seemed very hard to tell—a wonderful special provision of Providence to keep fresh the bloom which it had made; and Cosmo went home, thinking with enthusiasm that perhaps it was wrong to grudge all the poverty and trials which doubtless she had made beautiful and lighted up by her presence among them. Cosmo was very near writing some verses on the subject. It was a very captivating subject to a poet of his years—but blushed and restrained himself with a truer feeling, and only went to rest that night wondering how poor Mademoiselle Marie liked her omelette, and whether Madame Roche, the next time they met, would recognize him again.

CHAPTER LIII

The next day Cameron came up stairs to Cosmo's room, where the lad was writing by the window, with an open letter in his hand and rather a comical expression on his face.

"Here is for you, Cosmo," said Cameron. "The like of me does not captivate ladies. Macgregor and I must make you our reverence. We never would have got this invitation but for your sake."

"What is it?" cried Cosmo, rising eagerly, with a sudden blush, and already more than guessing, as he leaned forward to see it, what the communication was. It was a note from Madame Roche, oddly, yet prettily, worded, with a fragrance of French idiom in its English, which made it quite captivating to Cosmo, who was highly fantastical, and would not have been quite contented to find his beautiful old lady writing a matter-of-fact epistle like other people. It was an invitation to "her countrymen" to take a cup of tea with her on the following evening. She had heard from Baptiste and his wife that they were English travelers, and loved to hear the speech of her own country, though she had grown unfamiliar with it, and therewith she signed her name, "Mary Roche de St. Martin," in a hand which was somewhat stiff and old-fashioned, yet refined. Cosmo was greatly pleased. His face glowed with surprised gratification; he was glad to have his old heroine come up so entirely to his fancy, and delighted to think of seeing and knowing her, close at hand in her own home.

"You will go?" he said, eagerly.

Cameron laughed—even, if truth must be told, the grave Highlander blushed a little. He was totally unused to the society of women; he was a little excited by the idea of making friends in this little foreign town, and already looked forward with no small amount of expectation to Madame Roche's modest tea-drinking. But he did not like to betray his pleasure; he turned half away, as he answered:—

"For your sake, you know, laddie—Macgregor and I would have had little chance by ourselves—yes, we'll go," and went off to write a very stiff and elaborate reply, in the concoction of which Cameron found it more difficult to satisfy himself than he had ever been before all his life. It was finished, how ever, and dispatched at last. That day ended, the fated evening came. The Highland student never made nor attempted so careful a toilette—he, too, had found time to catch a glimpse of Cosmo's beautiful old lady, and of the pale, fragile daughter, who went out once a week to drive in the little carriage. Mademoiselle Marie, whom Cosmo had scarcely noticed, looked to Cameron like one of the tender virgin martyrs of those old pictures which had impressed his uncommunicative imagination without much increasing his knowledge. He had watched her, half lifted, half helped into the little carriage, with pity and interest greater than any one knew of. He was a strong man, unconscious in his own person of what illness was—a reserved, solitary, self-contained hermit, totally ignorant of womankind, save such as his old mother in her Highland cottage, or the kind, homely landlady in the High Street whose anxiety for his comfort sometimes offended him as curiosity. A lady, young, tender, and gentle—a woman of romance, appealing unconsciously to all the protecting and supporting impulses of his manhood, had never once been placed before in Cameron's way.

So Cosmo and his friend, with an interest and excitement almost equal, crossed the little street of St. Ouen, towards Madame Roche's second floor, in the early darkness of the February night, feeling more reverence, respect, and enthusiasm than young courtiers going to be presented to a queen. As for their companion, Cameron's pupil, he was the only unconcerned individual of the little party. *He* was not unaccustomed to the society of ladies—Madame Roche and her daughter had no influence on his imagination; he went over the way with the most entire complacency, and not a romantical sentiment within a hundred miles of him; he was pleased enough to see new faces, and share his own agreeable society with some one else for the evening, and he meant to talk of Italy and pictures and astonish these humble people, by way of practice when he should reach home—Macgregor was not going to any enchanted palace—he only picked his steps over the causeway of the little street of St. Ouen, directing his way towards Madame Roche's second floor.

This chamber of audience was a small room, partly French and party English in its aspect; the gilded clock and mirror over the mantel-piece— the marble table at the side of the room—the cold polished edge of floor on which Cameron's unwary footsteps almost slid—the pretty lamp on the table, and the white maze of curtains artistically disposed at the window, and looped with pink ribbons, were all indigenous to the soil; but the square of thick Turkey carpet—the little open fire-place, where a wood fire burned and crackled merrily, the warm-colored cover on the table, where stood Madame Roche's pretty tea equipage, were home-like and "comfortable" as insular heart could wish to see. On a sofa, drawn close to the fire-place, half sat, half reclined, the invalid daughter. She was very pale, with eyes so blue, and mild, and tender, that it was impossible to meet their gentle glance without a rising sympathy, even though it might be impossible to tell what that sympathy was for. She was dressed—the young men, of course, could not tell how—in some invalid dress, so soft, so flowing, so seemly, that Cameron, who was as ignorant as a savage of all the graces of the toilette, could not sufficiently admire the perfect gracefulness of those most delicate womanly robes, which seemed somehow to belong to, and form part of, this fair, pale, fragile creature, whose whole existence seemed to be one of patience and suffering. Madame Roche herself sat on the other side of the table. She was not in widow's dress, though she had not been many years a widow. She wore a white lace cap, with spotless, filmy white ribbons, under which her fair hair, largely mixed with silver, was braided in soft bands, which had lost nothing of their gloss or luxuriance. Her dress was black satin, soft and glistening—there was no color at all about her habiliments, nothing but soft white and black. She did not look younger than she was, nor like any thing but herself. She was not a well-preserved, carefully got-up beauty. There were wrinkles in her sweet old face, as well as silver in her hair. Notwithstanding, she sat there triumphant, in the real loveliness which she could not help and for which she made no effort, with her beautiful blue eyes, her soft lips, her rose cheek, which through its wrinkles was as sweet and velvety as an infant's, her pretty white hands and rosy finger tips. She was not unconscious either of her rare gift—but bore it with a familiar grace as she had borne it for fifty years. Madame Roche had been beautiful all her life—she did not wonder nor feel confused to know that she was beautiful now.

And she received them, singular to say, in a manner which did not in the slightest degree detract from Cosmo's poetic admiration, asking familiar questions about their names, and where, and how, and why they traveled, with the kindly interest of an old lady, and with the same delightful junction of English speech with an occasional French idiom, which had charmed the lad in her note. Cameron dropped shyly into a chair by the side of the couch, and inclined his ear, with a conscious color on his face, to the low voice of the invalid, who, though a little surprised, took polite pains to talk to him, while Cosmo as shyly, but not with quite so much awkwardness, took up his position by the side of Madame Roche. She made no remark, except a kindly smile and bow, when she heard the names of Cameron and Macgregor, but when Cosmo's was named to her she turned round to him with a special and particular kindness of regard.

"Ah! Livingstone!" she said; "I had a friend once called by that name," and Madame Roche made a little pause of remembrance, with a smile and a half sigh, and that look of mingled amusement, complacence, gratitude, and regret, with which an old lady like herself remembers the name of an old lover. Then she returned quietly to her tea-making. She did not notice Macgregor much, save as needful politeness demanded, and she looked with a little smiling surprise into the shadow where Cameron had placed himself by the side of her daughter, but her own attention was principally given to Cosmo, who brightened under it, and grew shyly confidential, as was to be looked for at his age.

"I have seen you at your window," said Madame Roche. "I said to Marie, this young man, so modest, so ingenuous, who steals back when we come to the window, I think he must be my countryman. I knew it by your looks—all of you, and this gentleman, your tutor—ah, he is not at all like a Frenchman. He has a little forest on his cheeks and none on his chin, my child—that is not like what we see at St. Ouen."

The old lady's laugh was so merry that Cosmo could not help joining in it—"He is my dear friend," said Cosmo, blushing to find himself use the adjective, yet using it with shy enthusiasm; "but he is only Macgregor's tutor not mine."

"Indeed! and who then takes care of you?" said the old lady. "Ah, you are old enough—you can guard yourself—is it so? Yet I know you have a good mother at home."

"I have indeed; but, madame, how do you know?" cried Cosmo, in amazement.

"Because her son's face tells me so," cried Madame Roche, with her beautiful smile. "I know a mother's son, my child. I know you would not have looked down upon an old woman and her poor daughter so kindly but for your mother at home; and your good friend, who goes to talk to my poor Marie—has he then a sick sister, whom he thinks upon when he sees my poor wounded dove?"

Cosmo was a little puzzled; he did not know what answer to make—he could not quite understand, himself, this entirely new aspect of his friend's character. "Cameron is a very good fellow," he said, with perplexity; but Cosmo did not himself perceive how, to prove himself a good fellow, it was needful for Cameron to pay such close reverential regard to the invalid on her sofa, whom he seemed now endeavoring to amuse by an account of their travels. The reserved and grave Highlander warmed as he spoke. He was talking of Venice on her seas, and Rome on her hills, while Marie leaned back on her pillows, with a faint flush upon her delicate cheek, following his narrative with little assenting gestures of her thin white hand, and motions of her head. She was not beautiful like her mother, but she was so fragile, so tender, so delicate, with a shadowy white vail on her head like a cap, fastened with a soft pink ribbon, which somehow made her invalid delicacy of complexion all the more noticeable, that Cosmo could not help smiling and wondering at the contrast between her and the black, dark, strong-featured face which bent towards her. No—Cameron had no sick sister—perhaps the grave undemonstrative student might even have smiled at Madame Roche's pretty French sentiment about her wounded dove; yet Cameron, who knew nothing about women, and had confessed to Cosmo long ago how little of the universal benevolence of love he found himself capable of, was exerting himself entirely out of his usual fashion, with an awkward earnestness of sympathy which touched Cosmo's heart, for the amusement of the poor sick Marie.

"We, too, have wandered far, but not where you have been," said Madame Roche. "We do not know your beautiful Rome and Venice—we know only the wilderness, I and my Marie. Ah, you would not suppose it, to find us safe in St. Ouen; but we have been at—what do you call it?—the other side of the world—down, down below here, where summer comes at Christmas—ah! in the Antipodes."

"And I would we were there now, mamma," said Marie, with a sigh.

"Ah, my poor child!—yes, we were there, gentlemen," said Madame Roche. "We have been great travelers—we have been in America—we were savages for a long time—we were lost to all the world; no one knew of us—they forgot me in my country altogether; and even my poor Jean— they scarce remembered *him* in St. Ouen. When we came back, we were like people who drop from the skies. Ah, it was strange! His father and his friends were dead, and me—it was never but a place of strangers to me—this town. I have not been in my country—not for twenty years; yet I sometimes think I should wish to look at it ere I die, but for Marie."

"But the change might be of use to her health," said Cameron, eagerly. "It often is so. Motion, and air, and novelty, of themselves do a great deal. Should you not try?"

"Ah, I should travel with joy," said Marie, clasping her white, thin hand, "but not to Scotland, monsieur. Your fogs and your rains would steal my little life that I have. I should go to the woods—to the great plains—to the country that you call savage and a wilderness; and there, mamma, if you would but go you should no longer have to say—'Poor Marie!'"

"And that is—where?" said Cameron, bending forward to the bright sick eyes, with an extraordinary emotion and earnestness. His look startled Cosmo. It was as if he had said, "Tell me but where, and I will carry you away whosoever opposes!" The Highlandman almost turned his back upon

Madame Roche. This sick and weak Marie was oppressed and thwarted in her fancy. Cameron looked at her in his strong, independent manhood, with an unspeakable compassion and tenderness. It was in his heart to have lifted her up with his strong arms and carried her to the place she longed for, wherever it was—that was the immediate impulse upon him, and it was so new and so strange that it seemed to refresh and expand his whole heart. But Marie sank back upon her pillows with a little movement of fatigue, perhaps of momentary pettishness, and only her mother spoke in quite another strain.

"You do not know my country, my child," said Madame Roche. "I have another little daughter who loves it. Ah, I think some day we shall go to see the old hills and the old trees; but every one forgets me there, and to say truth, I also forget," said the old lady, smiling. "I think I shall scarcely know my own tongue presently. Will you come and teach me English over again?"

"You should say Scotch, madam—it is all he knows," said Cameron, smiling at Cosmo, to whom she had turned. It was an affectionate look on both sides, and the boy blushed as he met first the beautiful eyes of his lovely old lady, and then the kind glance of his friend. He stammered something about the pleasure of seeing them in Scotland, and then blushed for the common-place. He was too young to remain unmoved between two pair of eyes, both turned so kindly upon him.

"He is his mother's son, is he not?" said Madame Roche, patting Cosmo's arm lightly with her pretty fingers. "I knew his name when I was young. I had a friend called by it. You shall come and talk to me of all you love—and you and I together, we will persuade Marie."

Cameron glanced as she spoke, with a keen momentary jealous pang, from the handsome lad opposite to him, to the invalid on the sofa. But Marie was older than Cosmo—a whole world apart, out of his way, uninteresting to the boy as she lay back on her cushions, with her half-shut eyes and her delicate face. It was strange to think how strong and personal was this compassion, the growth of a day, in the Highlander's stern nature and uncommunicating heart.

CHAPTER LIV

The days glided on imperceptibly over the travelers as they rested in St. Ouen—rested longer than there seemed any occasion for resting, and with so little inducement that Macgregor began to grow restive, and even Cosmo wondered; Cameron was no longer the same. The fiery heart of the Highlander was moved within him beyond all power of self-restraint. He was calm enough externally by the necessity of his nature, which forbade demonstration—but within, the fountains were breaking, the ice melting, a fiery and fervid activity taking the place of the long quiescence of his mind. He neither understood it himself nor reasoned upon it. He yielded because he could not help yielding. An arbitrary, imperious impulse, had taken possession of him, strengthening itself in his own strength and force, and taking into consideration no possibility of obstacles. His big, strong heart yearned over the tender weakness which could not help itself—he could think of nothing but of taking it up in his powerful arms and carrying it into safety. It was the first awakening of his native passionate fervor—he could acknowledge nothing, perceive nothing to stand in the way. He was as unreasonable and arbitrary as the merest boy—more so, indeed, for boys do not know emotions so stormy and violent. It had an extraordinary effect altogether upon this grave, reserved, toil-worn man; sometimes he was capricious, impatient, and fitful in his temper—at other times more tender than a woman—often half ashamed of himself—and only clear about one thing as it seemed, which was, that he would not go away.

Another point he was angrily jealous upon; he neither lingered in Baptiste's room himself, nor, if he could possibly prevent it, permitted Cosmo to do so. He would have no questions asked, no gossiping entered into about Madame Roche. "These ladies should be sacred to us—what they wish us to know they will tell us," said Cameron almost haughtily, on one occasion, when he interrupted a conversation between the cobbler and his young companion. Cosmo was half disposed to resent at once the interference, and the supposition that he himself would gossip about any one, or acquire information by such undignified means—but the serious feeling in his friend's face, almost stern in its earnestness, impressed the lad.

It was evidently of tenfold importance to Cameron more than to himself, much as he was interested in his beautiful old lady. Cosmo yielded with but little demonstration of impatience and wonder, half-guessing, yet wholly unable to comprehend what this could mean.

Another day, when Cosmo sat by his little window in the corner, to which he had been shy of going since he knew Madame Roche, but which had still a great attraction for him, Cameron entered his room hurriedly and found him at his post. The Highlandman laid his powerful hand roughly on the lad's shoulder, and drew him away, almost in violence. "How dare ye pry upon them?" he cried, with excitement; "should not their *home* be sacred, at least?" Almost a quarrel ensued, for Cosmo struggled in this strong grasp, and asserted his independence indignantly. He pry upon any one! The lad was furious at the accusation, and ready to abjure forever and in a moment the friend who judged him so unjustly; and had it not been that Cameron himself melted into an incomprehensible caprice of softness, there must have been an open breach and separation. Even then, Cosmo could scarcely get over it; he kept away from his window proudly, was haughty to his companions, passed Baptiste without the civility of a recognition, and even, in the strength of his ill-used and injured condition, would not go to see Madame Roche. Out of this sullen fit the lad was awakened by seeing Cameron secretly selecting with his uncouth hands such early flowers as were to be found in the market of St. Ouen, and giving shy, private orders about others, more rare and delicate, which were to be sent to Madame Roche, in her second floor. Cosmo was very much perplexed, and did not comprehend it, any more than he comprehended why it was that the Highlandman, without motive or object, and in face of the protestations of his pupil, persisted in lingering here in St. Ouen.

Thus a week passed—a fortnight, and no period was yet assigned for their stay. They became familiar with that pretty, little, half French, half English apartment, where poor Marie lay on the sofa, and her mother sat working by the window. Madame Roche was always kind, and had a smile for them all. Marie was sometimes vivacious, sometimes fatigued, sometimes broke forth in little outbursts of opposition to mamma, who was always tender and forbearing to her! sometimes Cosmo thought the gentle invalid was even peevish, lying back among her cushions, with her half closed eyes, taking no notice of any one. This poor Marie was not only weak in frame— she was unsatisfied, discontented, and had "something on her mind." She started into sudden effusions of longing and weariness, with eager wishes to go away somewhere, and anticipations of being well, if mamma would but consent, which Madame Roche quietly evaded, and, during which, Cameron sat gazing at her with all his heart inquiring in his eyes, where? But Marie showed no inclination to make a confidant of her mother's countryman. She listened to him with a languid interest, gave him a partial attention, smiled faintly when her mother thanked him for the flowers he sent, but treated all these marks of Cameron's "interest" in herself with a fatal and total indifference, which the Highlandman alone either did not or would not perceive. It did not even appear that Marie contemplated the possibility of any special reference to herself in the stranger's courtesies. She treated them all alike; paying no great regard to any of the three. She was amiable, gentle, mild in her manners, and pleasant in her speech; but throughout all, it was herself and her own burdens, whatever these might be, that Marie was thinking of. Perhaps they were enough to occupy the poor tender spirit so closely confined within those four walls. Cosmo did not know—but *his* sympathies were with the bright old mother, whose beautiful eyes always smiled, who seemed to have no time to spend in impatience or discontent, and whose perpetual care was lavished on her daughter, whether Marie was pleased or no.

Madame Roche, it would appear, was not too sensitive—her husband, who loved and was jealous of her, and who died and left her a widow, had not broken her heart; neither could her child, though she was ill and peevish, and not very grateful. Perhaps Cosmo would rather, in his secret spirit, have preferred to see his beautiful old lady, after all her hard life and troubles, and with still so many cares surrounding her, show greater symptoms of heart-break, but Madame Roche only went on working and smiling, and saying kind words, with an invincible patience, which was the patience of a natural temper, and not of exalted principle. She could not help her sweetness and affectionate disposition any more than she could help the beauty which was as faithful to her in age as in youth. She was kind even to Macgregor, who was totally indifferent to her kindness; perhaps she might be as kind to the next wandering party of travelers who were thrown in her way. Cosmo would not allow himself to believe so, yet, perhaps, it was true.

And in the meantime Macgregor grumbled, and wrote discontented letters home; and even Cosmo could give no reason to himself for their stay in St. Ouen, save Madame Roche and her daughter—a reason which he certainly would not state to the Mistress, who began to be impatient for her boy's return. Cameron had no letters to write—no thoughts to distract him from the one overpowering thought which had taken possession of his mind. The arbitrary fancy, absolute and not to be questioned, that his own errand in the little Norman town was to restore liberty, health, content, and comfort to Marie Roche de St. Martin. He felt he could do it, as his big heart expanded over Madame Roche's "wounded dove"—and Cameron, on the verge of middle age, experienced by privations and hardships, fell into the very absoluteness of a boy's delusion. He did not even take into account that, upon another capricious, willful, human heart depended all his power over the future he dreamed of—he only knew that he could do it, and therefore would, though all the world stood in his way. Alas, poor dreamer! the world gave itself no trouble whatever on the subject, and had no malice against him, nor doom of evil for Marie. So he went on with his imperious determination, little witting of any obstacle before him which could be still more imperious and absolute than he.

CHAPTER LV

On one of these days Cameron came again to Cosmo with a letter in his hand. His look was very different now—it was grave, resolute, determined, as of a man on the verge of a new life. He showed the letter to his young companion. It was from Macgregor's father, intimating his wish that they should return immediately, and expressing a little surprise to hear that they should have remained so long in St. Ouen. Cameron crushed it up in his hand when it was returned to him; a gesture not so much of anger as of high excitement powerfully restrained.

"We must go, then, I suppose?" said Cosmo; but the lad looked up rather doubtfully and anxiously in his friend's face—for Cameron did not look like a man obedient, who was ready to submit to a recall.

"I will tell you to-morrow," said the Highlander; "yes—it is time—I don't resent what this man says—he is perfectly right. I will go or I will not go to-morrow."

What did this mean? for the "will not go" was a great deal more than a passive negative. It meant—not a continued dallying in St. Ouen—it meant all that Cameron imagined in that great new torrent of hopes, and loves, and purposes, which he now called life. Then he went to Cosmo's window and glanced out for a moment; then he returned with a deep, almost angry flush on his face, muttering something about "never alone,"—then he thrust his arm into Cosmo's, and bade him come along.

"I am going to see Madame Roche," cried Cameron, with a certain recklessness of tone. "Come—you're always welcome there—and four is better company than three."

It was no little risk to put Cosmo's temper to—but he yielded, though he was somewhat piqued by the address, feeling an interest and anxiety for something about to happen, which he could not perfectly define. They found Madame Roche alone, seated by the window working, as usual—but Marie was not there. The old lady received them graciously and kindly, as was her wont. She answered to Cameron's inquiries that Marie's headache was more violent than usual, and that she was lying down. Poor Marie! she was very delicate; she suffered a great deal, the dear child!

"Invalids have sometimes a kind of inspiration as to what will cure them," said Cameron, steadily fixing his eyes upon Madame Roche, "why will you not let her go where she wishes to go? Where is it? I should think the trial worth more than fatigue, more than labor, ay—if man had more to give—more even than life!"

Madame Roche looked up at him suddenly, with a strange surprise in her eyes—a painful, anxious, terrified wonder, which was quite inexplicable to Cosmo.

"Alas, poor child!" she said hurriedly, and in a low voice. "I would grudge neither fatigue nor labor for my Marie; but it is vain. So you are going away from St. Ouen? ah, yes, I know—I hear every thing. I saw your young Monsieur Macgregor half an hour ago; he said letters had come, and you were going. We shall grieve when you are gone, and we shall not forget you, neither I nor my Marie."

Cameron's face changed; a sweetness, an elevation, a tender emotion, quite unusual to those strong features, came over them.

"It is by no means certain that I shall go," he said, in a low and strangely softened voice.

"Does Mademoiselle Marie know?"

And once more he glanced round the room, and at her vacant sofa, with a tender reverence and respect which touched Cosmo to the heart, and filled the lad with understanding at once and pity. Could he suppose that it was hearing of this that aggravated Marie's headache? could he delude himself with the thought that she was moved by the prospect of his departure? Poor Cameron! Madame Roche was looking at him too with a strange anxiety, trying to read his softened and eloquent face. The old lady paused with an embarrassed and hesitating perplexity, looking from Cosmo to Cameron, from Cameron back again to Cosmo. The lad thought she asked an explanation from him with her eyes, but Cosmo had no explanation to give.

"My friend," said Madame Roche, at last, trying to recover her smile, but speaking with an evident distress which she endeavored in vain to conceal—"you must not say *Mademoiselle* Marie. The people do so, for they have known her as a girl; but they all know her story, poor child! I fancied you must have heard it from Baptiste or Margot, who love to talk. Ah! have they been so prudent?—it is strange."

Madame Roche paused again, as if to take breath. Cosmo instinctively and silently moved his chair further away, and only looked on, a deeply-moved spectator, not an actor in the scene. Cameron did not say a word, but he grasped the little marble table with a hand as cold as itself, and looked at Madame Roche with the face of a man whose tongue clove to his mouth, and who could not have spoken for his life. She, trembling a little, afraid to show her emotion, half frightened at the look of the person she addressed, proceeded, after her pause, with a rapid, interrupted voice.

"My poor, tender Marie—poor child!" said the mother. "Alas! she is no more mademoiselle—she is married; she was married years ago, when she was too young. Ah, it has wrung my heart!" cried the old lady, speaking more freely when her great announcement was made; "for her husband loves her no longer; yet my poor child would seek him over the world if she might. Strange—strange, is it not? that there should be one most dear to her who does not love Marie?"

But Cameron took no notice of this appeal. He still sat gazing at her, with his blank, dark face, and lips that were parched and motionless. She was full of pity, of distress, of anxiety for him; she went on speaking words which only echoed idly on his ear, and which even Cosmo could not attend to, expatiating in a breathless, agitated way, to cover his emotion and to gain a little time, upon the troubles of Marie's lot, upon the desertion of her husband, her broken health and broken heart. In the midst of it, Cameron rose and held out his hand to her. The trembling mother of Marie took it, rising up to receive his farewell. She would have made a hundred anxious apologies for the involuntary and unconscious deceit from which he had suffered, but dared not. He shook hands with her hastily, with an air which could not endure speaking to.

"I shall leave St. Ouen so soon, that I may not be able to see you again," said Cameron, with a forcible and forced steadiness which put all her trembling compassion to flight; and he looked full in her eyes, as if to dare her suspicions. "If I can not, farewell, and thank you for your kindness. I can but leave my best wishes for—Mademoiselle Marie."

Before Cosmo could follow him—before another word could be said, Cameron was gone. They could hear him descending the stair, with an echoing footstep, as they stood together, the old lady and the lad, in mutual distress and embarrassment. Then Madame Roche turned to Cosmo, took his hand, and burst into tears.

"Could I tell?" cried Marie's mother—"alas, my child! could I think that your tutor, so grave, so wise, would be thus moved? I am beside myself! I am grieved beyond measure! Alas, what shall I do?—a good man is in distress, and I am the cause!"

"Nay, it is not your fault, madame," said Cosmo; "it's no one's fault—a mistake, a blunder, an accident; poor Cameron!" and the lad had enough ado to preserve his manhood and keep in his own tears.

Then Madame Roche made him sit down by her and tell her all about his friend. Cosmo would rather have gone away to follow Cameron, and know his wishes immediately about leaving St. Ouen, but was persuaded, without much difficulty, that it was kinder to leave the Highlander alone in the first shock of the discovery he had made. And Madame Roche was much interested in the story of the student, whose holiday had ended so sadly. She wished, with tears in her eyes, that she could do any thing to comfort, any thing to help him on. And in turn she told the story of her own family to Cosmo; how Marie's husband had turned out a vagabond, and worthless; how he had deserted his girlish wife in the beginning of her illness, leaving her alone and unattended, at a distance even from her mother; how they had heard nothing of him for three years—yet how, notwithstanding all, the poor Marie wept for him constantly, and tried to persuade her mother to set out on the hopeless enterprise of finding him again.

"My poor child!" said Madame Roche; "she forgets every thing, my friend, but that she loves him. Ah, it is natural to us women; we remember that, and we remember nothing more."

Cosmo could not help a momentary spark of indignation. He thought Marie very selfish and cold-hearted, and could not forgive her his friend's heart-break:—

"Mademoiselle Marie should not forget *you*," he said.

Though he dealt with such phenomena occasionally in his verses, and made good sport with them, like other young poets, Cosmo was, notwithstanding, too natural and sensible, not to pause with a momentary wonder over this strange paradox and contradiction of events. To think of such a man as Cameron losing his wits and his heart for love of this weak and perverse woman, who vexed her mother's heart with perpetual pining for the husband who had ill-used and deserted her! How strange it was!

"Marie does not forget me, my child; she is not to blame," said Madame Roche; "it is nature; do not I also know it? Ah, I was undutiful myself! I loved my poor Jean better than my father; but I have a little one who is very fond of me; she is too young for lovers; she thinks of nothing but to make a home in my own country for Marie and me. My poor Marie! she can not bear to go away from St. Ouen, lest he should come back to seek her; she will either go to seek *him*, or stay; and so I can not go to Desirée nor to my own country. Yet, perhaps, if Marie would but be persuaded! My little Desirée is in Scotland. They think much of her where she is. It is all very strange; she is in a house which once was home to me when I was young. I think it strange my child should be there."

"Desirée?" repeated Cosmo, gazing at his beautiful old lady with awakened curiosity. He remembered so well the pretty little figure whose bearing, different as they were otherwise, was like that of Madame Roche. He looked in her face, anxious, but unable, to trace any resemblance. Desirée! Could it be Joanna's Desirée—the heroine of the broken windows—she who was at Melmar? The lad grew excited as he repeated the name—he felt as though he held in his hand the clue to some secret—what could it be?

"Do you know the name? Ah, my little one was a true Desirée," said Madame Roche; "she came when the others were taken away—she was my comforter. Nay, my friend—she wrote to me of one of your name! One—ah, look at me!—one who was son of my old friend. My child, let me see your face—can it be you who are son of Patrick, my good cousin? What!—is it then possible? Are you the young Livingstone of Norlaw?"

Cosmo rose up in great excitement, withdrawing from the half embrace into which Madame Roche seemed disposed to take him; the lad's heart bounded with an audible throb, rising to his throat:—

"Do you know me? Did you know my father? Was he your cousin?" he cried, with an increasing emotion. "He was Patrick Livingstone, of Norlaw, a kinsman of the old Huntleys; and you—you—tell me! You are Mary of Melmar! I know it! I have found you! Oh, father! I have done my work at last."

The lad's voice broke into a hoarse cry—he had no words to express himself further, as he stood before her with burning cheeks and a beating heart, holding out his hands in appeal and in triumph. He had found her! he could not doubt, he could not hesitate—gazing into that beautiful old face, the whole country-side seemed to throng about him with a clamorous testimony. All those unanimous witnesses who had told him of her beauty, the little giant at the smithy to whom her foot rung "like siller bells," the old woman who remembered her face "like a May morning," rushed into Cosmo's memory as though they had been present by his side. He cried out again with a vehement self-assurance and certainty, "You are Mary of Melmar!" He kissed her hand as if it had been the hand of a queen—he forgot all his previous trouble and sympathy—he had found her! *his* search had not been made in vain.

"I am Mary Huntley, the daughter of Melmar," said the old lady, with her beautiful smile. "Yes, my child, it is true—I left my father and my home for the sake of my poor Jean. Ah, he was very fond of me! I am not sorry; but you sought me?—did you seek me?—that is strange, that is kind; I know not why you should seek me. My child, do not bring me into any more trouble—tell me why you sought for *me?*"

"I sought you as my father sought you!" cried Cosmo; "as he charged us all to seek you when he died. I sought you, because you have been wronged. Come home with me, madame. I thank God for Huntley that he never had it!—I knew I should find you! It is not for any trouble. It is because Melmar—Melmar itself—your father's house—is yours!"

"Melmar—my father's house—where my Desirée is now?—nay, my friend, you dream," said the old lady, trying to smile, yet growing pale; she did not comprehend it—she returned upon what he said about his father; she was touched to tears to think that Norlaw had sought for her—that she had not been forgotten—that he himself, a young champion, had come even here with the thought of finding her;—but Melmar, Melmar, her father's house! The old Mary of Melmar, who had fled from that house and been disinherited, could not receive this strange idea—Melmar! the word died on her lip as the voice of Marie called her from an inner chamber. She rose with the promptness of habit, resuming her tender mother-smile, and answering without a pause. She only waved her hand to Cosmo as the boy left her to her immediate duties. It was not wonderful that she found it difficult to take up the thread of connection between that life in which she herself had been an only child, and this in which she was Marie's nursing Mother. They were strangely unlike indeed.

CHAPTER LVI

Cosmo ran down the stairs, and out of the gate of Madame Roche's house, much too greatly excited to think of returning to his little room. The discovery was so sudden and so extraordinary that the lad was quite unable to compose his excitement or collect his thoughts. Strange enough, though Mary of Melmar had been so much in his mind, he had never once, until this day, associated her in the smallest degree with the beautiful old lady of St. Ouen. When he began to think of all the circumstances, he could not account to himself for his extraordinary slowness of perception. At, least a score of other people, totally unlikely and dissimilar, had roused Cosmo's hopes upon his journey. Scarcely a place they had been in which did not afford the imaginative youth a glimpse somewhere of some one who might be the heroine; yet here he had been living almost by her side without a suspicion, until a sudden confidence, given in the simplest and most natural manner, disclosed her in a moment—Mary of Melmar! He had known she must be old—he had supposed she must have children—but it was strange, overpowering, a wild and sudden bewilderment, to find in her the mother of Desirée and Marie.

Cosmo did not go home to his little room—he hurried along the narrow streets of St. Ouen, carried on by the stress and urgency of his own thoughts. Then he emerged upon the river side, where even the picturesque and various scene before him failed to beguile his own crowding fancies. He saw without seeing the river boats, moored by the quay, the Norman fishermen and market-women, the high-gabled houses, which corresponded so pleasantly with those high caps and characteristic dresses, the whole bright animation and foreign coloring of the scene. In the midst of it all he saw but one figure, a figure which somehow belonged to it, and took individuality and tone from this surrounding;—Mary of Melmar! but not the pensive, tender Mary of that sweet Scottish country-side, with all its streams and woodlands—not a Mary to be dreamt of any longer on the leafy banks of Tyne, or amid those roofless savage walls of the old Strength of Norlaw. With an unexpressed cry of triumph, yet an untellable thrill of disappointment, the lad hurried along those sun-bright banks of Seine. It was this scene she belonged to; the quaint, gray Norman town, with its irregular roofs and gables, its cathedral piling upward to a fairy apex those marvelous pinnacles and towers, its bright provincial costume and foreign tints of color, its river, bright with heavy picturesque boats, and floating baths, and all the lively life of a French urban stream. It was not that meditative breadth of country, glorious with the purple Eildons and brown waters, sweet with unseen birds and burns, where the summer silences and sounds were alike sacred, and where the old strongholds lay at rest like old warriors, watching the peace of the land. No—she was not Mary of Melmar—she was Madame Roche de St. Martin, the beautiful old lady of St. Ouen.

When Cosmo's thoughts had reached this point, they were suddenly arrested by the sight of Cameron, standing close to the edge of the quay, looking steadily down. His remarkable figure, black among the other figures on that picturesque river-side—his fixed, dark face, looking stern and authoritative as a face in profile is apt to look—his intense, yet idle gaze down the weather-stained, timber-bound face of the river-pier, startled his young companion at first into sudden terror. Cosmo had, till this moment, forgotten Cameron. His friendship and sympathy woke again, with a touch of alarm and dread, which made him sick. Cameron!—religious, enthusiastic, a servant of God as he was, what was the disappointed man, in the shock of his personal suffering, about to do? Cosmo stood behind, unseen, watching him. The lad did not know what he feared, and knew that his terror was irrational and foolish, but still could not perceive without a pang that immovable figure, gazing down into the running river, and could not imagine but with trembling what might be in Cameron's thoughts. He was of a race to which great despairs and calamities were congenial. His blood was fiery Celtic blood, the tumultuous pulses of the mountaineer. Cosmo felt his heart beat loud in his ears as he stood watching. Just then one of the women he had been in the habit of buying flowers from, perceived Cameron and went up to him with her basket. He spoke to her, listened to her, with a reckless air, which aggravated Cosmo's unreasonable alarm; the lad even heard him laugh as he received a pretty bouquet of spring flowers, which he had doubtless ordered for Marie. The woman went away after receiving payment, with a somewhat doubtful and surprised face. Then Cameron began to pull the pretty, delicate blossoms asunder, and let them fall one by one into the river—one by one—then as the number lessened, leaf by leaf, scattering them out of his fingers with an apparent determination of destroying the whole, quite unconscious of the wistful eyes of two little children standing by. When the last petal had fallen into the river, and was swept down under the dark keel of one of the boats, the Highlander turned suddenly away—so suddenly, indeed, that Cosmo did not discover his disappearance till he had passed into the little crowd which hung about a newly-arrived vessel lower down the quay;—his step was quick, resolute, and straightforward—he was going home.

And then Cosmo, brought by this means to real ground, once more began to think, as it was impossible to forbear thinking, over all the strange possibilities of the new events which had startled him so greatly. If Marie had not been married—if Cameron had wooed her and won her—if, strangest chance of all, it had thus happened that the poor Highland student, all unwitting of his fortune had come to be master of Melmar! As he speculated, Cosmo held his breath, with a sudden and natural misgiving. He thought of Huntley in Australia—his own generous, tender-hearted brother. Huntley, who meant to come home and win Melmar, and who already looked upon himself as its real master—Huntley, whose hopes must be put to an absolute and instant conclusion, and were already vain as the fancies of a child. He thought of his mother at home in Norlaw, thinking of the future which waited her son, and refusing to think of the woman who had inflicted upon her the greatest sufferings of her life—he thought of Patie, who, though much less concerned, had still built something upon the heirship of Melmar. He thought of the sudden change to the whole family, who, more or less unconsciously, had reckoned upon this background of possible enrichment, and had borne their real poverty all the more magnanimously, in consideration of the wealth which was about to come—and a sudden chill came to the lad's heart. Strange perversity! Cosmo had scorned the most distant idea of Huntley's heirship, so long as it was possible; but now that it was no longer possible, a compunction struck him. This prospect, which cheered Huntley in his exile, and put spirit into his labor—this, which encouraged the Mistress, for her son's sake, to spare and to toil—this, which even furthered the aims of Patie in his Glasgow foundery—this it was *his* ungracious task to turn into vanity and foolishness. His step slackened unconsciously, his spirit fell, a natural revulsion seized him. Madame Roche de St. Martin—the poor sick Marie, who loved only herself and her worthless French husband, who doubtless now would find his way back to her, and make himself the real Lord of Melmar! Alas, what a change from Cosmo's picturesque and generous dreams among the old walls of Norlaw! When he thought of the vagabond Frenchman, whose unknown existence had made Cameron miserable, Cosmo made an involuntary exclamation of opposition and disgust. He forgot *that* Mary of Melmar who was now an imaginary and unsubstantial phantom; he even forgot the beautiful old lady who had charmed him unawares—he thought only of the French Marie and her French husband, the selfish invalid and the worthless wanderer who had deserted her. Beautiful Melmar, among its woods and waters, to think it should be bestowed thus!

Then Cosmo went on, in the natural current of his changed thoughts, to think of the present family, the frank and friendly Joanna, the unknown brother whom bowed Jaacob respected as a virtuoso, and who, doubtless, firmly believed himself the heir—the father who, though an enemy, was still a homeborn and familiar countryman. Well, *that* household must fall suddenly out of prosperity and wealth into ruin—his own must forego at once a well-warranted and honorable hope—all to enrich a family of St. Ouen, who knew neither Melmar nor Scotland, and perhaps scorned them both! And it was all Cosmo's doing!—a matter deliberately undertaken—a heroical pursuit for which he had quite stepped out of his way! The lad was quite as high-minded, generous, even romantic, in the streets of St. Ouen as he had been in his favorite seat of meditation among the ruins of Norlaw; but somehow, at this moment, when he had just succeeded in his enterprise, he could not manage to raise within his own heart all the elevated sentiments which had inspired it. On the contrary, he went slowly along to his lodgings, where he should have to communicate the news to Cameron, feeling rather crest-fallen and discomfited—not the St. George restoring a disinherited Una, but rather the intermeddler in other men's matters, who gets no thanks on any hand. To tell Cameron, who had spent the whole fiery torrent of that love which it was his nature to bestow, with a passionate individual fervor, on one person and no more—upon the capricious little French Marie, who could not even listen, to its tale! Cosmo grew bitter in his thoughts as he took down the key of his chamber from the wall in Baptiste's room and received a little note which the cobbler handed him, and went very softly up stairs. The note was from Madame Roche, but Cosmo was misanthropical, and did not care about it. He thought no longer of Madame Roche—he thought only of Marie, who was to be the real Mary of Melmar, and of poor Cameron heart-broken, and Huntley disappointed, and the French vagabond of a husband, who was sure to come home.

CHAPTER LVII

Cameron was not visible until the evening, when he sent for Cosmo to his own room. The lad obeyed the summons instantly; the room was rather a large one, very barely furnished, without any carpet on the floor, and with no fire in the stove. It was dimly lighted by one candle, which threw the apartment into a general twilight, and made a speck of particular illumination on the table where it stood, and by which sat Cameron, with his pocket-book and Baptiste's bill before him. He was very pale, and somehow it seemed impossible to see his face otherwise than in profile, where it looked stern, rigid, and immoveable as an old Roman's; but his manner, if perhaps a little graver, was otherwise exactly as usual. Cosmo was at a loss how to speak to him; he did not even like to look at his friend, who, however, showed no such embarrassment in his own person.

"We go to-morrow, Cosmo," said Cameron, rather rapidly; "here is Baptiste's bill to be settled, and some other things. We'll go over to Dieppe the first thing in the morning—every thing had better be done to night."

"The first thing in the morning! but I am afraid I—I can not go," said Cosmo, hesitating a little.

"Why?" Cameron looked up at him imperiously—he was not in a humor to be thwarted.

"Because—not that I don't wish to go, for I had rather be with you," said Cosmo—"but because I made a discovery, and a very important one, to-day."

"Ah?" said Cameron, with a smile and a tone of dreary satire; "this must have been a day for discoveries—what was yours?"

"It was about Madame Roche," said Cosmo, with hesitation—he was afraid to broach the subject, in his anxiety for his friend, and yet it must be told.

"Just so," said Cameron, with the same smile; "I knew it must be about Madame Roche—what then? I suppose it is no secret? nothing more than everybody knew?"

"Don't speak so coldly," entreated Cosmo, with irrestrainable feeling; "indeed it is something which no one could have dreamed of; Cameron, she is Mary. I never guessed or supposed it until to-day."

Something like a groan burst from Cameron in spite of himself. "Ay, she's Mary!" cried the Highlander, with a cry of fierce despair and anguish not to be described, "but laddie, what is that to you?"

They were a world apart as they sat together on either side of that little table, with the pale little light between them—the boy in the awe of his concern and sympathy—the man in the fiery struggle and humiliation of his manhood wrung to the heart. Cosmo did not venture to look up, lest the very glance—the water in his eyes, might irritate the excited mind of his friend. He answered softly, almost humbly, with the deep imaginative respect of youth.

"She is Mary of Melmar, Cameron—the old lady; my father's kinswoman whom he was—fond of—who ran away to marry a Frenchman—who is the heir of Melmar—Melmar which was to be Huntley's, if I had not found her. It can not be Huntley's now; and I must stay behind to complete the discovery I have made."

Perhaps Cosmo's tone was not remarkably cheerful; the Highlander looked at him with an impatient and indignant glance.

"Why should it be Huntley's when it is hers?" he said, almost angrily. "Would you grudge her rights to a helpless woman? you, boy! are even *you* beguiled when yourself is concerned?"

"You are unjust," said Cosmo. "I do not hesitate a moment—I have done nothing to make any one doubt me—nor ever will."

The lad was indignant in proportion to his uneasiness and discomfort in his discovery, but Cameron was not sufficiently at rest himself to see through the natural contradictions of his young companion. He turned away from him with the half-conscious gesture of a sick heart.

"I am unjust—I believe it," he said, with a strange humility; "lands and silver are but names to me. I am like other folk—I can be liberal with what I have not—ay, more! I can even throw away my own," continued Cameron, his strong voice trembling between real emotion and a bitter self-sarcasm, "so that nobody should be the better for the waste; that's *my* fortune. Your estate will be of use to somebody—take comfort, callant; if you are disappointed, there's still some benefit in the gift. But ye might give all and no mortal be a gainer—waste, lavish, pour forth every thing ye have, and them the gift was for, if ever they knew, be the worse and not the better! Ay! that's some men's portion in this life."

Cosmo did not venture to say a word—that bitter sense of waste and prodigality, the whole treasure of a man's heart poured forth in vain, and worse than in vain, startled the lad with a momentary vision of depths into which he could not penetrate. For Cameron was not a boy, struggling with a boy's passion of disappointment and mortification. He was a strong, tenacious, self-concentrated man. He had made a useless, vain, unprofitable holocaust, which could not give even a moment's pleasure to the beloved of his imagination, for whom he had designed to do every thing, and the unacceptable gift returned in a bitterness unspeakable upon the giver's heart. Other emotions, even more heavy and grievous, struggled also within him. His old scruples against leaving his garret and studies, his old feelings of guilt in deferring voluntarily, for his own pleasure and comfort, the beginning of his chosen "work," came back upon his silent Celtic soul in a torrent of remorse and compunction, which he could not and would not confide to any one. If he had not forsaken the labors to which God had called him, could he have been left to cast his own heart away after this desperate and useless fashion? With these thoughts his fiery spirit consumed itself. Bitter at all times must be the revulsion of love which is in vain, but this was bitterer than bitterness—a useless, unlovely, unprofitable sacrifice, producing nothing save humiliation and shame.

"I see, Cosmo," he said, after a little pause, "I see that you can not leave St. Ouen to-morrow. Do your duty. You were fain to find her, and you have found her. It might be but a boy's impulse of generosity, and it may bring some disappointment with it; but it's right, my lad! and it's something to succeed in what you attempt, even though you do get a dinnle thereby in some corner of your own heart. Never fear for Huntley—if he's such as you say, the inheritance of the widow would be sacred to your brother. Now, laddie, fare you well. I'm going back to *my* duty that I have forsaken. Henceforth you're too tender a companion for the like of me. I've lost—time, and such matters that you have and to spare; you and I are on different levels, Cosmo; and now, my boy, fare ye well."

"Farewell? you don't blame *me*, Cameron?" cried Cosmo, scarcely knowing what he said.

"*Blame* you—for what?" said the other, harshly, and with a momentary haughtiness; then he rose and laid his hand with an extreme and touching kindness, which was almost tender, upon Cosmo's shoulder. "You've been like my youth to me, laddie," said the Highlandman; "like a morning's dew in the midst of drouth; when I say fare ye well I mean not to say that we're parted; but I must not mint any more at the pathways of your life—mine is among the rocks, and in the teeth of the wind. I have no footing by nature among your primroses. That is why I say—not to-morrow in the daylight, and the eyes of strangers, but now when you and me and this night are by ourselves—fare ye well, laddie! We're ever friends, but we're no more comrades—that is what I mean."

"And that is hard, Cameron, to me," said Cosmo, whose eyes were full.

Cameron made no answer at all to the boy; he went to the door of the dim room with him, wrung his hand, and said, "Good night!" Then, while the lad went sadly up the noisy stair-case, the man turned back to his twilight apartment, bare and solitary, where there was nothing familiar and belonging to himself, save his pocket-book and passport upon the table, and Baptiste's bill. He smiled as he took that up, and began to count out the money for its payment; vulgar, needful business, the very elements of daily necessity—these are the best immediate styptics for thrusts in the heart.

Cosmo, to whom nothing had happened, went to his apartment perhaps more restlessly miserable than Cameron, thinking over all his friend's words, and aggravating in imagination the sadness of their meaning. The lad did not care to read, much less to obey the call of Madame Roche's pretty note, which bade him come and tell her further what his morning's communication meant. For this night, at least, he was sick of Madame Roche, and every thing connected with her name.

CHAPTER LVIII

The morning brought feelings a little more endurable, yet still, very far from pleasant. Very early, while it was still dark, Cosmo saw his companions set off on their journey home, and was left to the cold dismal consciousness of a solitary day just beginning, as he watched the lights put out, and the chill gray dawn stealing over the high houses. The first ray of sunshine glimmered upon the attic windows and burned red in the vane over the dwelling-place of Madame Roche. This gleam recalled the lad's imagination from a musing fit of vague depression and uneasiness. He must now think no more of Cameron—no more of those strange breakings off and partings which are in life. On the contrary, his old caprice of boyish generosity laid upon him now the claim of an urgent—almost an irksome—duty, and he, who went upon his travels to seek Mary of Melmar with all the fervor of a knight-errant, turned upon his heel this cold spring dawn with an inexpressible reluctance and impatience, to go to her, in obedience to her own summons. He would rather have been with Cameron in his silent and rapid journey—but his duty was here.

When Cosmo went to Madame Roche, which he did at as early an hour as he thought decorous, he found her alone, waiting for him. She came forward to receive him with rather an anxious welcome. "I almost feared you were gone," said the old lady, with a smile which was less tranquil than usual. "When I saw your friends go, I said to myself, this boy is but a fairy messenger, who tells of a strange hope, and then is gone and one hears no more of it. I am glad you have not gone away; but your poor friend, he has left us? I thought it best, my child, to say nothing to Marie."

Cosmo's heart swelled a little in spite of himself; he could not bear the idea of the two women gossiping together over his friend's heart-break, which was the first thought that occurred to him as Madame Roche spoke, and which, though it was certainly unjust, was still partly justified by the mysterious and compassionate tone in which the old lady mentioned Cameron's name.

"I am not aware that there is any occasion for saying any thing, madame," said Cosmo, with a little abruptness. Madame Roche was not remarkably quick-sighted, yet she saw through the lad's irritation—the least smile in the world came to the corner of her lip. She did not think of the great pang in the Highlander's heart—she knew very little indeed of Cameron—she only smiled with a momentary amusement at Cosmo's displeasure, and a momentary sense of womanish triumph over the subjugated creature, man, represented in the person of this departed traveler, who, had just gone sadly away.

"Do not quarrel with me, my child," she said, her smile subsiding into its usual sweetness; "the fault was not with me; but tell me once more this strange news you told me last night. Melmar, which was my father's, I was born heiress of it—did you say it was mine—*mine*? for I think I must have mistaken what the words mean."

"It is quite true," said Cosmo, who had not yet quite recovered his temper, "your father left it to you if you were ever found, and if you were not found, to *my* father, and to Huntley Livingstone, his heir and eldest son. My father sought you in vain all his life; he never would put in his own claim lest it should injure you. When he died, Huntley was not rich enough to go to law for his rights, but he and everybody believed that you never would be found, and that he was the heir. He thinks so now; he is in Australia working hard for the money to maintain his plea, and believing that Melmar will be his; but I have found you, and you are the lady of Melmar; it is true."

"You tell me a romance—a drama," cried Madame Roche, with tears in her eyes. "Your father sought me all his life—*me*? though I was cruel to him. Ah, how touching! how beautiful!—and you, my young hero!—and this Huntley, this one who thinks himself the heir—he, too, is generous, noble, without selfishness—I know it! Oh, my child, what shall I do for him? Alas, Marie! She is my eldest child, and she is married already—I never grieved for it enough till now."

"There is no need, madame," said Cosmo, to whom these little sentences came like so many little shooting arrows, pricking him into a disappointed and vexed resentment. "Huntley needs nothing to make him amends for what is simply justice. Melmar is not his, but yours."

This speech, however, which was somewhat heroical in tone, expressed a most uncomfortable state of mind in Cosmo. He was angry at the idea of rewarding Huntley with the hand of Marie, if that had not been given away already. It was a highly romantic suggestion, the very embodiment of poetic justice, had it been practicable; but somehow it did not please Cosmo. Then another suggestion, made by his own fancy, came dancing unsolicited into the lad's mind. Desirée, perhaps, who was not married, might not *she* be compensation sufficient for Huntley? But Cosmo grew very red and felt exceedingly indignant as he thought of it; this second reward was rather more distasteful than the first. He paid very little attention, indeed, to Madame Roche, who, much excited, smiled and shed tears, and exclaimed upon her good fortune, upon the kindness of her friends, upon the goodness of God. Cosmo put his hands in his pockets and did not listen to her. He was no longer a young poet, full of youthful fervor and generosity. The temper of the British lion began to develop itself in Cosmo. He turned away from Madame Roche's pretty effusion of sentiment and joy, in a *huff* of disenchantment, discontented with her, and himself, and all the world.

Perhaps some delicate spirit whispered as much in the old lady's ear. She came to him when her first excitement was over, with tender tears in her beautiful old eyes.

"My child, you have found a fortune and a home for me," said Madame Roche, "but it is to take them away from your brother. What will your mother say at home?"

"She will say it is right and just, madame, and I have done my duty," said Cosmo, briefly enough.

Then Madame Roche bent forward and kissed his young cheek, like a mother, as she was.

"We are widow and orphans," she said, softly. "God will bless you—He is the guardian of such; and He will not let Huntley suffer when He sees how all of you do justice out of a free heart."

Cosmo was melted; he turned away his head to conceal the moisture in his own eyes—was it out of a free heart? He felt rebuked and humbled when he asked himself the question; but Madame Roche gave him no time to think of his own feelings. She wanted to know every thing about all that had occurred. She was full of curiosity and interest, natural and womanly, about not only the leading points of the story, but all its details, and as Marie did not appear, Cosmo by himself, with his beautiful old lady, was soon reconciled to the new circumstances, and restored to his first triumph. He had done what his father failed to do—what his father's agents had never been able to accomplish—what newspaper advertisements had attempted in vain. He had justified his own hope, and realized his own expectation. He had restored home and fortune to the lost Mary of Melmar. A night and a morning were long enough for the sway of uncomfortable and discontented feelings. He gave himself up, once more, to his old enthusiasm, forgetting Huntley's loss and Cameron's heart-break, and his mother's disappointment, in the inspiration of his old dreams, all of which were now coming true. The end of this conversation was, that Cosmo—charged with Madame

Roche's entire confidence, and acting as her representative—was to follow his former companions and return to Edinburgh as speedily as possible, and there to instruct his old acquaintance, Cassilis, to take steps immediately for the recovery of Melmar. He parted with the old lady, who was, and yet was not, the Mary of his fancy, that same evening—did not see Marie, who was fortunately kept in her room by an access of illness or peevishness, took leave of Baptiste and the old streets of St. Ouen with great content and exhilaration, and on the very next morning, at an hour as early, as chilly, and as dark as that of Cameron's departure, began his journey home.

CHAPTER LIX

The streets of Edinburgh looked strange and unfamiliar to Cosmo Livingstone when he stood in them once more—a very *boy* still in heart and experience, yet feeling himself a traveled and instructed man. He no longer dreamed of turning his steps towards Mrs. Purdy's in the High Street; he took his carpet bag to a hotel instead, half wondering at himself for his changed ideas. Cameron's ideas too, probably, were equally changed. Where was he, or how had he managed to reconcile the present with the past? But Cosmo had no time to inquire. He could not pause in Edinburgh for any thing but his needful business, which was to see Mr. Cassilis, and to place in his hands the interests of Madame Roche.

The young lawyer received him with a careless kindness not very flattering to Cosmo's dignity, but was greatly startled by the news he brought. Once only he paused in taking down all the facts of the case which Cosmo could give him, to say:—

"This discovery will be a serious loss to your brother;" but Cosmo made no reply, and with that the comment ceased. Huntley and his heirship melted away out of sight in the strangest manner while this conversation went on. Cosmo had never realized before how entirely it separated him and his from all real connection with Melmar. The sensation was not quite satisfactory, for Melmar, one way or another, had borne a most strong and personal connection with all the thoughts and projects of the family of Norlaw for a year or two past; but that was all over. Cosmo alone now had any interest in the matter, and that solely as the representative of Madame Roche.

When he had fully informed the young lawyer of all the needful points in the matter, and formally left the cause in his hands, Cosmo left him to secure a place in the first coach, and to hasten home with all the speed he could make. He could scarcely have felt more strange, or perceived a greater change upon every thing, if he had dropped from the skies into Kirkbride; yet every thing was precisely the same, so clearly and broadly recognizable, that Cosmo could not understand what difference had passed upon them, and still less could understand that the difference was in himself. His mother stood waiting for him at the door of the Norlaw Arms. It was cold March weather, and the Mistress had been sitting by the fire, waiting the arrival of the coach. She was flushed a little with the frosty air and the fire, and looked disturbed and uneasy. Cosmo thought he could fancy she turned a jealous eye upon himself as he sprang from the coach to meet her, which fancy was perfectly true, for the Mistress was half afraid that her son who had been abroad might be "led away" by his experiences of travel, and might have become indifferent or contemptuous about his home. She was a little displeased, too, that he had lingered behind Cameron. She was not like Madame Roche—all-enduring sweetness was not in this old-fashioned Scottish mother. She could not help making a strong personal claim of that arbitrary love which stinted nothing in bestowing upon those who were her own, and opened her heart only slowly and secondarily to the rest of the world.

"So you're hame at last!" was the Mistress's salutation; though her eye was jealous, there was moisture in it, as she looked at her boy. Cosmo had grown in stature for one thing; he was brown with exposure, and looked manly and strong; and, not least, his smooth cheeks began to show evidence of those symptoms of manhood which boys adore. There was even a something not to be described or defined upon Cosmo's upper lip, which caught his mother's eye in a moment, and gave a tangible ground for her little outburst of half-angry fondness.

"You're no' to bring any of your outlandish fashions here!" said the Mistress, "though you have been in foreign parts. I'll have no person in my house bearded like a Frenchman. Can you no' carry your bag in your ain hand, laddie? Come away, then; you can shake hands with other folk another time."

As the Mistress spoke, a figure strange to Kirkbride stalked through the circle of lookers-on. Nothing like that bearded face and wide cloak had been known to Cosmo's memory in the village or the district. He turned unconsciously to look after the stranger. Further down on the road before were two girls whom Cosmo recognized with a start; one was Joanna Huntley, the other there was no possibility of mistaking. Cosmo gazed after her wistfully—a blush of recollection, of embarrassment, almost of guilt, suddenly rising to his face. Bowed Jaacob stood at his smithy door, with the fiery glow of the big fire behind him, a swart little demon gazing after her too. Desirée! Was she the desired of this unknown figure in the cloak, who went languidly along to join her? Cosmo stood silent for a moment, altogether absorbed by the junction of old and new thus strangely presented to him. Familiar Kirkbride, with Jaacob at the smithy door, and that graceful little figure of romance, whose story no one but Cosmo knew, followed by the other stranger figure which he was entirely unacquainted with. He started when his mother repeated her imperative summons—the color on his cheeks looked guilty and troubled; he had his secret on his heart, and knew beforehand that it would not be agreeable to the Mistress. So he did the very worst thing he could have done—postponed the telling of it to a more convenient season, and so went uncomfortably, and with a visible restraint, which vexed his mother's soul within her, home to Norlaw.

Patie, as it happened, had come home a few days before on a brief visit; and when they met round the fire that first evening, every one's thought instinctively was of Huntley. When Marget came in, disturbing the gloamin quietness with lights, her long-drawn sigh and involuntary exclamation:—

"Eh, sirs! if Master Huntley were but here!" startled the little family group into open discussion of the subject which was in all their hearts.

"Huntley's been further than you, Cosmo," said the Mistress, "and maybe seen mair; but I wouldna wonder if Huntley thinks yet, as he thought when he left Norlaw, that there's no place equal to hame."

"Huntley's in the bush; there's not very much to make him change his opinion there, mother," said Patrick.

"Ay, but Huntley's heart is ever at hame," said the Mistress, finding the one who was absent always the dearest.

"Mother," said Cosmo, his courage failing him a little, "I have something to tell you—and it concerns Huntley, too, mother. Mother, I have found the lady, the heir—she whom we have all heard so much about; Patie, *you* know?"

"What lady? what heir? and how does Patie know?" asked the Mistress; then she paused, and her countenance changed. A guess at the truth occurred to her, and its first effect was an angry flush, which gradually stole over her face. "Patie is no a romancer, to have to do with heirs and ladies," she added, quickly; "nor to have strange folk in his thoughts the first hour he's at home. I canna tell wherefore any one of you should have such wandering fancies; it's no' like a bairn of mine."

"Mother, I've learnt something by it," said Cosmo; "before I went away, I thought it worth hunting over all the world to find her—for no reason that I can tell, except that she was wronged, and that we might be the better if she never came back; but now I have found her—I know where Mary of

Melmar is, and she knows she's the heir; but ever since my thought has been of Huntley. Huntley could have had no pleasure in Melmar, mother, if it were not justly his own."

The Mistress raised her head high as Cosmo spoke. Anger, great disappointment, of which she was half ashamed, and a pride which was resolute to show no sign of disappointment, contended in her face with that bitter dislike and repugnance to the lost Mary which she had never been able—perhaps had seldom tried to conquer. "I have heard plenty of Mary of Melmar," said the Mistress, hastily; "ae time and another she's been the plague of my life. What, laddie! do you mean to say you left me, and your hame, and your ain business, to seek this woman? What was she to you? And you come back and tell me you've found her, as if I was to rejoice at the news. You ken where she is, and she kens she's the heir; and I crave ye to tell me what is that to me? Be silent, Patie! Am I her mother, or her sister, or her near friend, that this lad shall come to bring the news to me?"

"It's poor news," said Patie, who did not hesitate to look gravely annoyed and disappointed, as he was; "very poor news for all of us, mother; but at least it's better that Cosmo found her than a stranger—if found she was to be." .

The Mistress paused a moment, subdued by this suggestion. "Poor news! I kenna what you both mean," she said, with pride; "what concern is it of ours? Would my Huntley ever put hand or touch upon another person's gear? Let her come back the morn, and what the waur are we? Do you think I envied her Melmar, or her land? Do you think I would have made my son rich at *her* cost, that never was a friend to me? You may ken many things, laddies, but you dinna ken your mother. Me!—I wouldna take blade o' grass or drop of water belonging to her, if you asked me; and I'm thankful to tell ye baith my Huntley is Huntley Livingstone of Norlaw, and needs to be indebted to no person in this whole country-side."

The Mistress rose up in the fervor of her indignant disappointment; vexation and mortified feeling brought the water to her eyes. She felt aggrieved and wronged, not only in this setting aside of Huntley, but in the very fact that Mary of Melmar was about to return. This Mary, for whose unthankful sake her husband had neglected *her* honest love and faithful heart, had at last lured even her son, her youngest and best beloved, away from her, and was coming back triumphant to the inheritance which might have been Huntley's. The Mistress's heart rose in a tumult of pride, love, indignation, and bitterness. She said "*my* son," and "*my* Huntley," with a proud and tender emphasis, an involuntary, anxious impulse to make amends to him for the hope he had lost—yet with an equally natural feeling rejected indignantly all sympathy for him, and would not permit even his brothers to speak of disappointment or loss to Huntley in this new event. She went away across the room, breaking up the fireside circle by the hasty movement, to seek out in her basket the stocking which she was knitting—for the Mistress's eyes began to fail her in candlelight with all her more delicate industries—and coming back to the table, began to knit with absorbed attention, counting the loops in the heel as if she had no care for the further particulars which Cosmo, encouraged by Patie, proceeded to tell. Yet she did hear them notwithstanding. But for the presence of Patie's practical good sense, Cosmo and his mother might have had painful recollections of that night; but his brother's steady look and sober attention kept Cosmo from indulging the irritation and wounded feeling which he might have felt otherwise. He went on with his story, gradually growing interested in it, and watching—as a dramatist might watch his first audience—the figure of the Mistress, who sat almost with her back to him, knitting assiduously, the light of the candle throwing a great shadow of her cap upon the wall, and her elbow moving slightly with the movement of her wires. Cosmo watched how the elbow moved irregularly at certain points of his tale, how it was still for an instant now and then, as the interest grew, and the boy-poet was pleased and forgave his mother. At last the stocking fell from the Mistress's hand—she pushed back her chair, and turned round upon him with a half-scream.

"Desirée!" cried the Mistress, as she might have exclaimed at the crisis of a highly interesting novel, "it's her that's at Melmar—whisht!—dinna speak to me—I'm just as sure as that we're a' here—it's her ain very bairn!"

After this, Cosmo's tale ended with a great success; he had excited his mother—and the truth began to glide into her unwilling heart, that Mary of Melmar was, like herself, the mother of fatherless children, a widow, and poor. She heard all the rest without a word of displeasure; she became grave, and said nothing, when her sons discussed the matter; she nodded her head approvingly when Patie repeated rather more strongly than before his satisfaction that Cosmo had found the lost Mary, since she was to be found. The Mistress was thinking of something—but it was only after she had said good night to them that the youths discovered what it was.

"Bairns," said the Mistress then, abruptly pausing upon the stair, with her candle in her hand, "that bit lassie at Melmar is in the dwelling of the enemy—and if it were not so, the mother canna make war on the house where her bairn has shelter. You're her nearest kinsmen that I ken of, to be friends as well—she'll have to come here."

"Mother!" cried Cosmo, in delight and surprise, and compunction, "can you ask her here?"

"Ay, laddie—I can do mony things, mair than the like of you ken of," said the Mistress; and, saying so, she went slowly up stairs, with the light in her hand, and her shadow climbing the wall after her, leaving no unkindness in the echo of her motherly good night.

CHAPTER LX

During all these months Desirée had led a strange life at Melmar. She had never told any one of the revelation, painful and undesired, the miserable enlightenment which Aunt Jean's story had brought. What Cosmo told Madame Roche months after, Madame Roche's little daughter knew on that winter night by the Kelpie, when the tale of Aunt Jean, and all its confirming circumstances, stung her poor little heart with its first consciousness of falsehood and social treachery. After that she was ill, and they were kind to her at Melmar, and when she recovered Desirée still did not tell her mother. People did not write so many letters then as they do now, in these corresponding days—Madame Roche certainly did not hear oftener than once a fortnight, sometimes not more than once a month from her daughter, for Melmar was nearly as far from St. Ouen in *those* days as India is now. Many a painful thought it cost poor Desirée as she stole out by herself, avoiding every one, to the side of Tyne. Oswald Huntley, after her recovery, had resumed his manner of devotion toward her—but Desirée's eyes were no longer touched with the fairy glamour of her first dream. She had not been "in love," though the poor child imagined she had—she had only been amused by that dream of romantic fancy to which seventeen is subject, and touched into gratitude and pleasure by the supposed love she had won—yet, even while she scorned his false pretense of tenderness, that very disdain made Desirée shrink from the thought of injuring Oswald. She was sadly troubled between the two sentiments, this poor little girl, who was French, and Madame Roche's child, and who consequently was much tempted by the dangerous intoxications of feeling. What was barely, simply, straightforwardly *right* might have satisfied Joanna; but Desirée could not help thinking of self-sacrifice and suffering for others, and all the girlish heroics common to her age. She could not live in their house and betray the family who had sheltered and were kind to her. She seemed to be tempted to avenge herself on Oswald by righting her mother at his expense; so for feeling's sake Desirée kept herself very unhappy, saying nothing to her mother of the discovery she had made, unable to resume her old cordiality with the Huntleys, ill at ease in her own mind, and sadly solitary and alone. If it had been any mere piece of information—or had the injury to be done been her own, Desirée would have seen what was right, plainly enough—but as it was, she only thought of the cruel difference to the family of Melmar, which a word of hers might make, and of the selfish advantage to herself; and feeling conscious of the sacrifice she made for them—a sacrifice which nobody knew or appreciated, and which her conscience told her was even wrong—Desirée's mind grew embittered against them and all the world; and her poor little heart, uneasy, cross, and restless, consumed itself. As the struggle continued it made her ill and pale, as well as disturbed in mind; nobody could tell what ailed her—and even Aunt Jean, with her keen black eyes, could not read Desirée. She had "something on her mind."

When one day she was startled by the arrival of a visitor, who asked to see *her*, and was put into a little waiting-room—a cold little room, without a fire, into which the March sunshine came chill, with no power of warmth in it—to wait for the little governess. Desirée was much amazed when she entered here to see the ruddy and comely face of the Mistress looking down upon her, out of that black bonnet and widow's cap. It was a face full of faults, like its owner, but it was warm, bright, kind, full of an unsubduable spirit and intelligence, which had long ago attracted the eye of the vivacious little Frenchwoman, who, however, did not know Mrs. Livingstone, except by sight. They looked at each other in silence for the first moment—one amazed, and the other thoughtful—at last the Mistress spoke.

"Maybe I may not name you right," she said; "I have nae knowledge of your tongue, and no' much of strangers, whatever place they come from; but my son Cosmo has seen your mother, in foreign parts, and that is the reason that brings me here."

Desirée started violently; for the moment it seemed to her that this was her true and fit punishment. Her mother, whom she might have been with—who might have been here had Desirée but spoken—was sick, was dying, and a stranger brought her the news! She grew very pale and clasped her little French hands in a passion of grief and self-upbraiding.

"She is ill!" cried Desirée, "ill, and I am here!"

"Na—no' that I ken of," said the Mistress; "stranger news than that; do you know of any bond between your mother and this house of Melmar? for that is what I am come to tell you of now, as maybe she has done herself before this time by hand of write."

From pale, Desirée's cheeks became burning red—her eyes sank beneath the look of the Mistress, her heart beat loud and wildly. Who had found her out? but she only turned her head aside with an uneasy movement and did not speak.

"I may guess you've heard tell of it by your face," said the Mistress; "Melmar was left by will to my family—to my Huntley, the eldest and the heir—failing your mother, that was thought to be lost. When he heard tell of that, my Cosmo would not rest till he was away on his travels seeking her. He's been through France and Italy, and I ken not what unlikely places a' to look for your mother, and at last he's found her; and she's coming home with little mair delay to be enfeoffed in her ain lands and prove herself the heir."

Bitter tears, which still had a certain relief in them, fell heavy from Desirée's eyes—she had known it all, but had not been the means of bringing this fortune to her mother. Her first impulse was not the delighted surprise which the Mistress expected, but she threw herself forward, after a moment's pause, at her visitor's feet, and seized her hand and cried—"Is it true?" with a vehemence which almost scandalized the Mistress. Cosmo's mother took her hand away involuntarily, but moved by the girl's tears laid it on her head, with a hasty but kindly motion.

"It's true," said the Mistress; "but being true do you no' see you canna stay here? It is your mother's house—but though I hold this Me'mar for little better than a knave, yet I would not deceive him. You canna remain here when your mother's plea against him is begun. You should not stay another day without letting him ken who you are—and that is why I'm here to bid you come back with me to Norlaw."

"To Norlaw!" cried Desirée, faintly; she had no words to express her amazement at the invitation—her shame for the deceit which she had practiced, and which was worse than any thing the Mistress supposed possible—her strange humiliation in comparing herself, Oswald Huntley, every one here, with Cosmo; somehow when this sudden burst of honest daylight fell upon her, Desirée felt herself as great a culprit as Melmar. Her place seemed with him and with his son, who knew the truth and concealed it—not with the generous and true hearts who relinquished their own expectations to do justice to the wronged. In an agony of shame and self-disgust, Desirée hid her face in her hands—she was like Oswald Huntley whom she despised—she was not like Cosmo Livingstone nor Cosmo's mother.

"Ay—to Norlaw," said the Mistress, ignorant of all this complication of feeling and with a softening in her voice; "Norlaw himself, that's gane, was near of kin to your mother; your grandfather, auld Melmar, was good to us and ours; my sons are your nearest kinsmen in these parts, and I'm their mother. It's mair for your honor and credit, and for your mother's, now when you ken, to be there than here. Come hame with me—you'll be kindly welcome at Norlaw."

"And yet," said Desirée, lifting her tearful eyes, and her face flushed with painful emotion; "and yet but for us, all this fortune would have gone to your son. Why are you kind to me? you ought to hate me."

"Na!" said the Mistress, with proud love and triumph; "my Huntley is nane the waur—bairn, do you think the like of you could harm my son, that I should hate you? Na! he would work his fingers to the bone, and eat dry bread a' his days before he would touch the inheritance of the widow—loss of land or loss of gear is no such loss to my Huntley that I should think ill of any person for its sake and you're my son's kinswoman, and I'm his mother. Come hame with me till your ain mother is here."

Without a word Desirée rose, dried her eyes, and held out her little hand to the Mistress, who took it doubtfully.

"I will be your daughter, your servant!" cried the little Frenchwoman, with enthusiasm; "I will come to learn what truth means. Wait but till I tell them. I will stay here no longer—I will do all that you say!"

In another moment she darted out of the room to prepare, afraid to linger. The Mistress looked after her, shaking her head.

"My daughter!" said the Mistress to herself, with a "humph!" after the words—and therewith she thought of Katie Logan; where was Katie now?

CHAPTER LXI

The Melmar family had just concluded their luncheon, and were still assembled in the dining-room—all but Mrs. Huntley, who had not yet come down stairs—when Desirée, flushed and excited from her interview with the Mistress, who waited for her in the little room, came hastily in upon the party; without noticing any of the others Desirée went up at once to the head of the house, who glared at her from behind his newspaper with his stealthy look of suspicion and watchfulness, as she advanced. Something in her look roused the suspicions of Mr. Huntley; he gave a quick, angry glance aside at Oswald, as if inquiring the cause of the girl's excitement, which his son replied to with a side-look of sullen resentment and mortification—an unspoken angry dialogue which often passed between the father and son, for Melmar had imposed upon the young man the task of keeping Desirée in ignorance and happiness, a charge which Oswald, who had lost even the first novelty of amusing himself with her found unspeakably galling, a constant humiliation. The little Frenchwoman came up rapidly to her host and employer—her cheek glowing, her eye shining, her small foot in her stout little winter-shoe sounding lightly yet distinctly on the carpet. They all looked at her with involuntary expectation. Something newly-discovered and strange shone in Desirée's face.

"Sir," she said, quickly, "I come to thank you for being kind to me. I come because it is honest to tell you—I am going away."

"Going away? What's wrong?" said Melmar, with a little alarm; "come into my study, mademoiselle, and we will put all right, never fear; that little deevil Patricia has been at her again!"

Desirée did not wait for the burst of shrewish tears and exclamations which even Patricia's extreme curiosity could not restrain. She answered quickly and with eagerness,

"No, no, it is not Patricia—it is no one—it is news from home; *you* know it already—you know it!" cried the girl. "My mother! She is poor; I have had to come away from her to be a governess; and you, alas, knew who she was, but said nothing of it to me!"

And involuntarily Desirée's eyes sought, with a momentary indignant glance, the face of Oswald. He sat perfectly upright in his chair staring at her, growing red and white by turns; red with a fierce, selfish anger, white with a baffled, ungenerous shame, the ignominy, not of doing wrong, but of being found out. But even in that moment, in the mortifying consciousness that this little girl had discovered and despised him—the revenge, or rather, for it was smaller—the spite of a mean mind, relieved itself at least in the false wooer's face. He turned to her with the bitterest sneer poor Desirée had ever seen. It seemed to say, "what cause but this could have induced me to notice *you*?" She did not care for him, but she thought she once had cared, and the sneer galled the poor little Frenchwoman to the heart.

"You are ungenerous—you!" she exclaimed, with a fiery vehemence and passion, "you delude me, and then you sneer. Shall I sneer at you, you sordid, you who wrong the widow? But no! If you had not known me I should have thanked you, and my mother would never, never have injured one who was good to Desirée; but now it is war, and I go. Farewell, Monsieur! you did not mean to be kind, but only to blind me—ah, I was wrong to speak of thanks—farewell!"

"What do you mean? who has deceived you?" cried Joanna, stepping forward and shaking Desirée somewhat roughly by the arm; "tell us all plain out what it is. I'm as sure as I can be that it's him that's wrong—and I think shame of Oswald to see him sit there, holding his tongue when he should speak; but you shanna look so at papa!"

And Joanna stood between Melmar and her excited little friend, thrusting the latter away, and yet holding her fast at arm's length. Melmar put his arm on his daughter's shoulder and set her quietly aside.

"Let us hear what this discovery is," said Mr. Huntley; "who is your mother, mademoiselle?"

At which cool question Desirée blazed for an instant into a flush of fury, but immediately shrunk with a cool dread of having been wrong and foolish. Perhaps, after all, they did not know—perhaps it was she who was about to heighten the misfortune of their loss and ruin by ungenerous insinuations. Desirée paused and looked doubtfully in Melmar's face. He was watching her with his usual stealthy vigilance, looking, as usual, heated and fiery, curving his bushy, grizzled eyebrows over those keen cat-like eyes. She gazed at him with a doubtful, almost imploring, look—was she injuring him?—had he not known?

"Come, mademoiselle," said Melmar, gaining confidence as he saw the girl was a little daunted, "I have but a small acquaintance in your country.

Who was your mother? It does not concern us much, so far as I can see, but still, let's hear. Oswald, my lad, can't you use your influence?—we are all waiting to hear."

Oswald, however, had given up the whole business. He was pleased to be able to annoy his father and affront Desirée at last. Perhaps the rage and disappointment in his heart were in some sort a relief to him. He was at least free now to express his real sentiments. He got up hastily from his chair, thrust it aside so roughly that it fell, and with a suppressed but audible oath, left the room. Then Desirée stood alone, with Melmar watching her, with Patricia crying spitefully close at hand, and even Joanna, her own friend, menacing and unfriendly. The poor girl did not know where to turn or what to do.

"Perhaps I am wrong," she said, with a momentary falter. "There was no reason, it is true, why you should know mamma. And perhaps it is unkind and ungenerous of me. But—ah, Joanna, you guessed it when I did not know!—you said she must have been here—you are honest and knew no harm! My mother was born at Melmar; it is hers, though she is poor— and she is coming home."

"Coming home! this is but a poor story, mademoiselle," said Melmar. "*That* person died abroad long ago, and was mother to nobody; but it's clever, by George! uncommonly clever. Her mother's coming home, and my land belongs to her! cool, that, I must say. Will you take Patricia for your lady's maid, mademoiselle?"

"Ah, you sneer, you all sneer!" cried Desirée. "I could sneer too, if I were as guilty; but it is true, and you know it is true; you, who are our kinsman and should have cared for us—you, who have planned to deceive a poor stranger girl—you know it is true!"

"If he does," cried Joanna, "*you're* no' to stand there and tell him. He has been as kind to you as if you belonged to us—you don't belong to us—go— go away this moment. I will not let you stay here!"

And Joanna stamped her foot in the excess of her indignation and sympathy with her father, who looked on, through all this side-play of feelings, entirely unmoved. Poor little Desirée, on the contrary, was stung and wounded beyond measure by Joanna's violence. She gave her one terrified, passionate look, half reproachful, half defiant, had hard ado to restrain a burst of girlish, half-weeping recrimination, and then turned round with one sob out of her poor little heart, which felt as though it would burst, and went away with a forlorn, heroical dignity out of the room. Poor Desirée would not have looked back for a kingdom, but she hoped to have been called back, for all that, and could almost have fallen down on the threshold with mortification and disappointment, when she found that no one interfered to prevent her withdrawal. The poor child was full of sentiment, but had a tender heart withal. She could not bear to leave a house where she had lived so long after this fashion, and but for her pride, Desirée would have rushed back to fall into Joanna's arms, and beg everybody's pardon; but her pride sustained her in the struggle, and at length vanquished her "feelings". Instead of rushing into Joanna's arms, she went to the Mistress, who still waited for her in the little room, and who had already been edified by hearing the fall of Oswald's chair, and seeing that gentleman, as he went furiously forth, kicking Patricia's lap-dog out of his way in the hall. The Mistress was human. She listened to those sounds and witnessed that sight with a natural, but not very amiable sentiment. She was rather pleased than otherwise to be so informed that she had brought a thunderbolt to Melmar.

"Let them bear it as they dow," said the Mistress, with an angry triumph; "neither comfort nor help to any mortal has come out of Me'mar for mony a day;" and she received the unfortunate little cause of all this commotion with more favor than before. Poor little Desirée came in with a quivering lip and a full eye, scarcely able to speak, but determined not to cry, which was no small trial of resolution. The family of Melmar were her mother's enemies—some of them had tried to delude, and some had been unkind to herself—yet she knew them; and the Mistress, who came to take her away, was a stranger. It was like going out once more into the unknown world.

So Desirée left Melmar, with a heart which fluttered with pain, anger, indignation, and a strange fear of the future, and the Mistress guided to Norlaw almost with tenderness the child of that Mary who had been a lifelong vexation to herself. They left behind them no small amount of dismay and anxiety, all the house vaguely finding out that something was wrong, while Joanna alone stood by her father's side, angry, rude, and careless of every one, bestowing her whole impatient regards upon him.

CHAPTER LXII

"Happened!" said bowed Jaacob, with a little scorn; "what should have happened?—you dinna ca' this place in the world—naething, so far as I can tell, ever happens here except births and deaths and marriages; no muckle food for the intelleck in the like of them, though I wouldna say but they are necessary evils—na, laddie, there's little to tell you here."

"Not even about the Bill?" said Cosmo; "don't forget I've been abroad and know nothing of what you've all been doing at home."

"The Bill—humph! it's a' very weel for the present," said Jaacob, with a twinkle of excitement in his one eye, "but as for thae politicians that ca' it a final measure, I wouldna gie that for them," and Jaacob snapped his fingers energetically. "It hasna made just a' that difference in the world ane would have expected, either," he added, after a moment, a certain grim humor stealing into his grotesque face; "we're a' as nigh as possible just where we were. I'm no' what you would ca' a sanguine philosopher mysel'. I ken human nature gey weel; and I canna say I ever limited my ain faith to men that pay rent and taxes at so muckle a year; but it doesna make that difference ane might have looked for. A man's just the same man, callant— especially if he's a poor creature with nae nobility in him—though you do gie him a vote."

"Yet it's all the difference," cried Cosmo, with a little burst of boyish enthusiasm, "between the freeman and the slave!"

Jaacob eyed him grimly with his one eye. "It's a' the like of you ken," said the cynic, with a little contempt, and a great deal of superiority; "but you'll learn better if ye have the gift. There's a certain slave-class in ilka community—that's my conviction—and I wouldna say but we've just had the good fortune to licht upon them in thae ten-pound householders; oh, ay, laddie! let the aristocrats alane—they're as cunning as auld Nick where their ain interest's concerned, though nae better than as mony school-boys in a' greater concerns. Catch them extending the suffrage to the real *men*, the backbane of the country! Would you say a coof in the town here, that marries some fool of a wife and gets a house of his ain, was a mair responsible person than *me*! Take it in ony class you please—yoursel' when you're aulder—na,

Me'mar's son even, that's nearer my age than yours—ony Willie A' thing of a shopkeeper gets his vote—set him up! and his voice in the country—but there's nae voice for you, my lad, if ye were ane-and-twenty the morn—nor for the young laird."

The mention of this name instantly arrested Cosmo's indignation at his own political disabilities. "You say nothing has happened, Jacob," said Cosmo, "and yet here is this same young laird—what of him?—is he nothing?—he ought to rank high in Kirkbride."

"Kirkbride and me are seldom of the same opinion," said the little Cyclops, pushing his red cowl off his brow, and proceeding carelessly to his work, which had been suspended during the more exciting conversation. "I canna be fashed with weakly folk, women or men, though it's more natural in a woman. There's that bit thing of a sister of his with the pink e'en—he's ower like her to please me—but he's a virtuoso. I've been ca'ed one mysel. I've mair sympathy with a traveled man than thae savages here. You see I wouldna say but I might think better of baith him and his father if I'm right in a guess o' mine; and I maun admit I'm seldom wrang when I take a thing into my mind."

"What is it?" said Cosmo, eagerly.

"There's a young lass there, a governess," said Jaacob; "I couldna tell, if I was on my aith, what's out of the way about her. She's no' to ca' very bonnie, and as for wut, that's no' to be looked for in woman—and she's French, though I'm above prejudice on that score; but there's just something about her reminds me whiles of another person—though no mair to be compared in ae way than a gowan to a rose. I'm no' very easy attractit, which is plain to view, seeing, for a' I've met with, I'm no' a married man, and like enough never will be—but I maun admit I was taken with her mysel'."

Cosmo's face was crimson with suppressed anger and laughter both combined.

"How dare you?" he cried at last, with a violent and sudden burst of the latter impulse. Bowed Jaacob turned round upon him, swelling to his fullest stature, and settling his red cowl on his head with an air of defiance, yet with a remote and grim consciousness of fun in the corner of his eye.

"Daur!" exclaimed the gallant hunchback. "Mind what you say, my lad! Women hae ae gift—they aye ken merit when they see it. I've kent a hantle in my day; but the bonniest of them a' never said 'How daur ye' to me."

"Very well, Jacob," said Cosmo, laughing; "I had forgotten your successes. But what of this young lady at Melmar, and your guess about Oswald Huntley? I know her, and I am curious to hear."

"Just the lad yonder, if you will ken, is taken with her like me—that's a'. I advise you to say 'you daur' to him," said Jaacob, shortly, ending his words with a prolonged chorus of hammering.

An involuntary and unconscious exclamation burst from Cosmo's lips. He felt a burning color rise over his face. Why, he could not tell; but his sudden shock of consternation and indignant resentment quite overpowered his composure for the moment—a thrill of passionate displeasure tingled through his heart. He was violently impatient of the thought, yet could not tell why.

"Whatfor no?" said Jaacob. "I'm nane of your romantic men mysel'— but I've just this ae thing to say, I despise a lad that thinks on the penny siller when a woman's in the question. I wouldna tak a wife into the bargain with a wheen lands or a pickle gear, no' if she was a king's daughter— though she might be that, and yet be nae great things. Na, laddie, a man that has the heart to be real downricht in love has aye something in him, take my word for't; and even auld Me'mar himsel'—"

"The old villain!" cried Cosmo, violently; "the mean old rascal! That is what he meant by bringing her here. It was not enough to wrong the mother, but he must delude the child! Be quiet, Jaacob! you don't know the old gray-haired villain! They ought to be tried for conspiracy, every one of them. Love!—it is profanation to name the name!"

"Eh, what's a' this?" cried Jaacob. "What does the callant mean by conspiracy?—what's about this lassie? She's gey bonnie—no' to say very, but gey—and she's just a governess. I respect the auld rascal, as you ca' him—and I wouldna say you're far wrang—for respecting his son's fancy. The maist o' thae moneyed men, I can tell ye, are as mean as an auld miser; therefore ye may say what ye like, my lad. I'm friends with Me'mar and his son the noo."

Jaacob went on accordingly with his hammering, professing no notice of Cosmo, who, busy with his own indignant thoughts, did not even observe the vigilant, sidelong regards of the blacksmith's one eye. He scarcely even heard what Jaacob said, as the village philosopher resumed his monologue, keeping always that solitary orb of vision intent upon his visitor. Jaacob, with all his enlightenment, was not above curiosity, and took a very lively interest in the human character and the concerns of his fellow-men.

"And the minister's dead," said Jaacob. "For a man that had nae experience of life, he wasna such a fuil as he might have been. I've seen waur priests. The vulgar gave him honor, and it's aye desirable to have a man in that capacity that can impose upon the vulgar;—and the bairns are away. I miss Katie Logan's face about the town mysel'. She wasna in my style; but I canna deny her merits. Mair folks' taste than mine has to be consulted. As for me, I have rather a notion of that French governess at Melmar. If there's onything wrang there, gie a man a hint, Cosmo, lad. I've nae objection to cut Oswald Huntley out mysel'."

"Find some other subject for your jests," cried Cosmo, haughtily; "Mademoiselle Desirée's name is not to be used in village gossip. I will not permit it while I am here."

Jaacob turned round upon him with his eye on fire.

"Wha the deevil made you a judge?" said Jaacob; "what's your madame-oiselle, or you either, that you're ower guid for an honest man's mouth? Confound your impidence! a slip of a callant that makes verses, do ye set up your face to me?"

At this point of the conversation Cosmo began to have a glimmering perception that Desirée's name was quite as unsuitable in a quarrel with Jaacob as in any supposed village gossip; and that the dispute between himself and the blacksmith was on the whole somewhat ridiculous. He evaded Jaacob's angry interrogatory with a half laugh of annoyance and embarrassment.

"You know as well as I do, Jacob, that one should not speak so of young ladies," said Cosmo, who did not know what to say.

"Do I?" said Jaacob; "what would ye hae a man to talk about? they're no muckle to crack o' in the way o' wisdom, but they're bonnie objecks in creation, as a'body maun allow. I would just like to ken, though, my lad, what's a' your particular interest in this madame-oiselle?"

"Hush," said Cosmo, whose cheeks began to burn; "she is my kinswoman; by this time perhaps she is with my mother in Norlaw; she is the child of—"

Cosmo paused, thinking to stop at that half-confidence. Jaacob stood staring at him, with his red cowl on one side, and his eye gleaming through the haze. As he gazed, a certain strange consciousness came to the hunchback's face. His dwarf figure, which you could plainly see had the strength of a giant's, his face swart and grotesque, his one gleaming eye and puckered forehead, became suddenly softened by a kind of homely pathos which stole over them like a breath of summer wind. When he had gazed his full gaze of inquiry into Cosmo's face, Jaacob turned his head aside hurriedly.

"So you've found her!" said the blacksmith, with a low intensity of voice which made Cosmo respectful by its force and emotion; and when he had spoken he fell to upon his anvil with a rough and loud succession of blows which left no time for an answer. Cosmo stood beside him, during this assault, with a grave face, looking on at the exploits of the hammer as if they were something serious and important. The introduction of this new subject changed their tone in a moment.

When Jaacob paused to take breath he resumed the conversation, still in a somewhat subdued tone, though briskly enough.

"So she's aye living," said Jaacob; "and this is her daughter? A very little mair insight and I would have found it out mysel'. I aye thought she was like. And what have you done with her now you've found her? Is she to come hame?"

"Immediately," said Cosmo.

"She's auld by this time, nae doubt," said Jaacob, carelessly; "women are such tender gear, a'thing tells upon them. It's *their* beauty that's like a moth—the like of me wears langer; and so she's aye to the fore?—ay! I doubt she'll mind little about Me'mar, or the folk here about. I'm above prejudices mysel', and maybe the French are mair enlightened in twa three points than we are—I'll no' say—but I wouldna bring up youngsters to be natives of a strange country. So you found her out with your ain hand, callant, did you? You're a clever chield! and what's to be done when she comes hame?"

"She is the Lady of Melmar, as she always was," said Cosmo, with a little pride.

"And what's to become of the auld family—father and son—no' to say of the twa sisters and the auld auntie," said Jaacob, with a grim smile. "So that's the story! Confound them a'! I'm no' a man to be cheated out of my sympathies. And I'm seldom wrang—so if you've ony thoughts that way, callant, I advise ye to relinquish them. Ye may be half-a-hunder' poets if ye like, and as many mair to the back o' that, but if the Huntley lad liket her she'll stick to him."

"That is neither your concern nor mine!" cried Cosmo, loftily. But, as Jaacob laughed and went on, the lad began to feel unaccountably aggravated, to lose his temper, and make angry answers, which made his discomfiture capital fun to the little giant. At length, Cosmo hurried away. It was the same day on which the Mistress paid her visit to Desirée, and Cosmo could not help feeling excited and curious about the issue of his mother's invitation. Thoughts which made the lad blush came into his mind as he went slowly over Tyne, looking up at that high bank, from which the evening sunshine, chill, yet bright, was slowly disappearing—where the trees began to bud round the cottages, and where the white gable of the manse still crowned the peaceful summit—that manse where Katie Logan, with her elder-sister smile, was no longer mistress. Somehow, there occurred to him a wandering thought about Katie, who was away—he did not know where—and Huntley, who was at the ends of the earth. Huntley had not actually lost any thing, Cosmo said to himself, yet Huntley seemed disinherited and impoverished to the obstinate eyes of fancy. Cosmo could not have told, either, why he associated his brother with Katie Logan, now an orphan and absent, yet he did so involuntarily. He thought of Huntley and Katie, both poor, far separated, and perhaps never to meet again; he thought of Cameron in his sudden trouble; and then his thoughts glided off with a little bitterness, to that perverse woman's love, which always seemed to cling to the wrong object. Madame Roche herself, perhaps, first of all, though the very fancy seemed somehow a wrong to his mother, Marie fretting peevishly for her French husband, Desirée giving her heart to Oswald Huntley. The lad turned upon his heel with a bitter impatience, and set off for a long walk in the opposite direction as these things glided into his mind. To be sure, he had nothing to do with it; but still it was all wrong—a distortion of nature—and it galled him in his thoughts.

CHAPTER LXIII

The presence of Desirée made no small sensation in the house of Norlaw, which did not quite know what to make of her. The Mistress herself, after that first strange impulse of kin and kindness which prompted her to bring the young stranger home, relapsed into her usual ways, and did not conceal from either son or servant that she expected to be "fashed" by the little Frenchwoman; while Marget, rather displeased that so important a step should be taken without her sanction, and mightily curious to know the reason, was highly impatient at first of Desirée's name and nation, and discontented with her presence here.

"I canna faddom the Mistress," said Marget, angrily; "what she's thinking upon, to bring a young flirt of a Frenchwoman into this decent house, and ane of our lads at home is just beyond me. Do I think her bonnie? No' me! She's French, and I daur to say, a papisher to the boot; but the lads will, take my word for it—callants are aye keen about a thing that's outray. I'm just as thankfu' as I can be that Huntley's at the other end of the world—there's nae fears of our Patie—and Cosmo, you see, he's ower young."

This latter proposition Marget repeated to herself as she went about her dairy. It did not seem an entirely satisfactory statement of the case, for if Cosmo was too young to be injured, Desirée was also a couple of years his junior, and could scarcely be supposed old enough to do any great harm.

"Ay, but it's in them frae their cradle," said the uncharitable Marget, as she rinsed her great wooden bowls and set them ready for the milk. The honest retainer of the family was quite disturbed by this new arrival. She could not "get her mouth about the like of thae outlandish names," so she never called Desirée any thing but Miss, which title in Marget's lips, unassociated with a Christian name, was by no means a title of high respect, and she grumbled as she was quite unwont to grumble, over the additional trouble of another inmate. Altogether Marget was totally dissatisfied.

While Desirée, suddenly dropped into this strange house, every custom of which was strange to her, and where girlhood and its occupations were unknown, felt somewhat forlorn and desolate, it must be confessed, and sometimes even longed to be back again in Melmar, where there were many women, and where her pretty needle-works and graceful accomplishments were not reckoned frivolous, the Mistress was busy all day long, and when she had ended her household employments, sat down with her work-basket to mend shirts or stockings with a steadiness which did not care to accept any assistance.

"Thank you, they're for my son, Huntley; I like to do them a' mysel'," she would answer to Desirée's offer of aid. "Much obliged to you, but Cosmo's stockings, poor callant, are no work for the like of you." In like manner, Desirée was debarred from the most trifling assistance in the house. Marget was furious when she ventured to wash the Mistress's best tea-service, or to sweep the hearth on occasion.

"Na, miss, we're no' come to that pass in Norlaw that a stranger visitor needs to file her fingers," said Marget, taking the brush from Desirée's hand; so that, condemned to an uncomfortable idleness in the midst of busy people, and aware that the Mistress's "Humph!" on one occasion, at least, referred to her pretty embroideries, poor little Desirée found little better for it than to wander round and round the old castle of Norlaw, and up the banks of Tyne, where, to say truth, Cosmo liked nothing better than to wander along with her, talking about her mother, about St. Ouen, about his travels, about every thing in earth and heaven.

And whether Cosmo was "ower young" remains to be seen.

But Desirée had not been long in Norlaw when letters came from Madame Roche, one to the Mistress, brief yet effusive, thanking that reserved Scottish woman for her kindness to "my little one;" another to Cosmo, in which he was called my child and my friend so often, that though he was pleased, he was yet half ashamed to show the epistle to his mother; and a third to Desirée herself. This was the most important of the three, and contained Madame Roche's scheme of poetic justice. This is what the Scotch-French mother said to little Desirée:—

"My child, we, who have been so poor, are coming to a great fortune. It is as strange as a romance, and we can never forget how it has come to us. Ay, my Desirée, what noble hearts! what princely young men! Despite of our good fortune, my heart bleeds for the generous Huntley, for it is he who is disinherited. Must this be, my child? He is far away, he knows not we are found; he will return to find his inheritance gone. But I have trained my Desirée to love honor and virtue, and to be generous as the Livingstones. Shall I say to you, my child, what would glad my heart most to see? Our poor Marie has thrown away her happiness and her liberty; she can not reward any man, however noble; she can not make any compensation to those whom we must supplant, and her heart wanders after that vagabond, that abandoned one! But my Desirée is young, only a child, and has not begun to think of lovers. My love, keep your little heart safe till Huntley returns—your mother bids you, Desirée. Look not at any one, think not of any one, till you have seen this noble Huntley; it is the only return you can give—nay, my little one! it is all *I* can do to prove that I am not ungrateful. This Melmar, which I had lost and won without knowing it, will be between Marie and you when I die. You can not give it all back to your kinsman, but he will think that half which your sister has doubly made up, my child, when I put into his hand the hand of my Desirée; and we shall all love each other, and be good and happy, like a fairy tale.

"This is your mamma's fondest wish, my pretty one: you must keep your heart safe, you must love Huntley, you must give him back half of the inheritance. My poor Marie and I shall live together, and you shall be near us; and then no one will be injured, but all shall have justice. I would I had another little daughter for the good Cosmo, who found me out in St. Ouen. I love the boy, and he shall be with us when he pleases, and we will do for him all we can. But keep your heart safe, my Desirée, for Huntley, and thus let us reward him when he comes home."

Poor Madame Roche! she little knew what a fever of displeasure and indignation this pretty sentimental letter of hers would rouse in her little daughter's heart. Desirée tore the envelope in pieces in her first burst of vexation, which was meant to express by similitude that she would have torn the letter, and blotted out its injunctions, if she dared. She threw the epistle itself out of her hands as if it had stung her. Not that Desirée's mind was above those sublime arrangements of poetic justice, which in this inconsequent world are always so futile; but, somehow, a plan which might have looked pretty enough had it concerned another, filled Madame Roche's independent little daughter with the utmost shame and mortification when she herself was the heroine.

"Let him take it all!" she cried out half aloud to herself, in her little chamber. "Do I care for it? I will work—I will be a governess; but I will not sell myself to this Huntley—no, not if I should die!"

And having so recorded her determination, poor little Desirée sat down on the floor and had a hearty cry, and after that thought, with a girlish effusion of sympathy, of poor Cosmo, who, after all, had done it all, yet whom no one thought of compensating. When straightway there came into Desirée's heart some such bitter thoughts of justice and injustice as once had filled the mind of Cosmo Livingstone. Huntley!—what had Huntley done that Madame Roche should dedicate her—*her*, an unwilling Andromeda, to compensate this unknown monster; and Desirée sprang up and stamped her little foot, and clapped her hands, and vowed that no force in the world, not even her mother's commands, should compel her to show her mother's gratitude by becoming Huntley's wife.

A most unnecessary passion; for there was Katie Logan all the time, unpledged and unbetrothed, it is true, but thinking her own thoughts of some one far away, who might possibly break in some day upon those cares of elder-sisterhood, which made her as important as a many-childed mother, even in those grave days of her orphan youth; and there was Huntley in his hut in the bush, not thriving over well, poor fellow, thinking very little of Melmar, but thinking a great deal of that manse parlor, where the sun shone, and Katie darned her children's stockings—a scene which always would shine, and never could dim out of the young man's recollection. Poor Madame Roche, with her pretty plan of compensation, and poor Desirée, rebelliously resistant to it, how much trouble they might both have saved themselves, could some kind fairy have shown to them a single peep of Huntley Livingstone's solitary thoughts.

CHAPTER LXIV

Five years had made countless revolutions in human affairs, and changed the order of things in more houses than Melmar, but had not altered the fair face of the country, when, late upon a lovely June evening, two travelers alighted from the coach at the door of the Norlaw Arms. They were not anglers, nor tourists, though they were both bronzed and bearded. The younger of the two looked round him with eager looks of recognition, directing his glances to particular points—a look very different from the stranger's vague gaze at every thing, which latter was in the eyes of his companion. At the manse, where the white gable was scarcely visible through the thick foliage of the great pear-tree—at the glimmering twilight path through the fields to Norlaw—even deep into the corner of the village street, where bowed Jaacob, with his red cowl pushed up from his bullet head behind, stood, strongly relieved against the glow within, at the smithy door. To all these familiar features of the scene, the new-comer turned repeated and eager glances. There was an individual recognition in every look he gave as he sprang down from the top of the coach, and stood by with a certain friendly, happy impatience and restlessness, not easy to describe, while the luggage was being unpacked from the heavy-laden public conveyance; that was a work of time. Even now, in railway days, it is not so easy a matter to get one's portmanteau embarked or disembarked at Kirkbride station as one might suppose; and the helpers at the Norlaw Arms were innocent of the stimulus and external pressure of an express train. They made a quantity of bustle, but did their business at their leisure, while this new arrival, whom none of them knew, kept looking at them all with their names upon his lips, and laughter and kindness in his eyes. He had "seen the world," since he last saw these leisurely proceedings at the Norlaw Arms—he had been on the other side of this big globe since he last stood in the street of Kirkbride; and the young man could not help feeling himself a more important person now than when he set out by this same conveyance some seven years ago, to make his fortune and his way in the world.

Huntley Livingstone, however, had not made his fortune; but he had made what he thought as much of—a thousand pounds; and having long ago, with a tingle of disappointment and a flush of pride, renounced all hopes of the Melmar which belonged to Madame Roche, had decided, when this modest amount of prosperity came to him, that he could not do better than return to his homely little patrimony, and lay out his Australian gains upon the land at home. It is true we might have told all this much more dramatically by bringing home the adventurer unexpectedly to his mother, and leaving him to announce his riches by word of mouth. But Huntley was too good a son to make dramatic surprises. When he made his thousand pounds, he wrote the Mistress word of it instantly—and he was not unexpected. The best room in Norlaw was prepared a week ago. It was only the day and hour of his return which the Mistress did not know.

So Huntley stood before the Norlaw Arms, while the gray twilight, which threw no shadows, fell over that leaf-covered gable of the manse; and gradually the young man's thoughts fell into reverie even in the moment and excitement of arrival. Katie Logan! she was not bound to him by the faintest far-away implication of a promise. It was seven years now since Huntley bade her farewell. Where was the orphan elder-sister, with her little group of orphan children now?

Huntley's companion was as much unlike himself as one human creature could be unlike another. He was a Frenchman, with shaved cheeks and a black moustache, lank, long locks of black hair falling into one of his eyes, and a thin, long, oval face. He was in short—except that he had no *habit de bal*, no white waistcoat, no bouquet in his buttonhole—a perfect type of the ordinary Frenchman whom one sees in every British concert-room as the conductor of an orchestra or the player of a fiddle. This kind of man does not look a very fine specimen of humanity in traveler's dress, and with the dust of a journey upon him. Huntley was covered with dust, but Huntley did not look dirty; Huntley was roughly attired, had a beard, and was somewhat savage in his appearance, but, notwithstanding, was a well-complexioned, pure-skinned Briton, who bore the soil of travel upon his surface only, which was not at all the case with his neighbor. This stranger, however, was sufficiently familiar with his traveling-companion to strike him on the shoulder and dispel his thoughts about Katie.

"Where am I to go? to this meeserable little place?" asked the Frenchman, speaking perfectly good English, but dwelling upon the adjective by way of giving it emphasis, and pointing at the moment with his dirty forefinger, on which he wore a ring, to the Norlaw Arms.

Huntley was a Scotsman, strong in the instinct of hospitality, but he was at the same time the son of a reserved mother, and hated the intrusion of strangers at the moment of his return.

"It's a very good inn of its kind," said Huntley, uneasily, turning round to look at it. The Frenchman shrugged his shoulders, and eyed the respectable little house with contempt.

"Ah! bah! of its kind—I believe it," said the stranger, kicking away a poor little dog which stood looking on with serious interest, and waiting for the fresh start of the coach; "I perceive your house is a chateau, an estate, my friend," he continued; "is there no little room you can spare a comrade? I come on a good errand, the most virtuous, the most honest! Madame, your mother, will give me her blessing—I go to seek my wife."

Huntley turned away to look after his trunks, but the stranger followed with a pertinacity which prevailed over Huntley. He gave a reluctant invitation at last, was restored to better humor by a sudden recognition from the landlord of the Norlaw Arms, and after pausing to receive the greetings and congratulations of everybody within hearing, set off, hastily accompanied by the Frenchman. Huntley endured his companion with great impatience, especially as they came within sight of home, and all the emotions connected with that familiar place rushed to the young man's heart and to his eyes. The Frenchman's voice ran on, an impertinent babble, while the gray old castle, the quiet house, with its pale vane pointing to the north, and the low hill-side, rustling to its summit with green corn, lay once more before the eyes which loved them better than any other landscape in the world. Then a figure became visible going in and out at the kitchen-door, a tall, angular form, with the "kilted" gown, the cap with its string pinned back, the little shawl over the shoulders, all of which homely details Huntley remembered so well. The young man quickened his pace, and held out his hands unconsciously. And then Marget saw him; she threw down her milk-pail, arched her hand over her eyes for a moment to gaze at him and assure herself and then with a loud, wild exclamation, rushed into the house. Huntley remembered no more, either guest or hospitality; he rushed down the little bank which intervened, splashed through the shallow Tyne, too much excited to take the bridge, and reached the door of Norlaw, as the Mistress, with her trembling hands, flung it unsteadily open to look for herself, and see that Marget was wrong. Too much joy almost fainted the heart of the Mistress within her; she could not speak to him—she could only sob out big, slow sobs, which fell echoing through the still air with the strangest pathos of thanksgiving. Huntley had come home.

"So you werna wrang, as it happened," said the Mistress, with dignity, when she had at last become familiar with the idea of Huntley's return, and had contented her eye with gazing on him; "you werna wrang after a'; but I certainly thought that myself, and me only, would be the person to get the first sight of my bairn. He minded you too, very well, Marget, which was less wonder than you minding him, and him such a grown man with such a black beard. I didna believe ye, it's true, but it was a' because I thought no person could mind upon him to ken him at a distance, but only me."

"Mind!" cried Marget, moved beyond ordinary patience; "did I no' carry the bairn in my arms when he was just in coats and put his first breeks upon him! Mind!—me that have been about Norlaw House seven-and-twenty years come Martinmas—wha should mind if it wasna me?"

But though this speech was almost concluded before the Mistress left the kitchen, it was not resented. The mother's mind was too full of Huntley to think of any thing else. She returned to the dining-parlor, where, in the first effusion of her joy, she had placed her first-born in his father's chair, and began to spread the table with her own hands for his refreshment. As yet she had scarcely taken any notice of the Frenchman. Now his voice startled her; she looked at him angrily, and then at her son. He was not quite such a person as fathers and mothers love to see in the company of their children.

"No doubt, Huntley," said the Mistress, at last, with a little impatient movement of her head—"no doubt this gentleman is some great friend of yours, to come hame with you the very first day, and you been seven years from home."

"Ah! my good friend Huntley is troubled, madame," interposed the subject of her speech; "I have come to seek my wife. I have heard she is in Scotland—she is near; and I did ask for one little room in his castle rather than go to the inn in the village. For I must ask you for my wife."

"Your wife? what should I know about strange men's wives?" said the Mistress; "Huntley's friends have a good right to be welcome at Norlaw; but to tell the truth he's new come home and I'm little accustomed to strangers. You used to ken that, Huntley, laddie, though you've maybe forgotten now; seven years is a long time."

"My wife," resumed the Frenchman, "came to possess a great fortune in this country. I have been a traveler, madame. I have come with your son from the other side of the world. I have been *bon camarade*. But see! I have lost my wife. Since I am gone she has found a fortune, she has left her country, she is here, if I knew where to find her. Madame Pierrot, my wife."

"I'm little acquaint with French ladies," said the Mistress, briefly; but as she spoke she turned from her occupation to look full at her strange visitor with eyes a little curious and even disquieted. The end of her investigation was a "humph," which was sufficiently significant. After that she turned her back upon him and went on with her preparations, looking somewhat stormy at Huntley. Then her impatience displayed itself under other disguises. In the first place she set another chair for him at the table.

"Take you this seat, Huntley, my man," said the Mistress; "and the foot of the table, like the master of the house; for doubtless Norlaw is yours for any person it's your pleasure to bring into it. Sit in to the table, and eat your supper like a man; and I'll put *this* back out of the way."

Accordingly, when Huntley rose, his mother wheeled back the sacred chair which she had given him in her joy. Knowing how innocent he was of all friendship with his companion, Huntley almost smiled at this sign of her displeasure, but, when she left the room, followed her to explain how it was.

"I asked him most ungraciously and unwillingly," said poor Huntley; "don't be displeased on account of that fellow; he came home with me from Australia, and I lost sight of him in London, only to find him again coming here by the same coach. I actually know nothing about him except his name."

"But I do," said the Mistress.

"You, mother?"

"Ay, just me, mother; and a vagabond he is, as ony person may well see," said the Mistress; "I ken mair than folk think; and now go back for a foolish bairn as you are, in spite of your black beard. Though I never saw the blackguard before, a' my days, I'll tell you his haill story this very night."

CHAPTER LXV

It was Saturday night, and in little more than an hour after Huntley's return, Cosmo had joined the little family circle. Cosmo was five years older by this time, three-and-twenty years old, a man and not a boy; such at least was his own opinion—but his mother and he were not quite so cordial and united as they had been. Perhaps, indeed, it was only while her sons were young, that a spirit so hasty and arbitrary as that of the Mistress could keep in harmony with so many independent minds; but her youngest son had disappointed and grieved her. Cosmo had relinquished those studies which for a year or two flattered his mother with the hope of seeing her son a minister and pillar of the Church. The Mistress thought, with some bitterness, that his travels had permanently unsettled her boy; even his verses began to flag by this time, and it was only once in three or four months that Mrs. Livingstone received, with any thing like satisfaction, her copy of the *Auld Reekie Magazine*. She did not know what he was to be, or how he was to live; at present he held "a situation"—of which his mother was bitterly contemptuous—in the office of Mr. Todhunter, and exercised the caprices of his more fastidious taste in a partial editorship of the little magazine, which had already lost its first breath of popularity. And though he came out from Edinburgh dutifully every Saturday to spend the day of rest with his mother, that exacting and impatient household ruler was very far from being satisfied. She received him with a certain angry, displeased affectionateness, and even in the presence of her newly-arrived son, kept a jealous watch upon the looks and words of Cosmo. Huntley could not help watching the scene with some wonder and curiosity. Sitting in that well-remembered room, which the two candles on the table lighted imperfectly, with the soft night air blowing in through the open window in the corner, from which the Mistress had been used to watch the kitchen door, and at which now her son sat looking out upon the old castle and the calm sky above it, where the stars blossomed out one by one—Huntley watched his mother, placing, from mere use and wont, her work-basket on the table, and seating herself to the work which she was much too impatient to make any progress with—launching now and then a satirical and utterly incomprehensible remark at the Frenchman, who yawned openly, and repented his contempt for the Norlaw Arms—sometimes asking hasty questions of Cosmo, which he answered not without a little kindred impatience—often rising to seek something or lay something by, and pausing as she passed by Huntley's chair to linger over him with a half expressed, yet inexpressible tenderness. There was change, yet there was no change in the Mistress. She had a tangible reason for some of the old impatience which was natural to her character, but that was all.

At length the evening came to an end. Huntley's uncomfortable companion sauntered out to smoke his cigar, and coming back again was conducted up stairs to his room, with a rather imperative politeness. Then the Mistress, coming back, stood at the door of the dining-parlor, looking in upon her sons. The shadows melted from her face, and her heart swelled, as she looked at them. Pride, joy, tenderness contended with her, and got the better for a moment.

"God send you be as well in your hearts as you are to look upon, laddies!" she said, hurriedly; and then came in to sit down at the table and call them nearer for their first precious family hour of mutual confidence and reunion.

"Seven years, Huntley? I canna think it's seven years—though they've been long enough and slow enough, every one; but we've thriven at Norlaw," said the Mistress, proudly. "There's guid honest siller at the bank, and better than siller in the byre, and no' a mortal man to call this house his debtor, Huntley Livingstone! which is a change from the time you gaed away."

"Thanks to your cares and labors, mother," said Huntley.

"Thanks to no such thing. Am I a hired servant that ye say such words to me? but thanks to Him that gives the increase," said the Mistress; "though we're no' like to show our gratitude as I once thought," and she threw a quick side-glance at Cosmo; "but Huntley, my man, have ye naething to tell of yourself?"

"Much more to ask than to tell," said Huntley, growing red and anxious, but making an effort to control himself, "for you know all of the little that has happened to me already, mother. Thankless years enough they have been. To think of working hard so long and gaining nothing, and to make all that I have at last by what looks like a mere chance!"

"So long! What does the laddie call long?—many a man works a lifetime," said the Mistress, "and even then never gets the chance; and it's only the like of you at your time of life that's aye looking for something to happen. For them that's out of their youth, life's far canniest when naething happens—though it is hard to tell how that can be either where there's bairns. There's been little out of the way here since this callant, Cosmo, gaed out on his travels, and brought his French lady and a' her family hame. Me'mar's in new hands now, Huntley; and you'll have to gang to see them, no doubt, and they'll make plenty wark about you. It's their fashion. I'm no much heeding about their ways mysel', but Cosmo has little else in his head, night or day."

Cosmo blushed in answer to this sudden assault; but the blush was angry and painful, and his brother eagerly interposed to cover it.

"The ladies that took Melmar from us!—let us hear about them, mother," said Huntley.

The Mistress turned round suddenly to the door to make sure it was closed.

"Take my word for it," she said, solemnly, and with emphasis, "yon's the man, that's married upon Marie."

"Who?" cried Cosmo, starting to his feet, with eager interest.

The Mistress eyed him severely for a moment.

"When you're done making antics, Cosmo Livingstone, I'll say my say," said his offended mother—"you may be fond enough of French folk, without copying their very fashion. I would have mair pride if it was me."

With an exclamation of impatience, which was not merely impatience, but covered deeply wounded feelings, Cosmo once more resumed the seat which he thrust hastily from the table. His mother glanced at him once more. If she had a favorite among her children, it was this her youngest son, yet she had a perverse momentary satisfaction in perceiving how much annoyed he was.

"You's the man!" said the Mistress, with a certain triumphant contempt in her voice; "just the very same dirty Frenchman that Huntley brought to the house this day. I'm no mista'en. He's wanting his wife, and he'll find her, and I wish her muckle joy of her bonnie bargain. That's just the ill-doing vagabond of a husband that's run away from Marie!"

"Mother," said Cosmo, eagerly, "you know quite well how little friendship I have for Marie—"

When he had got so far he stopped suddenly. His suggestion to the contrary was almost enough to make his mother inform the stranger at once of the near neighborhood of his wife, and Cosmo paused only in time.

"The mair shame to you," said the Mistress, indignantly, "she's a suffering woman, ill and neglected; and I warn you baith I'm no' gaun to send this blackguard to Melmar to fright the little life there is out of a puir dying creature. He shall find out his wife for his ain hand; he shanna be indebted to me."

"It is like yourself, mother, to determine so," said Cosmo, gratefully. "Though, if she had the choice, I daresay she would decide otherwise, and perhaps Madame Roche too. You say I am always thinking of them, but certainly I would not trust to their wisdom—neither Madame Roche nor Marie."

"But really—have some pity upon my curiosity—who is Marie, mother?" cried Huntley, "and who is her husband, and what is it about altogether? I know nothing of Pierrot, and I don't believe much good of him; but how do *you* know?"

"Marie is the French lady's eldest daughter—madame would have married her upon you, Huntley, my man, if she had been free," said the Mistress, "and I woudna say but she's keeping the little one in her hand for you to make up for your loss, as she says. But Marie, she settled for hersel' lang before our Cosmo took news of their land to them; and it just shows what kind of folk they were when she took up with the like of this lad. I've little skill in Frenchmen, that's true; if he's not a common person, and a blackguard to the boot, I'm very sair deceived in my e'en; but whatever else he is, he's her man, and that I'm just as sure of as mortal person can be. But she's a poor suffering thing that will never be well in this world, and I'll no' send a wandering vagabond to startle her out of her life."

"What do you say, madame," screamed a voice at the door; "you know my wife—you know her—Madame Pierrot?—and you will keep her husband from her? What! you would take my Marie?—you would marry her to your son because she is rich? but I heard you—oh, I heard you! I go to fly to my dear wife."

The Mistress rose, holding back Huntley, who was advancing indignantly:—

"Fly away, Mounseer," said Mrs. Livingstone, "you'll find little but closed doors this night; and dinna stand there swearing and screaming at me; you may gang just when you please, and welcome; but we'll have none of your passions here; be quiet, Huntley—he's no' a person to touch with clean fingers—are you hearing me man? Gang up to your bed, if you please this moment. I give you a night's shelter because you came with my son; or if you'll no' go up the stairs go forth out of my doors, and dinna say another word to me—do you hear?"

Pierrot stood at the door, muttering French curses as fast as he could utter them; but he did hear notwithstanding. After a little parley with Huntley, he went up stairs, three steps at a time, and locked himself into his chamber.

"He's just as wise," said the Mistress, "but it's no' very safe sleeping with such a villain in the house;" which was so far true that, excited and restless, she herself did not sleep, but lay broad awake all night thinking of Huntley and Cosmo—- thinking of all the old grief and all the new vexations which Mary of Melmar had brought to her own life.

CHAPTER LXVI

For these five years had not been so peaceful as their predecessors—the face of this home country was much changed to some of the old dwellers here. Dr. Logan, old and well-beloved, was in his quiet grave, and Katie and her orphans, far out of the knowledge of the parish which once had taken so entire an interest in them, were succeeded by a new minister's new wife, who had no children yet to gladden the manse so long accustomed to young voices; and the great excitement of the revolution at Melmar had scarcely yet subsided in this quiet place;—least of all, had it subsided with the Mistress, who, spite of a lurking fondness for little Desirée, could not help finding in the presence of Mary of Melmar a perpetual vexation. Their French habits, their language, their sentiments and effusiveness—the peevish invalid condition of Marie, and even the sweet temper of Madame Roche, aggravated with a perennial agitation, the hasty spirit of Mrs. Livingstone. She could not help hearing every thing that everybody said of them, could not help watching with a rather unamiable interest the failings and shortcomings of the family of women who had dispossessed her son. And then her other son—her Cosmo, of whom she had been so proud—could see nothing that did not fascinate and attract him in this little French household. So, at least, his mother thought. She could have borne an honest falling in love, and "put up with" the object of it, but she could not tolerate the idea of her son paying tender court to another mother, or of sharing with any one the divided honors of her maternal place. This fancy was gall and bitterness to the Mistress, and had an unconscious influence upon almost every thing she did or said, especially on those two days in every week which Cosmo spent at Norlaw.

"It's but little share his mother has in his coming," she said to herself, bitterly; and even Marget found the temper of the Mistress rather trying upon the Sundays and Mondays; while between Cosmo and herself there rose a cloud of mutual offense and exasperation, which had no cause in reality, but seemed almost beyond the reach of either explanation or peace-making now.

The Sabbath morning rose bright and calm over Norlaw. When Huntley woke, the birds were singing in that special, sacred, sweetest festival of theirs, which is held when most of us are sleeping, and seems somehow all the tenderer for being to themselves and God; and when Huntley rose to look out, his heart sang like the birds. There stood the Strength of Norlaw, all aglist with early morning dews and sunshine, wall-flowers tufting its old walls, sweet wild-roses looking out, like adventurous children, from the vacant windows, and the green turf mantling up upon its feet. There ran Tyne, a glimmer of silver among the grass and the trees. Yonder stretched forth the lovely country-side, with all its wealthy undulations, concealing the hidden house of Melmar among its woods. And to the south, the mystic Eildons, pale with the ecstacy of the night, stood silent under the morning light, which hung no purple shadows on their shoulders. Huntley gazed out of his window till his eyes filled. He was too young to know, like his mother, that it was best when nothing happened; and this event of his return recalled to him all the events of his life. He thought of his father, and that solemn midnight burial of his among the ruins; he thought of his own wanderings, his hope and loss of wealth, his present modest expectations; and then a brighter light and a more wistful gaze came to Huntley's face. He, too, was no longer to be content with home and mother; but a sober tenderness subdued the young man's ardor when he thought of Katie Logan among her children.

Seven years! It was a long trial for an unpledged love. Had no other thoughts come into her good heart in the meantime? or, indeed, did she ever think of Huntley save in her elder-sisterly kindness as she thought of everybody? When this oft-discussed question returned to him, Huntley could no longer remain quiet at his window. He hastily finished his toilette and went down stairs, smiling to himself as he unbolted and unlocked the familiar door—those very same bolts and locks which had so often yielded to his restless fingers in those days when Huntley was never still. Now, by this time, he had learned to keep himself quiet occasionally; but the old times flashed back upon him strangely, full of smiles and tears, in the unfastening of that door.

Thinking certainly that at so early an hour he himself was the first person astir in Norlaw, Huntley was greatly amazed to find Cosmo—no longer choosing his boyish seat of meditation in the window of the old castle—wandering restlessly about the ruins. And Cosmo did not seem quite pleased to see *him*; that was still more remarkable. The elder brother could not help seeing again, as in a picture, the delicate fair boy, with his long arms thrust out of the jacket which was too small for him, with his bursts of boyish vehemence and enthusiasm, his old chivalrous championship of the unknown Mary, his tenacious love for the hereditary Norlaw. Huntley had not seen the boy grow up into the man—he had not learned to moderate his protecting love for the youngest child into the steady brotherly affection which should now acknowledge the man as an equal. Cosmo was still "my father's son," the youngest, the dearest, the one to be shielded from trouble, in the fancy of the elder brother. Yet, there he stood, as tall as Huntley, his childish delicacy of complexion gone, his fair hair crisp and curled, his dark eyes stormy and full of personal emotions, his foot impatient and restless, the step of a man already burdened with cares of his own. And, reluctant to meet his brother, his closest friend, and once his natural guardian! Huntley thrust his arm into Cosmo's, and drew him round the other side of the ruins.

"Do you really wish to avoid me?" said the elder brother, with a pang. "What is wrong, Cosmo?—can you not tell *me*?"

"Nothing is wrong, so far as I am aware," said Cosmo, with some haughtiness. His first impulse seemed to be to draw away his arm from his brother's, but, if it was so, he restrained himself, and, instead, walked on with a cold, averted face, which was almost more painful than any act to the frank spirit of Huntley.

"I will ask no more questions then," said Huntley, with some impatience; "I ought to remember how long I have been gone, and how little you know of me. What is to be done about this Pierrot? So far as I can glean from what my mother says, he will be an unwelcome guest at Melmar. What ground has my mother for supposing him connected with Madame Roche? What sort of a person is Madame Roche? What have you all been doing with yourselves? I have a hundred questions to ask about everybody. Even Patie no one speaks of; if nothing is wrong you are all strangely changed since I went away."

"I suppose the *all* means myself; I am changed since you went away," said Cosmo, moodily.

"Yes, you are changed, Cosmo; I don't understand it; however, never mind, you can tell the reason why when you know me better," said Huntley, "but, in the meantime, how is Patie, and where? And what about this Madame Roche?"

"Madame Roche is very well," said Cosmo, with assumed indifference, "her eldest daughter is married, and has long been deserted by her husband;

but I don't know his name—they never mention it. Madame Roche is ashamed of him; they were people of very good family, in spite of what my mother says—Roche de St. Martin—but I sent you word of all this long ago. It is little use repeating it now."

"Why should Pierrot be *her* husband, of all men in the world?" said Huntley; "but if he's not wanted at Melmar, you had better send the ladies word of your suspicions, and put them on their guard."

"I have been there this morning," said Cosmo, slightly confused by his own admission.

"This morning? you certainly have not lost any time," said Huntley, laughing. "Never mind, Cosmo, I said I should ask nothing you did not want to tell me; though why you should be so anxious to keep her husband away from the poor woman—How have they got on at Melmar? Have they many friends? Are they people to make friends? They seem at least to be people of astonishing importance in Norlaw."

"My mother," said Cosmo, angrily, "dislikes Madame Roche, and consequently every thing said and done at Melmar takes an evil aspect in her eyes."

"My boy, that is not a tone in which to speak of my mother," said Huntley, with gravity.

"I know it!" cried the younger brother, "but how can I help it? it is true they are my friends. I confess to that; why should they not be my friends? why should I reject kindness when I find it? As for Marie, she is a selfish, peevish invalid, I have no patience with her—but—Madame Roche—"

Cosmo made a full stop before he said Madame Roche, and pronounced that name at last so evidently as a substitute for some other name, that Huntley's curiosity was roused; which curiosity, however, he thought it best to satisfy diplomatically, and by a round-about course.

"I must see her to-morrow," he said; "but what of our old friend, Melmar, who loved us all so well? I should not like to rejoice in any man's downfall, but *he* deserved it, surely. What has become of them all?"

"He is a poor writer again," said Cosmo, shortly, "and Joanna—it was Joanna who brought Desirée here."

"Who is Desirée?" asked Huntley.

"I ought to say Miss Roche," said Cosmo, blushing to his hair. "Joanna Huntley and she were great friends at school, and after the change she was very anxious that Joanna should stay. *She* is the youngest, and an awkward, strange girl—but, why I can not tell, she clings to her father, and is a governess or school-mistress now, I believe. Yes, things change strangely. They were together when I saw them first."

"They—them! you are rather mysterious, Cosmo. What is the story?" asked his brother.

"Oh, nothing very remarkable; only Des—Miss Roche, you know, came to Melmar first of all as governess to Joanna, and it was while she was there that I found Madame Roche at St. Ouen. When I returned, my mother," said Cosmo, with a softening in his voice, "brought Desirée to Norlaw, as you must have heard; and it was from our house that she went home."

"And, except this unfortunate sick one, she is the only child?" said Huntley. "I understand it now."

Cosmo gave him a hurried jealous glance, as if to ask what it was he understood, but after that relapsed into uncomfortable silence. They went on for some time so, Cosmo with anger and impatience supposing his elder brother's mind to be occupied with what he had just told him; and it was with amazement, relief, but almost contempt for Huntley's extraordinary want of interest in matters so deeply interesting to himself, that Cosmo heard and answered the next question addressed to him.

"And Dr. Logan is dead," said Huntley, with a quiet sorrow in his voice, which trembled too with another emotion. "I wonder where Katie and her bairns are now?"

"Not very far off; somewhere near Edinburgh. I think Lasswade. Mr. Cassilis' mother lives there," said Cosmo.

"Mr. Cassilis! I had forgotten him," said Huntley, "but he does not live at Lasswade?"

"They say he would be glad enough to have Katie Logan in Edinburgh," said Cosmo, indifferently; "they are cousins—I suppose they are likely to be married;—how do I know? Well, only by some one telling me, Huntley! I did not know you cared."

"Who said I cared?" cried Huntley, with sudden passion. "How should any one know any thing about the matter—eh? I only asked, of course, from curiosity, because we know her so well—used to know her so well. Not you, who were a child, but we two elder ones. My brother Patie—I hear nothing of Patie. Where is *he* then? You must surely know."

"He is to come to meet you to-morrow," said Cosmo, who was really grieved for his own carelessness. "Don't let me vex you, Huntley. I am vexed myself, and troubled; but I never thought of that, and may be quite wrong, as I am often," he added, with momentary humility, for Cosmo was deeply mortified by the sudden idea that he had been selfishly mindful of his own concerns, and indifferent to those of his brother. For the time, it filled him with self-reproach and penitence.

"Never mind; every thing comes right in time," said Huntley; but this piece of philosophy was said mechanically—the first common-place which occurred to Huntley to vail the perturbation of his thoughts.

Just then some sounds from the house called their attention there. The Mistress herself stood at the open door of Norlaw, contemplating the exit of the Frenchman, who stood before her, hat in hand, making satirical bows and thanking her for his night's lodging. In the morning sunshine this personage looked dirtier and more disreputable than on the previous night. He had not been at all particular about his toilette, and curled up his moustache over his white teeth, the only thing white about him, with a most sinister sneer, while he addressed his hostess; while she, in the meantime, in her morning cap and heavy black gown, and clear, ruddy face, stood watching him, as perfect a contrast as could be conceived.

"I have the satisfaction of making my adieux, madame," cried Pierrot; "receive the assurance of my distinguished regard. I shall bring my wife to thank you. I shall tell my wife what compliments you paid her, to free her from her unworthy spouse and bestow your son. She will thank you—I will thank you. Madame, from my heart I make you my adieux!"

"It's Sabbath morning," said the Mistress, quietly; "and if you find your wife—I dinna envy her, poor woman! you can tell her just whatever you please, and I'll no' cross you; though it's weel to see you dinna ken, you puir, misguided heathen, that you're in another kind of country frae your ain. You puir Pagan creature! do you think I would ware my Huntley on a woman that had been another man's wife? or do you think that marriage can be broken *here*? but it's no' worth my while parleying with the like of you. Gang your ways and find your wife, and be good to her, if it's in you. She's maybe a silly woman that likes ye still, vagabone though ye be—she's maybe near the end of her days, for onything you ken. Go away and get some kindness in your heart if ye can—and every single word I've said to you you can tell ower again to your wife."

Which would have been rather hard, however, though the Mistress did not know it. The wanderer knew English better than a Frenchman often does, but his education had been neglected—he did not know Scotch—a fact which did not enter into the calculations of Mrs. Livingstone.

"Adieu, comrade!" cried Pierrot, waving his hand to Huntley; "when I see you again you shall behold a milor, a nobleman; be happy with your amiable parent. I go to my wife, who adores me. Adieu."

"And it's true," said the Mistress, drawing a long breath as the strange guest disappeared on the road to Kirkbride. "Eh, sire, but this world's a mystery! it's just true, so far as I hear; she does adore him, and him baith a mountebank and a vagabone! it passes the like of me!"

And Cosmo, looking after him too, thought of Cameron. Could that be the husband for whom Marie had pined away her life?

CHAPTER LXVII

It was Sabbath morning, but it was not a morning of rest; though it was Huntley's first day at home, and though it did his heart good to see his mother, the young man's heart was already astray and pre-occupied with his own thoughts; and Cosmo, full of subdued but unrecoverable excitement, which his mother's jealous eye only too plainly perceived, covered the face of the Mistress with clouds. Yet a spectator might have supposed that breakfast-table a very centre of family love and harmony. The snow-white cloth, the basket of brown oat-cakes and white flour scones, of Marget's most delicate manufacture, the great jug full of rich red June roses, which made a glory in the midst, and the mother at the head of her table, with those two sons in the bloom of their young manhood, on either side of her, and the dress of her widowhood throwing a certain, tender, pathetic suggestion into her joy and their love. It was a picture had it been a picture, which no one could have seen without a touching consciousness of one of the most touching sides of human life. A family which at its happiest must always recall and commemorate a perpetual lack and vacancy, and where all the affections were the deeper and tenderer for that sorrow which overshadowed them; the sons of their mother, and she was a widow! But, alas, for human pictures and ideals! The mother was restless and dissatisfied, feeling strange interests crowding in to the very hour which should be peculiarly her own; the young men were stirred with the personal and undisclosed troubles of their early life. They sat together at their early meal, speaking of common matters, eating daily bread, united yet separate, the peace of the morning only vailing over a surface of commotion, and Sabbath in every thing around save in their hearts.

"It's a strange minister—you'll miss the old man, Huntley," said the Mistress; "but you'll write down your thanksgiving like a good bairn, and put an offering in the plate; put your name, say, 'Huntley Livingstone returns thanks to God for his safe home-coming.' There would have been nae need for that if Dr. Logan had been to the fore; he aye minded baith thanks and supplications; and I'll never forget what petitions he made in his prayer the last Sabbath you were at hame. You're early stirring, Cosmo—it's no' time yet for the kirk."

"I am going to Melmar, mother," said Cosmo, in a low voice.

The Mistress made no answer; a flush came over her face, and her brow contracted, but she only said, as if to herself:—

"It's the Sabbath day."

"I went there this morning, to warn them of this man's arrival," said Cosmo, with excitement, "saying what *you* thought. I did not see any of them; but Marie has one of her illnesses. They have no one to support them in any emergency. I must see that he does not break in upon them to-day."

The Mistress still made no answer. After a little struggle with herself, she nodded hastily.

"If ye're a' done, I'll rise from the table. I have things to do before kirk-time," she said at length, pushing back her chair and turning away. She had nothing to say against Cosmo's resolution, but she was deeply offended by it—deeply, unreasonably, and she knew it—but could not restrain the bitter emotion. To be absent from the kirk at all, save by some overpowering necessity, was an offense to all her strong Scottish prejudices—but it was an especial breach of family decorum, and all the acknowledged sentiment and punctilio of love, to be absent to-day.

"Keep us a' patient!" cried Marget, in an indignant undertone, when Mrs. Livingstone was out of hearing; for Marget, on one pretense or other, kept going and coming into the dining-parlor the whole morning, to rejoice her eyes with the sight of Huntley. "Some women come into this world for nae good reason but to make trouble. To speak to the Mistress about an emergency! Whaever supported her in *her* troubles but the Almighty himsel' and her ain stout heart? I dinna wonder it's hard to bear! Some gang through the fire for their ain hand, and no' a mortal nigh them—some maun have a haill houseful to bear them up. Weel, weel, I'm no' saying any thing against it—it's kind o' you, Mr. Cosmo—but you should think, laddie, before you speak."

"*She* is not like my mother," said Cosmo, somewhat sullenly.

"Like your mother!" cried Marget, with the utmost contempt. "She would smile a hantle mair, and ca' ye mair dears in a day than *my* Mistress in a twelvemonth; but would *she* have fought and struggled through her life for a thankless man and thankless bairns—I trow no! Like your mother! She was bonnie when she was young, and she's maybe, bonnie now, for onything I ken; but she never was wordy to tie the shoe upon the foot of the Mistress of Norlaw!"

"Be silent!" cried Cosmo, angrily; and before Marget's indignation at this reproof could find itself words, the young man had hurried out from the room and from the house, boiling with resentment and a sense of injury. He saw exactly the other side of the question—his mother's jealous temper, and hard-heartedness and dislike to the gentle and tender Madame Roche—but he could not see how hard it was, after all, for the honest, faithful heart, which grudged no pain nor hardship for its own, to find their love beguiled away again and again—or even to suppose it was beguiled—by one who had never done any thing to deserve such affection.

And Cosmo hurried on through the narrow paths to Melmar, his heart a-flame with a young man's resentment, and impatience, and love. He scarcely could tell what it was which excited him so entirely. Not, certainly, the vagabond Pierrot, or any fears for Marie; not even the displeasure of his mother. He would not acknowledge to himself the eager, jealous fears which hurried him through those flowery bye-ways where the blossoms of the hawthorn had fallen in showers like summer snow, and the wild roses were rich in the hedgerows. Huntley!—why did he fear Huntley? What was the impulse of unfraternal impatience which made him turn with indignant offense from every thought of his brother? Had he put it into words, he would have despised himself; but he only rushed on in silence through the silent Sabbath fields and bye-ways to the house of Madame Roche.

It is early, early yet, and there is still no church bell ringing through the silence of the skies to rouse the farms and cottages. The whole bright summer world was as silent as a dream—the corn growing, the flowers opening, the sun shining, without a whisper to tell that dutiful Nature carried on her pious work through all the day of rest. The Tyne ran softly beneath his banks, the Kelpie rushed foaming white down its little ravine, and all the cool burns from among the trees dropped down into Tyne with a sound like silver bells. Something white shone upon the path on the very spot where Desirée once lay, proud and desolate, in the chill of the winter night, brooding over false friendship and pretended love. Desirée now is sitting on the same stone, musing once more in her maiden meditation. The universal human trouble broods even on these thoughts—not heavily—only like the shadow that flits along the trees of Tyne—a something ruffling the white woman's forehead, which is more serious than the girl's was, and disquieting the depths of those eyes which Cosmo Livingstone had called stars. Stars do not mist themselves with tender dew about the perversities of human kind as these eyes do; yet let nobody suppose that these sweet drops, lingering bright within the young eyelids, should be called tears.

Tears! words have so many meanings in this world! it is all the same syllable that describes the child's passion, the honey-dew of youth, and that heavy rain of grief which is able sometimes to blot out both the earth and the skies.

So, after a fashion, there are tears in Desirée's eyes, and a great many intermingled thoughts floating in her mind—thoughts troubled by a little indignation, some fear, and a good deal of that fanciful exaggeration which is in all youthful trials. She thinks she is very sad just now as she sits half in the shade and half in the sunshine, leaning her head upon her hand, while the playful wind occasionally sprinkles over her those snowy drops of spray from the Kelpie which shine on her hair; but the truth is that nothing just now could make Desirée sad, save sudden trouble, change, or danger falling upon one person—that one person is he who devours the way with eager, flying steps, and who, still more disturbed than she is, still knows no trouble in the presence of Desirée; and that is Cosmo Livingstone.

No; there is no love-tale to tell but that which has been told already; all those preliminaries are over; the Kelpie saw them pledge their faith to each other, while there still were but a sprinkling of spring leaves on those trees of June. Desirée; the name that caught the boy's fancy when he *was* a boy, and she unknown to him—the heroine of his dreams ever since then, the distressed princess to whom his chivalry had brought fortune—how could the young romance end otherwise? but why, while all was so natural and suitable, did the young betrothed meet here?

"I must tell your mother! I must speak to her to-day! I owe it both to myself and Huntley," cried Cosmo. "I can not go away again with this jealous terror of my brother in my heart; I dare not, Desirée! I must speak to her to-day."

"Terror? and jealous? Ah, then, you do not trust me," said Desirée, with a smile. Her heart beat quicker, but she was not anxious; she held up her hand to the wind till it was all gemmed with the spray of the waterfall, and then shook it over the head of Cosmo, as he half sat, half knelt by her side. He, however, was too much excited to be amused; he seized upon the wet hand and held it fast in his own.

"I did not think it possible," said Cosmo. "Huntley, whom I supposed I could have died for, my kind brother! but it makes me frantic when I think what your mother has said—what she *intends*. Heaven! if he himself should think of *you!*"

"Go, you are rude," said Desirée; "if I am so good as you say, he must think of me; but am *I* nothing then," she cried, suddenly springing up, and stamping her little firm foot, half in sport, half in anger; "how do you dare speak of me so? Do you think mamma can give me away like a ring, or a jewel? Do you think it will be different to me whether he thinks or does not think of Desirée? You make me angry, Monsieur Cosmo; if that is all you come to tell me, go away!"

"What can I tell you else?" cried Cosmo. "I must and will be satisfied. I can not go on with this hanging over me. Do you remember what you told me, Desirée, that Madame Roche meant to offer you—*you!* to my brother? and you expect me to have patience! No, I am going to her now."

"Then it is all over," cried Desirée, "all these sunny days—all these dreams! She will say no, no. She will say it must not be—she will forbid me meeting you; but if you do not care, why should I?" exclaimed the little Frenchwoman, rapidly. "Nay, you must do what you will—you must be satisfied. Why should you care for what *I* say? and as for me I shall be alone."

So Desirée dropped again upon her stone seat, and put her face down into her hands, and shed a few tears; and Cosmo, half beside himself, drew away the hands from her face, and remonstrated, pleaded, urged his claim.

"Why should not you acknowledge me?" said the young lover. "Desirée, long before I ventured to speak it you knew where my heart was—and now I have your own word and promise. Your mother will not deny you. Come with me, and say to Madame Roche—"

"What?" said Madame Roche's daughter, glancing up at him as he paused.

But Cosmo was in earnest now:—

"What is in your heart!" he said breathlessly. "You turn away from me, and I can not look into it. What is in your heart, whether it is joy, or destruction, I care not," cried the young man suddenly, "I must know my fate."

Desirée raised her head and looked at him with some surprise and a quick flush of anger:—

"What have I done that you dare doubt me?" she cried, clapping her hands together with natural petulance. "You are impatient—you are angry—you are jealous—but does all that change me?"

"Then come with me to Madame Roche," said the pertinacious lover.

Desirée had the greatest mind in the world to make a quarrel and leave him. She was not much averse now and then to a quarrel with Cosmo, for she was a most faulty and imperfect little heroine, as has been already confessed in these pages; but in good time another caprice seized her, and she changed her mind.

"Marie is ill," she said softly, in a tone which melted Cosmo; "let us not go now to trouble poor mamma."

"Marie! I came this morning to warn her, or rather to warn Madame Roche," said Cosmo, recalled to the ostensible cause of his visit. "A Frenchman, called Pierrot, came home with Huntley—"

But before he could finish his sentence, Desirée started up with a scream at the name, and seizing his arm, in her French impatience overwhelmed him with terrified questions:—

"Pierrot? quick! speak! where is he? does he seek Marie? is he here? quick, quick, quick, tell me where he is! he must never come to poor Marie! he must not find us—tell me, Cosmo! do you hear?"

"He spent last night at Norlaw—he seeks his wife," said Cosmo, when she was out of breath; at which word Desirée sprang up the path with excited haste:—

"I go to tell mamma," she said, beckoning Cosmo to follow, and in a few minutes more disappeared breathless within the open door of Melmar, leaving him still behind.

CHAPTER LXVIII

Madame Roche sat by herself in the drawing-room of Melmar—the same beautiful old lady who used to sit working behind the flowers and white curtains of the little second floor window in St. Ouen. The room itself was changed from the fine disorderly room in which Mrs. Huntley had indulged her invalid tastes, and Patricia read her poetry-books. There was no longer a loose crumb-cloth to trip unwary feet, nor rumpled chintz covers to conceal the glory of the damask; and there was a wilderness of gilding, mirrors, cornices, chairs, and picture-frames, which changed the sober aspect of Melmar, and threw a somewhat fanciful and foreign character upon the grave Scotch apartment, looking out through its three windows upon the solemn evergreens and homely grass-plot, which had undergone no change. One of the windows was open, and *that* was garlanded round, like a cottage window, with a luxuriance of honey suckle and roses, which the "former family" would have supposed totally unsuited to the "best room in the house." It was before this open window, with the sweet morning breeze waving the white curtains over her, and the roses leaning in in little crowds, that Madame Roche sat. She was reading—at least she had a book in her hand, among the leaves of which the sweet air rustled playfully; it was a pious, pretty book of meditations, which suited both the time and the reader, and she sat sometimes looking into it, sometime suffering her eyes and mind to stray, with a sweet pensive gravity on her fair old face, and tender, subdued thoughts in her heart. Madame Roche was not profound in any thing; perhaps there was not very much depth in those pious thoughts, or even in the sadness which just overshadowed them. Perhaps she had even a far-off consciousness that Cosmo Livingstone saw a very touching little picture, when he saw the mother by the window reading the Sabbath book in that Sabbath calm, and saying prayers in her heart for poor Marie. But do not blame Madame Roche—she still did say the prayers, and out of an honest heart.

When Desirée flew into the room, flushed and out of breath, and threw herself upon her mother so suddenly, that Madame Roche's composure was quite overthrown:—

"Mamma, mamma!" cried Desirée, in what was almost a scream, though it was under her breath, "listen—Pierrot is here; he has found us out."

"What, child? Pierrot? It is impossible!" cried Madame Roche.

"Things that are impossible are always true!" exclaimed the breathless Desirée; "he is here—Cosmo has seen him; he has come to seek Marie."

"Cosmo? is *he* here?" said Madame Roche, rising. The old lady had become quite agitated, and her voice trembled. The book had fallen out of the hands which she clasped tightly together, in her fright and astonishment. "But he is mistaken, Desirée; he does not know Pierrot."

When Cosmo, however, came forward to tell his own story, Madame Roche became still more disturbed and troubled:—

"To come now!" she exclaimed to herself with another expressive French pressure of her hands—"to come now! Had he come in St. Ouen, when we were poor, I could have borne it; but now, perceive you what will happen, Desirée? He will place himself here, and squander our goods and make us despised. He will call my poor Marie by his mean name—she, a Roche de St. Martin! and she will be glad to have it so. Alas, my poor deluded child!"

"Still though he is so near, he has not found you yet; and if he does find you, the house is yours, you can refuse him admission; let me remain, in case you should want me," said Cosmo eagerly; "I have been your representative ere now."

Madame Roche was walking softly about the room, preserving through all her trouble, even now when she had been five years in this great house, the old habit of restraining her voice and step, which had been necessary when Marie lay in the little back chamber at St. Ouen, within constant hearing of her mother. She stopped for an instant to smile upon her young advocate and supporter, as a queen might smile upon a partisan whose zeal was more than his wisdom; and then went on hurriedly addressing her daughter.

"For Marie, poor soul, would be crazed with joy. Ah, my Desirée! who can tell me what to do? For my own pleasure, my own comfort, a selfish mother, must I sacrifice my child?"

"Mamma," cried Desirée, with breathless vehemence, "I love Marie—I would give my life for her; but if Pierrot comes to Melmar, I will go. It is true—I remember him—I will not live with Pierrot in one house."

Madame Roche clasped her hands once more, and cast up her eyes with a gesture of despair. "What can I do—what am I to do? I am a woman alone—I have no one to advise me," she cried, pacing softly about the room, with her clasped hands and eyes full of trouble. Cosmo's heart was quite moved with her distress.

"Let me remain with you to-day," said Cosmo, "and if he comes, permit me to see him. You can trust *me*. If you authorize me to deny him admission, he certainly shall not enter here."

"Ah, my friend!" cried Madame Roche. "Ah, my child! what can I say to you? Marie loves him."

"And he has made her miserable," cried Desirée, with passion. "But, because she loves him, you will let him come here to make us all wretched. I knew it would be so. She loves him—it is enough! He will make her frantic—he will break her heart—he will insult you, me, every one! But Marie loves him! and so, though he is misery, he must come. I knew it would be so; but I will not stay to see it all—I can not! I will never stand by and watch while he kills Marie. Mamma! mamma! will you be so cruel? But I can not speak—I am angry—wretched! I will go to Marie and nurse her, and be calm; but if Pierrot comes, Desirée will stay no longer. For you know it is true!"

And so speaking Desirée went, lingering and turning back to deliver herself always of a new exclamation, to the door, out of which she disappeared at last, still protesting her determination with violence and passion. Madame Roche stood still, looking after her. There was great distress in the mother's face, but it did not take that lofty form of pain which her child's half-defiance might have produced. She was not wounded by what Desirée said. She turned round sighing to where Cosmo stood, not perfectly satisfied, it must be confessed, with the bearing of his betrothed.

"Poor child! she feels it!" said Madame Roche, "and, indeed, it is true, and she is right; but what must I do, my friend? Marie loves him. To see him once more might restore Marie."

"Mademoiselle Desirée says he will break her heart," said Cosmo, feeling himself bound to defend the lady of his love, even though he did not quite approve of her.

"Do not say mademoiselle. She is of this country; she is not a stranger," said Madame Roche with her bright, usual smile; "and he *will* break her heart if he is not changed; do I not know it? But then—ah, my friend, you are young and impatient, and so is Desirée. Would you not rather have your wish and your love, though it killed you to have it, than to live year after year in a blank peacefulness? It is thus with Marie; she lives, but her life does not make her glad. She loves him—she longs for him; and shall I know how her heart pines, and be able to give her joy, yet keep silence, as though I knew nothing? It might be most wise; but I am not wise—I am but her mother—what must I do?"

"You will not give her a momentary pleasure, at the risk of more serious suffering," said Cosmo, with great gravity.

But the tears came to Madame Roche's eyes. She sank into a chair, and covered her face with her hand. "It would be joy!—can I deny her joy? for she loves him," faltered Marie's mother. As he looked at her with impatient, yet tender eyes, the young man forgave Desirée for her impatience. How was it possible to deal calmly with the impracticable sentiment and "feelings" of Madame Roche?

"I came to speak to you of myself," said Cosmo. "I can not speak of myself in the midst of this trouble; but I beg you to think better of it. If he is all that you say, do not admit him here."

"Of yourself?" said Madame Roche, removing her hand from her face, and stretching out to him that tender white hand which was still as soft and fair as if it had been young instead of old. "My child, I am not so selfish as to forget you who have been so good to us. Tell me what it is about yourself?"

And as she smiled and bent towards him, Cosmo's heart beat high, half with hope half with shame, for he felt guilty when he remembered that neither himself nor Desirée had confessed their secret betrothal to Desirée's mother. In spite of himself, he could not help feeling a shadow of blame thrown upon Desirée, and the thought wounded him. He was full of the unreasonable, romantic love of youth. He could not bear, by the merest instinctive secret action of his mind, to acknowledge a defect in her.

"You say, 'Marie loves him'—that is reason enough for a great sacrifice from you," cried Cosmo, growing out of breath with anxiety and agitation; "and Desirée—and I,—what will you say to us? Oh, madame, you are kind, you are very kind. Be more than my friend, and give Desirée to me!"

"Desirée!"—Madame Roche rose up, supporting herself by her chair—"Desirée! but she knows she is destined otherwise—you know—Desirée!" cried Madame Roche, clasping her pretty hands in despair. "She is dedicated—she is under a vow—she has to do justice! My friend Cosmo—my son—my young deliverer!—do not—do not ask this! It breaks my heart to say no to you; but I can never, never give you Desirée!"

"Why?" said Cosmo, almost sternly. "You talk of love—will you deny its claim? Desirée does not say no. I ask you again, give her to me! My love will never wound her nor break her heart. I do not want the half of your estate, and neither does my brother! Give me Desirée—I can work for her, and she would be content to share my fortune. She *is* content—I have her own word for it. I demand it of you for true love's sake, madame—you, who speak of love! Give her to me!"

"Alas!" cried Madame Roche, wringing her hands—"alas! my child! I speak of love because Marie is his wife; but a young girl is different! She must obey her destiny! You are young—you will forget it. A year hence, you will smile when you think of your passion. No—my friend Cosmo, hear me! No, no, you must not have Desirée—I will give you any thing else in this world that you wish, if I can procure it, but Desirée is destined otherwise. No, no, I can not change—you can not have Desirée!"

And on this point the tender and soft Madame Roche was inexorable—no intreaty, no remonstrance, no argument could move her! She stood her ground with a gentle iteration which drove Cosmo wild. No, no, no; any thing but Desirée. She was grieved for him—ready to take him into her arms and weep over him—but perfectly impenetrable in her tender and tearful obstinacy. And when, at last, Cosmo rushed from the house, half mad with love, disappointment, and mortification, forgetting all about Pierrot and everybody else save the Desirée who was never to be his, Madame Roche sat down, wiping her eyes and full of grief, but without the faintest idea of relinquishing the plans by which her daughter was to compensate Huntley Livingstone for the loss of Melmar.

CHAPTER LXIX

When Cosmo rushed forth from Melmar with his heart a-flame, and made his way out through the trees to the unsheltered and dusty highway, the sound of the Sabbath bells was just beginning to fall through the soft summer air, so bright with the sunshine of the morning. Somehow, the sound seemed to recall him, in a moment, to the sober home life out of which he had rushed into this feverish episode and crisis of his own existence. His heart was angry, and sore, and wounded. To think of the usual familiar routine of life disgusted him—his impulse was to fly out of everybody's reach, and separate himself from a world where everybody was ready to sacrifice the happiness of others to the merest freak or crochet of his own. But the far off tinkle of the Kirkbride bell, though it was no wonder of harmony, dropped into Cosmo's ear and heart like the voice of an angel. Just then, his mother, proudly leaning upon Huntley's arm, was going up the bank of Tyne to thank God for her son's return. Just then, Desirée, who had left Melmar before him, was walking softly, in her white summer robes, to the Sabbath service, little doubting to see Cosmo there; and out of all the country round, the rural families, in little groups, were coming up every path, all tending toward the same place. Cosmo sprang impatiently over a stile, and made his way through a corn field, where the rustling green corn on either side of the path, just bursting from the blade, was almost as tall as himself. He did not care to meet the church goers, who would not have been slow to remark upon his heated and uneasy looks, or even upon the novel circumstance of his being here instead of at "the kirk." This same fact of itself communicated an additional discomfort to Cosmo. He felt in his conscience, which was young and tender, the unsabbatical and agitating manner in which he had spent the Sabbath morning, and the bell seemed ringing reproaches into his ear as he hastened through the rustling corn. Perhaps not half a dozen times before in his life, save during the time of his travels, had Cosmo voluntarily occupied the Sabbath morning with uses of his own. He had dreamed through its sacred hours many a time, for he was "in love", and a poet; but his dreams had gone on to the cadence of the new minister's sermon, and taken a sweeter echo out of the rural psalms and thanksgivings; and he felt as a Scottish youth of religious training was like to feel under such circumstances—his want of success and present unhappiness increased by the consciousness that he was using the weekly rest for his own purposes, thinking his own thoughts, doing his own business, and filling, with all the human agitation of fears and hopes, selfish and individual, the holy quiet of the Sabbath day.

And when Cosmo reached Norlaw, which was solitary and quiet like a house deserted, and when the little girl who helped Marget in the dairy rose from her seat at the clean table in the kitchen, where, with her Bible open before her, she was seeking out "proofs" for her "questions," to let him in, not without a wondering air of disapproval, the feeling grew even stronger. He threw himself into his mother's easy-chair, in the dining-parlor, feeling the silence grow upon him like a fascination. Even the Mistress's work-basket was put out of the way, and there was no open book here to be ruffled by the soft air from the open window. Upon the table was the big Bible, the great jug full of red roses, and that volume of *Hervey's Meditations*, which the Mistress had certainly not been reading—and the deep, unbroken Sabbath stillness brooded over him as if it were something positive and actual, and not a mere absence of sound. And as he thought of it, the French household at Melmar, with its fancies, its agitations, its romantic plans and troubles of feeling, looked more and more to Cosmo discordant and inharmonious with the time; and he himself jarred like a chord out of tune upon this calm of the house and the Sabbath; jarred strangely, possessed as he was by an irritated and injured self-consciousness—that bitter sensation of wrong and disappointment, which somehow seemed to separate Cosmo from every thing innocent and peaceful in the world.

For why was it always so—always a perennial conspiracy, some hard, arbitrary will laying its bar upon the course of nature? Cosmo's heart was sore within him with something more than a vexed contemplation of the anomaly, with an immediate, pursuing, hard mortification of his own. He was bitterly impatient of Madame Roche in this new and strange phase of her character, and strangely perplexed how to meet it. For Cosmo had a poetic jealousy of the honor and spirit of his best beloved. He felt that he could not bear it, if Desirée for his sake defied her mother—he could not tolerate the idea that she was like to do so, yet longed, and feared, and doubted, full of the most contradictory and unreasonable feelings, and sure only of being grieved and displeased whatever might happen. So he felt as he sat by himself, with his eyes vacantly fixed upon the red roses and the big Bible, wondering, impatient, anxious beyond measure, to know what Desirée would do.

But that whole silent day passed over him unenlightened; he got through the inevitable meals he could scarcely tell how—replied or did not reply to his mother's remarks, which he scarcely noticed were spoken *at*, and not to him, wandered out in the afternoon to Tyneside and the Kelpie, without finding any one there—and finally, with a pang of almost unbearable rebellion, submitted to the night and sleep which he could not avoid. To-morrow he had to return to Edinburgh, to go away, leaving his brother in possession of the field—his brother, to whom Madame Roche meant to *give* Desirée, in compensation for his lost fortune. Cosmo had forgotten all about Katie Logan by this time; it was not difficult, for he knew scarcely any thing; and with a young lover's natural pride and vanity, could not doubt that any man in the world would be but too eager to contend with him for such a prize as Desirée Roche.

And to-morrow he had to go away!—to return to Mr. Todhunter's office, to read all the trashy stories, all the lamentable criticisms, all the correspondence, making small things great, which belonged to the *Auld Reekie Magazine*. Cosmo had not hitherto during his life been under much compulsion of the *must*, and accordingly found it all the harder to consent to it now. And he was growing very weary of his occupation besides. He had got a stage beyond his youthful facility of rhyme, and was, to say the truth, a little ashamed now of his verses, and of those flowery prose papers, which the Mistress still read with delight. He began to suspect that literature, after all, was not his vocation, and at this moment would rather have carried a laborer's hod; or followed the plow, than gone to that merchandise of words which awaited him in Edinburgh. So he rose, sullen and discontented, ready to quarrel with any or every one who thwarted him, and feeling toward Huntley rather more like an enemy than like a brother.

And Cosmo had but just risen from the early breakfast table when a note was put into his hand. Marget brought it to him, with rather an ostentation of showing what she brought, and Cosmo had to read it under the eyes of his mother and Huntley, neither of whom could help casting many glances at the young man's disturbed face. It was the first letter he had ever received from Desirée—no wonder that he hurried out when he had glanced at it, and did not hear that the Mistress called him back; for it was a very tantalizing, unsatisfactory communication. This is what Desirée said:—

"I knew it would be so. Why are you so restless, so impatient—why do you not be calm and wait like me? Mamma has set her heart upon what she says. She will not yield if you pray to her forever. She loves me, she loves you; it would make her happy; but, alas, poor mamma! She has set her thoughts upon the other, and will not change. Why do you vex her, you, me, every one? Be silent, and all will be well.

"For I am not in haste, Monsieur Cosmo, if you are. I am able to wait—me! I know you went away in great anger, and did not come to church, and were cross all day, and your mother will think I am to blame. But if you *will* be impatient, am I to blame? I tell you to wait, as I shall, to be good and silent, and see what will happen; but you do not regard me.

"Farewell, then, for a week. I write to you because I can not help it this time, but I will not write again. Be content, then, restless boy; *au revoir!*

"Desirée."

Cosmo turned it round and round, and over and over, but nothing more was to be made of it. Desirée had not contemplated the serious discontent of her lover. She thought he would understand and be satisfied with her playful letter, and required nothing more serious. Perhaps, had she thought he required something more serious, the capricious little Frenchwoman would have closed her heart and refused it. But, however that may be, it is certain that Cosmo was by no means so much pleased as he expected to be when he saw the note first, and prepared himself to leave home with feelings scarcely at all ameliorated, shaking hands abruptly with Huntley, and having a very cold parting with his mother. He carried a discontented heart away with him, and left discontent and vexation behind, and so trudged into Kirkbride, and drove away to Edinburgh on the top of the coach, troubled with the people behind and the things before him, and in the most unamiable humor in the world.

CHAPTER LXX

"Well, Huntley, and what's your opinion of our grand new neighbors?" said the Mistress. They were returning together on that same Monday from a formal call at Melmar; perhaps the first time on which the Mistress's visit to Madame Roche had been made with any pleasure. Mrs. Livingstone came proudly through the Melmar grounds, leaning upon Huntley's arm. She had gone to exhibit her son; half consciously to exult over her richer neighbor, who had no sons, and to see with her own eyes how Huntley was pleased with his new friends.

"I think," said Huntley, warmly, "that it is no wonder people raved about Mary of Melmar. She is beautiful now."

"So she is," said the Mistress, rather shortly. "I canna say I am ony great judge mysel'. She's taen good care of her looks—oh ay, I dinna doubt she is."

"But her daughters don't seem to inherit it," added Huntley.

"Ay, lad—would ye say no'?—no' the little one?" said the Mistress, looking up jealously in his face. She was the very reverse of a matchmaker, but perhaps it is true that women instinctively occupy themselves with this interesting subject. The Mistress had not forgotten Katie Logan, but in the depths of her heart she thought it just possible that Huntley might cast a favorable eye upon Desirée.

"No, not the little one," said Huntley, laughing; "though I like her best of the two; and was it that invalid whom you supposed the wife of Pierrot? Impossible!—any thing so fragile and delicate would never have married such a fellow."

"She's delicate, no doubt," said the Mistress, "but to be weakly in body is no' to be tender in the mind. Eh, what's that among the trees?—black and ill favored, and a muckle cloak about him—it's just the villain's sel'!"

"Hush, he sees us," said Huntley; "let us meet him and hear if he is going to Melmar. It seems unbelievable that so gentle an invalid should be his wife."

The Mistress only said "Humph!" She was sorry for Marie, but not very favorable to her—though at sight of the Frenchman all her sympathies were immediately enlisted on behalf of his devoted wife. Pierrot would have avoided them if he could, but as that was impossible, he came forward with a swaggering air, throwing his cloak loose, and exhibiting a morning toilette worthy of an ambitious tailor or a gentleman's gentleman. He took off his hat with elaborate politeness, and made the Mistress a very fine bow, finer than any thing which she had seen in these parts for many a day.

"Let me trust you found Madame Pierrot, my charming wife, well and visible," said the adventurer, with a second ironical obeisance, "and my gracious lady, her mamma, and pretty Desirée? I go to make myself known to them, and receive their embraces. I am excited, overjoyed—can you wonder? I have not seen my wife for ten years."

"And might have suffered that trial still, if it had not been for the siller," said the Mistress; "eh, man, to think of a woman in her senses taking up with the like of you!"

Fortunately the Mistress's idiomatic expressions, which might not have been over agreeable had they been understood, were not quite comprehensible to Monsieur Pierrot. He only knew that they meant offense, and smiled and showed his white teeth in admiration of the malice which he only guessed at.

"I go to my castle, my chateau, my fortune," he said; "where I shall have pleasure in repaying your hospitality. I shall be a good host. I shall make myself popular. Pierrot of Melmar will be known everywhere—it is not often that your dull coteries are refreshed by the coming of a gentleman from my country. But I am too impatient to linger longer than politeness demands. I have the honor to bid you very good morning. I go to my Marie."

Saying which, he swaggered past with his cloak hanging over his shoulders—a romantic piece of drapery which was more picturesque than comfortable on this summer day. The Mistress paused to look after him, clasping with rather an urgent pressure her son's arm, and with an impulse of impatient pity moving her heart.

"I could never bear a stranger nigh in *my* troubles," she cried, at last, "but yon woman's no' like me. She's used to lean upon other folk. What can she do, with that poor failing creature at one side of her and this villain at the other? Huntley, my man! she's nae friend of mine, but she's a lone woman, and you're her kinsman. Go back and give her your countenance to send the vagabone away!"

"Mother, I am a stranger," cried Huntley, with surprise and embarrassment; "what could I do for her? how could I venture indeed to intrude myself into their private affairs? Cosmo might have done it who knows them well, but I—I can not see a chance of serving them, perhaps quite the reverse. If you are right, this man belongs to the family, and blood is thicker than water. No, no; of course I will do what you wish, if you wish it; but I do not think it is an office for me."

And the Mistress, whose heart had been moved with compassion for the other widow who had no son, and who had suggested voluntarily that Huntley should help her, could not help feeling pleased nor being ashamed of her pleasure, when he declined the office. He, at least, was not "carried away" by the fascinations of Mary of Melmar. She took a secret pleasure in his disobedience. It soothed the feelings which Cosmo's divided love had aggrieved.

"Weel, maybe it's wisest; they ken best themselves how their ain hearts are moved—and a strange person's a great hindrance in trouble. *I* couldna thole it mysel'," said the Mistress; "I canna help them, it's plain enough—so we'll do little good thinking upon it. But, Huntley, my man, what's your first beginning to be, now that you are hame?"

At this question, Huntley looked his mother full in the face, with a startled, anxious glance, and grew crimson, but said not a word; to which the Mistress replied by a look, also somewhat startled, and almost for the moment resentful. She did not save him from his embarrassment by introducing then the subject nearest to his heart. She knew, and could not doubt what it was, but she kept silent, watching him keenly, and waiting for his first words. Madame Roche would have thrown herself into his arms and wept with an effusion of tenderness and sympathy, but this was the Mistress, who was long out of practice of love-matters, and who felt her sons more deeply dear to her own heart than ever lover was in the world. So it was with a little faltering that Huntley spoke.

"It is seven years since I went away, and she was only a girl then—only a girl, though like a mother. I wonder what change they have made upon Katie Logan, these seven years?"

"She's a good lassie," said the Mistress; "eh, Huntley, I'm ower proud!—I think naebody like my sons; but she's a very good lassie. I havena a word to say against her, no' me! I canna take strangers easy into my heart, but Katie Logan's above blame. You ken best yoursel' what you've said to one another, her and you—but I canna blame ye thinking upon her—na," said the Mistress, clearing her throat, "I am thankful to the Almighty for putting such a good bairn into your thoughts. I'm a hard woman in my ain heart,

Huntley. I'll just say it out once for a'. You've a' been so precious to me, that at the first dinnle I canna bide to think that nane of you soon will belong to your mother. That's a' —for you see I never had a daughter of my ain."

The Mistress ended this speech, which was a long speech for her, with great abruptness, and put up her hand hurriedly to wipe something from her eye. She could be angry with Cosmo, who confided nothing to her, but her loving, impatient heart could not stand against the frankness of his brother. She made her confession hurriedly, and with a certain obstinate determination—hastily wiped the unwilling tear out of the corner of her eye, and the next moment lifted her head with all her inalienable spirit, ready, if the smallest advantage was taken of her confession, to gird on her armor on the moment, and resist all concessions to the death.

But Huntley was wise. "We have said nothing to each other," he answered quickly, "but I would fain see Katie first of all."

This was about the sum of the whole matter—neither mother nor son cared to add much to this simple understanding. Katie had been absent from Kirkbride between four and five years, and during all that time the Mistress had only seen her once, and not a syllable of correspondence had passed between her and Huntley. It might be that she had long ago forgotten Huntley; it might be that Katie never cared for him, save with that calm regard of friendship which Huntley did not desire from her. It was true that the Mistress remembered Katie's eyes and Katie's face on that night, long ago, when a certain subtle consciousness of the one love which was in the hearts of both, gave the minister's daughter a sudden entrance into the regard of Huntley's mother. But the Mistress did not tell Huntley of that night. "It's no for me to do," said the Mistress to herself, when she had reached home, with a momentary quiver of her proud lip. "Na, if she minds upon my Huntley still—and wha could forget him?—I've nae right to take the words out of Katie's mouth; and he'll be all the happier, my puir laddie, to hear it from hersel'."

It was a magnanimous thought; and somehow this self-denial and abnegation—this reluctant willingness to relinquish now at last that first place in her son's heart, which had been so precious to the Mistress, shed an insensible brightness that day over Norlaw. One could not have told whence it came; yet it brightened over the house, a secret sunshine, and Huntley and his mother were closer friends than, perhaps, they had ever been before. If Cosmo could but have found this secret out!

CHAPTER LXXI

In the meantime, Cosmo, angry with himself and everybody else, went into Edinburgh to his weekly labor. It was such lovely summer weather, that even Edinburgh, being a town, was less agreeable than it is easy to suppose that fairest of cities; for though the green hill heights were always there to refresh everybody's eyes, clouds of dust blew up and down the hilly streets of the new town, which had even still less acquaintance then than now with the benevolent sprinkling of the water-carts. If one could choose the easiest season for one's troubles, one would not choose June, when all the world is gay, and when Nature looks most pitiless to sad hearts. Sad hearts! Let every one who reads forgive a natural selfishness—it is the writer of this story, who has nothing to do with its events, who yet can not choose but make her sorrowful outcry against the sunshine, sweet sunshine, smiling out of the heart of heaven! which makes the soul of the sorrowful sick within them. It is not the young hero in the agitation of his young troubles—warm discontents and contests of life—the struggles of the morning. Yet Cosmo was vexed and aggravated by the light, and heat, and brightness of the fair listless day, which did not seem made for working in. He could not take his seat at Mr. Todhunter's writing-table, laden with scraps of cut-up newspapers, with bundles of "copy," black from the fingers of the printers, and heaps of proof sheets. He could not sit down to read through silly romances, or prune the injudicious exuberance of young contributors. Unfortunately, the contributors to the *Auld Reekie Magazine* were almost all young; it had not turned out such an astounding "start" as the *Edinburgh Review*; it had fallen into the hands of young men at college, who, indisputably, in that period of their development, however great they may become eventually, are not apt to distinguish themselves in literature; and Cosmo, who had just outgrown the happy complacence of that period, was proportionately intolerant of its mistakes and arrogances, and complained (within himself) of his uncongenial vocation and unfortunate fate. He was not fit to be editor of the *Auld Reekie*. He was not able for the labor dire and weary woe of revising the papers which were printed, and glancing over those which were not—in short, he was totally dissatisfied with himself, his position and his prospects, very probably, but for his love-dream, Cosmo would have launched himself upon the bigger sea in London, another forlorn journeyman of literature, half conscious that literature was not the profession to which he was born; but the thought of Desirée held him back like a chain of gold. He could see her every week while he remained here, and beyond that office of Mr. Todhunter's in which perseverance and assiduity, and those other sober virtues which are not too interesting generally to young men, might some time make him a partner, Cosmo could not for his life have told any one what he would do.

After he had endured his work as long as he could in this quiet little den, which Mr. Todhunter shared with him, and where that gentleman was busy, as usual, with paste and scissors, Cosmo at last tossed an unreadable story into the waste-paper basket, and starting up, got his hat. His companion only glanced up at him with an indignant reproof.

"What! tired? Are they so *awful* bad?" said Mr. Todhunter; but this model of a bookseller said no more when his young deputy sallied out with a nod and a shrug of his shoulders. The proprietor of the *Auld Reekie Magazine* was one of those rare and delightful persons—Heaven bless their simple souls!—who have an inalienable reverence for "genius," and believe in its moods and vagaries with the devoutness of a saint.

"Of course I would exact common hours from a common young man," said Mr. Todhunter, "but a lad of genius is another matter. When he's in the vein, he'll get through with his work like a giant. I've seen him write four papers with his own hand after the twenty-third of the month, and the magazine as sharp to its time, notwithstanding, as if he had been a year preparing. He's not a common lad, my sub-editor;"—and Cosmo quite took credit with his employer on the score of his fits of varying energy and his irregular hours.

Cosmo, however, sauntered away through the bright and busy streets without giving himself so much credit. The young man was thoroughly uncomfortable, self-displeased, and aggravated. He knew well enough that it was not the impatience of genius, but only a restless and disturbed mind, which made his work intolerable on that long summer afternoon. He was thinking of Desirée, who would not bear thinking of, and whom he supposed himself to have bitterly and proudly relinquished—of Madame Roche, with her ridiculous fancy in respect to Huntley—and of Huntley himself, who it was just possible might accept it, and take Desirée's reluctant hand. It seemed to Cosmo the strangest, miserable perversion of everybody's happiness; and he could not help concluding upon all this wrong and foolishness coming to pass, with all the misanthropical certainty of disappointed youth. Cosmo even remembered to think of Katie Logan, by way of exaggerating his own discontent—Katie, who quite possibly had been faithful to Huntley's memory all these seven long years.

He was thus pondering on, with quick impatient step, when he caught a glimpse of some one at a distance whose appearance roused him. The figure disappeared down the Canongate, which Cosmo was crossing, and the young man hastened to follow, though this famous old street is by no means a savory promenade on a hot summer afternoon. He pushed down, notwithstanding, along the dusty burning pavement, amid evil smells and evil sounds, and passengers not the most agreeable. Women on the outside stairs, with dirty babies in their arms, loud in gossip, and unlovely in apparel—ragged groups at the high windows, where noble ladies once looked out upon the noble highway, but where now some poor housemother's washing, thrust out upon a stick, dallied with the smoky air, and was dried and soiled at the same moment—hopeless, ill-favored lads and girls, the saddest feature of all, throwing coarse jokes at each other, and, indeed, all the usual symptoms of the most degraded class of town population, which is much alike everywhere. Cosmo threaded his way among them with disgust, remembering how he had once done so before with Cameron, whom he was now pursuing, and at a time when his own anticipations, as well as his friend's, pointed to the sacred profession in which the Highlandman now toiled. That day, and that conversation, rose vividly before Cosmo. It sickened his sensitive heart to realize the work in which Cameron was employed; but when his mind returned to himself, who had no profession, and to whose eyes no steady aim or purpose presented itself anywhere, Cosmo felt no pleasure in the contrast. This was not the sphere in which a romantic imagination could follow the footsteps of the evangelist. Yet, what an overpowering difference between those steps and the wanderings of this disturbed trifler with his own fortune and youth.

But Cameron still did not reappear. Somewhat reluctantly Cosmo entered after him at the narrow door, with some forgotten noble's sculptured shield upon its keystone, and went up the stair where his friend had gone. It was a winding stair, dark, close, and dirty, but lighted in the middle of each flight by a rounded window, through which—an extraordinary contrast—the blue sky, the June sunshine, and a far-off glimpse of hills and sea, glanced in upon the passenger with a splendor only heightened by the dark and narrow frame through which the picture shone. Cosmo paused by one of these windows with an involuntary fascination. Just above him, on the dusky landing, were two doors of rooms, tenanted each by poverty and labor, and many children, miserable versions of home, in which the imagination could take no pleasure. In his fastidious distaste for the painful and unlovely realities, the young man paused by the window;—all the wealth of nature glowing in that golden sunshine—how strange that *it* should make its willing entrance here!

He was arrested by a voice he knew—subdued, but not soft by nature, and sounding audibly enough down the stairs.

"*I* don't know if he can do them harm—very likely no'—I only tell you I heard somebody speak of him, and that he was going to Melmar. Perhaps you don't care about the family at Melmar? I am sure, neither do I; but, if you like, you can tell Cosmo Livingstone. It's nothing to me!"

"I'll tell him," said Cameron. "Who was the man? Do you know?"

"He was French; and I'm sure a vagabond—I am sure a vagabond!" cried the other. "I don't know if *you* can mind me, but Cosmo will—I'm Joanna Huntley. I care for none of them but Desirée. Her mother and her sister may take care of themselves. But we were great friends, and I like her; though I need not like her unless I please," added Joanna, angrily; "it's no' for her sake, but because I canna help it. There—just tell Cosmo Livingstone! Perhaps it's nothing, but he might as well know."

"I'll tell him," said Cameron, once more.

Then there came a sound of a step upon the stair—not a light step, but a prompt and active one—and Joanna herself, grown very tall, tolerably trim, rather shabby, and with hair of undiminished redness, came rapidly down the narrow side of the spiral stair, with her hand upon its rib of stone. She started and stopped when she had reached almost as far as Cosmo's window—made as though she would pass him for the first moment, but finally drew up with considerable hauteur, a step or two above him. Joanna could not help a little offense at her father's conqueror, though she applauded him in her heart.

"I've been in London," said Joanna, abruptly, entering upon her statement without any preface. "I saw a man there who was inquiring about Melmar—at least about the eldest daughter, for he did not know the house—and Oswald directed him every step of the way. I'll no' say he was right and I'll no' say he was wrong, but I tell *you*; the man was a rascal, that's all I know about him—and you can do what you like now."

"But stop, Miss Huntley; did you seek Cameron out to tell him?" said Cosmo, with gratitude and kindness.

"I *am* Miss Huntley now," said Joanna, with an odd smile. "Patricia's married to an officer, and away, and Oswald's in London. My brother has great friends there. Did I seek Mr. Cameron out? No. I was here on my own business, and met him. I might have sought you out, but not him, that scarcely knows them. But it was not worth while seeking you out either," added Joanna, with a slight toss of her head. "Very likely the man is a friend of theirs—they were but small people, I suppose, before they came to Melmar. Very likely they'll be glad to see him. But Oswald was so particular telling him where they were, and the man had such an ill look," added Joanna, slowly, after a pause, "that I can not think but that he wanted to do them an ill turn."

"Thank you for warning them. He had come yesterday, and I fear he will do Marie a very ill turn," said Cosmo; "but nobody has any right to interfere—he is a—a relation. But may I tell Desirée—I mean Miss Roche— any thing of yourself? I know she often speaks, and still oftener thinks, of you."

"She has nothing to do with us that I know of," said Joanna, sharply; "good day to you; that was all I had to say," and she rushed past him, passing perilously down the narrow edge of the stair. But when she had descended a few steps, Joanna's honest heart smote her. She turned back, looking up to him with eyes which looked so straightforward and sincere, in spite of their irascible sparkle, that Joanna's plain face became almost pretty under their light. "I am sure I need not quarrel with you," she said with a little burst of her natural frankness, "nor with Desirée either. It was not her fault—but I was very fond of Desirée. Tell her I teach in a school now, and am very happy—they even say I'm clever," continued the girl, with a laugh, "which I never was at Melmar; and mamma is stronger, and we're all as well as we can be. You need not laugh, Cosmo Livingstone, it's true!" cried Joanna, with sudden vehemence, growing offended once more; "papa may have done wrong whiles, but he's very good to us; and no one shall dare throw a stone at him while I'm living. You can tell Desirée."

"I will tell Desirée you were very fond of her—she will like that best," said Cosmo.

Whereupon the vail, which had been hanging about her bonnet, suddenly dropped over Joanna's face; it is to be supposed from the suppressed and momentary sound that followed, that, partly in anger, partly in sorrow, partly in old friendship and tenderness, she broke down for the instant, and cried—but all that could clearly be known was, that she put out her hand most unexpectedly, shook Cosmo's hand, and immediately started down the stair with great haste and agitation. Cosmo could not try to detain or follow her; he knew very well that no such proceeding would have found favor in the eyes of Joanna; and Cameron at that moment came in sight from the upper floor.

Cosmo never could tell by what sudden impulse it was that he begged his old friend to return with him to his lodgings and dine; he had no previous intention of doing so—but the idea seized him so strongly, that he urged, and almost forced the half reluctant Highlandman into compliance.

Perhaps the listless loveliness of the day affected Cameron, in a less degree, somewhat as it affected his more imaginative companion—for, at length, after consulting his note-book, he put his strong arm within Cosmo's, and went with him. Cameron, like everybody else, had changed in these five years. He was now what is called a licentiate in the Church of Scotland— authorized to preach, but not to administer the sacraments, an office corresponding somewhat with the deacon's orders of the English Church. And like other people, too, Cameron had not got his ideal fortune. The poor student had no patronage, and the Gaelic-speaking parish among his own hills, to which his fancy had once aspired, was still as distant as ever from the humble evangelist. Perhaps Cameron did not even wish it now— perhaps he had never forgotten that hard lesson which he learned in St. Ouen—perhaps had never so entirely recovered that throwing away of his heart, as to be able to content himself among the solitudes of the hills. But, at least, he had not reached to this desired end—and was now working hard among the wynds and closes of old Edinburgh, preaching in a public room in that sad quarter, and doing all that Christian man could do to awaken its inhabitants to a better life.

"It is good, right, best! I confess it!" cried Cosmo, in a sudden *accés* of natural feeling, "but how can you do it, Cameron?—how is it possible to visit, to interest, to woo, such miserable groups as these? Look at them!" exclaimed the young man. "Mean, coarse, brutal, degraded, luxuriating in their own wretchedness, knowing nothing better—unable to comprehend a single refined idea, a single great thought. Love your neighbor—love *them*?—is it in the power of man?"

Cameron looked round upon them, too; though with a different glance.

"Cosmo," said the Highlandman, with that deep voice of his, to which additional years and personal experience had given a sweeter tone than of old, "do you forget that you once before asked me that same question? Love is ill to bind, and hard to draw. I love few in this world, and will to the end; but first among them is One whose love kens no caprice like to ours. I tell you again, laddie, what I tell them forever. Can *I* comprehend it?—it's just the mystery of mysteries—*He* loves them all. I have room in my goodwill, if not in my heart, for them that *you* love, Cosmo; and what should I have for them that He loved, and loved to the death? That is the secret. My boy, I would rather than gear and lands that you found it out for yourself."

"I can understand it, at least," said Cosmo, grasping his friend's hand; "but I blush for myself when I look at your work and at mine. They are different, Cameron."

"A lad may leave the plow in mid-furrow for a flower on the brae or a fish in the water," said Cameron, with a smile; "but a man returns to the work he's put his hand to. Come back, my boy, to your first beginning—there's time."

And Cosmo was almost persuaded, as they went on discussing and remonstrating to the young man's lodging, where other thoughts and other purposes were waiting for them both.

CHAPTER LXXII

For on Cosmo's table lay a letter, newly arrived, and marked *immediate*. Cosmo felt himself forewarned by the sudden tremor which moved him, as he sprang forward to take it up, that it was from Madame Roche. Perhaps some strange instinct suggested the same to Cameron, for he withdrew immediately from his friend's side, and went away to Cosmo's book-shelf in the corner without a word. Then, perhaps, for the first time, any unconcerned spectator looking on might have perceived that Cameron looked weary, and that, besides the dust upon his boots and black coat, the lines in his face were deeper drawn than his years and strength warranted, and told of a forlorn fatigue somewhere which no one tried to comfort. But he did not say any thing—he only stood quietly before the book-shelf, looking over Cosmo's books.

Cosmo, on the contrary, his face flushed with excitement and expectation, and his heart beating high, opened the letter. As he ran over it, in his haste and anxiety, the flush faded from his face. Then he read it seriously a second time—then he looked at his friend.

"Cameron!" said Cosmo.

But it seemed that Cameron did not hear him till he was called a second time, when he looked round slowly; and, seeing Cosmo holding towards him the letter which he had just read so eagerly, looked at it with a strange confusion, anxiety, and embarrassment, half-lifting his hand to take it, and saying "Eh?" with a surprised and reluctant inquiry.

"It concerns you as well as me. Look at it, Cameron," said the young man.

It was from Madame Roche; and this is what Cameron read:—

"Cosmo—my son, my friend! come back and help us! Pierrot—he of whom you warned us—has come; and I, in my folly—in my madness, could not deny to Marie to see him. You will ask me why? Alas! he is her husband, and she loves him! I thought, in my blindness, it might make her well; but we have known her illness so long, we have forgotten how great it is; and the shock has killed her—ah, me! unhappy mother!—has stricken my child! She was very joyful, the poor soul!—she was too happy!—and he who is so little deserving of it! But it has been more than she could bear, and she is dying! Come!—sustain us, comfort us, Cosmo, my friend! We are but women alone, and we have no one who will be so tender to us as you! It was but Monday when he came, and already she is dying!

"I have another thing to say. My poor Marie spoke to me this morning. I could not tell my child how ill, how very ill she was—I, her mother! but she has learned from our sad looks, or, perhaps, alas, from the wretch, Pierrot, that she is in danger. She spoke to me this morning. She said, 'Mamma, will no one speak to me of heaven? Alas, I know not heaven. How shall I know the way? Send for the Englishman—the Scottishman—the traveler who came with Cosmo to our old house. I remember how he spoke—he spoke of God as one might who loved Him. None but he ever spoke so to me. Send mother—if he loves God he will come.' Alas, my friend! could I say to her on her sick bed, 'My child, this good Monsieur Cameron loved *you*. I can not break his heart over again, and ask him to come.' No! I could not say it. I can but write to you, Cosmo. Speak to this good Cameron—this man who loves God. Ah, my friend, can you not think how I feel now that I am ignorant, that I am a sinner—that I, who am her mother, have never taught my Marie? Tell it to your friend—tell him what she has said—she knows not, my poor child, what thoughts might once have been in his heart. Let him come, for the love of God."

Cosmo scarcely ventured to look at his friend while he read this letter; and as for Cameron himself, he raised it in his hands so as to shade his face, and held it so with strong yet trembling fingers, that nobody might see the storm of passionate emotions there. Never before in his life, save once, had the vehement and fiery nature of the Highlandman been subject to so violent a trial, and even that once was not like this. A great sob rose in his throat—his whole passionate heart, which had been strained then in desperate self-preservation, melted now in a flood of sudden grief and tenderness, ineffable and beyond description. Marie, upon whom he had wasted his heart and love—Marie, whose weakness had filled him with a man's impulse of protection, sustenance, and comfort—Marie! Now at last should it be his, in solemnwise, to carry out that love-dream—to bring her in his arms to the feet of the Lord whom he loved—to show the fainting spirit where to find those wings of a dove, by which she might fly away and be at rest. Great over-brimming tears, big as an ocean of lighter drops, made his eyes blind, but did not fall. He sat gazing at the conclusion of the letter long after he had read it, not reading it over again like Cosmo— once had been enough to fix the words beyond possibility of forgetting upon Cameron's heart—but only looking at it with his full eyes, seeing the name, "Mary Roche de St. Martin," glimmering and trembling on the page, now partially visible, now altogether lost. When Cosmo ventured at last to glance at his friend, he was still sitting in the same position, leaning both his elbows upon the table, and holding up the letter in his hands to screen his face. Cosmo was aware of something strangely touching in the forced, strained, spasmodic attitude, but he could not see the big silent sob that heaved in his friend's strong heart, nor the tears that almost brimmed over but did not fall out of Cameron's eyes.

Presently the Highlandman folded up the letter with care and elaboration, seemed to hesitate a moment whether he would keep it, and finally gave it over with some abruptness to Cosmo. "Relics are not for me," he said, hastily. "Now, when you are ready, let us go."

"Go?—to Melmar!" said Cosmo, faltering a little.

"Where else?" asked Cameron, sternly—"is that a summons to say no to? I am going without delay. We can get there to-night."

"The coach will not leave for an hour—take some refreshment first," said Cosmo; "you have been at work all day—you will be faint before we get there."

Cameron turned towards him with a strange smile:—

"I will not faint before we get there," he said slowly, and then rose up and lifted his hat. "You can meet me at the coach, Cosmo, in an hour—I shall be quite ready; but in the first place I must go home; make haste, my boy; *I* will go, whether you are there or not."

Cosmo gazed after him with something like awe; it was rather beyond romance, this strange errand—and Cameron, in spite of the fervid Highland heart within him did not look a very fit subject for romance; but somehow Cosmo could not think what personal hopes of his own might be involved in this relenting of Madame Roche—could not think even of Desirée, whose name was not once mentioned in the letter, could think of nothing but Cameron, called of all men in the world to *that* bedside to tell the dying Marie where to find her Lord.

They left Edinburgh accordingly within the hour. Cameron had entirely recovered his usual composure, but scarcely spoke during the whole journey, in which time Cosmo had leisure to return to his own fortune, with all its perplexities. Even Marie's illness was not likely to form reason enough in the eyes of the Mistress for his abrupt and unexpected return, and he could hardly himself see what good his presence could do Madame Roche, with dangerous illness, perhaps death, and a disagreeable son-in-law in her house. Take him at his worst, Pierrot, who was Marie's husband, had a more natural place there than Cosmo, who was only Desirée's lover—a lover rejected by Madame Roche; and Desirée herself had not intimated by word or sign any desire for his presence. The whole aspect of things did not conduce to make Cosmo comfortable. It seemed almost a necessity to go to Melmar, instantly, instead of going to Norlaw; but what would the Mistress think of so strange a proceeding? And Huntley and Patie now, it was to be presumed, were both at home. What a strange, disturbing influence had come among the brothers! Cosmo began to contemplate his own position with a certain despair; he knew well enough by this time the unreasoning sentiment of Madame Roche; he knew very well that though she relieved herself in her trouble by writing to him, and made a solemn appeal for his services, that it by no means followed when this emergency was past, that she would confirm his sonship by giving him her daughter, or relinquish her past idea for the sake of the hopes she might have excited; and in the second place Cosmo could not tell for his life what use he was likely to be to Madame Roche, or how he could sustain her in her trouble—while the idea of being so near home without going there, and without the knowledge of his mother, aggravated all his other difficulties. He went on, however, with resignation, got down with the calmness of despair and bewilderment at Kirkbride, walked silently towards Melmar, guiding Cameron along the silent leafy ways, and yielding himself, whatever that might be, to his fate.

CHAPTER LXXIII

And there stood the house of Melmar, resting among its trees, in the soft sweet darkness of the June night.

Perhaps Cameron's heart failed him as he came so near—at least Cosmo reached the house first. The foliage was so thick around that the darkness seemed double in this circle round the house. You could only see the colorless, dark woods, stretching back into the night, and the gleam of blue sky over head, and the lighted windows in the house itself—lights which suggested no happy household meeting, but were astray among different windows in the upper story, telling their own silent tale of illness and anxiety. Cosmo, standing before the door which he knew so well, could only tell that Tyne was near by the low, sweet tinkle of the water among the sighing leaves, and was aware of all the summer flush of roses covering that side of the house by nothing save the fragrance. He stood there gazing up for a moment at one light which moved about from window to window with a strange restlessness, and at another which burned steadily in Marie's bed-chamber. He knew it to be Marie's chamber by instinct. A watch-light, a death-light, a low, motionless flame, so sadly different from the wavering and brightening of that other, which some anxious watcher carried about. Cosmo's heart grew sad within him as he thought of this great solemn death which was coming on Marie. Poor Marie, with her invalid irritability, her little feverish weakness, her ill-bestowed love! To think that one so tender and wayward, from whom even reason and sober thought were not to be expected, should, notwithstanding, go forth alone like every other soul to stand by herself before her God, and that love and pity could no longer help her, let them strain and struggle as they would! The thought made Cosmo's heart ache, he could not tell why.

Madame Roche met them at the door. She was not violently affected as Cosmo feared—she only kept wiping from her eyes the tears which perpetually returned to fill them, as he had seen his own mother do in her trouble—and perhaps it is the common weeping of age which has no longer hasty floods of youthful tears to spend upon any thing. She gave a cry of joy when she saw Cameron.

"Ah, my friend, it is kind—God will reward you!" said Madame Roche, "and you must come to her—there is little time—my child is dying."

Cameron did not answer a word—he only threw down his hat and followed her, restraining his step with a painful start when he heard it ring against the pavement. Cosmo followed, not knowing what else to do, to the door of the sick room. He did not enter, but as the door opened he saw who and what was there. And strange to her son sounded the voice which came out of that sad apartment—the voice of the Mistress reading with her strong Scottish accent and old fashioned intonation, so different from the silvery lady's voice of Madame Roche, and the sweet tones of Desirée. Spread out before her was the big Bible, the family book of old Huntley of Melmar, and she was seated close by the bedside of the sufferer, who lay pallid and wasted, with her thin hands crossed upon the coverlet, and her whole soul in an agony of *listening* not to be described. Close by the Mistress, Desirée was kneeling watching her sister. This scene, which he saw only in a momentary glance before the door was closed, overpowered Cosmo. He threw himself down upon a window-seat in the long corridor which led to this room, and covered his face with his hands. The sudden and unexpected appearance of his mother brought the young man's excitement to a climax. How unjust, unkind, ungenerous now seemed his own fears!

Madame Roche was one of those women who fear to meet any great emergency alone. In the first shock of dismay with which she heard that Marie's life was fast hastening to its end, she wrote to Cosmo; and before it was time for Cosmo to arrive—while indeed it was impossible that he could even have received her letter—the poor mother, with an instinct of her dependent nature, which she was not aware of and could not subdue, hastened to send for the Mistress to help her to bear that intolerable agony in which flesh and heart faint and fail—the anguish of beholding the dying of her child. The Mistress, who under similar circumstances would have closed her doors against all the world, came, gravely and soberly to the call of this undeniable sorrow. In face of that all the bitterness died out of her honest heart. Madame Roche had already lost many children. "And I have all mine—God forgive me—I ken nothing of *that* grief," cried Mrs. Livingstone, with a sob of mingled thankfulness and terror. It was not her vocation to minister at sick-beds, or support the weak; yet she went without hesitation, though leaving Huntley to do both. And even before Madame Roche sent for her, Desirée, who understood her character, had run over by herself early in the morning, when, after watching all night, she was supposed asleep, to tell the Mistress that her mother had written to Cosmo. So there was neither cause nor intention of offense between the sad family at Melmar and that of Norlaw. When she came to Marie's sick-bed, the Mistress found that poor sufferer pathetically imploring some one to tell her of the unknown world to which she was fast approaching—while Madame Roche, passionately reproaching herself for leaving her daughter uninstructed, mingled with her self-accusations, vague words about heaven and descriptions of its blessedness which fell dull upon the longing ears of the anxious invalid. The harps and the white robes, the gates of pearl and the streets of gold were nothing to Marie—what are they to any one who does not see there the only presence which makes heaven a reality? The Mistress had no words to add to the poor mother's anxious eager repetition of all the disjointed words, describing heaven, which abode in her memory—but instead, went softly down stairs and returned with the big Bible, the old, well remembered book, which never failed to produce a certain awe in Madame Roche—and this was how it happened that Cosmo found his mother reading to Marie.

When Cameron entered the room, the Mistress, who had not paused, continued steadily with the reading of her gospel. He, for his part, did not interrupt her—he went to the other side of the bed and sat down there, looking at the white face which he had never seen since he saw it in St. Ouen, scarcely less pale, yet bright enough to appear to his deluded fancy a star which might light his life. That was not an hour or place to think of those vain human dreams. Sure as the evening was sinking into midnight, this troubled shadow of existence was gliding on toward the unspeakable perfection of the other life. A little while, and words would no more vail the face of things to this uninstructed soul—a little while—but as he sat by Marie's death-bed the whole scene swam and glimmered before Cameron's eyes—"A little while and ye shall not see me—and again a little while and ye shall see me." Oh these ineffable, pathetic, heart breaking words! They wandered out and in through Cameron's mind in an agony of consolation and of tears. He heard the impatient anxious mother stop the reading—he felt her finger tap upon his arm urging him to speak—he saw Marie turn her tender, dying eyes toward him—he tried to say something but his voice failed him—and when at last he found utterance, with a tearless sob, which it was impossible to restrain, the words which burst from his lips with a vehement outcry, which sounded loud though it was nearer a whisper, were only these:—"Jesus! Jesus! our Lord!"

Only these!—only that everlasting open secret of God's grace by which He brings heaven and earth together! The gentle, blue eyes, which were no longer peevish, brightened with a wistful hope. There was comfort in the very name; and then this man—who labored for the wretched—whom himself could not force his human heart to love, because his Master loved them—this man, whom poor Marie never suspected to have loved her in *her* selfish weakness with the lavish love of a prodigal, who throws away all—this man stood up by the bedside with his gospel. He himself did not know what he said—perhaps neither did she, who was too far upon her way to think of words—but the others stood round with awe to hear. Heaven? No, it was not heaven he was speaking of—there was no time for those celestial glories, which are but a secondary blessing; and Cameron had not a thought in his heart save for this dying creature and his Lord.

Was it darker out of doors under the skies? No; there was a soft young moon silvering over the dark outline of the trees, and throwing down a pale glory over this house of Melmar, on the roof, which glimmered like a silver shield; and, in the hush, the tinkling voice of Tyne and the breath of the roses, and a sweet white arrow of moonlight, came in, all mingled and together, into the chamber of death. Yet, somehow, it is darker—darker. This pale figure, which is still Marie, feels it so, but does not wonder—does not ask—is, indeed, sinking into so deep a quiet, that it does not trouble her with any fears.

"I go to sleep," she says faintly, with the sweetest smile that ever shone upon Marie's lips, "I am so well. Do not cry, mamma; when I wake, I shall be better. I go to sleep."

And so she would, and thus have reached heaven unawares, but for the careless foot which pushed the door open, and the excited figure which came recklessly in. At sight of him, Cameron instantly left the bedside—instantly without a word, quitted the room—and began to walk up and down the corridor, where Cosmo stood waiting. Pierrot began immediately to address his wife:—His wife!—his life!—his angel! was it by her orders that strangers came to the house, that his commands were disobeyed, that he himself was kept from her side? He begged his adored one to shake off her illness, to have a brave spirit, to get up and rouse herself for his sake.

"What, my Marie! it is but courage!" cried her husband. "A man does not die who will not die! Up, my child! Courage! I will forsake you no more—you have your adored husband—you will live for him. We shall be happy as the day. Your hand, my angel! Have courage, and rise up, and live for your Emile's sake!"

And all the peace that had been upon it fled from Marie's face. The troubled eagerness of her life came back to her. "Yes Emile!" she whispered, with breathless lips, and made the last dying effort to rise up at his bidding and follow him. Madame Roche threw herself between, with cries of real and terrified agony; and the Mistress, almost glad to exchange her choking sympathy for the violent, sudden passion which now came upon her, went round the bed with the silence and speed of a ghost, seized his arm with a grip of imperative fury not to be resisted, and, before he was aware, had thrust him before her to the door. When she had drawn it close behind her, she shook him like a child with both her hands. "You devil!" cried the Mistress, transported out of all decorum of speech by a passion of indignation which the scene almost warranted. "You dirty, miserable hound! how daur you come there? If you do not begone to your own place this instant—Cosmo, here! She's gone, the poor bairn. He has nae mair right in this house, if he ever had ony—take him away."

But while this violent scene disturbed the death calm of the house, it did not disturb Marie. She had seen for herself by that time, better than any one could have told her, what robes they wore and what harps they played in the other world.

CHAPTER LXXIV

That same night, while they watched their dead at Melmar, the young moon shone kindly into the open parlor window of a pretty cottage, where some anxiety, but no sorrow was. This little house stood upon a high bank of the river Esk, just after that pretty stream had passed through the pretty village of Lasswade. The front of the house was on the summit of the height, and only one story high, while the rapid slope behind procured for it the advantage of two stories at the back. It was a perfectly simple little cottage, rich in flowers, but nothing else, furnished with old, well-preserved furniture, as dainty, as bright, and as comfortable as you could imagine, and looking all the better for having already answered the wants of two or three generations. The window was open, and here, too, came in the tinkle of running water, and the odor of roses, along with the moonlight. Candles stood on the table, but they had not been lighted; and two ladies sat by the window, enjoying the cool breeze, the sweet light, the "holy time" of evening—or, perhaps, not aware of enjoying anything, busy with their own troubles and their own thoughts.

"I doubt if I should advise," said the elder of the two, "but though I'm an old maid myself, I am not prejudiced either one way or another, my dear. I've lived too long, Katie, to say this or that manner of life's the happiest; it does not matter much whether you are married or not married, happiness lies aye in yourself. It's common to think a single woman very lone and dreary when she comes to be old; but I'm not afraid for you. Somebody else will have bairns for you, Katie, if you do not have them for yourself. Solitude is not in your cup, my dear—I'm prophet enough to read that."

Her companion made no answer; and in the little pause which ensued, the Esk, and the roses, and the moonlight came in as a sweet unconscious chorus, but a chorus full of whispers which struck deeper than those quiet words of quiet age.

"But on the other side," continued the old lady, "Charlie is as good a fellow as ever lived—the best son, the kindest heart! I would not trust myself praising him any more than praising you, my dear. You are both a comfort and a credit to us all, and maybe that is why we should like to make the two of you one. We're no' so very romantic, Katie, in our family—that is to say," continued the speaker, with sudden animation, "the women of us—for if Charlie, or any lad belonging to the house, was to offer himself without his whole heart and love, he had better never show his face to me."

"But, auntie," said the younger lady, with a smile, "would it be right to take a whole heart and love, and only have kindness to give in exchange?"

"Women are different, my dear," said Katie Logan's maiden aunt; "I will confess I do not like myself to hear young girls speaking about love—I would never advise a *man* to marry without it—nay, the very thought makes me angry; but—perhaps you'll think it no compliment to us, Katie—women are different; I have no fears of a good woman liking her husband, no' even if she was married against her will, as sometimes happens. I would advise you not to be timid, so far as that is concerned. Charlie's very fond of you, and he's a good lad. To be married is natural at your age, to have a house of your own, and your own place in this world; and then there are the bairns. Colin will soon be off your hands, but the other three are young. Do you think it would not be best for them if you married a *friend*?"

Katie did not reply; but perhaps it was this last argument which moved her to a long low sigh of unwelcome conviction. The old lady's emphatic *friend* was Scotch for a relative. Would it indeed be better for them that Katie's husband should be her cousin?

"Unless," said her aunt, rising up to light the candles, yet pausing to give effect to this last precaution; "unless, my dear, there should be a single thought of any other man resting in your mind. If there is, Katie, think no more of Charlie Cassilis. I'm willing you should marry him first and grow fond of him after; but, my dear, stop and think—do you like any other person better than him?"

"Maybe I do, auntie," said the low voice, softly; and Katie shook her head thoughtfully in the darkness, with a half melancholy, half pleased motion; "maybe I do."

"Then, for pity's sake, not another word!" cried the old lady; and that kindest of aunts rustled out of the pretty parlor, taking one of the candlesticks in her hand, with a commotion and haste which showed that Katie's quiet half confession had by no means pleased her, in spite of her avowed impartiality. Lucifer, son of the morning, had not fallen at that time into such degrading familiarity with housekeepers and housemaids as has chanced now to that unhappy spirit. Matches were none in all the village of Lasswade, nor throughout the kingdom, save slender slips of wood anointed with brimstone, and bearing the emphatic name of *spunk* in all the regions north of the Tweed. So Katie's respectable aunt, who was kind to her servants, rustled along the passage to the kitchen to light the candle, and on the way there and the way back recovered her temper—which was all the better for Katie; and by-and-bye the quiet maiden household shut itself up and went to sleep.

And perhaps when Katie knelt by her bedside that night to say her prayers—by the white bed where little Isabel slept the deep sleep which all the children sleep, thank Heaven, when we are awake with our troubles—a little weariness of heart made a sigh among her prayers. She was not romantic—the women of her family were otherwise disposed, as good Auntie Isabel said, who had not a single selfish impulse in her composition; and Katie was grieved to disappoint Cousin Charlie, and perhaps feared, as women always do, with an unconscious vanity, for the consequences of his disappointment; was she right to damage his happiness, to refuse a supporter for herself, a protector for her children, all for the sake of Huntley, who might perhaps have forgotten her years ago? Katie could not answer her own question, but she did what was the wisest course under the circumstances—laid her head resolutely down, on her pillow and fell asleep, leaving time and the hour to solve the question for her, and only sure of one thing—that her impulse was right.

But the question returned to her when she opened her eyes, in the morning, in those first waking moments, when, as Béranger says, all our cares awake before us, assault afresh, and, as if the first time, the soul which has escaped them in the night. Was she right? All through her early morning duties this oft-repeated question beset the mind of Katie; and it needs only to see what these duties were, to acknowledge how pertinacious it was. The cottage belonged to Aunt Isabel, who had received gladly her orphan nieces and nephews after the death of Dr. Logan. Aunt Isabel's spare income was just enough for herself and her maid, who, heretofore, had been sole occupants of the pretty little house, and Katie and her orphans managed to live upon theirs, which was also a very small income, but marvelously taken care of—and pleasantly backed by the gooseberry-bushes and vegetable beds of the cottage garden, which riches their mistress made common property. On Katie's advent, Aunt Isabel retired from the severe duties of housekeeping in her own person. It was Katie who made the tea and cut the bread and butter, and washed with her own hands the delicate cups and saucers which Aunt Isabel would not trust to a servant. Then the elder sister had to see that the boys were ready, with all their books strapped on their shoulder, and their midday "piece" in their pocket, for school. Then Isabel's daintier toilet had to be superintended; and if Katie had a weakness, it was to see her sister prettily dressed, and "in the fashion"—and that little maiden sent forth fair and neat to the ladies' seminary which illustrated the healthful village of Lasswade; and then Katie went to the kitchen, to determine what should be had for dinner, and sometimes to lend her own delicate skill to the making of a pudding or the crimping of a frill. When all was done, there was an unfailing supply of needlework to keep her hands employed. On this particular morning, Aunt Isabel meditated a call upon Miss Hogg, in Lasswade, and Katie had been so much persecuted by that question which some malicious imp kept always addressing to her, that she felt heated and out of breath in the pretty parlor. So she took up her work, put her thread and scissors in her pocket, and went out to the garden to sit on a low garden seat, with the grass under her feet, and the trees over her, and sweet Esk singing close at hand, thinking it might be easier to pursue her occupation there.

Perhaps that was a mistake. It is not easy to sew, nor to read, nor even to think, out of doors on a June morning, with a sweet river drowsing by, and the leaves, and the roses, and the birds, and the breeze making among them that delightful babble of sound and motion which people call the quiet of the country. Still Katie *did* work; she was making shirts for Colin, who had just gone into Edinburgh to Cousin Charlie's office;—stitching wristbands! and in spite of the sunshine and her perplexed thoughts, Katie's button-holes were worth going ten miles to see.

But was she right? Search through all the three kingdoms and you could not have found a better fellow than Cousin Charlie, who was very fond of Katie Logan, and had been for years. The elder sister liked him heartily, knew that he would be kind to her orphans, believed him every thing that was good in man; but while she reasoned with herself, the color wavered upon her cheek, and somewhere in heart a voice, which might have been the Esk river, so closely its whisper ran with her thoughts, kept saying, "Dinna forget me, Katie!" till, by dint of persistence, all the other meditations yielded, and this, with a triumphant shout, kept the field. Oh, Huntley Livingstone! who had, just as like as no', forgotten Katie—was she right?

He could not have come at a better time—he came quite unannounced, unintroduced, so suddenly that Katie made an outcry almost of terror— one moment, nobody with her but the Esk, and the roses, and her own thoughts—not a shadow on the grass, not a step on the road. The next moment, Huntley, standing there between her and the sky, between her and home, shutting out every thing but himself, who had to be first attended to. If she had only seen him a moment sooner, she might have received him quite calmly, with the old smile of the elder-sister; but because of the start, Katie getting up, dropping her work, and holding out her hands, looked about as agitated, as glad, as tearful, as out of herself, as even Huntley was.

"I have come home—to Norlaw—to remain," said Huntley, when he began to know what he was saying, which was not just the first moment; "and you are not an old Katie in a cap, as you threatened to be; but first I've come to say out what I dared not say in the manse parlor—and you know what that is. Katie, if you have forgotten me—Heaven knows I never will blame you!—it's seven weary years since then—if you have forgotten me, Katie, tell me I am not to speak!"

Katie had two or three impulses for the moment—to tell the truth, she was quite happy, rejoiced to be justified in the unsolicited affection she had given, and entirely contented in standing by this sudden Œdipus, who was to resolve all her doubts. Being so, she could almost have run away from the embarrassment and gravity of the moment, and made a little natural sport of the solemnity of the lover, who stood before her as if his life depended on it. Perhaps it was the only coquettish thought which Katie Logan ever was guilty of. But she conquered it—she looked up at him with her old smile.

"Speak, Huntley!" she said; and having said so much, there was not, to tell the truth, a great deal more necessary. Huntley spoke, you may be sure, and Katie listened; and the very roses on the cottage wall were not less troubled about Cousin Charlie for the next hour than she was. And when Aunt Isabel returned, and Katie went in with a blush, holding Huntley's arm, to introduce him simply as "Huntley Livingstone," with a tone and a look which needed no interpretation, there was no longer a doubt in Katie's mind as to whether she was right.

But she did not think it needful to tell Huntley what question she was considering when his sudden appearance startled her out of all her perplexities; and it is very likely that in that, at least, Katie was perfectly right.

CHAPTER LXXV

A very sadly different scene; no young hopes blossoming towards perfection—no young lives beginning—no joy—has called together this company, or makes this room bright; a dark house, shrouded still in its closed curtains and shutters, a wan light in the apartment, a breathless air of death throughout the place. Outside, the tawdry Frenchman, with a long crape hatband, knotted up in funeral bows, as is the custom in Scotland, walking up and down smoking his cigar, angry at finding himself excluded, yet tired of the brief decorum into which even he has been awed, and much disposed to amuse himself with any kitchenmaid whom he may chance to see as he peers about their quarters, keeping at the back of the house. But the maids are horrified and defiant, and the affair is rather dull, after all, for Monsieur Pierrot.

The company are all assembled in the drawing-room, as they have returned from the funeral. The minister, the doctor, a lawyer from Melrose, Cameron, and the three brothers Livingstone. Madame Roche, her black gown covered with crape, and every thing about her of the deepest sable, save her cap; the white ribbons of which are crape ribbons too, sits, with her handkerchief in her hand, in an easy chair. The Mistress is there, too, rather wondering and disapproving, giving her chief attention to Desirée, who sits behind her mother quietly crying, and supposing this solemn assembly is some necessary formality which must be gone through.

"Is it to read the will?" asks the minister, who suggests that her husband had better be present; but no, there is no will—for poor Marie had nothing and could leave nothing. When they have been all seated for a few minutes, Madame Roche herself rises from her chair. Though the tears are in her eyes, and grief in her face, she is still the beautiful old lady whom Cosmo Livingstone loved to watch from his window in St. Ouen. Time himself, the universal conqueror, can never take from Mary of Melmar that gift which surrounded her with love in her youth, and which has lighted all her troubled life like a fairy lamp. The sweet soft cheek where even wrinkles are lovely, the beautiful old eyes which even in their tears can not choose but smile, the footstep so light, yet so firm, which still might ring "like siller bells," though its way is heavy. Every one was looking at her, and as they looked, every one acknowledged the unchanging fascination of this beautiful face.

"Gentlemen," said Madame Roche with a little tremor in her voice, "I would speak to you all—I would do my justice before the world; you have heard what I was in my youth. Mary Huntley of Melmar, my father's heiress. I was disobedient—I went away from him—I knew he disowned me, and knew no more than an infant that he relented in his heart when he died. I was poor all my life—my Marie, my dear child!" and here Madame Roche paused to sob aloud, and Desirée laid her head upon the knee of the Mistress and clutched at her dress in silent self-control; "it was then she married this man—married him to break her heart—yet still loved him to the last. Ah, my friends, I was thus a widow with my sick child in my husband's town. My Jean was dead, and she was forsaken—and my Desirée was gone from me to serve strangers—it was then that one came to my house like an angel from heaven. Cosmo, my friend, do you blush that I should name your name?

"And what a tale he told me!" cried poor Madame Roche, whose tears now filled her eyes, and whose lips quivered so that she had to pause from moment to moment; "I, who thought me a lonely woman, whom no one cared for;—my father had thought upon me—my kinsman, Patrick Livingstone, had sought me to give me back my lands—my young hero was seeking me then; and his brother, yes, Huntley, his noble brother, was ready to renounce his right—and all for the widow and her children. I weep, ah, my friends, you weep!—was it not noble? was it not above praise? When I heard it I made a vow—I said in my heart I should repay this excellent Huntley. I had planned it in my mind—I said in my thoughts, my Marie, my blessed child, must have half of this great fortune. She is married, she can not make compensation—but the rest is for Desirée, and Desirée shall give it back to Huntley Livingstone."

Every one of her auditors by this time gazed upon Madame Roche. Desirée, sitting behind her, lifted her face from the lap of the Mistress; she was perfectly pale, and her eyes were heavy with crying. She sat leaning forward, holding the Mistress's gown with one hand, with sudden dismay and terror in her white face. Just opposite her Cameron sat, clenching his hand. What *he* was thinking no one could say—but as Madame Roche spoke of Marie he still clenched his hand. Then came the strangers, surprised and sympathetic, Patrick Livingstone among them. Then Huntley, much startled and wondering, and Cosmo, with a face which reflected Desirée's, dismayed and full of anxiety, and the attitude of a man about to spring up to defy, or denounce, or contradict the speaker. The Mistress behind sat upright in her chair, with a face like a psalm of battle and triumph, her nostril dilating, her eyes shining. For the first time in her life, the Mistress's heart warmed to Mary of Melmar. She alone wanted no explanation of this speech—she alone showed no surprise or alarm—it was but a just and fit acknowledgment—a glory due to the sons of Norlaw.

"But, alas," cried Madame Roche; "God has looked upon it, and it has not been enough. He has broken my heart and made my way clear; pity me, my friends, my Marie is in heaven and her mother here! And now there is but one heir. My Desirée is my only child—there is none to share her inheritance. Huntley Livingstone, come to me! I have thought and I have dreamed of the time when I should give you my child—but, alas! did I think it should be only when Marie was in her grave? Huntley Livingstone! you gave up your right to me, and I restore it to you. I give you my child, and Melmar is for Desirée. There is no one to share it with you, my daughter and my son!"

Huntley had risen and approached to Madame Roche, though with reluctance, when she called him. Now she held his hand in one of hers, and stretched out the other for that of Desirée—while Huntley, confounded, confused, and amazed beyond expression, had not yet recovered himself sufficiently to speak. Before he could speak Cosmo had sprung to the side of Desirée, who stood holding back and meeting her mother's appeal with a look of dumb defiance and exasperation, which might be very wrong, but was certainly very natural. Every one rose. But for the grief of the principal actors, and the painful embarrassment of all, the scene might almost have been ludicrous. Cosmo, who had grasped at Desirée's hand, did not obtain it any more than her mother. The girl stood up, but kept her hold of the Mistress's gown, as if for protection.

"No, no, no, no!" said Desirée, in a low, hurried, ashamed voice; "mother, no—no—no! I will not do it! Mamma, will you shame me? Oh, pity us! Is it thus we are to weep for Marie?"

"My child, it is justice," cried Madame Roche, through her tears; "give him your hand—it is that Huntley may have his own."

"But there is some strange mistake here," said Huntley, whose brow burned with a painful flush; "Melmar was never mine, nor had I any real right to it. Years ago I have even forgotten that it once was possible. Be silent for a moment, Cosmo, I beg of you, and you, Mademoiselle Desirée, do not fear. Madame Roche, I thank you for your generous meaning, but it is an entire mistake in every way—let me explain it privately. Let us be alone first;—nay, nay, let me speak, then! I am my father's heir, and our house is older than Melmar; and nothing in the world, were it the hand of a queen, could tempt me to call myself any thing but Livingstone of Norlaw!"

The Mistress had been standing up, like everybody else, an excited spectator. When Huntley said these words she sat down suddenly, with a glow and flush of triumph not to be described—the name of her husband and her son ringing in her ears like a burst of music; and then, for the first time, Desirée relinquished her hold, and held out her hand to Huntley, while Cosmo grasped his other hand and wrung it in both his with a violent pressure. The three did not think for that moment of Madame Roche, who had been looking in Huntley's face all the time he spoke to her, and who, when he ended, dropped his hand silently and sank into her chair. She was leaning back now, with her white handkerchief over her face—and the hand that held it trembled. Poor Madame Roche! this was all her long thought of scheme had come to—she could only cover her face and forget the pang of failure in the bigger pang of grief—she did not say another word; she comprehended—for she was not slow of understanding—that Huntley's little effusion of family pride was but a rapid and generous expedient to save him from a direct rejection of Desirée. And poor Madame Roche's heart grew sick with the quick discouragement of grief. She closed her eyes, and heavier tears came from them than even those she had shed for Marie. She had tried her best to make them happy, she had failed; and now they for whose sake alone she had made all this exertion neglected and forgot her. It was too much for Madame Roche.

"Mamma, listen," whispered Desirée, soothingly. "Ah, mamma, you might force mine—I should always obey you—but you can not force Huntley's heart—he does not care for *me*; bah, that is nothing!—but there *is* one whom he cares for—one whom he has come home for—Katie, whom they all love! Mamma, you were right! he is noble, he is generous; but what is Melmar to Huntley? He has come back for Katie and his own home."

"Katie?—some one else? My darling, does he love her?" said Madame Roche. "Then it is God who has undone all, Desirée, and I am content. Let him come to me, and I will bless him. I will bless you all, my children," she said, raising herself up, and stretching her hands toward them. "Ah, friends, do you see them—so young and so like each other! and it was *he* who sought us, and not Huntley; and it is I who am wrong—and God is right!"

Saying which, Madame Roche kissed Huntley's cheek, dismissing him so, and took Cosmo into her arms instead. Her sweet temper and facile mind forgot even her own failure. She put back Cosmo's hair tenderly from his forehead and called him her hero. He was her son at least; and Desirée and Melmar, the two dreams of his fancy, between which, when he saw the girl first, he suspected no possible connection, came at once, a double gift, the one eagerly sought, the other totally unthought of, into the Benjamin's portion of Cosmo Livingstone.

CHAPTER LXXVI

"There's aye plenty fools in this world," said bowed Jaaoob; "a'thing else that's human fails; but that commodity's aye ready. I had my hopes of that laddie Livingstone. He has nae discrimination, and hasna seen the world, like some other folk, but for a' that I thought I could perceive a ring of the right metal in him, and I'm no' often wrang. And so Cosmo's to be marriet! I dinna disapprove of his taste—that's a different matter. I even had a great notion of *her* mysel'; but when the lad's married there's an end of him. Wha ever heard tell of a man coming to distinction with a wife at his tail?—na! I wash my hands of Cosmo—he shall never mair be officer of mine."

Jaacob did not address himself to any one in particular. The news with which Kirkbride was ringing was great news in its way, and a little crowd had collected in the corner, close by the smithy, to discuss it, a crowd composed chiefly of women, chief among whom, in a flush of triumph and importance, stood Marget of Norlaw. Jaacob did not often concern his lofty intelligence with the babble of women, but the little giant was interested in spite of himself, and had a warm corner in his heart for both the heroes who were under present discussion. A lusty blacksmith apprentice puffed at the great bellows within that ruddy cavern, and Jaacob stood at the door, with one or two male gossips lingering near him, which was a salve to his dignity; but Jaacob's words were not addressed even to his own cronies; they were a spontaneous effusion of observant wisdom, mingled with benevolent regret.

"The man's in a creel!" cried the indignant Marget—"an officer of yours, Jaacob Bell?—*yours*, ye objeck! and I would just like to ken wha gave the like of you ony right to ca' *our* son by his christened name? Na, sirs, ye're a' wrang—it just shows how little folk ken about onything out of their ain road; and canna haud their peace either, or let them speak that have the knowledge. The auld lady—her that was Mary of Melmar—would have given our Huntley baith the land and the bonnie lass, if it had been *her* will, for she's a real sensible woman, as it's turned out, and kens the value of lads like ours. But Huntley Livingstone, he said no. He's no' the lad, our Huntley, to be ony wife's man—and he has his awn yestate, and an aulder name and fame than Melmar. There's no' an auld relick in the whole country-side like our auld castle. I've heard it from them that ken; and our Huntley would no mair part with the name than wi' his right hand. Eh! if auld Norlaw, puir man, had but lived to see this day! Our Cosmo is very like his father. He's just as like to be kent far and near for his poems and his stories as Walter Scott ower yonder at Abbotsford. It's just like a story in a book itsel'. When he was but a laddie—no' muckle bigger than bowed Jaacob—he fell in with a bonnie bit wee French lady, in Edinburgh. I mind him telling me—there's never ony pride about our sons—just as well as if it was yesterday. The callant's head ran upon naething else—and wha was this but just Miss Deseera! and he's courted her this mony a year, whaever might oppose; and now he's won and conquered, and there's twa weddings to be in Kirkbride, baith in the very same day!"

"In Kirkbride? but, dear woman, Miss Logan's no' here," suggested one of the bystanders.

"Wha's heeding!" cried Marget, in her triumph, "if ane's in Kirkbride, and ane in anither kirk, is that onything against the truth I am telling? Sirs, haud a' your tongues—I've carried them a' in my arms, and told them stories. I've stood by them and their mother, just me and no other person, when they were in their sorest trouble; and I would like to hear wha daur say a word, if Norlaw Marget is just wild and out of her wits for aince in her life to see their joy!"

"I never look for discretion at a woman's hand mysel'," said bowed Jaacob, though even Jaacob paused a little before he brought the shadow of his cynicism over Marget's enthusiasm; "they're easy pleased, puir things, and easy cast down—a man of sense has aye a compassion for the sex—it's waste o' time arguing with them. Maybe that's a reason for lamenting this lad Livingstone. A man, if he's no' a' the stronger, is awfu' apt to fall to the level of his company—and to think of a promising lad, no' five-and-twenty, lost amang a haill tribe—wife, mother, mother-in-law, sister-in-law, and gude kens how many friends forbye—it's grievous—that's just what it is; a man goes down, a man comes to the calibre of the woman. For which cause," said bowed Jaacob, thrusting his cowl on one side of his head, twisting still higher his high shoulder, and fixing a defiant gaze upon the admiring crowd with his one eye; "in spite of mony temptations—for I'll say that for the women, that they ken a man of sense when they see him—I'm no', and never will be, a marrying man mysel'!"

"Eh, but Jaacob," cried a saucy voice, "if you could have gotten her, you might have put up with Miss Roche."

"Humph—I had a great notion of the lassie," said Jaacob, loftily; "men at my years get above the delusion of looking for a woman as a companion. It makes nae muckle matter whether she's ca'ed a foolish woman or a sensible ane; its naething but a question of degree; and when a man finds that out, he has a right to please his e'e. When you hear of me married, it's a wife of sixteen, that's what I'll have gotten; but you see, as for Miss Deeseera, puir thing, she may be breaking her heart, for onything I ken. I'm a man of honor, and Cosmo's a great friend of mine—I wouldna, for twenty Melmars, come between my friend and his love."

And amid the laughter which echoed this magnanimous speech, bowed Jaacob retired into the ruddy gloom of the smithy and resumed his hammer, which he played with such manful might and intention upon the glowing iron, that the red light illuminated his whole swarthy face and person, and the red sparks flashed round him like the rays round a saint in an old picture. He was not in the least a saintly individual, but Rembrandt himself could not have found a better study for light and shade.

A little time sufficed to accomplish these momentous changes. The Mistress gave up her trust of Norlaw, the cows and dairies which were the pride of her heart, the bank-book, with its respectable balance, and all the rural wealth of the farmsteading, to her son. And Huntley warned the tenants to whom his mother had let the land that he should resume the farming of it himself at the end of the year, when their terms were out. Every thing about Norlaw began to wear signs of preparation. The Mistress spoke vaguely of going with Patie, the only one of her sons who still "belonged to his mother"—and making a home for him in Glasgow. But Patie was an engineer, involved over head and ears in the Herculean work of the new railways; he was scarcely three months in the year, take them altogether, at the lodging which he called his head quarters—and perhaps, on the whole, he rather discouraged the idea.

"At least, mother, you must wait to welcome Katie," said this astute and long-headed adviser of the family—and the Mistress, with her strong sense of country breeding and decorum, would not have done less, had it broken her heart. But she rather longed for the interval to be over, and the matter concluded. The Mistress, somehow, could not understand or recognize herself adrift from Norlaw.

"But I dinna doubt it would be best—it's natural," said the Mistress— "they should have their good beginning to themselves," and with that she sighed, and grew red with shame to think it was a sigh, and spoke sharply to Marget, and put the old easy chair which had been "their father's!" away into a corner, with a little momentary ebullition of half resentful tears. But she never lost her temper to Huntley—it was only Nature, and not her son who was to blame.

It was early in August when Katie came home. The Mistress stood at the door waiting to receive her, on a night which was worthy such a homecoming. Just sunset, the field-laborers going home, the purple flush folded over the Eildons like a regal mantle, the last tender ray catching the roofless wall of the Strength of Norlaw, and the soft hill rising behind, with yellow corn waving rich to its summit, soon to be ripe for the harvest. Tears were in the Mistress's heart, but smiles in her face; she led her new daughter in before even Huntley, brought her to the dining-parlor, and set her in her own chair.

"This is where I sat first myself the day I came home," said the Mistress, with a sob, "and sit you there; and God bless my bairns, and build up Norlaw—amen!"

But Katie said the amen too, and rose again, holding the Mistress fast and looking up in her face.

"I have not said mother for ten years," said Katie. "Mother! do you think dispeace can ever rise between you and me, that you should think once of going away?"

The Mistress paused.

"No dispeace, Katie—no, God forbid!" said Huntley's mother, "but I'm a hasty woman in my speech, and ever was."

"But not to me," said the Katie who was no more Katie Logan—"never to me! and Huntley will be a lonely man if his mother goes from Norlaw, for where thou goest I will go, and where thou dwellest I will dwell. Mother, tell me! is it Patie or poor Huntley who is to have you and me?"

The Mistress did not say a word. She suffered herself to be placed in the chair where she had placed Katie, and then put her apron over her face and wept, thinking strangely, all at once, not of a new daughter-in-law and a changed place, but of him who lay sleeping among the solemn ruins at Dryburgh, and all the sacred chain of years that made dear this house of Norlaw.

The other marriage took place after that, with much greater glory and distinction, to the pride of the Mistress's heart. It was a great festival when it came—which was not till the season of mourning was over—to all of whom Madame Roche could reach. Even Joanna Huntley and Aunt Jean were persuaded to come to gladden the wedding of Desirée and Cosmo; and it is even said that Joanna, who is of a very scientific turn of mind, and has a little private laboratory of her own, where she burns her pupils' fingers, was the finder of that strange little heap of dust and cinders which revealed to Huntley the mineral wealth in the corner of the Norlaw lands, which now has made him rich enough to buy three Norlaws. At any rate, Joanna was put into perfect good humor by her visit, and thenceforward, with the chivalry of a knight-errant, worshiped above all loveliness the beautiful old face of Madame Roche.

This is about all there is to tell of the Livingstone family. They had their troubles, and are having them, like all of us; but, like all of us, have great joy-cordials now and then to make them strong; and always Providence to work a clear web out of the tangled exertions which we make without witting, and which God sorts into His appointed lot.